Praise for *King's Fool*

"...The author presents an absorbing picture of King Henry VIII and his court... Through [Somers'] shrewd and observing eyes the reader gains not only an intimate view of each of the monarch's six wives but also a remarkably honest and human portrait of Henry."
—*Booklist*

"All should be warned that, despite the title, they will not encounter the traditional fool."
—*Chicago Tribune*

"Using the bright threads of historical fact, Margaret Campbell Barnes, one of the abler practitioners of the costume novel, has woven a regal tapestry of pomp and circumstance."
—*Philadelphia Inquirer*

"For anyone who thinks of Henry VIII as a violent and tempestuous king, this novel opens another side. The violence is there, but it is tempered by an almost pitiful tenderness which only those closest to him ever found."
—*Free Press* (Winnipeg, Canada)

"Margaret Campbell Barnes has written a novel in which warmth of feeling and imaginative perception have been skillfully blended with historical research."
—*Gazette Montreal*

Temple City Library 628
County of Los Angeles Public Library
5939 Golden West Avenue
Temple City CA 91780
Phone: (626) 285-2136

FIC BARNES
BARNES, MARGARET
CAMPBELL
KING'S FOOL   FEB 11 2010

king's fool

king's fool

A Notorious King, His Six Wives, and the
One Man Who Knew All Their Secrets

MARGARET CAMPBELL BARNES

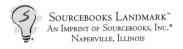

SOURCEBOOKS LANDMARK™
AN IMPRINT OF SOURCEBOOKS, INC.®
NAPERVILLE, ILLINOIS

Copyright © 1959, 2009 by Margaret Campbell Barnes
Cover and internal design © 2009 by Sourcebooks, Inc.
Cover photo © Portrait of Catherine Parr (1512-48), 1545 (coloured
engraving) by Master John (fl.1544) (after)
Private Collection/ The Stapleton Collection/ The Bridgeman Art Library
Nationality / copyright status: English / out of copyright

Sourcebooks and the colophon are registered trademarks of Sourcebooks,
Inc.

All rights reserved. No part of this book may be reproduced in any form or
by any electronic or mechanical means including information storage and
retrieval systems—except in the case of brief quotations embodied in crit-
ical articles or reviews—without permission in writing from its publisher,
Sourcebooks, Inc.

The characters and events portrayed in this book are fictitious or are used ficti-
tiously. Apart from well-known historical figures, any similarity to real persons,
living or dead, is purely coincidental and not intended by the author.

Published by Sourcebooks Landmark, an imprint of Sourcebooks, Inc.
P.O. Box 4410, Naperville, Illinois 60567–4410
(630) 961–3900
Fax: (630) 961–2168
www.sourcebooks.com

Originally published in 1959 by Macdonald & Co.

Library of Congress Cataloging-in-Publication Data

Barnes, Margaret Campbell.
  King's fool : a notorious king, his six wives, and the one man who knew all
their secrets / Margaret Campbell Barnes.
     p. cm.
 1. Henry VIII, King of England, 1491-1547—Fiction. 2. Courts and courtiers—Fiction. 3. Great Britain—History—Henry VIII, 1509-1547—Fiction.
I. Title.
 PR6003.A72K56 2008
 823'.912—dc22
                              2008038834

Printed and bound in the United States of America.
                VP 10 9 8 7 6 5 4 3 2 1

Also by Margaret Campbell Barnes
Brief Gaudy Hour
My Lady of Cleves
The Tudor Rose

In grateful memory

of my parents,

CHARLES and EMILY WOOD

The Wives and Family of King Henry VIII

Henry Tudor
King Henry VII
(b. 1457;
r. 1485–1509)

=

Elizabeth of York
(1466–1503)
daughter of Edward Plantagenet
King Edward IV of England

Arthur (1) = Katherine of (1) = **Henry VIII** = (2) Anne Boleyn = (3) Jane Seymour
Tudor   Aragon   (b. 1491;   (m. 1533;   (m. 1536;
(1486–1502) (1485–1536;   r. 1509–1547)   e. 1536)   d. 1537)
            div. 1533)

= (4) Anne of Cleves
  (m. & div. 1540
  d. 1557)

= (5) Katherine Howard
  (m. 1540; e. 1542)

= (6) Katherine Parr
  (m. 1543; d. 1548)

Philip I of Spain = Mary I   Elizabeth I   Edward VI
                    (b. 1516   (b. 1533   (b. 1537
                    r. 1553–1558)   r. 1558–1603)   r. 1547–1553)

WILL SOMERS

"Few men were more beloved than was this fool

Whose merry prate kept with the King much rule.

When he was sad the King with him would rhyme;

Thus Will exil'd sadness many a time.

"The King would ever grant what he did crave,

For well he knew Will no exacting knave,

But wish'd the King to do good deeds great store,

Which caused the Court to love him more and more."

Contemporary verse by Robert Armin in

Nest of Ninnies, 1608.

Author's Note

That Will Somers was friend as well as fool to the Tudor family seems to be proved not only by the many stories told of him at the time, but also by the fact that he was painted with Henry the Eighth for one of the few illustrations in the King's own psalter, which is now in the British Museum, and that he appears in the background of other Tudor family groups. He knew all six of Henry's wives and lived just long enough to see each of his three children come to the throne. Queen Mary the First and Queen Elizabeth the First each gave Will an annuity.

The outline of his life and many of the incidents and conversations used in my story are founded on contemporary records, and the way in which several writers mentioned him, both then and later, shows him to have been a popular and well-loved character. The main facts about his first master, Richard Fermor, are authentic; but as nothing is known of Will's love story, this is purely fictional. There is an excellently preserved brass of Richard Fermor at Easton Neston in Northamptonshire, and a mural tablet to William Somers in St. Leonard's, Shoreditch, London, where he was buried in 1560. Richard Tarleton, Queen Elizabeth's jester, and James Burbage, the actor, were also buried there, and the registers and several memorials were preserved when the church was rebuilt by Dance in 1740.

My sincere thanks are due to the Staff of the Manuscripts Department and the Prints and Drawings Department of the

British Museum. Also to the County Librarian and Staff of the County Seely Library in Newport and Freshwater, Isle of Wight, for their help in getting me reference books.

Yarmouth, I.o.W.
M. C. B.

Chapter One

I WAS SHROPSHIRE BORN, essentially a country lad, brought up to take my place among the new middle class which Tudor rule begat. Under the Plantagenets there had been titled folk and peasants. But when Henry the Seventh defeated the last of them on Bosworth field and filched dead Richard's crown he changed all that. With his encouragement of merchants and explorers, and this new printing, and learning for the sons of solid citizens, he opened up life for those who knew how to profit by it. Perhaps a prince who has known exile and hardship is apt to have new and wider ideas. And I was particularly fortunate in this matter of learning because my father taught the choristers of Wenlock Priory, and every day I went with him to be schooled in Latin and calculus and other clerkly knowledge as well as music. From boyhood I knew the grandeur of architecture as well as the beauty of the countryside.

But though I was fortunate in one way I was misfortunate in another, for I was an only child and my mother died of the plague when I was four. She was a Welsh woman from over the border and it must have been from her, folks said, that I inherited my dark leanness and love of music. Although I respected my father, I had no particular love for him, so mine was a lonely childhood. While often poking fun at my schoolmates, I envied them secretly and fiercely because they had real homes. Not just a house swept by a hired woman, and empty to come back to. But warm, candlelit homes full of family bickering and laughter, with some mothering person at the heart of it. It would have been easier for me, I sometimes think, had my mother died a year earlier so that I could not remember her at all. For then my mind would not always have been searching for, or my heart hungering for, a shadowy, half-remembered presence, never completely visualised yet all-pervading. A childish hungering of the heart which went on throughout my youthful life.

Because I am hardier than I look some of my happiest hours were spent helping with the work at my Uncle Tobias's farm. Gathering the golden harvest through long summer days leaves a lasting sweetness to ripen in a man's soul. The smell of newly carted hay can be a lasting memory even in strange cities. The indiscriminating hospitality of my uncle's wife, feeding willing helpers as if they were her own strapping sons, taught me the core of kindness. The glowing companionship of harvest suppers established a belief in humanity against the mean buffets of the years. I shall always remember the glow of these sunsets over Wenlock Edge, and the gloaming covering the softly thatched houses like a gradual benediction. The rough voices of the farm lads and the giggling of the lasses handing round the ale pots making a homely kind of music as precious as the chanting of the monks; the older folk sitting around the cleared trestles afterwards, and the lads drawing the lasses away into the warm darkness. The shrieks and stifled laughter coming from the deeper shadow of the great tithe barn, and then the stillness and the rustling in the straw stack. That was the time I half dreaded. I'd always been the life and soul of the party with my mimicry and quips, and the topical jingling rhymes that even then came to me so easily. But the girls with whom I was popular enough in the day-time had no use for me under a hedge or in the hay. My awkward attempts had always been rebuffed, and I was never one to press myself where I was not wanted. Perhaps they felt me to be different, being the schoolmaster's son, or maybe it was just because I was plain, with quick mind and tongue, and unreddened skin drawn tight across my cheekbones.

So when the lasses and lads paired off with that excited catch in their voices and the glitter of expectation in their eyes I would invent some face-saving errand to the elder folk, and slip away through the beauty of the summer night to listen to the spilled-out ecstasy of nightingales and watch the great gold-white moon sail up behind the branches of the trees. Lonely, I was, and aching for I know not what. But because such beauty could lift the soul clear out of my scrawny body in ecstasy—because I had found celestial beauty in the stone lacework of soaring arches or in the echo of some lingering chord—I seldom hankered for long after the coarse, comely, sweat-soaked bodies and the toil-hardened limbs of the kind of girls I knew. I thought, Heaven help me, that I was immune and never could be driven crazy by a woman.

And so it happened that when I left Shropshire I was still inexperienced and fancy-free.

Until I was fourteen the highlights of my life had been during High Mass or Vespers, when I sent the pure treble of my carefully trained voice soaring up in praise to the very roof of the Priory, or muted it to plead for God's compassion so that it filled the dimness of arcaded aisles with sweet sound. How my world seemed to shatter about me when my voice broke! How restlessly I waited through those awkward months of adolescence when any remark I made croaked between childish treble and manhood gruffness, when I felt like an outcast waiting to creep back into the choir among the alto line. My secret hope was that one day I should be able to sing the tenor solos on Saints' days, or even in the new anthem which my father told us the King himself had composed. But to my bitter disappointment my voice never came again. Oh, of course it was trained and true, good enough to warble a love song as I went about my work, but never again to draw the hearts out of worshippers in a Cluniac priory famous for its music.

Although this was no fault of my own my father was unforgivingly disappointed, lacking the imagination to conceive how much worse it was for me. Half the tragedy of youth is that it has no measuring stick for grief. With a mother I might have talked some of mine out of my heart, bringing it into lighter proportion—indeed, I think that mothers sense such things without being told. But our musical work as master and pupil was the sole thing my father and I had in common. So I tried to assuage my frustration by sitting moodily strumming my shabby lute when I ought to have been chopping logs for winter fuel, or wandering over the hills making up ribald couplets about my betters when I was supposed to be construing Latin, or—with a sudden change of mood—driving the neighbours to distraction with practical jokes and leading the other lads in wild bursts of revelry. By then my poor father—God rest his soul!—was not only disappointed in me, but exasperated and bewildered beyond measure, not knowing what devil possessed me so to dishonour his standing in our little Shropshire town. Twice he beat me, grown lad as I was. Once for hanging a pewter chamber pot on a gable of our Guildhall, and once for releasing a pretty drab from the stocks to annoy our pompous beadle. And Heaven knows the parental chastisements were well deserved! "What is modern youth coming to?" my father would mutter, running a scholarly hand through his rapidly greying hair. So that I imagine he must have been much relieved to send me away into another county to learn better manners.

Actually it was my simpler-minded and more practical Uncle Tobias who brought this about. With more free time on my hands I was often helping him at Frith Farm and, although my thoughts wandered far farther than theirs, I enjoyed the company of my sturdy, uncomplicated cousins. With the failure of my voice I had fallen between two stools, as it were, being neither scholarly enough to teach nor robust enough to make a full-time farmer. And so it happened that I was up a ladder searching for one of my aunt's hens when a strange gentleman came galloping into the yard, and by the wayward chance of a nit-wit bird going broody on a half-cut straw-stack the whole course of my life was altered and enriched.

"Ho, you up there!" I heard him calling urgently. "Find your master and tell him that one of my men has broken his ankle getting a sheep out of a road-side ditch, and by his good leave we are bringing him into the house."

I came down the ladder in haste, with the clucking hen clutched against the front of my borrowed smock.

The stranger was of middle height and mud-bespattered, soberly dressed for riding, but obviously accustomed to command. So I let the hen flop squawking on to a heap of midden and sprinted across the yard to the house, calling to one of my cousins to bring a hurdle as quickly as he could. And in no time at all we had brought the young shepherd into the warm kitchen and my aunt was fussing over him with strips of torn linen, essence of mandrake and the like. He was not much older than I but twice as robust-looking, even with the colour blanched from his cheeks.

"He'll need to rest that ankle for weeks, Sir," prophesied Uncle Tobias, hurrying in from the stable.

"I'm afraid you are right, my friend," agreed the lad's master, passing an experienced hand over the swollen flesh. "If you and your good wife here will be so kind as to keep him until he is fit to follow us, I will send back a doctor as we pass through Bridgnorth."

"Do you have far to go?" asked my uncle.

"Across two counties to Easton Neston near Towcester in Northamptonshire."

My uncle's round red face lit up with pleased surprise. "Then you'll be Master Richard Fermor, who knows more about the wool trade than any other land-owner in the Midlands?"

Master Fermor nodded, and while he shook a generous cascade of silver from his pouch on to the kitchen table, the black-visaged man who appeared to be his bailiff surveyed the groaning lad gloomily. "Old Hodge and the collies be keeping the flock together out there now, but how we be goin' to get 'em home without this agile young 'un beats me," he said.

It was then, following the two men out into the yard, that we became aware of concerted bleating from the direction of the Bridgnorth road, and Master Fermor explained how he had made the journey into Wales to visit his old home and to buy some strong mountain ewes to improve his own flocks in Northamptonshire. "But they need careful handling on the roads, being less tame than ours," he added, obviously sharing his bailiff's anxiety. "I suppose you good Shropshire folk could not spare me one of those strapping sons of yours to help drive them? I'd make it worth your while and send him back with all speed."

My uncle scratched his sandy-coloured head, torn between practical necessity and his habitual desire to oblige. His gaze roved over his few newly ploughed fields from which, even with free grazing on Frith Common, he barely managed to scrape a living for his hard-working family. "Well, scarcely, Sir, what with seed time comin' along an' all—" he began regretfully. And then his eyes must have fallen upon me, gazing like a goon at the gentleman's fine bearing. "But there's my nephew here—" he added, well aware that my willing agricultural efforts would scarcely be missed.

Richard Fermor turned to look at me, too, and a poor, uninviting sight I must have made with my thin, gangling limbs and straw wisps still in my hair.

"Be he much good?" demurred the bailiff.

"Well, only middlin'," admitted my uncle, being essentially a truthful man.

Master Fermor smiled, though not unkindly. "Middling farm hands are no good to me with shiploads of the best quality wool to be sent abroad, and all the keen cloth competition in Flanders."

"Hundreds of fleeces to be sheared and carted and shipped, as well as a clowder of other goods," elaborated Jordan, the bailiff.

I could see my cousins grinning at my discomfiture, but some eagerness in my stance or some understanding of my father's disappointment in me must have moved my invaluable Uncle Tobias to make another try. "At least he could count 'em," he urged. "The lad has learning, his father being the schoolmaster up to Wenlock Priory."

Master Fermor seemed to take a new interest in me then. "He certainly had his wits about him in getting help so quickly just now. Perhaps he could stay with us and help you with your accounts, Jordan," he suggested. "What is your name, lad?"

"William Somers, Sir," I told him.

"If you want work I suppose I could use you. Before leaving Neston I ridded myself of a young clerk because he cheated me of a shilling. Of a single shilling," he repeated, although he had generously left an uncounted pile of them upon the table. "I suppose you can assure me, William Somers, that though you may be but middling with the sheep, you are more than middling honest?"

"Utterly honest," I heard my uncle vouch for me firmly. And because I suddenly wanted to start out in the service of this gentleman more than I had ever wanted anything except to see my mother and to send my voice singing up to the Priory roof, I stopped slouching by the rain butt and pulled myself erect and looked him straight in the eyes. "I may be a fool, but God strike me dead if I ever wittingly cheat you," I heard myself saying in a choky sort of voice that seemed to run up several octaves beyond my control. I suppose my absurd youthful earnestness must have touched him. I remember wondering at the time whether it was because he happened to have a son or daughter of about my age. And in a daze of incredulity I soon found myself showing him and his disapproving bailiff the way to the school cottage, where my father greeted him with great respect and seemed willing enough for me to go. Although, to give him his due, I do not think he would have sent me away had he not already heard tell of the squire of Easton Neston and felt sure that all would be well with me. "As good a man as ever God made, if report speaks truly, and trades in silks and wheat as well as wool," he assured me as, with a sudden wave of homesickness, I went around the familiar rooms hurriedly gathering up my lute and a few other personal possessions. "See that you make good use of so fine a chance and prove a credit to me and to the good mother who bore you."

It was usual enough for lads of sixteen or so who were not destined to help in the forge or follow the plough to be placed in some gentleman's household. I know now that my father acted wisely in taking the sudden chance, and for me it proved a gateway to the world. To a world of loves and cruelties and ambitions beyond my adolescent understanding, to rare experiences which could not fail to teach even a fool some sort of wisdom, and to success in a guise which neither he nor I nor any of the good people of Wenlock could possibly have foreseen.

Chapter Two

HELPING TO DRIVE SHEEP across two counties tried my strength to the uttermost, as my inexpert efforts must have tried even old Hodge's patience. Mercifully the spring sun shone and the ruts in the road were not too full of water. And weary as I was I felt keenly interested in the journey, never having been so far from home before. I marvelled at the pink and white froth of fruit blossom in the Worcestershire orchards, and stared at the stateliness of Warwick Castle dominating the town through which we dodged laden carts and pack-horses. Even when trudging in a cloud of dust behind an incessantly bleating flock I could not help noticing how farms and towns and manors gradually took on a more prosperous appearance as we travelled in the direction of the trading wealth of East Anglia. Hodge and I moved perforce as slowly as our sheep, and once we were in Northamptonshire our master and his bailiff rode ahead, so by the time we arrived the village people of Easton Neston, by Towcester, were on the look out for us, and many of them left their weaving and came running out from neatly timbered cottages to welcome the well-loved old shepherd and to enquire after the lad whose place I had taken. "There be master's manor at last," Hodge told me as we turned aside towards the large farm buildings, and looking through the main gateway I saw that delectable house with its stonework and latticed windows bathed in the pink light of sunset.

I remember little of that first evening save that I was treated kindly and given food, and that almost before swallowing the last mouthful I must have thrown myself down thankfully to sleep beside the embers of the stockman's kitchen fire.

It was a good life, a bustling kind of life, at Neston, lived among people too fully occupied by the numerous branches of their master's business to have time for petty meannesses. In the employ of a prosperous merchant farmer who is as zealous about the quality of the wheat and wool he trades to Flanders as he is about the rich silks and spices which his ships bring back from Venice there are a dozen ways in which a young man who is not work-shy can make himself useful and get on. Particularly if he has sufficient enthusiasm and imagination to see his own small piece of work as something that will help to enlarge his world. Even counting sheep as they were passed through the shearing dip, which was all I was called upon to do at first, I felt remotely connected with the foreign ports to which the woollen cloth would ultimately go. Later in the summer, making out bills of lading at some quiet desk from which I could see the strings of pack-horses being laden, I could almost hear the wind in the rigging of the ship to whose hold the bales of merchandise would be lowered at some East Anglian port. Coming from a sleepy village, I found each day exciting, and experienced a new sense of elation because almost anything might happen on the morrow.

At first I had been shy and often homesick, and tired out with farm work too heavy for my frame. It was then that Father Thayne, the village priest, was so good to me. More than once he invited me into his house where, finding that I could read Latin, he allowed me to browse among his meagre store of books. I think it must have been he who reminded Jordan that a more clerkly occupation had been promised me. And once, when he must have seen the tears in my eyes, he took me up to the Manor because he had remembered—or invented—a bit of carpentry that was needed to the bracket of the chapel hour-glass. He left me there, and while I was struggling with it—perhaps by his invention, too—a girl of about my own age came in, carrying a bowl of fragrant buds from the rose garden. I guessed that she must be Master Fermor's only unmarried daughter Joanna whom I had heard my work-mates speak of as "the young mistress." She paused, surprised at finding me there, so that I saw her that first time standing framed in the archway of the open door with the morning sunlight making a radiance about her head. I thought her more beautiful than any stained-glass angel in the windows of Wenlock Priory, and I think so still.

"Are you the young man my father brought back from Shropshire in poor Cob Woodman's place?" she asked, coming into the cool shadow of the chapel.

I stepped down from the bench I had been standing on and stood before her, hammer in hand and very conscious of my wind-tousled hair and stained farm clothes. "Yes, milady," I said, not knowing how else to address her.

"Then you must be a long way from home. I trust you are settling into our busy ways?" she said, with an air of responsibility which sat oddly upon her slender youth.

"Everyone has been very kind," I answered stiffly.

She tilted her golden head a little on one side as though catching some unexpected gentleness in my speech, just as the priest had done. "Father Thayne spoke to me about you yesterday," she said, regarding me with less conventional concern and more personal interest. "He thought you were homesick. Are you wishing very much that you could leave us and go back there?"

I was sure then that the good man, knowing her to be young and kind, had manoeuvred our meeting, and blessed him for it. And surprised myself by saying vehemently, "I have no real home, and would not leave here for anything!"

She laughed at my unexpected vehemence, her carefully assumed role of chatelaine broken up by merriment. Then, as though suddenly remembering the consecrated place in which we stood, she turned to the small carved statue of our Lady and set down her flowers at its foot. Crossing herself, she knelt in prayer, and, thinking she had forgotten my existence, I laid down my tools for later use and tip-toed to the door so as not to disturb her. Coming out from dimness into the sunny manor courtyard,

I almost tripped over her deerhound bitch, and sat down on the chapel steps to fondle the lovely, cream-coloured creature while I waited. To my surprise, when her mistress joined us, she had not forgotten our brief conversation. "What did you mean just now when you said you had no real home?" she asked.

I scrambled to my feet while Blanchette, the hound, gathered up her graceful limbs more leisurely.

I felt the shamed blood burn my face for so angling for her feminine sympathy. "I lied," I said, almost sullenly. "I have always had a home with good food and books and music, and a father who kept me far better fettled than I deserved. It is only that—none of these benefits seem to make a real home if one has no mother." Half smiling, I raised my eyes to hers. "But that must sound foolishness to you."

"To *me?*" The words were full of reproach and pained surprise; and suddenly I remembered Jordan telling me the very first evening I arrived that Master Fermor was but recently widowed, and how the stockman's wife had complained that the maidservants were growing pert and out-of-hand because there was no chatelaine. No one but Mistress Joanna and a spinster relative who had always lived with them. But I must have been too sleepy to take in what they said. "Forgive me," I stammered foolishly. "I have thought of you only as the daughter of a fine house...."

"And do you imagine that griefs are not felt in fine houses?" she asked angrily. She had been trying to take her mother's place, to show a kindly interest in her father's servants, and I had behaved like a clumsy, heartless dolt. I had thrown away the comfort of her sweet kindness which Father Thayne had wished for me. What mattered far more, I must have hurt her. But before I slunk away she turned and laid a hand, light as a petal, on my bare brown arm. "Do not be unhappy," she said softly. "I know what it is to be lonely. I offered a prayer for you just now, to our Lady."

She had prayed for me, though she did not even know my name. After that there was no more homesickness. Lying in the attic which I now shared with some of the house servants, long after their bawdy gossip had turned into healthy snores, I felt the cool touch of her fingers on my flesh. During the day-time I watched for a glimpse of her, walking on the terrace or riding out of the gates, and instead of finishing up my food with the farm-workers in the great kitchen I would hover by the opening of the serving screens to catch a glimpse of her at board. Because she had seemed to care I felt myself bound to Neston Manor and challenged to do well in her father's service. I often worked on by candle-light at dull account books as if on me alone, an insignificant clerk, depended the weal of the Fermor family, even discovering a fault or two in my dishonest predecessor's untidy reckoning. Although Jordan grudged me the intimacy of estate affairs which such work entailed, he was no scholar himself, and had the good sense to realise that by relying on me more and more he was left freer for the over-seeing of more important business. When our master came home from a visit to his other property in East Anglia I secretly hoped that he would commend me, but beyond a kindly word in passing and an enquiry as to whether Jordan found me satisfactory he took no particular notice of me. And, as I have often confessed to Father Thayne, I am one of those miserable sinners who hunger to be noticed. I need to bolster up my inadequacy with applause, as stronger men need breath.

Although I was now living in the Manor itself it was, quite naturally, the bailiff who took the books to his master's room and the bailiff who discussed profits and prices, and it was not long before I suspected that he must have passed off all those hardly-laboured-over columns of figures as his own. But, fume as I might, I dared say nothing.

Always careful for others, Mistress Joanna must have sensed my depression. "Is my father pleased with you?" she asked, one sunny morning, as I forestalled her groom at the mounting block to hold her stirrup.

"How should I know when he has scarcely spoken to me since he employed me?" I answered ungraciously, without raising my head.

"If you employed as many people as he does or had as many important concerns on your mind you might understand," she said sharply, and beckoning to her tardy groom she wheeled her mare so that the mud from her fresh heels splashed me in the face.

The well-merited rebuke kept me in gloom all morning but next day I learned from Jordan that a ship was in from Venice bringing some of our merchandise and Master Fermor was off to Norwich almost immediately. And scarcely had I sat down to my work next morning before Mistress Emotte, the stern, middle-aged aunt who had been nurse to all the Fermor children and who was now in some sort housekeeper, poked her horse-like face in at the window where we worked. "Master Jordan," she called, "the young mistress wants you to spare her that new young clerk who works for you. She has all the household lists to make out for her father's ordering while in Norwich, and as usual all laid on inexperienced young shoulders on the spur of the moment."

"You mean young Somers here?" temporised Jordan, loath to let me go on a busy morning.

The woman's hawk eyes swivelled round upon me, obviously disapproving of what they saw. "I have no notion what his name is," she said tartly, "nor what sort of use he is likely to be to her. But my mistress has taken the fancy to employ him."

So I gathered up pen and paper and followed the gaunt, straight-backed old lady to a kind of store-room between the buttery and the kitchen. Sun shone through a small, open casement and outside in the herb garden thrushes were singing, and there was Mistress Joanna, looking very young and rather flushed and harassed, with an assortment of food-stuffs laid out on a great table before her and the head cook at her side. "Scarcely enough honey to last the winter, do you think, Diggory?" she was saying, in business-like tones ridiculously like her father's. "We had better order some of that sugar from one of the Italian merchants. How much do you use in a week?"

"Brown sugar for the wassail bowl at Christmas," Mistress Emotte reminded her.

They began earnestly discussing first this commodity and then that, and Mistress Joanna waved a hand in my direction without looking round. "Write down the quantities as I say them," she directed. "And when you have a moment count those jars of mulberry preserve on that shelf."

I had thought her to be lily-handed, never realising the responsibilities that the chatelaine of a large manor has to shoulder. A household of twenty or so to be fed, not counting the farmhands, the visitors, the merchants and their clerks who came on business, our own pack-horse drivers, the grooms and the village poor. And the unspeakable, inhospitable shame of running out of anything not grown on the estate which could not be replenished without sending to Northampton, or Norwich perhaps, or even London.

"Some more of those spices with which the Master likes me to dress his meat," Diggory was suggesting.

"Pepper, cinnamon, and ginger root for a good caudle if anyone should fall sick," enumerated Mistress Joanna.

"Dates, and those oranges that you love, Madam—"

"We can get all the tallow candles we need from the chandler here," decided Mistress Joanna, peering into a deep cupboard. "But Father Thayne was saying we shall soon need some tall wax ones for the altar. Write down two score, Will. And now for the cellar. Where is Simon? How much red wine do we need, Simon? I hear there will be a ship in from Bordeaux—"

Two of the maidservants were called in to go hastily through boxes where silks and needles were kept, and so the animated conversation went on while I tried to keep account of the quantities.

"You will need a new gown for Christmas, Madam."

"Some of that new scarlet brocade I should like, all shot with gold threads. Master Purdy said when he was last here from Norwich that he could get me some from Florence—"

"And pins—"

"And a new basting spoon."

"And shoes for us maids."

"Yes, yes, I will buy you some. And we must not forget some strong wooden shoes for old Hodge when he has to go out in the snow."

"You're sure you've written down milady's dress length, young fellow?" demanded Emotte.

"Scarlet and gold for Christmas," repeated my lady, with a lilt in her voice.

The hour sped by and we were scarcely finished before the Master of the House came striding in through the open door, cloaked for riding, and briskly impatient. "Well, my sweeting, what commissions have you for me?" he asked. "I cannot wait long. They are bringing the horses round now."

"Thanks to my new clerk we have finished in time for once," said Mistress Joanna, with a prodigious sigh of relief. "Give the list to your master, Will."

She might just as easily have handed it to him herself since it lay before her on the table, but she chose that moment to sink down on a chest of bed linen with a dramatic gesture of exhaustion so that the neat sheet of words and figures, as I handed it, seemed to be particularly of my own making. A satisfaction which that curmudgeon Jordan had never permitted me.

Master Fermor stood reading it through. "Six score hogshead of wine at eightpence a gallon. Do we keep the King's bodyguard?" he grumbled, half humorously, as breadwinners will the world over. "Ah, well, I will see what I can do." He folded the list and thrust it into the velvet travelling wallet which I had so much admired when I had first seen him in Shropshire, and turned to me with an approving grin. "Very well set out, young man," he said. "I can see that I shall have to take you with me next time I go abroad on business."

I stood tingling with pleasure while he bade farewell to his daughter and to Emotte, and almost before the door closed behind him Mistress Joanna was kneeling on the window-seat with her head thrust out in all the blustering rain and wind, waving to him as he mounted outside in the courtyard. "Be sure that you sleep in a well-aired bed tonight," she called, much as her mother must have done, as his little cavalcade began to clatter off across the wet and slippery stones. "And I pray you do not forget my dress length."

By the time she turned back into the room Emotte had hurried after the cook for some last-minute conference and, my little lady's thoughts being still with the departing travellers, she seemed surprised to find me still waiting there.

"I stayed to thank you," I said. "You called me in purposely—out of kindness—and then let me hand it to him."

"But see how you helped us!" she protested laughingly, tucking a rain-glistening curl back beneath her demure headdress. "It was but a small thing to do," she added more seriously. "I hate injustice."

"If it was a small thing I am hugely grateful," I said. And this time my voice did not go croaking and squeaking as it still did sometimes through nervousness, but sounded deep and true with a man's emotion. "And if ever Life should grant me some service which I can render you, I shall remember."

From that day I felt myself to be truly one of the household. Master Fermor must have left orders that I was to eat in hall. Oh, only at the end of a lower table, of course, between the head carpenter and the falconer's assistant. But I no longer had need to peer round the screens, roundly cursed by the hurrying servants as they bore in the dishes. From where I sat I could see my lady, every meal time, sitting at the family table beside her father, talking to him or helping to entertain their guests. If I could not hear what she said at least I could watch her lively movements and sometimes catch the bright music of her laughter.

Chapter Three

I T WAS THE FOLLOWING spring, in the throes of first love, that I
began composing love songs. Mere snatches of song they were,
that kept dancing through my brain as lightly as moonlight on
swaying branches. But being begot of true emotion, they were not
without some small, transient beauty. Although the composing of
verse was all the fashion among the gallants at court and in great
houses, I should have been laughed at for an affected ninny had my
comrades in a plain, commercially minded household overheard
me. So each evening when my compulsory archery practice was
done, and the other young men were still competing at the butts
or dancing to a fiddle in some barn, I would slip away to a deserted
corner I had discovered and sit on an old bench beneath that very
window of the store-room from which Mistress Joanna had looked
out, waving goodbye to her father. It was sheltered on one side by
an angle of the kitchen wall and on the other by the high box hedge
of the herb garden, and where the land stretched away behind that
western wing of the house there was an unimaginably lovely view.
So there I would loiter, wallowing in the enjoyable melancholy of
youth which a lovely sunset engenders, or, supposing myself to be
alone save for sleepy birds, I would strum my lute and give voice to
my love-sick vapours.

And it was there that my lady first came to me of her own
free will. She must have been walking in the herb garden and
heard me.

> *"You move in grace so far above*
> *Such thoughts as I may dare,*
> *So far beyond my humble love*
> *You smile, all unaware,"*

I sang, and it was only when my fingers had thrummed the last yearning chord that I looked down and saw the shadow of her gown against the dipping sun, and realised that she must have been standing there for some time.

"How amazingly sweetly you sing, Will!" she said. She was evidently surprised at hearing so trained a voice in the vicinity of the buttery windows, but mercifully did not ask me who composed the words.

I sprang up, pulling the fustian cap from my head. "My father taught me. He is choir-master at Wenlock Priory," I told her with pardonable pride.

"So *that* is how you came by your gentle speech and your Latin," she answered with a smile. "Why do you sit here all alone?"

"I did not know that you—that any of the family—ever walked here," I apologised in confusion.

"Oh, I was not chiding you. You are free to come here whenever you like. I merely wondered why you prefer this place."

I pointed to the little river shimmering through the valley and a distant farmstead half gathered into a fold of the darkening hills. "It is so peacefully beautiful in this evening light."

Perhaps the fact that such an aesthetic consideration should concern me surprised her as much as my singing. She did not answer immediately but seated herself on the bench I had vacated, thoughtfully spreading her skirts around her. "Those are the very words my mother used. She often came here at this time of the day, although *she* had all the rose garden and terrace to choose from."

I drew nearer, forgetting everything except that we were two young people with some similarity of thought drawing us together. "You loved her very much?" I asked gently.

"Yes."

"I scarcely remember mine."

"That is perhaps worse. It must do something to a child, having no memories of what you called a *real* home."

"It makes one feel—different."

"Have you no brothers or sisters?"

I shook my head. "At least you have an elder brother," I said, having frequently heard people speak of the heir, Master John, who was abroad.

"And two married sisters, but I do not often see them. And a young brother with the same name as you who is being brought up in my Uncle William's household right away in Somerset. The others died."

"And that day by the chapel I spoke as if you knew nothing of grief!"

We had been talking quietly to match the evening hour and our mood, and she dismissed my former *bêtise* with a shrug. "My brother John will be coming home soon, and everything will be bustle and entertainment. You will have to make music for us sometimes when we have company. But tell me about your life in Shropshire and how you came to be driving our sheep home when you can write clerkly Latin," she invited.

So I told her about our lovely priory, and the harvest suppers, and imitated our pompous beadle hauling a poacher before the Mayor, and my uncle arguing with Sir James Tyrrell about the boundaries of Frith Common, until she laughed aloud and the sun sank down below the rich fields in a blaze of splendour and we could hear Emotte's shrill voice calling. "I must go. The dear old dragon is always terrified lest I catch a chill as my mother did," she said. "But I shall have to ask my father if you can amuse us with some of your crazy mimicry in hall."

It is easy enough to be amusing when one is happy. Because I was at ease, all the absurd antics with which I had entertained the folk at Wenlock came back to me. Rhyming couplets slipped involuntarily from my tongue, through sheer lightness of spirit. But now, because I was happy, there was no malice in them. Save for the rare occasions when I was stirred to anger and meant to leave my sting, I found that

I could mock without giving offence. Almost affectionately I could mimic our beloved Father Thayne torn between making his theological point and watching the hour-glass, or even Master Fermor himself trying to avoid the determined efforts of local ladies who felt that it was high time he married again, and I teased that forbidding woman Emotte until, ceasing to fear her sharp tongue, I found her soft heart. Because people of all degrees love to laugh, I became popular in kitchen, stables or hall. If I heard Mistress Joanna laugh I was well rewarded, but I fed on the applause, too. And sometimes of an evening I was called into my master's private room to sing my songs, and that often mended my conceit, because some of the French and Italian merchants, cultured by travel, knew far more about music than I. And I noticed how some of the titled gallants from neighbouring manors made languishing eyes at Joanna as they sang, which was something which I, poor loon, was not in a position to do.

I began to long to travel. To speak easily of foreign parts, and wear a modish doublet, as they did. And when I was trusted enough to be sent on some errand into Northampton I spent what time I dared looking covetously at the tailors' wares.

Was I spoiled at Neston? Given too much liberty? Perhaps. But people have ever been kind to me.

I shall always hold in my memory an evening just before Master John came back from Florence, and was to stay at Neston before going home to his wife in London. All day the women had been in a turmoil of preparation, and as soon as my work for Jordan was done I had been pressed into helping them to unfold and hang the best set of arras for the walls of the guest chamber. When the last heavy length had been stretched and pegged in place, the great four-poster made ready and logs piled high in the fireplace, Emotte, outraged because moths had got at the bed-hangings, had sent me to tell Mistress Joanna that she and one of the maids would be staying to repair them before daylight gave out.

I found my lady in the family room sitting in rare idleness before the fire. "What it is to be the eldest son! A good thing perhaps that he does not come home every week or we should all be prostrate," she exclaimed, half rueful and half laughing. "Oh, I am tired, Will! Are not you?"

"A little," I confessed, for it was I who had been up and down the ladder stretching those tapestries from peg to peg because Emotte and her maids had declared that I climbed like a monkey.

"Then stay awhile and sing to me," invited Mistress Joanna.

"Here?" I faltered, never having been with her alone in this luxurious room before.

"Yes, here," she decreed. "It is lonely sometimes when my father is busy with his papers, and now Emotte will be darning till her eyes drop out. Sing that one I specially love about the May Queen and the miller's son. Take my brother's old lute from the shelf. He has bought himself a new one now."

I went to the hearth first and carefully shook the wall dust from the plain, clerkly garments which my master had provided for me. Then, fetching the beribboned and ill-used instrument, I squatted cross-legged on a stool beyond the pool of firelight and sang as she bade me. She listened with her head resting against a cushion, and her eyes half closed. So when I ran out of her favourite songs, I went on improvising softly on the strings. I thought I had lulled her to sleep, but when I stopped she roused herself with a sigh. "That was very beautiful. How did I manage to pass the winter evenings before you came, Will Somers?"

Her words filled me with a rush of happiness. From my lowly seat in the shadows I allowed my eyes to devour her loveliness—a dangerous delight which I should have known better than to allow myself. "Your brother will be home tomorrow and then you will not need me," I said, my voice sharpened by a pang of jealousy.

If she recognised the impertinence of my feelings she ignored it. "You will have to imitate Jordan paying the wages for him. We used to laugh so much when we were all at home together," she said. As though suddenly rested, she clapped her hands and leaned forward, all childlike eagerness. "We must devise some special entertainment for his homecoming. We ought to be doing it now instead of idling. My father means to invite all our best friends to sup in a few days' time. Why should we not perform a masque?"

"A masque?" I repeated stupidly. "Like they do at Court, you mean?"

"Oh, not so *grand*, of course."

"But—we have never been there," I objected. "I do not know the first thing—"

"No, but I do. My brother's wife has described them to me. She is sister to Lord Vaux, and she has been to Court and saw two masques performed last Christmas, and the little Princess Mary danced in one of them while the King and Queen watched. Maud—my sister-in-law—said it was the loveliest thing she had ever seen. The costumes were unbelievable, and they had a mountain built at one end of the hall to represent Olympus, with real sheep grazing on it. And when the three goddesses all in white samite came dancing down the side of the mountain poor Paris—the shepherd boy, you know—had to choose which one to give the apple to. Juno, the Goddess of Heaven, Minerva, the Goddess of Wisdom, or Venus, the Goddess of Beauty."

I sprang up eagerly. "If I had been Paris—" I began, thinking that she had never looked more beautiful. But she was too full of her project to be interested in what I might or might not have done in ancient Greece.

"They performed something about the Virtues and the Vices, too, with all the good people dressed in white and all the bad ones dressed in black. And an ingenious wooden Hell that opened, and a Devil with tail and pitchfork. I don't think I should like that so much, but we could do Persephone and Pluto, and her poor mother Ceres trying to prevent him from dragging her from Earth down to his Underworld, and then their arranging that she should live half the year in each place. There would have to be girls dressed as Spring, of course, and men as cruel Winter. And plenty of singing and dancing. *You* must make up the songs, Will."

Her enthusiasm was catching. We both of us were of the temperament to be fired by some crazy idea. And besides wanting to please her I knew, quite suddenly and surely, that this was the sort of thing that I should be better at than clerking. That it would be something which I could take great joy in doing, apart from wanting all the approval and applause. "I doubt not I could make some sort of show with the words and tunes," I boasted. "But never in my life have I had the chance to learn a proper dance step."

"But you can *caper*," she insisted. "You know, Will, how you made everyone in hall nearly choke over their wassail with your absurd capering last Christmas." I remembered only too well, for had she not worn the new scarlet and gold gown and looked radiant? "And as for the Spirits of Spring," she went on, "I can devise some measure and ask some of my friends to come and practise it. Something light-hearted and rustic."

She lifted her skirts above her little ankles and began to try out a kind of morris dance, and her slender body was so full of verve and joyousness that soon she had passed from that to the role of Persephone. "Look! I am flying from the thought of living in the Underworld and crying out to Ceres to plead for me—my hair should be unbound and flying in the wind—and Pluto is chasing me!" she cried breathlessly, pulling off her headdress and throwing convincing glances of terror over her shoulder. "Come, come, Will, don't stand there like a moonstruck dolt! Be Pluto, and give chase. Caper if you cannot dance...."

Round and round the room she danced, and I after her, capering and leering like a devil because I had no other conception of how the Lord of the Underworld might have looked. Until, turning, she caught sight of me and missed her own steps for laughing. "Will, Will, you are the realest devil rather than a god!" she cried breathlessly. "I swear I can almost smell the brimstone." She held her nose, and realistically, with raised arms and clawing fingers, I made a fantastic grab at her and caught her so that she shrieked in feigned, delighted terror. Breathless, laughing, she leaned against me. And I held her. Unplanned, frolic turned to passion. For a brief mad moment torn out of the sanity of time I held her warm, human fragrance in my arms, with her tumbled, golden hair against my cheek. God knows I tried to remember my place, to be respectful, not to let her feel how crazed I was at the touch of her. I believe that her innocent unawareness was not so much as singed by the brimstone. It was I who was burned. Burned to the realisation of manhood, to the depth of my being and for all time. Yet I shall ever draw self-respect from the fact that I had made myself release her before the door opened and my master came in.

I swung round at once, but Joanna had not heard because she was still laughing with her face up-turned to mine.

"Why are you almost in the dark?" he asked.

"We had not noticed," she said, hurrying to greet him. "Will is helping me to plan a masque for John's homecoming, and Mottie is so busy I expect she forgot to tell them to bring the candles."

"That woman is always busy. She should be here with you," Master Fermor said sharply. I think it must have been then that the thought first crossed his over-occupied mind that we two were too much together.

When a servant had brought in the lighted candles and departed he laid a present on the table for his daughter, but he was staring across the room at me. Quite understandably my humble position in his household, and my plainness perhaps, had excluded such a thought before; but now he was taking no chances. He looked at me as appraisingly as he looked for possible bad points in a stallion before buying. Joanna had run to the mirror to try on the necklace he had brought her, and he turned to admire the effect. "It will look even better with your hair bound up seemingly," he said, but softened the reproof by adding, "Perhaps you would like to ride with me to invite some of our friends to sup with us next week?"

She threw herself upon him with a cry of joy. "I have the kindest father in England!" she cried, in that extravagant way of hers, standing on tip-toe the better to strangle him with her embrace.

He detached her clinging arms and kissed her and, without looking in my direction, said, "Then you had better leave your mummery, Will, and tell them to have Mistress Joanna's jennet ready saddled with my roan as soon as it is light tomorrow. And be sure to have that invoice ready for me to take to the Vintners' Guild while I am in Northampton."

I knew that without any unjust show of displeasure he was putting me in my place, and I bade them both a respectful good-night. "You have forgotten to put away Master John's lute," he added, with an arm still about his daughter and not knowing, perhaps, how coldly he spoke nor how protective his strong arm looked. I removed the lute from the stool where, in my perturbed state, I had left it, and setting it carefully on a shelf, closed the door behind me with a mixture of reluctance and relief. It hurt damnably to feel myself firmly excluded from that pleasant family room, but even then I had enough loyalty and sense to acknowledge that Richard Fermor was kind and practical and wise. "Oh, most assuredly he was wise!" I muttered, beating with angry fists against the prickly straw of my mattress that night. For what was I but a clerk in his household, whose blood ran too hot at times to have much wisdom of his own?

Chapter Four

ONCE THE MARRIED SON of the house was back from abroad on a visit there was plenty for all of us to do. There was hunting and hawking and feasting, and Neston Manor seemed always to be full of people—younger and more fashionable people than we usually saw, who made the fine hall ring with their gaiety after supper. Mistress Joanna was the life of the party, never sparing herself to make her brother's visit a success, but sometimes I thought she looked tired and somehow the masque which we had half-planned was never performed. Master John always had more modern ideas of his own.

He was fair and good to look upon like the rest of his family; clever and self-confident, yet somehow lacking the dependable firmness of his father. His fine leather boots were tooled in Florence, his cardinal red hose were the latest craze in Rome, and his slashed doublets could only have been cut in Paris. Athletic as he looked, he used some womanish kind of perfume and liked to impress the ladies by introducing Italian words into his conversation with seeming casualness. Or was I being unfair to him because I have never had the advantages of a rich man's son?

The truth is I did not like him from the first. Perhaps I was jealous of him because, with him and his fine friends about, Mistress Joanna had no need of my company. He knew all the latest songs from Paris, and smiled tolerantly at our homespun kind of entertainment.

Actually, even had he invited me to help with their merrymaking, I should have been far too much occupied. For weeks I was kept busy checking the bales of silk and boxes of delicious-smelling spices which had filled the hold of the ship in which he had sailed home. Besides which it fell to my share to cope with a mass of figuring concerning some deal which he had made in Florence on his father's behalf, this being rendered the more complicated because he had bought at lower prices than we were accustomed to, and Master Fermor, being the honest trader he was, altered all his own prices to regular customers accordingly.

Master John talked a good deal about that cheap contract, though I had the feeling that my master was not altogether happy about it. But what Master John talked about most in company was how he had met our Cardinal Wolsey's agent, John Clark, in Florence, and on what friendly terms he and this confidential agent were. When it came down to facts it appeared that young Fermor, finding him financially embarrassed in a foreign country, had lent him money. And always we were hearing how beholden this John Clark had been to him, and—what was far more important, I suppose, to anyone who went to Court—how beholden the great, all-powerful Cardinal himself would be when he came to hear of it. Without doubt Master John's high-born in-laws, the Vaux family of Harroden, would be mightily pleased. But unfortunately it was his own father's money that had bought the gratifying situation.

"How much *did* you let him have?" asked Master Fermor anxiously, that last evening when the guests his son had been bragging to were finally gone. Because his son had avoided talking business until almost the moment of his departure and I had stayed up late to bring my master the account books he had asked for, I could not but overhear.

"Nearly two hundred pounds," Master John admitted. "That was why I could not buy the silks from Barbarino's of Venice as usual."

"But Barbarino's stuff is *good*. Whereas I know nothing of this new Florentine merchant, save that his prices are cheaper—"

"But do you not understand, Sir, how much more important this was than a mere trade deal?" explained the son of the house, with scarcely veiled impatience. "Cardinal Wolsey is the coming man of Europe. Between ourselves, his agent was over there negotiating for the Papacy. His gentleman usher, Cavendish, told me when I was last in London that they have very high hopes. Think what it would mean to us to have the Pope himself remembering your obligingness!"

The prospect was so amazing that I admit I upset an ink-horn and started repairing my clumsiness in order to delay my departure, and so heard my master mutter something about a bird in the hand being worth two in the bush and there being a regular clutch of ambitious cardinals to choose from. And Master John, who obviously considered anyone to be old-fashioned who was not in the swim of Court life, said in his cocksure way, "Well, in any event, I acted wisely. Even from a trade point of view alone I was looking after your interests. For this clerk of his was so grateful that he has promised to bring our name before milord Cardinal next time it comes to ordering silks for those rich robes he wears. And we all know how wealthy Thomas Wolsey is. And how extravagant he can be! Why, this new house he is building at Hampton will be grander than the King's palace at Greenwich."

"Let us hope that this man Clark remembers," said Richard Fermor, only partly mollified. "Men have short memories, I often find, when they are no longer needing anything."

"You will get the order, never fear," his son assured him. "And in the meantime there on your table is the residue of your money which I brought back after paying off the ship's master."

"His freight charges were higher this time," commented my master, lifting up a rather meagre bag of coins and motioning to me to wait just as I reached the door.

"Iniquitous, I call them," agreed Master John. "You know, Sir, you should really lay down more ships of your own instead of chartering. All the other merchants of your standing do."

"I already have six," commented his father, with a wry smile.

"Well, at least there are fifty sovereigns towards the seventh," laughed Master John, indicating the moneybag.

Whether his father thought this much or little to bring back I do not know. "Have you counted them?" he asked.

"Hurriedly, before joining the others for the hunt yesterday morning. But I am no clerk. Better check them again." Thanks to his father's exertions John Fermor had married into a titled family and his mind was never seriously on the family business. Indeed, he affected to despise it. He was so much interested in social advancement that the more solid romance of commerce passed him by. After he had taken an airy leave before returning to his real interests in London it was as if some whiff of Court life were gone and his father's room looked solid and ordinary again, yet somehow remarkably comfortable. "Here, Will, take this money with you and count it before entering it in the foreign ledger, and then put it in my strong room," ordered its owner as soon as we were left alone. Normally he would have locked it away himself, but there was a weariness of disappointment in his voice. To rear a son who grows too grand for gratitude could be, I thought, more bitter than to lose him, still warmly loving, in battle.

Although I had sometimes counted the contents of money bags before, this was the first time that ever I was entrusted with the strong-room key. I thrust it into the wallet hanging from my belt and carried the bag down to the deserted estate office and, untying its leather thong, spread a flood of glittering sovereigns across my table. Fifty of them, and some silver, according to the accompanying statement. It might not seem much to the Fermors, but to me—who had seldom had the handling of more than a few shillings of my own—it looked enticing as the wealth of all the Indies. I set to and counted it and had half risen again, prepared to sweep it all back into the soiled leather bag, when suddenly I stopped in surprise. I had counted fifty-six sovereigns. Six sovereigns too many. Nearly thrice as much as my wages for a year. Master John, in his careless haste, must have reckoned them wrongly. Instinctively I rose to run and tell him, but remembered that he had already gone. I had heard the horses. And in any case what would six of his father's sovereigns be to him? In his gay life and the excitement of returning to London and of reunion with his wife he was not likely ever to think of that grubby money-bag again.

And then the despicable thought came to me that neither his father nor the bailiff need ever know either. Jordan had been out since morning settling a dispute about some straying cattle, and Master Fermor was on the point of riding into Northampton to catch up on some business which had been delayed during his son's visit. I—and I alone—knew about those six odd pounds.

I came slowly to my feet and stood with them spread out temptingly along my outstretched palm. Balancing the forces of good and evil, as one might say—the white and black spirits, as Mistress Joanna had said they were portrayed in that royal masque. The thought of her, so honestly fought against during my preoccupation with affairs, rushed back into my mind. Now that her brother was gone and life would be falling into a normal routine she would probably be needing me again. Asking me to sing to her some evening when the day's work was done, in that well-furnished family room when her father was away, perhaps.

With six golden sovereigns in my pocket I could go into the best tailor's shop in Northampton and buy myself a velvet doublet— even a velvet doublet with slashed sleeves. I could buy a pretty fairing and appear before her, not in the guise of an insignificant clerk, but like those sons of neighbouring land-owners who had been bringing her gifts and with whom she had been laughing and talking so much of late. For only some devil of injustice knew why I, who loved her so much more ardently than any of them, must always appear at such a disadvantage! After all, I argued, though I might be plain of face, I had a reasonably good leg that would look the better in silk hose. Having been smiled at enticingly by the scatter-brained young sister of one of her brother's friends, I could not but realise that good living and responsibility must have improved me and given me poise.

The coins were half-way into my wallet and I had moved, dreaming of finding favour by such means, to the open window; and it must have been the sight of fields brown in furrow that brought me back to sanity. What sort of figure should I, Will Somers, who had once sweated at the plough, cut in a slashed velvet doublet? And somehow the sight of practical farm buildings brought back to my mind the day when I had stood beside Uncle Tobias's water butt and sworn to Richard Fermor in that cracked, adolescent voice of mine, "God strike me dead if I ever wittingly cheat you!" And should I now break my word to a master who had ever been just and considerate to me?

Far better that I should spend my small, honestly earned wages on taking that brown-eyed dairymaid who doted on me to the fair—except that brown eyes never did much move me.

I could hear the stable boy bringing round Master Fermor's horse. Clutching the bag in one hand and the odd coins in the other I made for the stairs and rushed up two at a time towards his room. "Sir—" I panted breathlessly, almost colliding with him at the top.

"Pardy, what is the hurry, Will?" he exclaimed, in annoyance.

"The money," I said, feeling that I could not rid myself of it quickly enough. I held out the sovereigns all sticky in my palm. "There are six more than Master John told you. He must have miscounted them."

My master stood at the top of the stairs, a man of medium height and age, good-looking, with gloves and riding crop in hand. A moment more and he, too, would have been gone. He frowned down at the money, annoyed as he always was by carelessness. I do not think that any other aspect of the matter occurred to him at that moment. If I had imagined—and half hoped—that he would tell me to keep some of the money as reward for my honesty, he did not. Richard Fermor either took honesty for granted in the people he employed, or was instantly rid of them. "Well, put it away now with the rest and give Jordan the key. And be sure to make the necessary alteration in the ledger," he instructed me, his frown relaxing into a half-smile. "I thought at least a hayrick was afire." And as I flattened my thinness respectfully against the wall, downstairs he went, seemingly all unaware that a mighty spiritual battle had been fought.

But I spoke of it to Father Thayne that Friday when I went to Confession. I had been badly shaken by the strength of the temptation and by how nearly I had come to falling, and kept imagining how I should feel now if I had. And, truth to tell, I was afraid for the future, lest, being over much trusted, some other time I might succumb. But that saintly man gave me then, as always, understanding reassurance. "Oh, no, my son. Dishonesty is alien to all your parentage and upbringing. That is one dragon which you have slain," he said. "Just as you will keep in honourable check the powerful force of affection which plagues you and which alone drove you to contemplate keeping your master's money."

"Then—you have guessed?" I whispered.

"And prayed that you might be given strength to keep it as something wholly beautiful and good. But always bear in mind, my son, that, being in his household, there are more serious and subtle ways in which you could cheat him than by stealing merely money."

Father Nicholas Thayne was right. Whatever temptations might assail me during the rest of my life—and they were legion—all temptation to line my own pocket dishonestly had retreated from me for ever. Somehow the incident had left me hardier spiritually and grown to manhood.

Perhaps my master sensed this growth in me. From then onwards he usually took me with him when he rode abroad on business. He would hand over to me customers' money uncounted, and in all matters of business he gave me his confidence as he would to Jordan—a confidence which I found to be more precious than a purse full of ill-gotten gold or any sense of importance or smiling favours which it might buy. More than once I went with him to East Anglia.

In Ipswich he pointed out to me the grazing land and house where Thomas Wolsey had been born, and I was amazed to see that it was no bigger than my Uncle Tobias's farm. And there I beheld the great trading ships which I, being inland bred, had always longed to see. He decided to take his son's advice, and in the yards on the River Orwell I watched the shipwrights laying down a new ship for him, and was allowed to clamber aboard and watch the massive timbers being bolted together for the deep, cavernous hold.

And never shall I forget the kindness I received at Neston when a travelling friar who had lain a night or two at Wenlock Priory brought me the news that my father was dead. About farm and buttery the dairy people did me small, simple kindnesses. That day Jordan somehow brought himself to admit gruffly that I had been of some use to him. My sweet young mistress had tears in her eyes when she spoke of my loss. And it was then that I discovered the warm heart beneath Emotte's severity. "You have no home or parents now, poor Will," she said, laying her hand on my arm in a rare gesture of emotion. "Because the good God has never given me the children I have longed for, you must come to me if there should ever be anything I can do for you."

In spite of her protests and to her huge delight I hugged her hard, and no man can have dared to do that in years. "I have the best home in the world here at Neston," I assured her.

My master, in his practical way, offered to lend me a horse to go back to Shropshire and see my friends and settle my father's affairs, and I would gratefully have gone; but it was just at that time that I first noticed Mistress Joanna began to look pale and listless. Perhaps I noticed it before the others, because I looked at her so often from my seat at the lower table. "Even *you* cannot make her laugh any more," whispered Emotte, beginning to grow worried.

"She will grow better as the warm spring weather comes," prophesied Father Thayne to comfort us.

She made so good a pretence at welcoming her father home from a journey to Norwich just before Christmas and at exclaiming over the exciting parcels he had brought that for the first few hours he noticed nothing amiss. But at supper, when she scarcely spoke and sat toying with her food, I saw him glancing anxiously at her from time to time during his jovial account of his doings. Next day Emotte prevailed upon her to stay in bed, maids scurried upstairs with hot bricks and possets, and towards evening, while I was working dejectedly by candlelight, my master came to me.

"Will, she is really sick," he said. "Take my roan Swiftsure and ride into Northampton to Doctor Mansard. Bring him back with you at once. It is blowing up for a foul night, but you will know how to persuade him."

I was up from my stool in a moment. "Are you afraid that it might be—"

"The same sickness that took my others? It could be. God knows she looks transparent enough."

"Or the fever that Master John spoke of on board his ship?"

"I, too, had thought of that. A man, without being sick himself, can be a carrier, they say."

"But it is surely too long since he was here."

We were talking in quick, half-finished sentences, as I struggled into coat and boots. He must have felt how mutual was our anxiousness. "Here, take my cloak," he said, dragging it from his own shoulders and setting it about my own. "I have told Jeremy to have Swiftsure ready saddled. And, Will," he added awkwardly, "I know that you care as I would have you care—that you would never spare yourself in her service. If I have ever misjudged you in this matter…"

His worried voice tailed off, and I was out of the door and then out in the blustering night, his cloak warm and comforting about me. I am no great horseman and was always terrified of that wicked-eyed roan, but somehow I urged him through that night of lashing rain, by some miracle not breaking our necks in ruts or potholes. And by morning light Doctor Mansard was by my little lady's bedside. He stayed at Neston for three anxious days and nights, caring for her with all his skill. Emotte nursed her devotedly. And by the end of a week the fever had abated and the patient smiled wanly and knew us all again. Her father must have told her that it was I who had fetched the doctor so swiftly, for she sent for me and thanked me, though the effort tired her.

There were no Christmas festivities at Neston Manor that year, but it was arranged that Master Fermor should take her to London in the summer.

"She grows stronger, and Emotte says she eats her food and takes the remedies Mansard ordered," he told me. "But she is so quiet, so listless—so unlike my laughing little wench. I must be growing old, for I cannot seem to rouse her. Something seems to be worrying her."

"Is it not possible that at a time like this she may still be fretting for her lady mother?" I suggested, out of my own experience.

We stood in silence. In that moment we were less master and clerk than two desperate men at the end of our resources. And then the idea came to me. "She used to laugh at a kind of play of shadows I made on the wall by candlelight," I recalled. "Would you allow me, Sir, to try to distract her?"

"Go to her now, Will, with your inane foolery," he said at once, but without much conviction.

I think Emotte was too worn out to make objections. And so I used to go to Mistress Joanna's bedchamber every hour that I could spare from my work. By candlelight I would make a shadow with my hands against the wall. I invented grotesque birds feeding their young, rabbits sitting up to scratch their ears and dragons belching fire, until a small laugh would erupt from behind the half-drawn bed-curtains. By sunlight I would sing snatches of gay songs, make up doggerel about each member of the household, teach her deer-hound Blanchette's puppies to do tricks—anything I could devise to make her laugh and bring back the colour to her cheeks.

"Anything and everything until his head nearly rolls to his breast with weariness after a hard day's work," Emotte would say gruffly, her own face strained with lack of sleep. "Go to your bed and get some sleep, Will Somers, and may the good God bless you!"

The good God blessed us all, for the beloved daughter of the house, who made its heart and sunshine, grew strong and well again. By May Day we saw her dancing with the other girls upon the green. My master sent a messenger with the good news to his son and daughter-in-law in London, Jordan stopped cuffing his subordinates, old Hodge started singing to his sheep, maids and men-servants began courting again, and Father Thayne, who had prayed unceasingly, held a thanksgiving service. It may have lacked the grandeur of the priory I had been accustomed to, but to me, grateful upon my knees, it was the most profound *Te Deum* of my life.

Chapter Five

ALTHOUGH MISTRESS JOANNA WAS restored to health the doctor would not hear of her going to London to visit her brother and sister-in-law and to be taken to Court. "Not with all that smoke-polluted air, and the crowded streets with their stinking gutters," he said firmly. "Let her get strong first in the good country air, and no doubt her father can arrange to take her next year or when he next goes on business."

A year seems a long time to wait when one is seventeen, and she had talked so often of the masques and tournaments which the Vaux side of the family had described, and of the splendid city of London of which her maternal grandfather, Sir William Brown, had been Lord Mayor. "Are you grievously disappointed?" I asked, after Doctor Mansard's mandate had gone forth. She was sitting on the sunny terrace and I had just come back from combining exercise for Blanchette and her two puppies with an errand for Mistress Emotte in Towcester.

"Of course I should love to see all the fine buildings, and the Palace and great Abbey at Westminster. And King Henry and Queen Katherine, and the Court ladies' lovely dresses," she admitted wistfully. "But in some ways I am relieved that it is not to be yet."

"Relieved?" I repeated, standing before her with a wriggling pup under either arm. We had grown to know each other so well by then that it seemed no impertinence to enquire into her affairs.

She explained then, slowly and reluctantly. "It was not only because of the tax which is owing that my father was going to London, nor so that I could visit my relatives. But so as to consult the Browns and the Vaux about arranging a suitable marriage for me."

I let the pups slide down my body to the paving stones and, standing there motionless in the warm morning sunlight, it was as if an arrow loosed by some unseen archer had pierced my heart. Heaven knows why I had never before thought about what was so inevitable. Nor why we had never before spoken of it. It could have been reluctance on her part. And as usual, almost before I had recovered from the piercing blow, her aspect of the matter seemed to me more important than my own. "I have often wondered how it must feel to be a girl of good family and have a husband—arranged," I managed to say, almost impersonally.

She bent over Blanchette, whose head rested against her knee, and began fondling her silken ears. "I think, perhaps, if our childhood homes have been happy, we try not to think of it," she said.

I took a turn about the terrace and came back to her. "Do you know what man it will be?" I asked, hating him as I had never hated any being before.

"Not yet. I do not think my father has decided. It was to have been a young relative of my mother's who would have inherited part of Sir William Brown's estate. I always hoped so."

"Because you loved him?" I asked, kicking viciously at an unoffending stone.

She looked up, puzzled, at my scowling visage. "Loved him?" she repeated, as if the question had scarcely occurred to her. "Not as you probably mean it. We were scarcely more than children when he was brought to stay here. So that we might get to know each other, I imagine. We used to go rowing on this little river and he gave me Blanchette."

"So that is why you care for her so much. Then why are you not going to marry him?" I asked brusquely.

"He was killed in the French wars."

I could have kicked myself, for this was yet another grief which I had never so much as guessed at. "I am sorry," I said inadequately.

"I suppose it is difficult for a man, who can more or less make his own life, to understand," she went on with spirit. "I *liked* him. We had interests in common. And just to have had the comfortable assurance that I should not have to go and live with some complete stranger who might be distasteful to me, or to play second wife to some rich old dotard as some of my friends have had to do—all this meant a great deal to me. To know that one must leave a home like this and perhaps go right away into some far county as my sisters have done is hard enough."

I began to surmise why depression had set in upon her after her illness. "But your father loves you dearly. He would not make an unhappy choice for you," I said, to comfort her.

She pushed Blanchette aside, got up with a sigh and went to lean against the terrace wall. "No, not *willingly*," she said. "But we merchants' daughters are assets of the business. All his friends who have traded successfully and built themselves comfortable manors try to marry their sons and daughters into the older, titled families. He saw to it that my elder sisters made what we call good marriages. It is a fair enough exchange, I suppose. The titled families want the money and we want to climb." She paused to pick thoughtfully at some stonecrop on the wall. "But sometimes it means misery for the daughters, and spoils the sons—as it has spoiled John."

I had never heard that cynical bitterness in her voice before. She seemed no more the laughing girl I had known. But if I was shocked by her outspoken comments I was learning at first hand my first valuable lesson about the power of ambition and the price which women are often called upon to pay for it. Our conversation had saddened me more than anything that had happened since I came. I joined her by the wall, staring out across the home meadow where the assistant falconer was training the fine hawk Master Fermor had given me, which up to that moment had been my pride, but he might as well have been scything grass for all I cared. "Then you will be leaving us?" I said blankly, although I ought to have been prepared to face up to it since the day I first saw her.

"Not going too far, I hope. I might well become mistress of one of these manors in Northamptonshire," she said, turning to me with an attempt at a smile.

"Then you will have to take me with you, as your clerk or your steward," I said, trying to play up to her.

"Or my jester. Have I not always said that you would make a marvellous jester, Will? Not that I am likely to marry into some ducal household and need one. Although it is true that Thomas Vaux keeps one. An amusing little dwarf, my brother says."

I was not particularly flattered by the association of ideas. "I shall come with you in some capacity or other," I insisted stubbornly.

"Will, Will, don't be absurd!" she rallied me. "You never would leave my father. You think so much of him, so why should you want to?"

"Because I could not bear to stay here without you."

The words were said. The truth was out. We stood facing each other, and a silence fell between us. For the first time we were man and maid, without any thought or barrier of difference in worldly position, and in that moment I am sure that she realised that I loved her. And that her instinctive liking for me was so strong that she dared not look ahead. For the first time the crazy hope leapt in me that in this modern world of opportunities, where merchants married into titled families, and cattle dealers' sons rose to be Cardinals, I might one day, by hard work and quick wits, become socially worthy of her. It was a mad and dangerous moment. Controlled by the training of wise parents, she cut it short. She stooped and gathered up the two importunate puppies, preparing to depart. "Because he is a widower my father will be very loath to part with me. It may be months and months before I marry," she said, gently putting our world back into sane and orderly perspective. And I felt that she was saying the words as much for her own comfort as for mine.

Strangely enough it was that same evening that Master Fermor came into the hall with a letter in his hand and a messenger whom we all recognised as Master John's groom by his side. After bidding the man sit down with us and sup, my master walked to the top table looking mightily pleased and began reading the letter to his daughter, and while he was still eating I could see him giving orders about something to Jordan and Mistress Emotte, and heard him call for horses to be ready in the morning. Sunk in despair, I was ready to believe that letter and journey were all in some way connected with Mistress Joanna's marriage. But as Jordan came stumping hurriedly out through the serving screens to attend to something or other, he thumped me on the shoulder in passing and said gruffly, "Master wants you in his room soon as supper is over. You're in luck, Will Somers!"

And there, in the private sitting-room, I found the family in an unusual state of excitement. Mistress Joanna was setting a maidservant to polish her father's best gold chain, he himself stood before the empty hearth, half in and half out of a doublet, while Emotte knelt before him with needle and scissors letting out the fastenings. It was a much grander doublet than I had ever seen him wear, with velvet bows and silk slashings. "Grown too heavy for it," he was grunting, struggling to hold his breath while Emotte got him into it at last. "Last time I wore the thing must have been at John's wedding."

"You should have a new one made in case John or Lord Vaux takes you to Court while you are there," Mistress Joanna admonished him.

"My dear foolish one, what time is there when I must be off first thing tomorrow morning?" he asked, chucking her chin in high good humour.

"Well, I believe Mottie is right. Old as it is, it looks well enough," she decided with good reason. "How brown velvet becomes you, Sir! Charles Brandon, the King's own friend, could not look more dignified, and he a Duke!"

"I feel like one of your peacocks with his tail spread," grumbled her father, obviously not ill-pleased. He turned to settle the garment more trimly over his firm, hard belly, and caught sight of me standing all goggle-eyed in the doorway. "I'm off to London in the morning, Will, to wait on milord Cardinal," he called out. "And you are coming with me."

"I?" If he had told me I was to sing a duet with his Holiness the Pope I could not have been more taken aback. Incredulity, excitement, pride and abashed terror all jostled together in my mind. It was the second shock I had sustained that day. But then anything can happen in a prosperous merchant's house.

"I must leave Jordan here to look after the farm," he said. "And I need someone who can calculate and write a fair hand. Besides, you think quicker. If you keep your wits about you, you may prove of more use to me."

"It is the scarlet silk," explained his daughter, taking pity on my mystification, and almost pink with excitement. "Cardinal Wolsey is buying it from us this time."

"My son was right, after all," said Richard Fermor, as if the reinstatement of his son in his good opinion meant more to him even than the money.

To me all that mattered was that commerce, not matrimony, was taking him so urgently to London.

"And what is Will to wear?" asked Emotte the practical, who had been sitting back on her ankles with her mouth full of pins.

The thought that I was going to see the capital of England was beginning to seep joyously into my mind, but the thought that anyone there was likely to notice my clothes seemed ridiculous.

"There is the plain worsted John used to wear for Sabbaths before he grew so tall," she suggested. "I folded it away myself and could lay my hands on it."

I was thankful that it was she and not Mistress Joanna who had thought of anything so utterly unwelcome to me.

"It would only cause delay, Sir," I pointed out before they could discuss the matter further. "I will brush the good suit you gave me last year, and go at once and see about any papers you may need."

"And while you are about it, make sure the saddle bags are properly packed," said my master, obviously relieved. "I am sure to be able to get a new suit of some kind for you in London."

"And I will see to it that I earn it," I called back from the door, being caught up in the general excitement which makes for friendly informality between master and man.

I worked until all hours making sure that everything was in order for our journey, and scarcely slept that night for excitement. And so special was the occasion that half the farm hands and servants were gathered out in the courtyard to bid us goodbye. Even Mistress Joanna had risen early.

"I feel a brute," I said to her penitently, when she had embraced her father and we had moved out of the way of his roan's restive hooves while he was giving some last-minute instructions to Jordan. "I, Will Somers, a nobody, going to see all those fine things you talked of while you, the Mistress of Neston, have to stay here!"

"She will be better here. Mistress Emotte and I will look after her," promised Father Thayne, as the four of us stood in a little group apart.

"And you must remember *everything*, Will," insisted Mistress Joanna gaily, trying to hide from us that her blue eyes were awash with tears of disappointment. "Notice the Queen and the little Princess and all the great personages we are always hearing about—the kind ones and the pompous ones and the funny ones—and when you come back you must keep us amused for weeks imitating them all in hall. Try to see the King himself."

"And the Cardinal," I added, strutting a pompous pace or two and sticking out my meagre paunch.

And so we were all laughing when we parted. Save that when a stable boy brought my sturdy little horse I bent a knee and asked our good Father for a blessing, suddenly feeling that I should have much need of it.

"We shall be back soon and we shall have all the summer to tell of our adventures," I said, springing into my saddle.

"And your new suit, Will?" called Mistress Joanna, following me a pace or two as though suddenly reluctant to part from me. "What colour will you get?"

"I have no idea," I shouted back over my shoulder, turning to wave the velvet cap into which dear Emotte had stitched a jaunty feather.

"Green. Get *green*," called back Joanna Fermor, cupping her pretty lips with both hands. "You being dark, it should become you."

But already her voice sounded thin and far off. I had to trot forward to catch up with my master. We passed through the gates with the groom and pack-horse clattering behind out on to the Northampton road, and Easton Neston was left behind.

We rode southwards through Buckinghamshire, putting up at comfortable country-town inns. It was very different from journeying on foot behind a flock of dusty, bleating sheep. Through Aldersgate we rode into the city of London with the spire of St. Paul's pointing like a finger into the sky, and then through Cheapside where there was more chaffering and buying than ever I could have imagined, with 'prentices crying their wares, and separate streets leading off the main thoroughfare for the bakers, the fishmongers, the ironmongers and such. My master pointed out to me the goldsmiths' splendid houses, and the Lord Mayor's stocks for evil doers, and the lovely open arcade from which royalty watched the city pageants, and the tall conduit from which all the bustling people in the streets and gabled houses drew their water. And soon we were clattering over London Bridge, narrow between its houses, with the swift Thames swirling through its arches below, and every now and then a glimpse of great warehouses on the banks and crowded shipping in the Pool.

Cardinal Wolsey, we had been told, was gone to Greenwich to transact some business for the King. They were always together these days, Wolsey gathering more and more of the affairs of the country into his capable hands, and King Henry only too pleased to have more time in which to enjoy the various sports at which he excelled. My master wanted to see the Cardinal about his silks, and the King, if possible, about his taxes. And when we had come by the Kentish bank of the river to Greenwich all that we had been told in London appeared to be true.

"Milord Cardinal will be closeted all morning with the French Ambassador but will no doubt see you tomorrow," his gentleman usher told my master. And when Master Fermor explained that he was acquainted with Lord Vaux, this usher added civilly that his Grace the King was out on the bowling green that lovely morning and without doubt young Lord Vaux would be out there, too, watching the play.

He sent a servant to show my master the way and, being eager to see the King and remembering Mistress Joanna's instructions, I followed at a respectful distance and mingled with a crowd of citizens and minor Court officials who appeared to be perfectly free to watch their sovereign and his gentlemen at play. And a fine sight it was with the verdure of the smoothly clipped grass and the bright silks and velvets of the players and the nimble, bright-faced pages retrieving and handing the woods. I saw Master Fermor join some spectators at the far end of the green, and quite close to me at the nearer end was the King himself. A man who towered over them all, fair skinned and ruddy, with the good looks of an athletic man in his prime. He was so close that I could even see the beads of sweat on his forehead and the sandy hairs on his strong hands.

Bowling was a game for the gentry. By his new law it was forbidden to most of us in order that we should spend much of our leisure at the butts and so be ready in the defence of our country, and no one grumbled because the Tudors kept no standing army, relying, since Crécy and Agincourt, upon the fact that the marksmanship of England was feared throughout the world. But I had watched my master bowling with his friends often enough to follow the finer points of the game. "It is almost the last end, and his Grace's and milord of Suffolk's team score almost even," a London craftsman told me with the camaraderie engendered by sport. And by the tenseness of players and spectators alike one might have guessed it. There was one fat, grey-haired little gentleman upon the Duke of Suffolk's side who kept muttering "Too short!" or "Too wide!" and urging his wood along with gestures of tragic despair, and a tall, lean nobleman in purple who never made a cast but what he pranced sideways after it, following its bias down the rink like an anxious crab. Their unconscious antics enthralled me, and it was all I could do to restrain my own limbs from imitating them.

The last end was excitingly close, with all the woods clustered in a bunch, and when the King himself scattered the lot of them with a final firing shot which carried the jack the tension finished in a deal of back-slapping and a burst of applause. Men threw their caps in the air and, for the benefit of the good-natured fellows about me—or for sheer *joie de vivre*—I stepped out on the grass in front of them and began imitating the players, particularly the tall, important-looking crab-like gentleman. For how was I to know that he was Thomas Howard, Duke of Norfolk, Hereditary Earl Marshal of England?

Everyone about me laughed or tittered, but the noise they made so spontaneously and tried to stifle so swiftly was drowned by a great guffaw of laughter from behind me. I swung round, and there was King Henry himself, leading the players off the green. A page was handing him his feathered velvet cap, and he was standing there within a few yards of me, bare bronze head thrown back, convulsed with mirth. "Beshrew me, cousin of Norfolk, if he hasn't got you to the life," he spluttered, seeming to relish the discomfiture of a powerful relative who probably had quite as much Plantagenet blood as he himself. "What is your name, young man?"

"William Somers, in the service of Master Richard Fermor of Easton Neston in Northamptonshire," I answered, snatching the cap from my own head, and trying to seize so auspiciously good-humoured a moment to draw his attention to my waiting master.

I knew that my quick seizing of the situation had been successful. I saw Lord Vaux step forward to present him. I saw my master bow, as fine a looking man as any of them in his brown velvet, and the King made a gracious gesture to them both to accompany him back to the palace. But his florid, laughing face was still turned towards me.

"By the Holy Rood, Will Somers, I like you for a witty, impudent knave! And by your master's leave, who brought you here," he said, to my utter dumbfounded amazement, "we will keep you at Court as our Jester."

Chapter Six

I FOUND THE MOTLEY spread out on a table in the little room they took me to. The servants who led me there were still babbling congratulations on my extraordinary good fortune, but I was longing to be alone in my bewilderment. I pushed them outside and stood staring with aversion at the strange trappings which were to be the sign of my new calling. The green worsted doublet stiffened with buckram and all fringed with bells to attract attention. The parti-coloured hose. The cap fashioned like a monk's cowl, but ornamented with a gaudy coxcomb. The belt with leather pouch and foolish wooden dagger. Most horrible of all, the painted bladder on a stick.

I picked up each symbol, one by one, and laid it down again. Once I had donned them should I become a different person? Should I never see Easton Neston again, nor any who lived there? I covered my face with my hands and sank down on a stool by a little lattice window overlooking the carpenter's courtyard. There I must have sat for hours trying to accept the fantastic change of fortune which had been thrust upon me. And there, just before twilight, my first master found me. He was on the point of leaving for London, but would not go without seeing me.

"Why, Will," he exclaimed, coming suddenly upon my obvious dejection where he had expected to find at least some measure of jubilation.

I rose stiffly and asked how he had fared. For him, it seemed, the day at Greenwich had been one vast success, as he deserved. He had spent some time with the great Cardinal who had thanked him for his son's financial help in Florence, and ordered one of his clerks to repay the loan. And Wolsey had also been delighted with the samples of Italian silk, and ordered more than one hundred and twenty pounds' worth of the scarlet alone, so that it seemed reasonable to suppose that Fermor ships would continue to supply the Papal Legate's needs. And the King himself had walked with Master Fermor from bowling green to palace, talking and laughing, and enquiring how trade went with Flanders. Being still in high good humour over his spectacular winning shot on the green, he had promised to persuade the Duchess Margaret of Savoy to allow my master to export a certain amount of wheat from Flanders free of tax. "When I explained that I needed this concession to offset the expense of laying down a new ship, his Grace readily understood that in the end this would bring in more trade," said Master Fermor. "He takes vast and knowledgeable interest in ships. 'The more the better, for they are our larder and our defence,' he said. So now everything should go well. What with gaining the Cardinal's custom and a hundred thousand bushels or so of wheat tax free from Flanders, my trading this year should be doubled."

"I am indeed glad for you, Sir," I said soberly.

"And to think that it all came about through your clowning, Will. As it happened, you could not have timed it better, for Lord Vaux and I were standing right beside his Grace when he stopped and laughed at you. 'We will keep that crazy mimic of yours as hostage for any future taxes you may incur,' he said jokingly afterwards, when I began thanking him. And here is your own fortune made too, Will. Though God knows I shall miss you," he added. "We shall all miss you grievously at Neston." And then, as I stood silent, the depth of my grief must have pierced his consciousness. The pleased smile left his face and he said with genuine regret, "My daughter will miss you."

But who was Richard Fermor to refuse a king? Or I, to refuse to stand hostage, even jokingly, for a good master's improbable debts?

"You will explain to my little lady that I had no choice—that I could not come back as I promised to—to make her see it all?"

"Yes, I will explain—everything," he promised. "I know that Neston has been a home to you, and am glad of it. But be a man, Will, and grasp at Life's opportunities. This is a chance in a million for you."

"If I can do it."

He slapped me on the back to cheer me. "I *know* that you can. Everyone in Neston knows it. And when I go home and tell them they will be so proud."

"I owe it to you, Sir," I said.

He must have remembered then how I had cheered his daughter back to health, for he answered very earnestly, "We owe much to each other." Now that it had come to parting we stood for a moment or two tongue-tied, and to hide how much he cared he pointed to the array of motley strewn across my bed and said laughingly, "You certainly earned your new suit, though it is not I who will be paying for it."

"At least it is the colour which Mistress Joanna advised," I answered, with an effort at equal levity. Green, she had said, and green it would be for years, perhaps. Tudor green.

Richard Fermor nodded and shook me by the hand. "Strange, that I once asked if you were honest," he muttered.

"Let me have news," I entreated, as he reached the door. He nodded and was gone. To visit his son, to see the sights of London, to be entertained by fellow merchants at their Guild, and then to ride quietly and contentedly home to Neston—without me.

Soon they came to call me to supper in the great hall. An uproarious mob of Court underlings, seemingly. I was far too emotionally upset to care who they were. With shouts of mirth they helped me to don my unfamiliar clothes, laughing all the more no doubt because of the tragic expression on my face. A clown, the saying goes, is always funniest when broken-hearted. "You have liberty to say anything you like," they kept repeating. "Things that neither blue-blooded old Thomas of Norfolk nor Charles Brandon of Suffolk, the King's familiar friend, would dare to say. Nor even milord Cardinal, Pope's Legate in this country as he is. Why, you can walk without knocking into the King's own private rooms. You can even call him Harry to his face."

They were telling me these things to please me. Or because they envied me, perhaps. But the bare thought of calling the King of England *Harry* filled me with terror. And how could I explain that not so long ago I had been cutting corn and catching broody hens in strawstacks?

I followed them along what appeared to be endless passages, my stomach seeming to turn to water at every step. At the entrance to the great hall they stopped and waited in respectful silence while I, who had free run of all the palace, cowered in a corner like a pickpocket awaiting ordeal before a justice of the peace. And presently there was a flutter in the assembled crowd and through an archway, with the swish of silk and the light tinkle of laughter, came an informal procession of ladies more grandly dressed than any I could have imagined. I shrank farther into the shadows as someone whispered with reverent affection, "Here comes the Queen." In the swift glance I took I saw a plain, middle-aged woman with the hereditary hauteur of Aragon in her gait and the sweetness of a girlhood spent in England in her face, and then I lowered my eyes so that I could see only the stiff brocade of her wide, swaying skirt. But to my amazement she noticed me and paused a moment to say with formal kindness, "If you are the new jester milord the King has told me of, I hope you will be happy with us." And then she added, so softly that only I and her nearest lady could have heard, "Do not be afraid." She must have seen how my limbs were shaking. Her voice was low-pitched and gentle, and rendered the more charming by a slight Spanish accent. I went down on my knees as she passed on her way to supper, and that has ever been the way I felt towards her. From her own incredible store of courage she ever sought to give some semblance of it to others. Strengthened by it, I seized my chance as the King himself came striding into the hall. Urged by some happy instinct I slipped into his procession immediately behind him, inserting my thin body between his back and the lords who followed closest. "You can go anywhere," my well-wishers had told me. So when he stopped in mid-hall and looked around him calling, "Where is that new jester of mine?" I slid between his wide-spaced, purple-hosed legs so that when he made to go forward again he suddenly found me begging like a grinning dog before him. He burst into a great guffaw at the unexpected manner of my arrival, and a great shout of laughter went up all round us at the way I had taken him by surprise. A poor, foolish trick indeed, but it set the ball of merriment rolling, and by the time the royal party were seated at the dais table Queen Katherine was laughing with the rest; less at my jests, I suspect, than because she was relieved that someone to whom she had been kind had so proven himself.

It seemed to me a fabulous meal, with the servants coming and going among the tables bearing all manner of princely dishes, and the courtiers and ladies, like a bevy of richly plumaged birds, making a pageant out of everyday chatter and movements.

Some of them I recognised as people I had seen out on the bowling green. There was also, sitting near the Queen, a young girl of about ten whom I took to be her daughter, the Princess Mary, and, deep in conversation with the King, the unmistakable scarlet-clad figure of the great Thomas Wolsey, who had entered the hall with a young man bearing his cardinal's hat on a cushion before him. The ceremony that surrounded him as Papal Legate appeared to be more ostentatious than the King's. Certainly his face was prouder and sterner. And, watching him converse graciously with men and women of noble lineage, I marvelled to myself, remembering that most unremarkable stretch of grazing land which Master Fermor had pointed out to me at Ipswich.

Dodging my way between servants bearing great dishes of boar's head and venison, I made myself stand in the midst of the company before the high table and, knowing that sooner or later I must bring myself to do this outrageous thing, I seized an empty beaker from some noisy gallant and, raising it aloft, shouted above all the conversational din, "Here's a right good health to you, Harry!"

I saw the proud Plantagenet lift of his close-cropped head as he turned, surprised, from some serious discourse with milord Cardinal, but all that was warm and Welsh in him was quick to smile at the licence of my impertinence. "What do you propose to drink it with?" he enquired, seeing my empty beaker.

"With a right good Will," I quipped.

He laughed, recalling my name with that invaluable royal flair for remembering even the humblest. "Will Somers," he corroborated. "May you indeed prove a right good Will and brighten all our days." He beckoned to a page to pour for me from his own flagon, and before returning to his conversation raised his gleaming golden goblet to me in return.

I felt the Queen's glance like beneficent encouragement upon me. I—plain Will of Shropshire—had called the King of England Harry to his face, and the Heavens had not fallen. Gratefully, I sank down on the lowest step of the dais at his feet and sipped at my brimming beaker. Its sparkling contents and his genial kindness warmed my apprehensive heart. Needless to say, I had never tasted such a witchery of wine. And soon after I had finished it and scooped up some well-spiced venison from a plate on my knees, the sweetmeats and pastries were being served, and through the door by the serving screens some misguided optimist had dragged in a performing bear to entertain the company. A mangy, sad-faced creature, whose clumsy antics could not evoke so much as a titter. Which misjudgment, coupled with the wine, gave me the idea to play lion, prowling up and down behind the sorry beast and waving my absurd jester's bladder for a tail, until the hall was in such an uproar of mirth that the poor devil of a bear-leader retired before my opposition.

Either from pity for the fellow, or because the noise disturbed his discourse, milord Cardinal evidently disapproved of my antics. "If the pushful rogue wishes to curry favour he would be better advised to counterfeit a dragon," I heard him remark to the Duke of Norfolk, while dipping his fingers fastidiously in a finger bowl.

"A ninny who relies on crude caricatures would scarcely have the wit to think of that," replied that tall, sour-looking peer whom I had inadvertently mimicked on the bowling green.

But before the heady encouragement of the King's best vintage could be altogether dissipated, a childish voice piped out, "Yes, be a dragon! Can you make a real dragon, Fool?" And I turned, enchanted, to see the young Princess Mary leaning across the table, her red-gold hair glittering beneath a demure little head-dress in the candlelight, and her Spanish brown eyes alight with eagerness.

I thought quickly. King, Queen and Cardinal were forgotten. My one desire was to please her. Had there not been splendid, life-like dragons carved on the lintel on the Chapter House at Wenlock? And had they not been a familiar, terrifying joy of my own childhood? "A green dragon belching fire," I promised her. And seizing a lighted candle and a scarlet kerchief which Thomas Wolsey had dropped, I held the shaded flame to my mouth and padded with reptilian sinuosity among the company, seeming to blow out fire so realistically that some of the women screamed at my approach, while men swivelled round on their stools forgetful of their food. The royal Tudor wench watched wide-eyed, and by the time I had handed back the ecclesiastical kerchief with an exaggerated flourish she was clapping vigorously. "It is the dragon rampant on my father's shield come to life!" she cried with delight.

"Well counterfeited indeed—except that it should be red," agreed her father, glancing round at the fierce-looking beast embroidered beside the Plantagenet lions on the canopy of state behind his chair.

"I, too, am half a Welshman," I told him, brazenly extending a hand across the table. And Henry Tudor grasped it good-naturedly and looked well pleased.

After that my success seemed to be assured. I felt that I had been accepted by the Court, and my torment of nervousness left me. Milord Chamberlain had had no time to explain the extent of my duties, but my fellows in the royal household had made it clear that I might go anywhere. A Fool's familiarity was, it seemed, taken for granted. So after supper I followed the family and a small group of relatives and favoured courtiers into a room which, for all its rich tapestries and wealth of carved chairs and chests, yet had the comfortable, lived-in look of that well-loved parlour at Neston. And all the more comfortable, thought I, because the energetic Cardinal had excused himself, making a great show of denying himself an evening's pleasure in order to attend to some weighty item of the King's business.

After his going, his Grace heaved a gusty sigh of gratitude that the matter should be taken from him, and settled his great frame in homely relaxation. Clearly, he wanted neither affairs of state nor professional fooling, but to talk with his friends at the close of the day as any lesser man might. He was soon reliving with them, as sportsmen will, the events of some recent tournament and then, with the younger men eager about him, making plans for the next one. And later on he was calling upon one of them, Master Thomas Wyatt, to recite to them his latest verses. Music, poetry—nothing came amiss to the gifted Tudor. There was still a kind of youthful zest about him. I heard him roaring with laughter at some whispered story of his cousin of Norfolk's which I felt sure concerned their mutual relative, the French King, and a few minutes later he had entered into a discussion with his wife about the new Lutheran doctrine of original sin, courteously including one or two of her plain elder ladies. Yet ever and anon he would throw a kindly, teasing word to the younger ones, some of whom were anything but plain.

Not knowing what else to do in such bewildering, brilliant surroundings I set myself as unobtrusively as possible to amuse the Princess, and whenever a spontaneous spurt of laughter broke from her I noticed how her parents, whatever their immediate preoccupations, would turn to glance at her with pleasure, as though she were the light of their lives. If her mother called her to order sometimes, forbearing to spoil her as her father did, it was clear to see that her Grace the Queen was all concern about her daughter's upbringing, and when I heard Queen Katherine telling the King what her lessons had been that day I realised with surprise that in certain subjects it was she herself who instructed their child.

"Recite to his Grace that lovely prayer of St. Thomas Aquinas which you have been learning this week," she bade Mary, and the ten-year-old's expressive face changed from gay to grave as she stood within the circle of her father's arm and spoke the Latin words right through with clear and sweet perfection.

"That is far more than I could do, poppet, and merits a reward," declared her uncle, Charles Brandon of Suffolk, handing her a box of comfits when she had finished. It was the kind of affection she was surrounded with, and clearly she loved him. All England knew how he had been sent to fetch home Henry's young widowed sister, after her husband, the doting old King of France, had died. And how he had braved Henry's wrath by marrying her in Paris— that first beloved Mary Tudor for whom our young Princess had been named—and so had graduated from King's friend to King's brother-in-law.

The long June evening was drawing to a close and the Countess of Salisbury, who had always had charge of her, summoned the child's ladies to take her to her bed. Her elders fell to talking quietly of personal matters, with an occasional nostalgic laugh at some foolish, threadbare family joke. A young man called Hal Norris stood by a darkening lattice singing softly in French to the accompaniment of his lute. And once the King, lured by the melody, joined in for the length of a stanza in a sweet, lingering tenor such as I would have given my ears to possess.

Looking around me and holding my peace I realised with a warm flood of reassurance that this place to which an incredible destiny had brought me was not a Court, but a home. And that, in the midst of it, the Queen herself stood as the epitome of motherhood for which I had always hungered.

Dog tired, grateful and unnoticed, I slipped away in the wake of the young Princess's women. Seldom can any one day in a man's life have brought him so much to think about. Neston seemed a lifetime and a thousand miles away. But I was weary beyond marvelling or grief. Carefully folding my fool's motley and as carefully avoiding my fellow members of the royal household, I lay down in shirt and hose to sleep among the King's spaniels on the rushes in the hall.

Chapter Seven

FROM THE FIRST KING Henry showed himself indulgent towards me. He often led the laughter at my quips and topical rhymings; but, at that time, having so many spontaneous friends and so few troubles, he had little time or need to talk to me. Nor did I dream that by reason of the apartness of his exalted state and the humble uniqueness of my own he might ever come to find solace in so doing.

But a King's jester, to be successful, must somehow keep abreast of all that goes on around him. He must have a finger on the pulse of both national events and private lives. For how else can he barb topical comedy with shrewd comment? I found my country up-bringing a disadvantage, and during my first homesick weeks at Court my greatest source of information was the unguarded conversation of the young men and women to whom time had not yet taught caution, who had perforce to idle away much of their time while waiting to attend upon the King or Queen.

There was one coterie of them who particularly attracted me. Beneath a surface gloss of careless frivolity they were nearly all gifted youngsters with ambitions of their own who, given the chance, might prove of value to their country. Being sprigs of families with vast country estates, many of them were related. All of them were modishly dressed and most of them were good to look upon. The most outstanding, perhaps, was that poet, Thomas Wyatt, whom I had heard reading his fine verses to the King and whose swordsmanship, I learned, was even finer. Then there were his cousins—a family trio from Kent—Mary, George and Anne Boleyn. Three modish sportsmen, Weston, Brereton and Bryan, and a sharp-nosed girl who, I gathered, might marry George Boleyn. Usually with them, when his duties permitted, was that likeable young gentleman-of-the-bedchamber, Hal Norris, who had been singing to his lute that first evening when I came. And sometimes the young Lord Vaux whose sister was married to Master John Fermor. I would find them grouped together, gossiping on some sunlit terrace, or sitting apart from the older courtiers at the end of one of the long galleries, the girls scarcely pretending to touch their embroidery frames and the men discussing anything from the bold anti-papal preaching of a German called Martin Luther to the King's bold innovation of putting guns on ships. They seldom bothered to lower their voices, and as often as not I was within hearing, waiting also for the coming of our royal master.

It was from their idle chatter that I first learned about the plans for the Princess Mary's marriage.

"A gold sovereign to that new falcon of yours the King won't want us at the tennis court this morning, Wyatt," wagered Francis Bryan. "Where is he, Hal?"

"Still closeted with Wolsey," Norris told them. "They are fuming with rage over this rumour that the Emperor Charles will refuse to marry our Princess."

"But they have been betrothed since she was six!" exclaimed the younger and more vivacious Boleyn girl.

"All the same, the Emperor is entering into negotiations for the hand of Isabel of Portugal. The Spanish Ambassador is in there with them now. Between Wolsey's blighting sarcasm and the King's storming, I would not for a fortune stand in his fine Cordova leather shoes!"

"This Isabel is said to be very beautiful and the Emperor Charles must be getting on for twenty years older than the lady Mary," said Sir Thomas Boleyn's elder daughter.

"As if that would deter him if he wanted the alliance!" scoffed her sister Anne. "You may be sure there is some deeper reason than that."

There were always men hanging around this sloe-eyed, slender Anne. Although to me Mary Boleyn seemed the more beautiful, there was a tired, defeated look about her, and she accepted her younger sister's pert superiority without protest. "If the King *does* come he will be in a vile temper!" she observed flatly.

"And small wonder, for this sudden spiteful unfriendliness will wreck all his efforts to balance the power in Europe," exclaimed Surrey indignantly. "And think what a position it puts our Queen in. She has always been set on a Spanish alliance and now it is her own nephew who throws this deadly insult at us."

"It will put her in a still more unenviable position, poor lady, if Wolsey persuades the King to angle for an alliance with rival France," observed George Boleyn.

Anne, who never let people forget that she had been with that first Mary Tudor when she was Queen of France, gave a contemptuous little laugh. "King Francis would not look at a chit of ten!" she said.

"Because he looked too often at you!" teased Sir Thomas Wyatt, leaning over the back of her chair.

"All the same," she went on, "Henry Percy, who as you know is in Wolsey's household, tells me that the Cardinal is so anxious for a French alliance that he plans—"

Before she could voice any further indiscretion her brother clapped a hand over her mouth, and Wyatt said sadly, "Harry Percy is another who has looked at you too often for my liking."

"If Henry Tudor wants a French marriage for their daughter, Queen Katherine will hide her hurts and do exactly as he wants," said Mary Boleyn, just as if neither of them had spoken.

She spoke with an odd kind of bitterness, and there followed a puzzling silence during which everyone seemed to avoid looking at *her*.

"Ah, well, mercifully our little Princess is too young to be overmuch hurt by all this," said Norris, moving away to throw open a casement to the beauty of the June morning.

But I was not too sure. A girl of ten who could speak four different languages and begin to read the classics must mature in mind if not in body. Standing there, half hidden by a tall armoire half-heartedly trying to jot down a line or two of topical doggerel which had occurred to me, I recalled how I had seen her earlier that morning coming from her mother's apartments and how, instead of hurrying back to the instructions of her learned Doctor Vives and her lesson books, she had stood quite still by an open garden door, leaving her women in an uncertain huddle behind her. Naturally I had supposed that she stopped to watch the birds fluttering between the budding roses and the low box hedges, but now I doubted if she had really seen any of these sweet things.

"How doth the beauty of an English rose
Beguile a maid from Latin prose!"

I had teased, breaking in upon her stillness like an ill-timed clock. For once she had not whirled lightly round, sparkling with answering fun. When she turned her brown eyes were set in a blind, bewildered stare, as though looking inward at her own destiny. I had felt momentary compassion, thinking that perhaps her parents, in their loving pride, had been forcing her to study too much. And then, to my surprise, the tall Countess of Salisbury had appeared, unattended and unannounced, motioning to the huddled women not to follow. She had smiled down at the child with infinite kind-ness, and taken her hand and led her out into the sunlit garden.

There had seemed to be no question of lessons this morning, and as they moved away I had overheard Mary Tudor say in the shocked voice of a hurt child who has hitherto known nothing but security and kindness, "I gave him an emerald ring and he promised to wear it always." Emerald green, so I had learned in my new fashionable environment, was the colour for constancy—a colour which she must often have heard her younger ladies reading about in romances, or seen exchanged by them in ribbons or posies with their lovers.

I had no idea then of whom she spoke. But I knew now that Queen Katherine must just have endured the painful duty of telling her beloved daughter that their own kinsman, the Emperor, had jilted her.

I do not pretend to follow all the political repercussions which followed, only the human ones which began to unfold themselves gradually before me like a play. The gay young Boleyn coterie had been right. Mary Tudor was too young for this matrimonial insult to cloud her gaiety for long. And the Emperor *did* have a reason for his behaviour which must have drawn the sting of resentment from his aunt's judgment of him, even while the reason itself appalled her. But while all this may have been discussed for weeks in higher circles, I stumbled on it by chance, which—before I acquired intimate friends at Court—was my usual way of gathering up the threads of Court life.

To my great delight and to the furtherance of my ambition I had been allowed to help Master John Thurgood, the Master of Revels, to devise and produce a masque in the gardens at Greenwich. It was to celebrate the King's birthday, and he and the Queen had both declared it to be one of the most effective pieces of play-acting they had ever seen. And all the guests who had flocked to Greenwich by road and water appeared to agree with them. "Almost as inventive as those I have taken part in in Paris!" admitted Mistress Anne Boleyn, as she ran past us afterwards with a bevy of water nymphs in clinging green draperies.

"Must all our fashions come from France?" demanded Thurgood, grimacing behind her back. "Give me an English morris dance any day!"

"Or a rousing Welsh part-song," I said. "But no wonder the scintillating lady is elated. She was right royally admired. Did you see the King call her father to sit by him?"

With his usual generosity, his Grace had called us to the royal stand and handed us each a bulging purse and congratulated us before all the fine company, and now, as the sun went down, actors and spectators were beginning to follow him back into the palace. The day's tension over and success assured, Thurgood and I sat down on the nearest piece of scenic rock to relax over a flagon of wine which our good friend the head cellarer had had the thought to send out to us. Because of the heat I had discarded my motley and had been rushing here, there and everywhere, directing and exhorting, in black hose and breeches and an old white shirt. And dressed like this I felt more truly myself than I had felt for weeks.

"You are a versatile fellow, Will!" said Thurgood, seeming to appreciate some hitherto unsuspected facet in my personality. "I believe you would sooner work behind the scenes on the music and sequences of a masque than quip your way to popularity in full blaze of the royal presence."

Because we were of the same kind of calling and he had never shown the least jealousy of my growing success—or because after some high excitement one is apt to relapse into complete natural-ness—I shared with him a soul-searching moment of truth. "We players live on applause," I said thoughtfully. "But the fooling has been forced upon me. As a lonely fellow's face-saver for other deficiencies, perhaps. I am a serious creature at heart, caring to the point of ecstasy for all beautiful things. Most of all for music, though to my deep regret I have no remarkable voice."

He answered nothing, but looked at me carefully as though wishing to remember me as he saw me revealed at that moment. He laid a hand momentarily upon my knee, in a gesture of promised friendship. And then we fell to discussing our recent dramatic creation, learning pointers for our next effort, as professional entertainers must, from its moments of success or failure. And presently Lord Vaux and my late master's son, who had been among the guests, strolled over to join us. Thomas Vaux, young as he was, was by way of becoming a patron of the arts, and royal approval had given me a new importance in John Fermor's eyes. I was amused to find how much less condescending his manner was than it had been when I was in his father's house. "The part of Neptune was excellently conceived, and my wife was enrap-tured by the little mermaids," he said.

"Master John Thurgood here was responsible for that," I told him as we both rose to our feet.

"But their singing in the caves was Will's," insisted Thurgood.

"A pleasant novelty," allowed Vaux. "But perhaps another time we might persuade my friend Wyatt to write the words."

"Ah, yes, indeed, milord," I agreed wholeheartedly. "If we can but find someone to speak them well enough. For my own part, I think the loveliest thing in all the afternoon was the Princess Mary dancing alone to her shadow in that stiff Spanish dress."

"A child item always steals the show," said Thurgood, smiling reminiscently.

We emptied our well-earned beakers, basking in general approval. "But that other child—the boy of about the same age—I have never seen him before," I demurred. "I heard some of the people at the back hissing. What made you put him in the place of the young Earl of Surrey, his Grace of Norfolk's son, who spoke the lines so much better at rehearsal, Thurgood?"

Both the young courtiers laughed. "Our shrewd Master of Revels probably knows that had that boy not taken part King Henry might not have been so extravagantly pleased," said Master John Fermor.

"Why, who is he?" I asked, annoyed that approval of our play should depend in any degree at all upon the indifferent acting of a peaky-looking boy.

"How country green you are, Will!" snickered John Fermor.

"He is the King's natural son," Lord Vaux told me more civilly.

"By Elizabeth Blount, who is now Lady Taillebois," elaborated Fermor, who always enjoyed seeming to be in the swim of things.

"No wonder some of the people hissed," I muttered to Thurgood, after they had turned aside to wait for their wives.

"Oh, I don't know," said that tolerant man, motioning to a posse of approaching servants that they might remove our rock. "The King has been happily married for sixteen years or more and this Fitzroy is the only by-blow that ever I heard of. Unless the elder Boleyn girl had one."

Mary Boleyn. I remembered how intimately she had spoken of the King's moods, and thought back on her jaded bitterness with new understanding. I was certainly learning my world. "I am not grass green enough to have meant that," I said. "But that the people must resent this Henry Fitzroy being brought to Court because of the discomfiture of the Queen and Princess."

"They are both exceedingly beloved, as we all know. But, however difficult it may be, Queen Katherine is always gracious to the lad and obedient to whatever the King may have in mind for him. And it may be much. Who ever heard of a woman inheriting? Particularly with so much trouble in Europe? Henry Tudor must be desperate for a son. And Queen Katherine, they say, is now too old—"

He ceased speaking abruptly as two ladies on their way back to the palace came within hearing. One of them I knew to be Elizabeth, Lady Vaux, the other I guessed must be his lordship's sister, whom John Fermor had been fortunate enough to marry. They stopped to thank us graciously for an afternoon of good entertainment, and Mistress Maud Fermor tarried behind a moment or two and smiled at me. "You must be the Will Somers whom I heard spoken of so often when I was at Easton," she said.

My whole being seemed to spring to life. "Have you been there recently, Madam?" I asked.

"Only on a passing visit," she said, smiling at my eagerness.

"Then you can tell me how my master fares?"

"Do you never remember that you have now risen up in the world?" she teased. "He is excellently well, and busy as ever. His new ship is nearly completed."

"How is she called?" I asked, remembering with what enthusiasm I had clambered about her half-built hull at Ipswich.

"The *Cast*."

I felt that I must say something—anything—to detain her. "And they still speak of me?"

"*Ad nauseam*," she assured me with a friendly smile. "My pretty little sister-in-law, Joanna—Mistress Mottie—that grumpy old Jordan, farmhands, servants—all of them."

"How is—Mistress Joanna?" I brought myself to ask at last.

"Much stronger in health. But dispirited, I thought. That kind old man, Father Thayne, says she misses the good cheer you made. It was he who told me to be sure to speak to you if I should see you."

Kind old man, indeed—kind and ever full of Heavenly understanding. I kissed Mistress Fermor's hand with a passionate gratitude which probably amazed her. "After today's entertainment I will believe all the good things they say of you," she vowed laughingly, before hurrying to rejoin her impatient husband.

I do not know how long I stood there, lost to my surroundings. The noble towers and gardens of Greenwich had faded into the beloved memory of Richard Fermor's manor. The diminishing chatter of departing courtiers and the advancing shouts and hammering of servants were lost in recollection of the homelier, more rural sounds of Easton Neston. Joanna remembered me, spoke of me, missed me....

"Had you not best get changed into your motley?" John Thurgood was urging.

"Hurry, Will, they are going in to hall for supper," some other kind fellow was warning me.

Could she, too, have remembered, when she told me to choose a green suit, that green was the colour for constancy?

My heart was warm with the thought that she cared, torn by the thought that she needed me to cheer her. And I must go to entertain a king. My desire was all to be with her, yet I must go and think up some damnable lunacy to make the great hall at Greenwich ring to the rafters with guffaws of laughter.

Chapter Eight

I T WAS TOWARDS THE close of Midsummer Day when I came upon the King's daughter sitting weeping on a stone bench by the sundial. She had been playing at shuttlecock, and her ladies were still playing on a river-side lawn near by. Thinking that she might have hurt herself, I stopped on my way to the landing-steps to ask what was amiss and whether I could call one of them to her.

"No, no. Please do not tell them," she begged.

I realised that royal ladies of Spanish descent, even at the tender age of ten, might be trained not to manifest their emotions. But I could not leave her in such distress. "Then why do you cry, my sweet poppet?" I asked, sitting down beside her as I would to comfort any child.

"B-because I do not want to leave my parents and go so f-far away," she answered, between sobs.

"But you will not have to. It is all finished now," I said, supposing that she spoke of the marriage with her cousin the Emperor.

"Oh, not across the sea to Spain. Only across the Severn to Ludlow."

"And only on a visit? Like you go sometimes to Westminster or Windsor," I said soothingly, not realising the implication.

"No. I am to live there. I am to have my own household. My father has just told me so. He is going to make me Princess of Wales. 'I love you dearly and will not see you humiliated,' he said.

'I will show the Emperor and the whole world that my daughter is of an estate fit to marry a King.'"

The King of France. The words sprang into my mind as they may well have entered hers. A gust of feminine laughter and the smart slap of parchment-covered battledores came from the near-by lawn and I thought, In truth, it is she who is the shuttlecock. Who would be a high-born girl, to be slapped so smartly from one prospective husband to another? And how often does worldly ambition pass for parental care?

"I am to hold my own Court and rule Wales. And I am so f-frightened. Oh, Will, I am so glad you came!" She threw her arms about my neck and sobbed afresh; then, with a brave effort at composure, pulled herself erect and settled her skirts sedately about her. "I must never show fear in front of my household," she said, as if reciting some oft-repeated lesson. "But I can tell you."

I was touched to the heart. There must be something about motley that sets a man apart, but I do not think it was wholly that. Whether I am wearing it or not, people do tell me things. And this tearful wench looked so pathetically young that I did not know whether to laugh or cry at the thought of her ruling Wales. She must have seen the painful working of my face. "Did *you* feel the same way when you came *here?*" she asked.

"I was gibbering with fright that first evening when I called your royal father *Harry*—"

"And made a dragon for me...."

At last she was smiling, and I jerked a silk kerchief from the little velvet pocket hanging from her belt and handed it to her so that she could dry her eyes. "I expect you had to leave people whom you loved dearly, too?" she said.

"God knows I did, my sweet lady. But we must both be brave and look for the happy things in our new lives," I said, realising as I spoke that I was only passing on to her some of the courage which her mother the Queen had inspired in me.

And then Mary Tudor said something which made me understand the root of her unhappiness. "They say that Ludlow is a fine castle, but my mother lived there when *she* was Princess of Wales and married to my late Uncle Arthur. He died there, so she has no happy recollections of the place." Seeing that her ladies had finished their game and were coming towards us, she dabbed hastily at her button of a nose and asked in a whisper, "Are my eyes still red, Will?"

"It is growing dusk, your Grace. No one will notice," I assured her. And springing up so that I shielded her from view, I seized a battledore from one of them and began a spirited attack upon the rising gnats, scratching myself the while, and so drew their laughing attention to myself until they all trooped indoors to bed.

What the Princess had told me in private was soon the talk of the whole country, and the Welsh were said to be wildly delighted. "It is high time they were properly requited for their loyalty when my late father landed at Pembroke and for the numbers of them who followed him to Bosworth," said King Henry to the Duke of Suffolk, whose father had been standard-bearer to his own at that momentous battle.

"You do for them now what was intended when your elder brother was sent," said Suffolk.

"It must have been a bitter blow to them when he died within a few months," sighed Henry. "So there must be nothing niggardly now."

"*Two groats for the Welshmen, three for the French,*" I dared to sing, parodying a popular ballad from my lowly stool. For I had already noticed how often the Tudor had two separate motives—one to further political ends, and one with which to salve his own conscience.

"The Princess of Wales will keep a revelry this coming Christmas which will be the talk of Europe," he went on, ignoring me. "I will not have her mope."

"Then she will need a jester," I said, letting my foolish heart spur me against my own interests.

"Not a bawdy one like you!" laughed Henry, recovering his good humour and making a pass at my backside with his hefty foot.

But the seed of the idea may have been sown, for the following evening the Queen sent for me and questioned me about homely things, such as my life in Shropshire, where I learned to sing so truly, and how I came to be in the merchant Fermor's household. And all the while I felt that she was assessing me. She asked if I were married or like to be, and because of her goodness I found myself telling her that there was one in Neston whom I loved and to whom I should ever remain constant.

"I will remember you in my prayers, that God will bring you together again and grant you both great happiness," she said.

"That is impossible, Madam, for she is far above me in estate," I told her.

"Nothing is impossible with God," she said. Words of faith and courage which I was to cling to through many a lonely hour of my life. And then she told me that she intended to try to persuade the King to send me with her daughter to Ludlow. "I want her to enjoy life, but if she is to dance and sing and take part in masques as young people now do, such entertainments must be presented with suitable restraint. I want her to grow up gay without becoming *légère*, as I am afraid some of my younger ladies have. She has taken a great liking to you, Will Somers, and I have observed how you can suit your fooling to catch a child's fancy, so that you may be able to help her if she should be unhappy."

"Your Grace fears that she will be very homesick?"

The Queen sighed profoundly. All day I had noticed how ill she looked, and could guess how much this parting tried her. "Perhaps I am foolishly apprehensive," she said. "But I have such unhappy memories of Ludlow. As you know, I spent the short six months of my first marriage there. I did not speak your language very well then and Prince Arthur was so ill all the time. How he suffered, poor lad!" The words were said involuntarily, as of one younger and weaker than herself, and the impersonal pity of them convinced me as no arguments or protestations could have done that poor fifteen-year-old Arthur Tudor had never been a husband to her.

"Her Grace is very young to rule a principality, even nominally," I ventured, being assured in my own mind that her mother felt the same.

"But the King thinks it will provide excellent training for one who may become a queen," said Katherine of Aragon, with that forthright honesty which must often have disconcerted his more tortuous mind. "She will have wise advisers in whose hands all practical matters will rest. And of course our well-beloved Countess of Salisbury will be with her, as she has always been."

I was duly presented to that great Plantagenet lady and to Sir John Dudley, who had been appointed Chamberlain to this newly founded Court. All manner of preparations were begun. Greenwich seethed with tailors, dressmakers and scurrying clerks. The Thames was congested with barges plying between our watergate and London. The King and Queen accompanied their daughter as far as Langley, and by the time we set out for the Welsh border there was certainly nothing niggardly about our cavalcade, which included more than a dozen ladies of honour and four bishops. "And if that does not keep you from telling the kind of stories with which you regale the King and his sporting friends..." chuckled John Thurgood, wringing my hand at parting.

Ludlow was certainly a fair castle. The King's father, Henry of Richmond, had restored it, but parts of it were much as they must have been when it was the Mortimers' border stronghold during the Wars of the Roses. "Milady of Salisbury says she can remember when the little princes lived here. They must have studied *their* lessons in this very room," the Princess told me when her tutor had departed and I had slipped in to lift her heavy, leather-bound books back from table to shelf.

"The little princes?" I repeated, my mind being on a jumble of newer things.

"Edward and Richard Plantagenet, of course. The young king and his brother who are said to have been murdered in the Tower of London. If they had lived I suppose my father could not have been king."

"You must not let that sadden your Grace," I said.

But I know that she often thought of them. And once I saw Margaret Plantagenet of Salisbury, who was their cousin, pass her long white hands along the table edge in a gesture of infinite pity, and then go and stand for a long time before the window from which their eager young eyes must so often have looked.

Yet life at Ludlow was far from being sorrowful. That lady, in her own wisdom, made sure that our young Princess walked in the sunshine, practised dancing and made music on her virginals, and, according to her mother's instructions, was never over-tired by her studies. And in spite of the heavy Latin books and the four bishops, I saw to it that there was plenty of revelry and that Christmas was kept right royally at Ludlow, as the King had ordered.

Two things happened during our sojourn there which gave me singular pleasure. I acquired and learned to play a small Welsh harp, an instrument little used in England but in which the King delighted. And I was able to visit my relatives at Much Wenlock. The Countess provided me with a fine suit of brown velvet for my journey, and Princess Mary had her ladies ransack the kitchens and stuff my saddle-bags with all manner of dainties for my aunt. "There is so much that you have done for me," she said. "Enjoy your visit, Will, but come back to us soon."

Bestriding a good horse, I found it was no more than a day's journey. But after life in a palace, how the farmhouse and fields seemed to have shrunk! Perhaps it was my imagination, but there seemed to be an air of poverty about the place. The haystacks looked smaller and the rain butt by the door, near which I had made my bid to serve Master Fermor, leaked from a broken stave. But the family welcome was as warm as the fire crackling on the hearth, and my Uncle Tobias, though his straw-coloured hair was beginning to grey, had always been kept fit by hard work. My cousins crowded round me, half over-awed by my good mount and my fine new clothes and covering their embarrassment with rough badinage. For, in spite of my new appointment, had I not always been the one to be teased? The clumsy dolt who could not plough a straight furrow? My aunt, recovering from my exuberant embrace, burst into tears at sight of all the good things I had brought them, and then, on hearing that our beloved Princess had sent them to her, seemed almost more inclined to keep them as objects of veneration than to allow her family to slake their ever-ready appetites. It was only when I was helping my cousins to put away the remnants of the feast for another day that it struck me how strangely bare the familiar old pantry looked. "Is the farm not paying as well as it used?" I asked anxiously, remembering how, during all my mother-less youth, Frith farm had seemed the home of plenty.

"'Tis the weevil," my eldest cousin Colin explained. "And with all that drought we'd a mighty poor harvest. But now we're making up a better herd and I've hired myself out to Squire Tyrrell till the new heifers be paid for."

I looked into his candid, patient eyes. "You must hate that," I said.

"But 'twill tide us over. And then I hopes to get wed—one of them Tarleton girls up at Condover. The tall, honey-haired one. Only thing is, Will, Squire Tyrrell be such a sly brute."

Around the fire that evening, when I had entertained them with some idea of my life at Greenwich, we talked of family affairs, and my uncle explained more fully how they had used more of their poor soil for growing cattle fodder and staked their savings on buying a bigger herd. "At least we have free grazing on the Frith Common," he said. "And as you may remember, my beasts have always brought in more money than the crops."

Next day I visited the old school cottage and spoke with my father's successor, and the whole village turned out to welcome me and to gape with pride and curiosity at a Wenlock man who was now the King's jester. "Is it true that you sit at meat with him?" they asked, crowding round me.

"Not quite," I had to admit, explaining how I usually had a stool placed for me before his table or squatted on the dais steps.

"And that you actually talk with him?" they asked, round-eyed.

"Aye. And call him Harry," I boasted.

The women fingered my fine doublet, and the children seemed to be disappointed because I had not travelled in cap and bells. Also, I imagine, that off duty I did not seem particularly funny.

I managed to give them all the slip and went alone to kneel in the Priory at High Mass. Once again I heard the exquisite music soaring up to the roof, and was soul-satisfied. Here was a beauty which nothing which I had seen or experienced of material grandeur could shrink. I had been brought up in invaluable proximity to perfection and, kneeling there, I understood in all humility that because I had been granted the sensitivity to appreciate it God would ask more of me than of some unheeding clod. King's fool as I was, a compassionate Christ could use me.

When I left Much Wenlock my aunt gathered all the best herbs from her poor garden and pressed them into my hands for the richest Princess in Christendom, and I rode back to Ludlow considerably wiser than when I came. For it is good for a man to know his roots, and to acknowledge them, even as he grows upwards.

Mary Tudor pressed some of the sprigs of lavender between the pages of her missal, because she was that kind of child, and listened carefully to all the details of my visit. She herself was full of the possibility of a visit from her own family. But before another Christmas came round we were all back at Greenwich because the French Ambassador was coming specially to see her. To look her over like a young mare at a fair, I supposed angrily. Because our clever Cardinal had at last persuaded King Francis the First to make a bid for her. Francis Capet, who was more than twenty years her senior and the Devil alone knows how many in dissolute experience.

Chapter Nine

THE EVENING AFTER THE French Ambassador's arrival we were waiting as usual to attend the King and his guests to supper. Word had gone round "Will Somers is back," several people greeted me with the welcome information that the Court had been a duller place without me, and to my surprise I found that now, possibly owing in part to Lord Vaux's patronage, I was more or less *persona grata* with that brilliant group of young courtiers whose conversation I had previously hung on from afar.

"Spain, France and England. The three countries between whom a balance of power must be adjusted if we are to have peace in Europe," Thomas Wyatt was explaining to me with his usual courtesy. "Any two of them tend to unite their weight against the third. And so you see, Will, how it is forced upon our King, having broken with a friendly Spain, to ally himself with our old foe France or stand odd man out."

"And against the security of a nation how can the feelings of his Spanish wife or the future happiness of his daughter matter very much?" added the elder Boleyn girl, who, after being for a short time the King's mistress, had disappointed her father's hopes by marrying a penniless younger son, and who was at last blissfully happy.

"All the world over, women are the pawns that rulers play with," sighed Hal Norris, too loyal to criticise his beloved master even among trusted friends.

"Why perturb yourselves about something which may never happen?" asked Anne Boleyn, not even troubling to lower her clear young voice. "Have I not wagered you that Francis will not marry her? His second son, Henry of Orleans, may be offered as a sop, perhaps."

"But after Francis has so far committed himself as to send this deputation?" objected Wyatt.

"He can always fall back on the old suggestion that she is a bastard."

"Nan, for Heaven's sake!" intervened her brother, glancing hastily over his shoulder to see who was within earshot. "Do you want to get us all beheaded?"

"*Mon cher* George, what cheerful things you suggest!" she exclaimed, stretching up a fondling white hand as if to press his own handsome head more firmly to his shoulders. "But whether I say it or not, surely all the world is aware that the Queen of England married her deceased husband's brother?"

"With a dispensation from the Pope," Norris reminded her firmly.

"Whose opulent Legate is approaching us at this moment," warned Wyatt.

With their flair for swift invention they had switched smoothly into an innocuous discussion about the merits of some lively poet called Skelton by the time Cardinal Wolsey came past. Wolsey, deep in conversation with the Bishop of Tarbes, and surrounded by gesticulating Frenchmen. Wolsey, resplendent in Richard Fermor's rustling silk, with his scarlet hat carried before him and his obsequious jester, Saxton, scampering behind. He seemed to wait with haughty impatience for the King's procession, after which came the Queen and her ladies bringing the Princess. A Princess who looked pale and remote, who did not even glance at me and who was dressed more grandly than I had ever seen her.

When they had all passed into the great hall I realised that for more than a year the merriment of the King's table must have been mainly in the hands of Saxton and a cumbersome, black-bearded fellow called Budge who had wormed his way into my place. With my mind still shocked by the cruel, careless words of Anne Boleyn, I was obliged to brace my wits for the fray so that now on my return I might recover my own secure place.

It had been easy enough to entertain a young Princess and her household, particularly in Wales where everyone could sing. Jesting for the King had suited my pattern, partly because of that odd blend of scholarship and simplicity which was in him, and partly because broad, good-natured English humour is much the same at Court as at any country fair. But the prospect of having to crack jokes which would be comprehensible to sardonic, sophisticated Frenchmen unnerved me. Yet somehow I must out-shine the two thrusters who had for months been feeding on my pastures. After a few laboured bits of buffoonery had fallen flat I tried popping out suddenly from behind a wall tapestry and firing a riddle at the resplendent company, and then retiring behind it again to give my audience time to call out their various answers and—more important still—to give myself time to devise the next one. By setting an eager page to time them by the King's gold clock, and by roping in John Thurgood to record all successful scores on a chequer-board, I found to my relief that I had introduced a game which gave French wits a chance to sparkle and which would probably help to pass our own winter evenings.

That supper was a vast success. Never had there been such a blending of French and English voices, such an unbending of politely veiled criticism and formality. And the King, in the heyday of his manhood, was the merriest of hosts. His Greenwich cooks had excelled themselves in providing an unending procession of fish and meats and venison. And while his guests were still admiring a marvellous sugared confection made in the shape of a fleur-de-lys, the musicians in the gallery above the serving screen struck up a favourite dance tune. King Henry, anxious to show off the maiden in the marriage market, danced with her himself. All his life he had loved dancing and excelled at it, but the sight of his tall, stalwart frame linked with her short, child-like one seemed to me, the professional showman, a ludicrous mistake. How much more to advantage she would have shown, I thought, if partnered by someone of her own age such as the young Earl of Surrey, or even by her half-brother, Henry Fitzroy.

"That lad is still at Court, I see," I muttered to Thurgood, who was counting out the wagers which had been thrown on to his chequer-board.

"And has been created Duke of Richmond since you left," he muttered back.

"And the Queen tolerates it?"

"What else can she do, poor lady? Could she but produce a son this Blount boy would soon be sent back to obscurity."

"And who is the demure-looking child sitting beside him?" I asked, looking round for fresh faces at Court while waiting for the royal dance to stop.

"Mary Howard, young Surrey's sister." Thurgood lowered his voice still more, so that I had to incline my head to catch his disturbing words. "Rumour has it that the King intends to marry her to this by-blow of his, and that her father, proud old Norfolk, jumped at the chance."

"The chance of a *crown*, you mean?" I gasped, incredulously, under cover of the music.

Thurgood shrugged. "A desperate solution. But bolstered by the Howards' Plantagenet blood—"

"But, John," I protested, "the people would never submit—"

"They hate the very thought. Many of them would sooner go back to the Plantagenets."

"But what of the Princess Mary for whom they shout themselves hoarse in the streets?"

"As to that," Thurgood reminded me, "if the result of all this lavish display proves successful her Grace will be living in France."

The sweetness of lutes and hautboys ceased. The dance was over. Mary Tudor made an enchanting curtsy to her father. And he, telling the company that she was his pearl beyond price, led her back to a chair beside the Queen. The servants were bringing in great gold dishes piled with grapes and Spanish oranges, and scarcely had the applause for the dancers died down before that bungler Budge was on his feet reciting some ill-scanned poem he had been concocting. So tedious was it that I recall no more than a few lines towards the end—something mawkish about "This king did dance with his fair flower, the mother standing by," and then, playing for popular approval with complete tactlessness, "I pray God, save father and mother, and this young dancer fair, and send her a brother to be England's *rightful* heir."

He stared pointedly at Fitzroy as he spoke the last line, and, turning, I saw the look on the Queen's tired face and the embarrassed fury on the King's. I overheard a man sitting just behind Budge mutter, "The time is gone past, you fool. The Queen is too old."

And the gay tinkle of Mistress Anne Boleyn's laughter as she leaned forward to whisper behind her hand, "You speak truth, Master. Doctor Butts says so. And being of the Queen's household I should know."

I had just begun to string together a short, stinging parody of Budge's illiterate verses, but in sudden pity for the King and Queen I abandoned it. Once again some words of Anne Boleyn's had shocked me into a presentiment of insecurity—not for myself, but for them, and for the whole of our familiar, comfortable life.

I sprang up on the dais, intent upon creating some diversion— anything to wipe that distressed look from the Queen's plain, motherly face. With no precise idea of my intentions I seized a dish of half-cold frumenty from a side table and began ladling some of the white milky stuff into four small bowls. "After sitting through so much poesy we need more sustenance, royalty and fools alike!" I declared. I handed a bowl to the suffering Queen, unobtrusively kissing her hand as I did so, and handed a second, on bended knee, to my frowning master. I set down one for myself and beckoned to my rival to come and take the fourth. He was nearly twice my size, with four times the self-complacency, and when he came strutting up to the top table I picked up his share and, driven by instinctive dislike, flung the whole helping in his silly face. The horrid glutinous mess hung upon his eyelashes and dribbled down his bristling beard to the tawdry finery of his coat. My motive was inexcusable, although the action itself passed for ordinary slapstick humour and raised a storm of cheap laughter from the lower tables.

But the victim was furious. Instead of meeting it with professional buffoonery before our public and making a great to-do of mopping up his face, he rushed at me in grim earnest and, with a flamboyant gesture, so far forgot where we were standing as to draw his sword. It was only the foolish wooden sword which some jesters wear as a part of their stock in trade. But instantly Henry Tudor roared to him to put up his weapon, and milord Chamberlain rapped out an order and the servants were bundling my unfortunate rival from the hall. Because I was but country bred, I took some moments to realise the enormity of the offence, and to remember that a sword drawn in anger in a sovereign's presence could mean death. But Henry was no longer gratefully amused. Briefly his glance met mine in a kind of reproach. Then, like a good host, he swept the incident lightly aside, bidding some official pay the unfortunate man his wages and let him go.

Only Sir Reginald Pole, the Countess of Salisbury's son, referred to the incident again that evening. "Why did you do it?" he asked, stopping to speak to me a few minutes later as he came down from the high table.

"Professional jealousy," I said jauntily, because my conscience was sick with shame.

"Or human pity for those in high places?" he suggested, laying one of his fine scholarly hands on my shoulder. "It is hard to see those whom we love hurt, and keep silence." He was recently home from Italy where, I understood, he had been studying for the priesthood, and when he was a very young man much of his time must have been spent in the company of the Queen and her infant daughter. He looked at me appraisingly and then, as if deciding that he could trust me, he broke through that barrier of shyness which held him from familiarity with most men. "The Queen and her daughter will soon have need of all their friends. Though I imagine," he added, with a singularly charming smile, "that we may be called upon to do more dangerous things than flinging bowls of frumenty in order to help them."

I stared after him. "Tall as a Pole" was how his young relative, Mary Tudor, had often teasingly, adoringly described him. Tall and slender, he was, with that red-gold hair, that effortless charm and that devastating smile. And belatedly the fact established itself in my rustic mind that he was pure Plantagenet—grandson of that murdered Duke of Clarence and great-nephew of two kings. And there followed a dangerously inevitable comparison between him and that over-dressed, newly ennobled youth, Fitzroy of Richmond.

One could not doubt Reginald Pole's unself-seeking sincerity. And how soon his warning was justified; and the Boleyn girl's disquieting prophecy fulfilled. Although how she, a mere Kentish knight's daughter, could know these things before the rest of us amazed me, unless she had some spy in the King's council chamber. It was soon common knowledge that Francis preferred to marry the widowed Queen of Portugal rather than a child Princess of England. And that in order to delay the present negotiations he had instructed the Bishop of Tarbes to question the legitimacy of the proffered bride.

We at Court were shocked and, as the news filtered through, the whole of the country was indignant. The King's Privy Council sat day after day, and an ecclesiastic enquiry was set up regarding the validity of her parents' marriage. Although King Henry must have tried to keep this from the Queen, she soon heard of it. She was sick abed at the time and one could only imagine her distress. And because she had never wanted this French alliance it must have been all the more bitter to find that Francis could be the cause of such hurtful humiliation.

"His Grace, to calm her natural distress, had assured her that he permitted the enquiry only to dispel all disadvantage towards their marriageable daughter," I overheard Wolsey assuring the anxious Lord Mayor of London, whose barge was often at the Greenwich watergate.

With the Queen sick, the King so preoccupied and all the festivities for the departed Frenchmen finished, a cloud of depression seemed to hang over the palace. Instead of hunting or playing in his newly roofed tennis court, my master seemed to be for ever closeted with the Cardinal or discussing his marriage and his conscience with the learned Doctor Longland, his confessor. He was seldom in the mood for merriment. "Devise something to cheer us, Will," he would say occasionally at supper, but he no longer joined in with that whole-hearted zest which had made our efforts go with a swing. But sometimes afterwards he would call me into his private room to play to him while he rested, withdrawn from statesmen and sports-loving friends alike. "You are half a Welshman, Will, and your music soothes me," he would say. And I would play tune after tune, softly, on my small Welsh harp. Every now and then he would join in and sing some of his favourites, but as often as not he would just sit pulling at his lip in thought or seem to be dozing.

"I have not been sleeping well," he explained one evening, rousing himself with a nod and a start.

The fire had burned low and the room was mostly in shadow, else I do not think he would have begun speaking before me as he did. Almost as if he were speaking to himself, saying over something for the hundredth time. "Small wonder that I sleep ill, with my conscience so troubling me. Suppose what Tarbes says be right, then I have been living in sin all these years. However wise my father's policy for Spain, I should not have obeyed him and taken Arthur's widow." His strong, square hands pushed restlessly up and down the carved arms of his chair, and presently he turned, aware of my sympathetic presence, and spoke as man to man. "But when I look back over all the sunlit years of our married life a priest's pedantic words seem to make little sense. Getting on for twenty years. That is a long time, Will. And it has been the kind of marriage that men pointed to with envy."

I laid aside my harp, and my heart throbbed with excitement that he should be talking to me so. He rose from his chair and stretched his great arms above his close-cropped head—arms which could throw most of his own archers in the wrestling ring. "Consider my vigour!" he challenged. "It is incredible that I cannot beget sons. I—who need them so desperately for England—when half my subjects' hovels crawl with 'em."

His massive shadow on the wall seemed to writhe in a fury of frustration. "You had Henry of Richmond," I dared to remind him.

His manhood clutched gratefully at the thought. "And again and again I begat sons on my own virtuous wife. But they all died—or never even breathed their way into this life. So this must be the hand of God, punishing us—punishing us for living all these twenty years in sin."

He slumped back into his chair. "Her Grace the Queen has been ailing for months," I pointed out.

"But she was radiant then." He sat upright, suddenly smiling at proud memories. "I can see her now, crowning me and Charles Brandon and the other winners at some tournament—golden-haired, gay and kind—"

A short silence fell. He was gazing into the dying embers and I guessed that he was still remembering those golden days. "Sir," I said—the familiar Harry being a word I would not presume to use in serious privacy—"you have her most lovable and accomplished daughter."

He laughed then, short and sure. "And what would happen to this country in the hands of a woman? With a new dynasty at home and all the powers of Europe yapping like hungry curs abroad? I tell you, Will, there never was such need for a strong hand and ruthless diplomacy."

I leaned forward from my shadowed stool, too absorbed to be afraid to voice my eager thoughts. "God grant your Grace long life. But come the time, there could be able men around her. Some of these brilliant young scions who are growing to maturity now."

He smiled and shrugged indulgently at my untutored visionary sophistry. "And because she is a woman they would all squander their brilliant abilities in struggling for precedence."

"But is it not conceivable—just conceivable—that a woman, not great in herself, could produce a great age? Being served by a very rivalry of chivalric love?"

"I might have imagined so once," he admitted, a little sad, perhaps, for his disillusionment. "But you talk out of romantic legend, Will. Take Wolsey—or that bull-faced secretary of his, Tom Cromwell—the new men of business ability whom it has suited us Tudors to use. By means of them my father amassed a fortune, broke the power of the contentious barons and the unending threat of civil war, and made England strong. But chivalry is not in their make-up. What woman, I ask you, could control them?"

"Or what man?" I thought, considering to what heights of power the Ipswich grazier's clever son had come. Or was it only that Wolsey *seemed* to rule both king and country? Was he, after all, perhaps only one of those able men whom Tudors use? I seemed to have learned more in this past half hour than in a lifetime. "And failing milady Mary there is no one?" I said, thirsting for knowledge and fearing that never again could I hope to stand so near the source.

"No one save that feckless boy I had of Bessie Blount—or a Plantagenet through the male line." The last words sounded like a muttered curse. The Tudor heaved himself out of his chair and padded with that panther-soft tread of his across to the moonlit window. I think he had momentarily forgotten me again, and, having risen when he rose, I stood there feeling as if I watched a piece of play-acting. He banged his fists with a kind of controlled and weary fury against the emblazoned glass. "After Bosworth— after all my father's careful building—*back to the Plantagenets!*"

I saw then the naked thing that nagged him. The usurper's fear which had driven his impostor-ridden father to murder Margaret of Salisbury's brother Warwick. The lurking canker that no one could suspect, seeing his boisterous splendid state. "What have I done worse than other men that God will not give me a legitimate son?" he demanded of the indifferent moon.

After a while he turned and stood staring into space, emotion abated, his strong hands slack at his sides. "The Princess Elizabeth of York, your Grace's mother, was a Plantagenet," I reminded him.

He crossed himself, remembering her with devotion. Perhaps he thought, too, of his favourite sister Mary, who had married Suffolk. I am sure that he thought, too, of Katherine the Queen. "I have been singularly blessed in my women," he said.

During that moment or two of reverie, love seemed to have subdued frustrated rage. He came back almost lightly to the hearth and to the former points of our incredible conversation. "And so you see, Will," he summed up, with a soft, sibilant intake of breath, "there is nothing for it but for me to marry again."

Chapter Ten

I FOUND IT DIFFICULT to believe that the King had told me of this momentous decision which Lord Mayor, prelates and people all hung upon. It was not so much that he liked my company, I told myself, as that he could be comfortably unaware of it. To him I must seem a familiar, impersonal being, midway between mountebank and monk, to whom he could lay bare his inmost thoughts. If they shocked me my reactions were too unimportant to matter, and if he suffered I could give him human understanding. He had taken me into his service as a jester, but it was rather my instinct for the moment to stop jesting which had brought us into touch. That, and our mutual love of music. And however much I strove not to become too puffed up, at least I knew that the King of England trusted me.

From that time I had no need to fear other entertainers, however ambitious and clever they might be. They performed their act, won their applause and passed on. But the Tudor family had accepted me as part of their daily life and I belonged. John Fermor, going home to visit Neston, could truthfully report to his father and Joanna that I was a success at Court.

And success, I found, can be judged as accurately by the attitude of one's fellows as by that of one's master. When it became known that I was sometimes called to spend quiet hours alone with the King all manner of people began to tell me of troubles and injustices in the hope that I could get them righted.

"But I am not the Chancellor of England!" I would protest.

"No," they would come back at me. "But you can say things to the King which even milord Chancellor Wolsey dare not."

This was true enough, providing that I chose my moment and wrapped the kernel of the grievance in good enough entertainment. Several times by cracking a topical joke about some unnoticed hardship I was able to draw royal attention to it. And sometimes, if he were in a good humour, Henry would rap out an order which would serve to remedy it. Not with the carefully weighed justice of Wolsey's law courts, but with the swift, more spectacular kindness of a king. And sometimes my sly efforts worked the other way, as when the royal auditors came bowing to their master and I was able to raise a laugh by forestalling the usher and announcing them as his Grace's *frauditors* because, as most of us knew, they were waxing fat on his careless extravagance and their needless cutting of a thrifty Queen's household allowance.

I would not accept bribes as Budge had, but because quite humble people often laid small offerings outside my door I was not surprised when an unknown woman followed me one afternoon along my favourite riverside path. The September sun was hot and I was tired with trying to distract an unusually irritable master, and when I stretched myself out on the grass and leaned against a stile I saw her standing by the oak tree beneath whose shade I lay. She had brought a cushion which she tucked deftly between my weary back and the hardness of the wood.

I suspected that the cushion was stolen, but it was soft, so I thanked her for her pains and settled to rest, but she would not move away. "What do you want with me?" I asked testily.

Solicitude for my comfort turned all too swiftly to supplication. "It is about my son," she said. And through half-closed eyelids I noticed her work-roughened hands twisting in a kind of vicarious agony against the soiled darkness of her skirt.

"Who told you that I come this way?" I snapped.

"I have a cousin among the scullions," she answered, as if that were immaterial. "My son is to be hanged tomorrow."

"Then he has probably done something that well merits it."

She did not deny it. "He is a sailor," she went on in the same urgent voice. "He was caught on a pirate ship which had sunk one of those accursed French merchantmen off Dover. Not so long ago he was sent to fight them. Now Chancellor Wolsey's new laws punish piracy with death."

"And quite rightly," I said, wanting only to be rid of her.

"And so he was dragged to London and is to be hanged at noon tomorrow."

"And, having brought him up badly, you come to plague me in my rare hour of peace and quiet."

"He is all I have."

I closed my eyes, but felt sure that she was still there.

"Have you a mother, Master Somers?"

"What is that to do with you?" I asked shortly, hating her persistency.

"Because if you have you must know that were your life in danger she would be as importunate for you."

It was a stab in the dark, but it went home. "Touché," I admitted. "What is your son's name and where is the hanging to be?"

She told me his name was Miles Mucklow and that it was to be at Blackwell and I calculated that, if I could catch the King's ear, it might not be too late to save the man. All the same I do not think that I should have bestirred myself to help if it had not been for the way in which she found opportunity to show her gratitude.

It was deliriously green and cool beneath the sun-dappled leaves of my oak tree, with the silver Thames rippling through brown rushes almost at my feet. I fell asleep and dreamed that I was with Joanna at Neston. But all too soon the snap of a twig wakened me and I saw that the woman had come back. "What is it now?" I grumbled.

"A man at the kitchen door."

"There must be scores every day."

"But he is a stranger. And he is asking for you."

"*Another* beggar," I said ungraciously.

"He is certainly crumpled looking, as if he had been sleeping out in the fields. That is why they are all laughing and throwing things at him. Because he looks so odd and says he is a relation of yours."

"An old ruse," I said, idly throwing a pebble into the water. "And where does this one say he comes from?"

"From Shropshire."

I sat up straight and really looked at her for the first time. She must have been handsome once, before the hardness of her life left her lined and scrawny. For the first time I saw her smile. "Like me, he will not go away however cruelly they bait him," she said. "So I thought perhaps he really *is* a relation and loves you."

"What is he like?" I asked.

"Short and fresh-faced, with straw-coloured hair and the funniest country hat."

In a moment I was on my feet and hurrying back along the path to the back premises of the palace, woman and cushion forgotten. But even as I neared the garden wall my eagerness became mixed with dismay, so that my pace slackened. Just as Frith farm had seemed poor compared with Court life, so would the social status of its owner. Hot into my mind shot the contemptuous epithets used by men who hated our up-climbing Cardinal. "Butcher's brat," "Ipswich cattle boy," and the like. My father had been possessed of dignity, but even in his own setting Uncle Tobias would have seemed a figure of fun had we not been so affectionately accustomed to him. And now the very cooks and scullions were laughing at him.

Reluctantly, I rounded the palace wall and looked through the open gateway. And there I saw him—hot, dishevelled, his strong country hose all torn by briars and his sun-baked face half hidden by a rustic hat. Smart kitchen underlings, in cheap clothes that aped the fashions of their betters, were mimicking his broad Shropshire accent, and scullions were pelting him with stinking wet refuse from their sinks. The dinner dishes were washed, the fires damped down, and here was a God-sent persistent old comic to provide their spot of afternoon amusement. "Says he's Will Somers's uncle, does he?" laughed the dapper Clerk of the Kitchen, happening to cross the courtyard at that moment. "Then I must be the Pope's grandfather!"

Shame and dismay possessed me. How unkind, how inconsiderate of such a relative to come, debasing me where I had so laboriously built up success. Were he to see me I could not be callous enough to disown him. But no one *had* seen me. And how easy it would be to slip away!

"The poor old man must have walked a long way," I heard someone murmur pityingly at my shoulder, and realised that the condemned man's mother must have followed me again. And, enlightened by her words, I noticed how, even with blobs of basting fat dripping down on to his broken shoes, my uncle held his ground. And how his resolution made his tormentors look like yapping, insignificant curs.

I walked briskly across the yard and swung him round to me, gripping him by the shoulders. "Uncle Tobias!" I called loudly, so that all should hear me. And the welcome sounded glad because I was thanking God that my treachery had been but momentary, in mind rather than fact. Even then I had sense enough to know that shame of family may be a sharp dismay, but that the memory of having felt it could stick in one's conscience all one's life.

"Will!" he cried, with so much relief that I am sure he had already forgotten this Court scum and all he had been through to reach me.

His tormentors had drawn back towards the kitchen doorway, gaping and abashed. Some young nitwit giggled, supposing my greeting to be part of a jester's play-acting. And so to leave no uncertainty in their minds I turned on them in anger. "Is this the way you represent the most hospitable Court in Europe?" I rated them. "Go back to your spits and sinks. And if you are so ignorant that you cannot read, then learn by rote the rules which milord Chamberlain finds it necessary to hang on the wall for such louts as you. 'Do not snot at table. Do not claw your back for fleas. Do not mock old men.' And now get out of my way, all of you, and bring my visitor something to eat."

I took him by the arm and hurried him along a passage to my little room overlooking the carpenter's court. "What brings you? And how come your shoes and hose to be in such a state?" I asked.

"Trouble brings me. And scarce was I out of Shropshire when my horse went lame. I had not the silver in my purse to hire, and so I walked."

"But could you not have sent one of my cousins?" I asked, seeing that however brave a face he might put on all his misadventures he was tired out.

"They had to stay and do the best they could for the herd."

With contrite celerity half a dozen shame-faced servants were setting up a table and laying the best dishes they could find before him and, instead of fogging him with foreign wines, an older man from the brew house produced a tankard of good Kentish ale. "Forgive us, Master Somers," he entreated before closing the door upon us. "It was just that we did not believe him." For which, upon reflection, I could scarcely blame them.

"Then learn to know an honest man when you see one," I admonished, with a friendly buffet and a groat or two for their pains.

Seeing that the honest man was famished, I did not plague him with questions, but as soon as he had laid down his knife and folded his hands across a comfortably filled stomach the explanation came. "It is that grasping landlord Tyrrell. He has enclosed the common which we small farmers have always had the use of for our cattle, we an' our fathers afore us. An' now there be nowhere for the fine herd I've spent my savings on to graze."

"Why did the old lick-penny do this?"

"Surely you know that the price of wool is soaring. 'Tis happening all over our part o' the country. The lords of the Manor always want to keep more sheep. Quick wool export, more profit and less labour. What easier than to fence in a bit here and a bit there of the village common-land? But this devil at Frith has taken the lot."

I sat in the window seat staring at him aghast. "But our commons were granted years ago by Royal Charter. It is plain robbery. And yet for stealing a loaf a tinker or a pedlar would have his ears cut off."

"Aye. An' that's not all of it. One old man with a good dog can care for a flock of sheep. So with our pastures gone where are our sons to get even hired work?"

I had been living in a world of luxury too long. It was not only a whole family's tragedy, but a menace to a whole hard-working rural class. "There be them as pulls up the stakes by night, but 'tis time someone did summat more permanent about it," he said, in that deliberate, determined way of his. "An' so I came to you, Will."

They all came to me—the man with royal favour and a foolish heart. And what was I to do? Yet something I *would* do in this case, having so often done small kindnesses for people who were nothing to me, while families like the Boleyns were forever begging favours for their kin. I now saw this upright, kind old relative through the clear eyes of long affection, unblurred by shibboleths of class. And I remembered that only by his recommendation, however characteristically impartial, had I got my chance in the world and met the girl I loved.

I slid briskly from the window seat. "We must go and see the King," I said.

"*I*—see the King?" he gasped. Then, supposing me to be joking, he laughed loudly, got up from the table and looked down ruefully at his stained and sorry garments. "In these rags? What would your aunt say, my lad, who keeps all our Sabbath wear so clean and patched?"

"No, not in those rags," I agreed, looking wildly round the bareness of my room for inspiration. "But we must go *now* if we are to catch him before he leaves the council chamber and goes hunting."

"You are serious, Will?" I have seen my uncle face a maddened bull with less terror on his face, but he had put himself in my hands and made no further protest.

I remembered that my new jester's suit had come from the tailor and was hanging, as yet unworn, behind the door. Quickly I bundled Uncle Tobias into it, struggling to make the green worsted doublet meet across his belly. It was lined with stiff buckram and fringed with red bells, and if he had looked a figure of fun before he looked even more ludicrous now. "Two of us?" he panted, looking from my shabbier motley to his creakingly new outfit.

"Yes, two—which is bound to attract the King's attention," I said firmly, pulling the hood more closely about his face. In spite of the difference between his ruddy face and my high cheek-bones and deep-set eyes there appeared to be some family resemblance which made us look alike.

Straight to the royal apartments I hurried, choosing all the most populated corridors and ante-rooms. "Make way! Make way for his Grace's jesters!" I shouted as I went. And high and low made way, stepping back to stare and then entering into the spirit of the thing without knowing quite what was afoot. "Way for my uncle, the King's new jester!" I called, coming within sight of the great closed door of the King's privy council chamber.

Some benevolent guardian angel must have flown down to open it at that very moment, and there in the doorway stood King Henry, flushed and frowning, with a handful of anxious lords and clerics behind him. At sight of us he stopped short in bewilderment and put up a hand to scratch at his auburn pate. "God save us, Will, are there two of you?" he exclaimed. "Did your mother have twins?"

"No, but she had a brother, and because he has come a long way to see you and his clothes are travel stained I have lent him the fine new suit you had made for me."

"And I hope you have given him some food," said Henry, his frown smoothing into a smile as he examined my double. "Is he as amusing as you are?"

"Not intentionally. In fact, Harry, he is a very sad man at this moment. But he has an interesting tale to tell."

"Then let us hear it," said the King, seating himself in a chair which a page had set before the hearth. "It is time we heard something more entertaining than fruitless conferences." He looked sourly at milord Cardinal and Bishop Fisher of Rochester, who excused themselves and moved away, presumably to confer apart.

My uncle looked imploringly at me, but I knew that his simple sincerity would be worth all my babbling. "It is about a farmer and some cows and a griping old miser," I said. "But he will tell it better than I."

And tell it better he did, for any man talking of his own trade is worth listening to. And Henry Tudor listened, for was it not a story of the ordinary, everyday workings of his kingdom? "What is this landlord's name?" he asked.

"Master Tyrrell, your Grace," said Uncle Tobias.

"And what Tyrrell ever did his king any good?" I put in, to help things along. And, seeing Henry look at me questioningly, I ventured to jog his memory with one of those items of history which had been dinned into me in my father's classroom. "Was it not a Sir Walter Tyrrell who shot King William Rufus through the eye?"

"An accident, when they were hunting in the New Forest," recalled Henry. But perhaps he felt the name boded him ill, for he sent for a clerk and there and then gave orders that the fencing was to be taken down. "Does that satisfy you?" he asked, scrawling his all-powerful signature across the paper.

To my amazement it did not, and Uncle Tobias, having once overcome his shyness, made no bones about saying so. "The old scurrimudgeon will but enclose all over again when your Grace has forgotten," he said bluntly.

The Tudor's sandy eyelashes blinked at him in surprise, but he was sportsman enough to appreciate a man who spoke his mind. "Can you write, Tobias?" he asked, after a moment's thought.

"Well enough to keep my farm accounts, since my brother-in-law was a schoolmaster," answered my uncle.

"Then I tell you what we will do," said Henry with a chuckle. "We will make you bailiff of this Frith Common. At a fee of twenty pounds a year. And I make no doubt you will know how to keep this Tyrrell on his own side of the fence."

My uncle was overcome with gratitude, but my own thanks had to wait. I remembered the woman who had pestered me by the riverside and how, but for her, my uncle would have suffered penury and I would have suffered shame. I must make an effort to save her son. And now, while the pen was in Henry's hand, was as good a moment as any. I hated asking for another boon, but somehow I managed it. A reprieve was signed and a royal servant sent with it to London.

"And what do I get out of all this?" my master asked, handing the pen back to his clerk and looking up at me with a rueful grin.

I joined my palms and bowed my head. "Your reward will be in Heaven," I said, in a really fine imitation of the Cardinal's most unctuous baritone.

Henry sprang up in exasperation. He gave me a friendly cuff on the shoulder, and even a friendly cuff from his massive hand could be painful. "So those sanctimonious advisers of mine are always telling me. But there are times in a man's life when he wants some of the reward here and now!"

And off he strode in a flurry of handsome brocade to join the merry group of youngsters clustered, as usual, around the tinkling laughter of Anne Boleyn.

Chapter Eleven

LTHOUGH KING HENRY WAS beginning to thicken into middle age, such was his vigour that he seemed to regain his youth when in the company of this group of gay young courtiers. More and more often he sought escape in their vivifying and irresponsible levity from the weightier matters thrust upon him by his counsellors. And in doing so he emphasised, all unconsciously perhaps, the difference in years between himself and his too rapidly ageing wife. When Cardinal Wolsey took up residence at his new Manor of Hampton and invited his royal master to a house-warming feast, it was an excited company of youngsters who crowded into the royal barges to escort him, while Queen Katherine, who was beginning to suffer from dropsy, stayed in her apartments to rest.

Seeing that Lord Vaux and Sir Thomas Wyatt and the Boleyn family had been invited into the King's own barge, I scrambled after him and squatted beside the gorgeously arrayed bargemaster in the stern. The sun was shining, and up river with the tide we went, the eight oarsmen with the great Tudor rose on their doublets pulling as one. Through a cluster of foreign shipping and past our own busy wharves where clerks and wherrymen all stopped work to gaze and cheer at the fine sight we made. Past the grim silence of the Tower. Then shooting skillfully through one of the arches of London Bridge, where the rush of water between the stone piers was so murderous that most of the women screamed—all except

Mistress Boleyn, whose slender body tensed adventurously to the thrill of swiftly approaching danger. Through the city of London itself, with the tall spire of St. Paul's on our right and the brothels of Bankside on our left. And then past the stately Palace of Westminster and out into the country between green meadows again until we came to Richmond.

"The lovely palace where I was born and where my mother lived," said Henry, and I swear that his thoughts were back in those gardens and galleries with her, for he never turned his gaze from them until we were past. "Only a good woman should live in that peaceful place," he added, with a sigh for his happy boyhood memories.

But almost immediately everyone was exclaiming at the beauty of Hampton as the tall gatehouse towers of Wolsey's new home came into view, and the portly prelate himself was seen to be standing at the top of his watergate steps to welcome his royal guest.

"Trust a churchman to find himself a fine site!" Sir Thomas Boleyn was saying enviously. "I am told that he bought the lease from the Knights Hospitallers."

"Who could scarcely refuse, seeing that he was the Pope's legate," laughed Wyatt. "But it was in sad repair, having been used as a kind of theological school, and one must admit that he has done wonders to it."

"It is fairer even than Greenwich!" exclaimed Anne Boleyn tactlessly.

"And so much more convenient for Westminster and the City," added Vaux, who was beginning to acquire the practical viewpoint of his merchant relatives.

> *"With all the wealth which a bishopric brings*
> *He makes him a mansion to rival the King's,"*

I chanted maliciously, from my precarious perch abaft.

A few months ago the King would not have tolerated such sly thrusts at his all-powerful Chancellor, and between us I scarcely think we had added to our prospective host's popularity. But it was true of Thomas Wolsey that although few men can have been more efficient, few men have been less loved. As a hard-working statesman he impressed all Europe, but as a priest he lacked spirituality. It always seemed to me that he was without a vestige of that rare virtue humility, which most inspires affection.

We were lavishly entertained at Hampton with banquets and jousting and dancing, and as usual I enjoyed pitting my wits against those of Saxton, the Cardinal's pretentious jester. During the days which we spent there we were shown all the fine features of the place. The exquisite linen-fold panelling and the gold and silver hangings in milord Cardinal's private apartments overlooking the river, and the splendid ceilings ornamented with the pillars and cross-keys of his badge. Men like Vaux and Wyatt, who were familiar with the famous buildings of Italy and France, admired the outer walls of the base court where narrow, dark-red bricks were patterned with black ones—an effect achieved locally by burning hay in the mortar, so Wolsey's usher Cavendish told us. And we could not but marvel at the two hundred and eighty rooms always kept in readiness for guests, and at the fine galleries which connected them and were lighted by beautiful mullion windows. Yet with such palatial impressiveness Wolsey had managed to preserve a kind of mellow homeliness.

It was a privilege to share so interesting a visit. Such a home was indeed a proud symbol of a successful career. Yet, watching milord Cardinal showing it off proudly to the royal master who had always been his friend, I thought involuntarily, "You learned Ipswich fool! Can you not see where friendship, over-taxed, begins to fray? Did you never hear, when you were a bright grammar-school boy, the good old adage 'Pride goes before a fall'?"

Perhaps Wolsey was always so busy advising Henry that he had less time to listen and to observe than those of us who earned our bread by waiting upon the King's pleasure and so had urgent need to find out what it really was.

Henry took his leave sooner than we expected. Although the entertainment was good, his laugh rang out less boisterously than usual. His farewell to his host was a shade less cordial. On his way to the water steps he looked back pensively at that attractive house, pulling at his small, pursed mouth with thumb and forefinger as he often did when his thoughts were none too pleasant. And when we were all back in the barge I overheard him say to Sir Thomas Boleyn, "As a second son I was trained for the Church and, by Heaven, I might have done better for myself had I remained in that lucrative profession!"

"What does a celibate priest need with all those guest rooms?" asked Anne Boleyn, in that clear, penetrating voice of hers. "Oh, of course, George, I know as well as anybody that he has not really been celibate," she added, seeing her brother grin. "But surely that Lark woman has been dead these many years?"

"Not dead, Nan, but comfortably married off to someone else," he told her.

"Perhaps our good Cardinal intends to take a second wife," laughed Henry, charmed back to good humour by her very impudence, and throwing a red rose from the prelate's garden into her lap.

Anne Boleyn sighed as she withdrew her gaze reluctantly from the receding beauty of Hampton. "I would almost marry him myself to become mistress of that manor," she declared, turning her dark eyes upon the King in a provocative manner which must have maddened her enamoured cousin, Wyatt.

And, numbskull that I was, I did not even then suspect that anything less natural than the need of sons drove the Tudor into contemplating divorce. That very evening, back at Greenwich, in full view of all, I made a cruel kind of blunder worthy of that clumsy, bearded Budge.

The Queen, pale-faced and bravely pretending to have recovered from her indisposition, appeared at supper in her usual place beside her husband. Kindly, ungrudgingly, she listened to all the accounts of our pleasant visit. And because my heart was full of pity for her I had squandered a week's wages on a basket of golden Spanish oranges, which she loved.

"See what the King has brought your Grace from Hampton," I said, sure that he had never once thought of her and that nothing would please her so much as the belief that he had.

She turned to smile at him, the warm light of pleasure beautifying her tired eyes. And then some nosey old busybody had to spoil it.

"Oranges and lemons
Said the bells of St. Clement's,"

he gurgled, having been too freely at the sack. "But I saw our Will buying them from a ship's master at the Fermor wharf." And instead of letting his tipsy *faux pas* go, I must needs enlarge upon it defensively.

"Better that poor Will should bring home an orange or two from the wharves than that the King should bring home a *leman* from Hampton," I said, making play with our popular word for a light o' love. And immediately I realised by the lack of laughter, the embarrassed titter or two, and the awkward silence that I had spoken amiss. Worse still, I saw the warm light die from the Queen's plain face, and the embarrassed red flush Henry's.

"You certainly exceeded your licence just now, Will," Lord Vaux warned me in an undertone as we all rose with a fluster of silks and a scraping of stools from the supper tables. "The most favoured of fools had better keep his tongue caged on the matter of mistresses."

Even then I thought he was just giving me a well-merited rebuke for the cheap coarseness of my *double entendre* before the Queen.

But I was to learn the enormity of my *bêtise* with blinding suddenness. Later that evening the Countess of Salisbury sent for me to come and sing to our young Princess, who had been asking for me because she had one of her bouts of toothache and could not sleep. There was no summons which I would have obeyed with more alacrity. But I remembered that in the hurry of setting off for Hampton I had left my harp in the King's ante-chamber, and hurried along the stairs and passages to reclaim it before his Grace should have retired to his bedchamber. It was quite dusk by then and some careless servant had forgotten to light the torch at the archway to the King's gallery—or so I thought. But it was not too dark for me to make out the tall figure of my master with a slender woman in his arms. Or to recognise the heart-shaped whiteness of Anne Boleyn's face. She appeared to be holding him off, but the urgent hunger of his embrace was unmistakable.

For a moment or two I stood rooted in the deep shadow of the archway. Then slipped away soft-footed, a wiser and a deeply troubled man.

I realised how my silly, tasteless words must have hurt the Queen, who undoubtedly knew that her husband really *had* brought home a leman, and from the same Kentish family as before. Or, at any rate, one whom he *desired* to make his mistress. I saw how well Wolsey had been serving his master's interests when he had so callously crushed Anne's betrothal to young Percy of Northumberland, and why so many favours were being shown to her ambitious father. And, retracing my steps more slowly to the Princess's apartments, I wondered sadly how this new complication in the lives of her elders would affect her.

But I had little time to dwell on this before I became involved in troubles of my own. Knowing the King's interests to be engaged elsewhere, I had more sense than to hang around to amuse him, and a day or two later when I went to my own room to read in peace, to my great surprise I found John Fermor waiting for me there.

"Master John! I did not know you were at Court," I exclaimed, surprised to find him sitting patiently in so humble a place.

But most of his uppishness seemed to have been shaken out of him. "I am not here to wait upon the King, but to see my brother-in-law—and you, Will," he admitted. "I have bad news from Neston."

"Not sickness? Not any of the family?" I blurted out, seeing him draw from his pouch a letter sealed with the crimson cock's head of the Fermors.

"No, no," he assured me. "But the new ship. The *Cast*. My father says here that she went aground off the Dutch coast in a raging gale. Half the sailors were drowned and all that valuable cargo of wheat lost!"

I sank down on the other stool and stared at him in dismay.

"The ship which was the pride of Master Fermor's heart and the cargo for which he had obtained free export," I recalled.

"My father is a rich man, but this must be a blow."

"And for more than financial reasons," I said, knowing how that upright merchant would feel about the lives of all those men.

"He warns me to curb my expenditure," went on his son, gloomily tapping the letter with an idler's bejewelled hand. "And seems to blame me for all those orders of silk which we have had from the Cardinal since I befriended his clerk in Florence."

"But surely they should help?"

"If they were paid for!"

"The silk not paid for!" I exclaimed incredulously. "But the Queen's ladies complain jokingly that they can scarcely hear themselves speak for the rustle of it. His splendour is the talk of half Europe. Only last week he invited the King and Court to see his new Manor at Hampton. I went with them. It is even finer than York House on the Strand and all his other places. It has everything that money can buy."

"Which is where much of his wealth is gone. He was always one for ostentation. Yet when, at my father's bidding, I had to go crawling to that odious secretary of his, this bull-faced Cromwell tells me bluntly that his master cannot at the moment pay—I am but now come from him."

I knew how much young Fermor must have hated this, and began to suspect that he had come to me in the hope of help, or at least advice. "If any two men have cause to detest the sight of me, they are Wolsey and his fool, for I am for ever poking fun at them," I pointed out.

"But you could drop a hint to the King, perhaps, in the clever way you sometimes do," he suggested.

"Even I have exceeded my licence in that quarter of late, as milord Vaux will tell you," I said, wishing with all my heart that I could find some way to help. "But after all, Thomas Cromwell said only that he could not make payment *now*. And milord Cardinal's credit must stand higher than any man's save the King's."

"But for how long? Thomas Vaux says that if the Butcher's Dog cannot bring about a royal divorce soon he will be kicked out of the kennel."

"But is not milord Cardinal doing everything he can to persuade the Pope?"

"Not quickly enough, it seems, now that the Tudor is hot on the scent of that Boleyn bitch."

"How should that affect Wolsey?" I asked. "The King would not want to *marry* her."

"No, I suppose not. Any more than her sister. But any passionate interlude at this juncture will make him yet more restive about his present bonds of matrimony."

"Everything Thomas Wolsey has is of the King—save his own ability," I agreed musingly, comparing his state with my own and glad that my own was so incomparably humbler. "To fall from such a height would be to shatter hopelessly."

We sat in silence for a minute or two, considering the consequences of such a wild possibility. Then John Fermor kicked back his stool and rose with a sigh, as one who has done all he can and now shrugs off further responsibility. "Well, all merchants have their mishaps," he said, almost cheerfully. "If Fermor trade be bad this year, now is the moment for my sister Joanna to make a wealthy marriage."

I, too, had risen to gather up his cloak and sword. "With whom?" I asked, and could feel the blood draining from my face.

"There are plenty of young blades in the county whose fathers have made bids for her, but she would do better to marry someone of importance in London. There is that old man Pickering, for instance, for whom my father is executor—wadded with money and recently widowed."

"And sixty if he is a day," I cried hotly.

"Well, well, she would see life and have all the jewels and gowns she wanted, and my wife could bring her to Court sometimes."

"Do you suppose that is all Mistress Joanna wants?"

"A girl must marry as her father thinks best. And last time I was with my father I strongly advocated this."

"He loves her and would not for any cause see her unhappy," I said, with more brave conviction than I felt. "And what would he do without her at Neston?"

John Fermor flung his modish cloak about his shoulders and laughed. "Marry again himself," he suggested. "Surely you know that Northamptonshire is full of rich widows who are only too willing to throw themselves at him for his likeable personality alone."

I knew it all too well. I was still holding the cocksure young fellow's sword in my hands and could cheerfully have murdered him with it. But he was my first master's son and I a kind of mountebank who had no right to mind whom my sweet Joanna married.

Chapter Twelve

I DO NOT KNOW how people tolerated me during that winter. My heart was sore and my tongue sharp. And specially I could not keep the edge of it off Wolsey. Because we all knew that he was trying to persuade the Pope to sanction a formal court of enquiry regarding the validity of the Queen's union, I had to twit him whenever I dared on the subject of his own wife's second marriage. She had borne him a son and a daughter, but as soon as the glaring light of fame began to search out the hidden corners of his life he had sacrificed her to his ambition, passing her on, complete with wedding dowry, to a wealthy landowner, called Lee. So my pointed little ditty, "With freedom not for you and me, the lark's now nesting on the lea," was quite popular about the palace, and must have enraged him every time he heard the pages whistling it.

And once when he was strolling in the privy garden with the King—suggesting, I dare swear, that our poor Queen might be persuaded to retire to some convent—I rushed up to them and announced that a crowd of people were asking for his Eminence at the kitchen court gate.

"What people?" demanded the King testily.

"His creditors," I told him, "all clamouring to be paid."

Wolsey turned on me like an enraged bull, for which I do not blame him. "I will wager anything—anything I possess—that I owe no man a penny," he declared pompously.

I shrugged as if the matter could not concern me less. "Your Eminence has so many enviable possessions, and the King may take you up on that. What will you have as wager, Harry?"

"His new manor at Hampton," answered Henry promptly, beginning to smile.

I turned and pointed along the low wall which separated garden from river, and from where we stood we could see a crowd of people waiting outside the back entrance by which my uncle had once entered. I knew, of course, that they were the daily horde of beggars waiting for the palace almoner to distribute bread and scraps of meat left over from the midday meal, and Henry must have known this, too. But probably the Cardinal did not.

"There seems to be a vast number of them," remarked his Grace, gamely playing up to me.

"There is one, for instance, who claims a considerable sum for silks," I said.

I do not know whether Wolsey really believed that some Fermor agent was waiting there, or whether he was merely embarrassed that I, who had been in their employ, should know of this debt and dare to bait him with it in the King's presence. He fished in some pocket deep within the folds of his voluminous soutane and threw six golden sovereigns on the flat coping of the wall. It must have been all that he had on him, for at that moment I am sure he would have paid anything to prevent further revelations in his royal master's presence. "Take these, you impudent knave, and send them all away!" he ordered, turning back hastily in the opposite direction.

"Then it seems that Hampton is yours, Harry!" I said, batting an eyelid at the grinning King as I gathered up the scattered coins.

How Thomas Wolsey must have hated the sight of me!

Left alone with the sovereigns glittering in my palm, I was suddenly reminded of those testing moments at Neston when I had held six of Richard Fermor's in my hand and been tempted to rob him. It seemed incredible now. A glad sense of spiritual freedom possessed me, and I found myself smiling with grateful affection at the memory of Father Thayne's words, "That is *one* dragon which you have slain, Will." God knows there were many more lurking in my soul needing the attack, but having won for myself some of my first master's integrity I hurried to divide my takings among the maimed and aged beggars at the King's gate.

Most of them knew and seemed to hold me in affection, and while the almoner's clerk doled out the food I tried to hearten them with a kindly jest or two. And while I stood there beneath the great archway leading to the kitchens a huge bearded man came rolling up to me with a seaman's gait. "Have you, too, come to say a *Deo Gratia?*" I asked, thinking that he looked too strong and well fed to be seeking alms.

"Aye," he answered. "But for more than bread. For life itself. I am Miles Mucklow, that pirate whose mother begged you to save him from the gallows."

"Then be good to her all the days of her life," I said, recalling the incident. "You have in her a consolation which I lack. But I thought they threw you into the Marshalsea prison in lieu of hanging?"

"I did not have to serve my time. I had the good fortune to save the prison master from two murderers who beset him and, having use for my strength, he made me one of his gaolers."

I told him I was glad to hear it.

"My life is yours," he said sententiously.

"And what should I do with it?" I asked, giving him a friendly shove. "I am at enough pains sometimes to live my own."

"The more reason why you should remember me if ever I can be of service to you," he pointed out, with something of his mother's flat persistency.

"I will remember you, Miles Mucklow, if only for your extraordinary name," I promised, and straightway went indoors and forgot all about him for many a month. For the thoughts and conversation of all of us within the palace were at that time centred upon this so-called "secret matter" of the King's divorce.

It was beginning to dawn upon those of us who were nearest to him that he had no intention of contracting the matrimonial alliance with France for which Wolsey was so devotedly trying to pave the way. And that Anne Boleyn was far too clever to allow herself to become his mistress. Of two things I felt certain. She had truly loved Percy of Northumberland, and she would never forgive Wolsey for so brutally breaking off their betrothal, although he had been but acting on the King's instructions.

When she first came back from France Anne Boleyn had been a gay, affectionate, high-spirited girl: but now she was growing into a calculating, cynical woman, with a wit as sharp as her pointed chin. With an ambitious father egging her on, she intended to recompense herself for lost happiness with more than a brief, gaudy hour of royal lust to be followed by the obscurity that was now her sister's. She was attractive enough, God knows, in her slender black and white way, to bewitch a man utterly. But it was now borne in upon us that she meant to keep her virtue until the Tudor's passion drove him to pay top price for it. Though how she held him off all those months I cannot imagine, for he could have crushed her between his ten strong fingers and was hot with desire for her.

The Queen herself must have been aware of her skittish maid's ambition, for I was in her apartments one evening when she and her ladies were playing those new card games which we had from France. The stakes ran high and some of us crowded round to watch. Katherine of Aragon laid down a queen with the face of her late mother-in-law Elizabeth of York painted upon it, as was the fashion. But Anne Boleyn, who was always lucky at games of chance, trumped that high card with the king of hearts, so winning both trick and game. "Ah, my lady Anne, I see that you will have a king or nothing," said her Grace with a wry smile, motioning to another of her ladies to pay the girl her winnings and rising wearily from the table.

But the getting of him was to be a more difficult sport, subject to plague and parting and procrastination. And for the poor Queen a long-played-out tragedy, subject to every kind of cruel delay.

Henry sent envoys to the Pope, entreating his Holiness to sanction a divorce and a second marriage to Mistress Boleyn so that he might beget an heir. And Wolsey, who had so glibly called Anne "a foolish girl about the Court" when rating Percy of Northumberland for wanting her, was obliged to arm them with a wordy testament lauding her gentle birth, her virginity and her virtue. But by the time the earnest prelates reached him poor Pope Clement had fled from the Castello Sant'Angelo in Rome and was the Emperor's prisoner in Oriento, and could receive them only in the shabbiest of rooms. He promised to send a wise old Cardinal called Campeggio to arbitrate, but so poor was his Holiness's state at that time that Wolsey had the choir in Canterbury cathedral sing *Ora pro papa nostro Clements* instead of *Ora pro nobis*.

And as if all this was not unfortunate enough for my royal master, here in England we had the plague. I well remember the heat that June, when the Fleet river almost dried up, the street runnels stank and the sweating sickness began to kill off the citizens of London like flies.

The King was staying at York House, Wolsey's riverside mansion by Westminster, and I had laid aside my motley and walked along the Strand into London in the hope of seeing my former master. Knowing the great pleasure that this would be to me, Father Thayne had asked one of the Neston grooms to bring me word that Master Fermor would be staying with his sister-in-law and her husband, John Brown, while attending to various affairs in the capital. It was not difficult to find Master Brown's whereabouts. As became a wealthy merchant whose father had been Lord Mayor, he lived in one of those fine, high-gabled houses in Aldermanbury near the Guildhall—a house all ornamented with richly coloured coats-of-arms and wooden carvings of men mounted on monstrous beasts. A few years ago such solid grandeur would have over-awed me to the point of retreat, but now I gave my name to an obliging servant and was allowed inside to wait, and presently my former master came into the great hall accompanied by two other gentlemen. He did not attempt to hide his pleasure at finding me there, and without any kind of condescension presented me to them. One I recognised instantly as a son of Sir William, from his portrait hanging at Easton Neston, and the other was Master Skevington, a lean, stooping old wine merchant, reported to be of great wealth. Both of them greeted me most pleasantly, making reference to my growing popularity at Court, and then, to my secret delight, excused themselves to Master Fermor as they had to attend some meeting at the Guildhall.

It was indeed good to be alone with him again. There was an air of solid efficiency about him which struck me afresh after living among the more foppish figures at Court. Although his brown doublet was of the finest Utrecht velvet and his matching hose of the best wool obtainable, he was content to look what he was—a busy merchant and land-owner—rather than to ape the courtiers, in the manner of his son.

It was too early in the day for the midday meal to be laid, so we sat at the end of the top table in that comfortable hall with a bottle of the vintner's own well-chosen wine which Master Brown had, before leaving, called to one of his servants to bring.

"It seems you have succeeded marvellously with the King, Will," he said heartily. "We in Northamptonshire are proud of you, and I find that some of your *bon mots* have already spread to other counties where I do business. You even have some influence with his Grace, my son tells me."

"I do at times have his ear, being often alone with him," I said. "But I would say rather that by some unaccountable favour of God I irritate him less than others."

"Which is quite understandable," said Fermor, with a reminiscent smile. "For you have a way of entering into the lives and loves of others."

"Having little of my own!" I thought sadly. And to amuse him rather than to exalt myself I related the incident of milord Cardinal and the creditors at the gate.

He threw back his head and laughed heartily, but almost immediately spoke with gravity. "Because I brought you to Court, Will, I would not have you ever feel constrained to beg anything for me. Not ever, in any circumstances whatever."

And there was Richard Fermor of Easton Neston speaking—the finest master man ever had—as opposed to all those favour-seeking climbers at Court, who so often showed me kindness for their own ends.

"There can never be any question of obligation or constraint," I heard myself saying, in the slow way one speaks when digging up a real thought from the banalities cluttering one's mind. "If you should ever be assailed by trouble, Richard Fermor, it would be to me as my own."

And speaking those words I knew that, in a different way, I, too, had grown to the pride of independent manhood. Across our brimming tankards we looked into each other's eyes and knew that we were no longer master and man, but friends. He stretched a strong brown hand across the polished surface of the table and gripped my bony one. We must have made an incongruous pair. We lifted our tankards and drank, and then fell to talking of more obvious things.

"I was grieved when Master John told me about the *Cast*."

"It was a bitter blow," he admitted thoughtfully, "but one of the hazards of commerce. And now the drought of this hot summer is like to spoil our harvest. But I have good men, and by dint of hard work we hope to make up for it next year. In the meantime I am short of ships for wool and wheat and have just gone into partnership with Master Skevington, whom you just now met, in the ownership of two brigs."

"I remember that when you first brought me to London he, like Master Pickering, had asked you to be his executor."

"So naturally I am assured that he is sound," grinned Richard Fermor. "Besides which, he is an old friend of my father-in-law."

I looked round the handsomely appointed hall. "It was here in his house that Mistress Joanna was to have stayed had she not been taken ill. How is she?" I said, in what sounded almost an ordinary sort of voice.

"Well and gay as ever. Growing uncommonly beautiful. And quite the woman."

"But not yet betrothed?" I forced myself to ask.

"No. All this *Cast* trouble put it from my mind. But I must not so selfishly keep her at home much longer. That is one of the things I have come to discuss with the Brown family. She must make a good marriage." It seemed to me that the sunlit lattices and the diligently polished silver dishes on the sideboard and the fine bright tapestries were all darkening, when a letter with the familiar cock's-head crest was thrust before my eyes. "Oh, before I forget," I heard Master Fermor saying, "Joanna asked me to give you this. She sat up late to write it the night before I left."

I tried not to clutch at it like a starving beggar at the royal almoner's bread. A perfectly good leather wallet hung at my belt, but I thrust the precious missive between the buttons of my doublet, warm against my heart. I would save it until I was alone, and live on it for weeks. "And Mistress Emotte? And Father Thayne? And Jordan? And old Hodge?" I gabbled.

He gave me news of them all, saying that Mistress Emotte was growing less domineering and our beloved Father more frail. And then he rose briskly, reminding me that he had many affairs to attend to and inviting me to accompany him down to the river to take a look at the two ships of which he was now part owner.

"Must you go down to the docks with all this sickness about?" I demurred.

"Of course. It is partly what I came for."

I swung into step beside him as we went out into the stifling heat and down towards his wharf near the busy steelyard where the Hanseatic traders berthed. "Is it true, all I hear from my London friends about a royal divorce?" he asked anxiously, as we hurried along Thames Street.

"Too true," I said, and told him all I knew.

"But our poor, good Queen. How can he repudiate her after all these years?" he asked, with the bewildered distress which was typical of all who lived too far from Court for the latest news of the matter to be daily meat. "His father would never have arranged her second marriage without the Pope's consent. He was far too anxious to establish the Tudor dynasty to take any chances. I remember being taken to see him when I was a lad, when he was issuing orders that all merchants' weights and measures should be strictly checked. A shrewd Welshman if ever there was one. No spectacular figure like his son. But he did more for our trade, with his lively interest in exploring and exporting, than any king we ever had. And now this power-drunk Cardinal-Chancellor ruins our Flemish market by picking war with Spain and then imposing impossible taxes to pay for it." He stopped to survey the Flemish ships, which were fewer than usual. "And he, an Ipswich grazier's son, who should know better!" he added with a sigh.

We were come to the wharf where Master Skevington's ships lay alongside his own, and after admiring them we bade each other a brisk farewell. Master Fermor was soon aboard discussing the size of hold and quantity of bales, while I was hurrying away to find some unused bollard further along the quay where I could sit alone to devour my lady's letter.

It was a very ordinary letter, I suppose—gay with foolish family jokes and practical with everyday happenings. She told me how the pups now had families themselves, how Jordan's new young clerk always muddled up her household orders, how the honeysuckle was blooming on the wall beyond the herb garden where we used to sit, how *dull* Christmas had been without me and how often my poor threadbare jests were quoted. Towards the end anxiety for our good Queen crept through, together with Mottie's fond instructions for my health. But as I sat there, all unaware of contagion and passing wherries, hustling seamen and laden porters, I was back in a world where all in retrospect seemed sunlit, and where I was still affectionately remembered. And my heart sang because Joanna herself still missed me, burning her candle late to bring our minds, if not our bodies, into contact.

A warning shout and a flung hawser drove me from my borrowed perch. Back from the comparative freshness of the river to York House. Picking my way along narrow riverside lanes towards Ludgate and the Strand, I was glad enough of the shade from closely overhanging upper stories, but not a breath of air stirred beneath them—only the stifling, stench-laden heat.

Inevitably, with all the coming and going of clerks and messengers and merchants, the plague soon spread to Greenwich. Several of the servants and two of the household died—swiftly and hideously. And the King of England, without waiting for so much as a change of clothing, mounted his horse and hurried off with his wife and his daughter and his physician to the Abbot of St. Alban's sequestered country place at Tittenhanger.

Henry Tudor's fear of sickness was not an edifying sight, and some years later I was to wonder if he had noticed how contemptuously that tall, proud Plantagenet woman, Margaret of Salisbury, looked at him as she stood in the sunlit courtyard bidding a calm farewell to her friend the Queen and to her young charge, the Princess.

To those of us who had scores of times watched him pitting his enormous strength against the finest wrestlers in the country and riding full tilt against deadly opponents in the lists, it seemed incredible that he should behave so anxiously and propitiatingly at Tittenhanger. He had even sent Mistress Boleyn home to Hever, although she was one of the Queen's ladies. But this may well have been because he loved her and wanted to keep her and her strange beauty safe. Instead of enjoying sports and dancing he was much with his confessor, and used to spend hours helping Doctor Butts to compound ointments and lotions against this sweating sickness. Of an evening he would sit dutifully discussing rather dull subjects with Queen Katherine, and of a morning he would attend Mass with her, as if he were seeking to shelter from the possible wages of sin beneath the wings of her unruffled goodness. But his health remained excellent and, before long, whenever he retired to his own room he would be writing love letters to Hever. That they were impassioned I know because often he would have me play softly to him while he wrote, and I would hear him sigh and see him draw a heart at the bottom of the paper with the lady's initials within. I believe that for greater privacy he often wrote to her in French, because sometimes he would break off and sit singing one of her favourite *chansons* in that sweet, soft tenor of his, or speak to me absently in French as though his thoughts lingered in that language. And when news came that, in spite of all his precaution, she and her father were suffering from the sickness he was nearly frantic and sent his own Doctor Butts to her without thought for himself, which showed the extraordinary measure of his love for her.

Although her sister's beloved husband Carey died, she and Sir Thomas Boleyn had the plague but slightly. With the cooler autumnal days the infection abated, and the Queen returned to Greenwich. But Henry, brooking no more parting from his beloved, furnished Suffolk House, beside the Thames, for the entire Boleyn family, and for himself borrowed York House, which stood near to it, from Wolsey. And at last Campeggio, the aged Cardinal, came. With Pope Clement's authority to arbitrate, it was said.

Being a prescient old man, he came reluctantly, after a long delay occasioned by what the Boleyn girl called "a convenient attack of gout." And he seemed to have hoped to smooth matters over by an assumption that Katherine of Aragon would make things easy for her husband by retiring into a convent. But nothing was going to be easy. "I have no vocation for the conventual life. I am a wife and mother, and my vocation is to be Queen of England," insisted that indomitable woman. "But if your Eminence decides that my husband and I have been living in sin, then as soon as the King goes into a monastery I will enter a nunnery." Which must have left the well-meaning old prelate speechless.

Incongruous pictures of Henry the Eighth as a monk would have provided me with rich sources of ribald merriment—had I dared to use them. But it was difficult to be amused by this valiant feminine riposte for long, for seldom have I seen anything more pitiful than her Grace's effort to refute Campeggio's suggestion by entering into a round of heart-broken gaiety which was quite in contrast to her desires and a great strain on her health. The King ceased to try to be kind to her, and all that her behaviour brought her was the first bitter intimation that her daughter might be taken from her. "The Aragon woman is a fool to withstand the King's will," stormed Wolsey, which in turn, when the Queen came to hear of it, brought *him* the most forthright dressing-down which he was ever likely to receive.

"Have I not been married to my lord the King nearly twenty years, and no objections made?" she cried, when both Cardinals went to badger her. "Are there not various prelates and lords yet alive who judged our marriage good and lawful? As all the world knows, our parents were neither unwise nor weak in judgment, and my father sent to Rome for a dispensation, which I have in my possession, showing my second marriage to be good and lawful."

And then she turned, perhaps with some unfairness, upon the hapless Wolsey. "For all this trouble I may thank you, my lord of York," she said, before all present. "I have ever wondered at your vain glory, and abhorred your voluptuous life, and cared little for your presumption and tyranny. Out of malice you have made all this great unhappiness for me owing to the great grudge you bear my nephew, the Emperor, because he would not gratify your ambition by using his influence to get you made Pope."

She said it right out like that to a pompous scholar who had been seeing himself as Pope for years. And I would have given a year's wages to hear her. I was not there, of course, but one of her ladies, shaken and breathless, almost swooned into my arms afterwards and, prompted by a comforting beaker of warm, spiced wine, relived the exhilarating scene for me. Never can any lonely, unprotected woman have shown such forthright courage. And never, I wager, had our magnificent, scarlet-clad Cardinal legate been so plainly spoken to in all his up and coming life.

Chapter Thirteen

Most decent Englishmen and all the women sympathised with Queen Katherine in their hearts. And
Henry could not have been unaware of it. So one foul
November Saturday, when thick mist swirled up from the river, he
called together all the great ones in the land in Bridewell Palace
and put his case before them. I was not among them, of course, but
more than one told me afterwards what took place. And a strange
experience it would have been for me, who, unimportant as I was,
had often looked behind the scenes at the man's passion, to hear
him so self-righteously setting forth his dilemma.

"If it be adjudged that the Queen is my lawful wife nothing will
be more acceptable to me," he assured them, so a clerk who had
been in the service of Lady Willoughby, the Queen's Spanish friend,
told me. And I could picture Henry Tudor saying it, with that self-
righteous expression on his florid face. "Besides her noble parentage
she is a woman of the utmost gentleness, humility and buxomness. If
I were to marry again I would choose her above all women."

"'If I were to marry again,' forsooth! When he is straining at
the leash like a dog who scents a bitch," sniggered a Captain of the
King's guard who had kept the door.

"But, wait, that is not all," said the clerk. "'Were I to marry
again I would choose her of all women,' he told them."

"May God forgive him!" I muttered—and meant it. For because
of his goodness to me my loyalties were torn.

"And then he assured us all that if their marriage should be against God's laws, because of her former union with Prince Arthur, he was prepared to part from her with sorrow, as from a good lady and a loving companion."

"And the strange thing is that he believes it all," I said.

"Believes it—with that Boleyn bitch all but in his bed!" exclaimed his Captain, who probably thought none the worse of him for that.

"Yes. The whole of it, just as he says it," I insisted. "For whereas you and I sin and know it, Captain, he must always persuade his conscience. Oh, none knows better than I that he can be kind to the likes of us, and spontaneously generous in sport and friendship. But for the bigger moves of life he must always have two reasons. One springing from his private needs, and one to hold before his own conscience as much as to show the world."

They thought that I exaggerated the King's complexity, but had I not heard him building up those reasons, brick by brick, as he paced terrace or gallery with Wolsey, his voice soft and sibilant as the swish of his companion's scarlet robes? Not the roaring, jolly voice familiar to so many across butts or bowling green, but the voice of a naturally naïve man clumsily acquiring self-interested slyness. I can hear it yet, trying to trick conscience. "There was that page, after the wedding night, who told everyone how my brother leaned out from the closed bed-curtains calling for a drink. 'I am thirsty,' Arthur is supposed to have said, 'for Spain is a hot place and I have been in the midst of it this night.' Stolid young Willoughby could not have invented that, could he?" They would pass on, the King and Wolsey, in their interminable pacing, beyond range of my pricking ears. And then when they came past again they would be discussing the verses in Leviticus about the man who marries his brother's wife and is cursed with childlessness, or the way in which all poor Katherine's babies had been either still-born or had died. All except Mary, and she a girl.

But sometimes alone in his own room of an evening Henry Tudor would sigh and lay down his book or his harp, and speak the bare, indisputable truth. Once he rose and crossed the room and for a long time stood leaning with bowed head against the great carved chimney hood. "It is a cursed thing indeed to be but the second sovereign of a disputable dynasty won by the sword, and to have no son," he groaned.

My heart yearned for him, but probably he had forgotten I was there.

In some way this urgent need for a male heir seemed to excuse his growing determination to marry Anne Boleyn. Though how he could stake everything on that highly-strung, narrow-hipped girl giving him one I never could imagine.

Now that his "secret matter" had been dragged out into the open, he courted her no longer by stealth. Most of his leisure hours were spent hunting, hawking, making music or rhyming among the gay company of her contemporaries. Hal Norris, Thomas Wyatt, Francis Weston, and her brother George, to name but a few. I must admit that he was the pleasanter for it, and the flame of Anne's inner excitement burned so brightly that none of them could take their eyes off her. Wyatt wrote love-sick verses to her which excelled the King's, and her chattering sister-in-law, Jane, was quite extinguished by her vivacity. But whatever other women whispered in the extremity of their jealousy, I do not believe that the brilliant Boleyn girl had ever loved any but young Percy of Northumberland, who had been denied her, or that she ever lay with any of those gifted, attractive young men, either then or later. I, who hated her for hurting the Queen and milady Mary and for breaking up my pleasant world, would wager my precious Welsh harp upon it. One had only to watch her to know that the pathway to intoxicating power stretched too clearly before her to allow her to make a false step, that the lure of a crown preoccupied her mind too constantly for any call of her body to tempt her very urgently.

And so we were come to this extraordinary pass—that a court was set up to try the validity of our sovereign's marriage and, as a natural sequence, the legitimacy of their beloved daughter. Out of doors the early summer sun shone, the scent of lilacs drifted from walled riverside gardens, the Maypole had scarcely been taken down from Charing village, and we might all have been much better employed. But inside the vast imposing hall of Blackfriars Palace two reluctant Cardinals—one silvery and frail, the other black-browed and strong—sat at judicially appointed tables. And at opposite sides of the hall on high, gold chairs of state sat our King and Queen, like commoners come to wash their domestic linen in public.

This time I managed to creep in unnoticed among his Grace's attendants, and, though the proceedings tore me to the heart, I would not have missed them for the world. It was like storing in one's mind a momentous hour of history, besides providing a scene more colourful and dramatic than the Master of Revels and I could ever hope to stage.

It all began with the usual legal bickering. Queen Katherine objected that the court was prejudiced because all the judges held appointments from the King. The two Cardinals denied her right to appeal over their heads to Rome. When the court crier called for "Henry of England" my royal master repeated that effective flood of conjugal eloquence which he had made before at Bridewell, lauding his wife's virtues and professing himself to be but the slave of conscience, because his brother had had her first.

When at last the Queen's name was called to answer, a great hush fell and men stood on tip-toe to peer over each other's shoulders. I suppose most of us expected her to employ some Spanish priest or clever lawyer. But she was the kind of woman who would speak in her own defence, or not at all.

She rose from her chair and crossed the hall. Being a proud daughter of Spain, she ignored the obstructive Cardinals and knelt, with infinite dignity, at the King's feet. "Sir, I beseech you, for all the loves there have been between us, and for the love of God, let me have some right and justice. I appeal to you, who should be head of justice in this realm." Although every inflection of her beautifully controlled southern voice was audible to the farthest ends of the hall, such was the personal nature of her appeal that they two might have been alone. "I take God and all the world to witness," she went on, "that for twenty years I have been a true, humble and obedient wife, ever compliant to your will and pleasure.

I have been pleased and contented with those things in which you took dalliance or delight. I loved all those whom you loved, for your sake." She spoke most movingly of their shared sorrow for their lost children, asking if it could be considered any fault of hers that they had died. And, looking around me, I saw tears standing in many a man's eyes, even where it was least to be expected. And one had only to look at the King himself to see how deeply he was affected—to know that this was no easy thing he did.

Still kneeling with her rich damask skirts about her, the Queen stretched wide her arms and, looking straight into his eyes, challenged him before us all. Coming direct to the crux of the matter, she reduced all their legal quibbling to feminine common sense. "I put it to your conscience, whether I came not to you a maid?" she said, asking straight out for the truth from the only other person who was likely to know.

But a terrible silence hung in the hall. Henry neither moved nor answered. Behind his rapidly blinking eyes the thought must have been scurrying through his mind that whichever way he answered, the words would condemn him. Either he must vindicate and keep her, or admit that instead of suffering some recent qualm of conscience he had deliberately, ever since his wedding night, been living in sin.

And presently, knowing the ethical limitations of her man, the Queen let her arms drop despairingly and went on to speak almost objectively of the world-renowned wisdom of both their parents, who had so carefully arranged their marriage. And to plead that judgment might be suspended until she, who stood so much alone, could be further advised by her friends in Spain. "If you will not extend to me this favour, then to God do I commit my cause," she said.

Even from my perch on the plinth of a pillar at the far end of the hall I could see that she was weeping when she arose, and I could think of nothing but how she had tried to inspire *me* with courage when I first came to Court and stood alone and friendless. Although it was clearly painful to her stiffening limbs, she made a deep obeisance to the King and, instead of returning to her seat, walked with unhurried composure to the great doors of the hall. "Katherine, Queen of England, come again into court!" called the crier in a fine fluster. They had not finished with her, all those learned argumentative men, although she had finished with them. But she did not so much as turn her head, and her retinue had perforce to follow her out.

It was bravely done. But afterwards, back in her apartment, she said in Spanish to Lady Willoughby, "Never before in all these years have I disputed the will of my husband," and went weeping to her private chapel. And Lady Willoughby—who had been Mary de Salines when she had come with her as a girl from sunny Spain— must have known how true this was.

After the Queen's most regal exit from Blackfriars, prelates and laymen seemed to shake themselves back into the lesser mould of legal hair-splitting and expediency. They had seen Truth personi-fied, but descended to the calling of doubtful witnesses about the amatory scufflings of a delicate, callow youth of sixteen with a prim, convent-bred girl behind drawn bed-curtains. A lady of the bedchamber testified to having left them alone and bedded. Several scurrilous old noblemen who ought to have known better vied with each other in recalling at how tender an age they had first known their unfortunate wives. Lord Fitzwalter corroborated Prince Arthur's youthful boast that he had been in Spain, and added to it an inconclusive remark made by the bridegroom at supper to the effect that being married was good sport. After which tasty tittle-tattle the Bishop of Ely's dull statement that the Queen, when younger, had more than once told him that her first marriage had never been really consummated fell singularly flat.

Henry, hating the whole proceedings, was all for a quick settlement. All he wanted was to get his hands on the paper signed by an imposing row of English bishops, confirming that in this matter they were on his side. And Warham, Archbishop of Canterbury, was pleased to hand it to him. A long list, seem-ingly, and all in convenient sympathy with his conscience. An expression of local clerical feeling unanimous enough, he hoped, to persuade Rome. All that remained now was to get back to

York House or Eltham or Windsor and ride out into the sunshine with a well-trained hawk—anywhere where one could forget Katherine's plain, good, tear-stained face. Like most big men, Henry hated to see a woman cry. She ought to have thought of that, because it would be something which through the years ahead he would find it uncomfortably difficult to forget. And she ought not to have cornered him in public with that embarrassing question—she, his Kate, who had always been so considerate of his comfort. But perhaps it didn't matter very much, because in the years ahead he was going to have ease and wit and gaiety and a sloe-eyed woman's clear, high laughter....

He began to fidget, impatient for the painful proceedings to end. Watching my royal master, I had so far entered into his thoughts, and he himself had half risen with Warham's welcome paper in his hand, when one of those unexpected things happened which will stay in my memory as long as Queen Katherine's courage and for all time be associated with it. The Archbishop was assuring Henry that he and his whole bench of bishops would give their consent to a divorce, when a tall, thin old man arose from their midst. He was so parchment-skinned that there seemed to be nothing of him save his burning conviction and the carrying quality of his cultured voice. "No, Sir, not I," he told his King. "Ye have not *my* consent thereto."

Men turned and stared, mouths agape, and all that was decent in most of us momentarily envied him from the safe distance of our contemptible subservience to easy living. He had been confessor to the King's learned grandmother, Margaret Beaufort, and had probably never hesitated to say what he really thought since Henry was small. He was John Fisher, Bishop of Rochester. His name should be written somewhere in gold. When his unequivocal words dropped into the murmuring stillness of the hall it was as if a shining sword had suddenly fallen point downwards from Heaven and pierced a pool of mud, striking it into alarming and prophetic flames.

The King swung round and glared at him but, seeing who it was, passed the matter off with admirable nonchalance. But even as he spoke, milord Bishop must have known that sooner or later sword or flame of bitter controversy must strike him, too. But, as I say, he was old; and even in this world walked so closely with rectitude and compassion and things of the spirit that probably being despatched with violent cruelty to his God would disturb him scarcely at all.

Chapter Fourteen

WHETHER THE BISHOPS AGREED or not, the trial was not conclusive. How could it be, with the Pope held prisoner by Queen Katherine's nephew? In order not to offend him, his Holiness recalled Campeggio without any decision having been made.

I was there when Wolsey brought his fellow Cardinal to take leave of the King. We had been dicing on the chances of a coming tournament—his Grace, milord of Suffolk, young Hal Norris and I—when they were announced. And they came in upon us with all Wolsey's usual fanfare of silver staves and scarlet hat and Great Seal of England carried before him, which made the elderly Italian look shabby. "God Almighty and Old Father Time!" I whispered, ducking behind the nearest arras and peering out in pretended terror. And poor Norris, who was Gentleman Usher, had to rise and bow them in while struggling to hide his irreverent laughter. But laughter was soon wiped from the faces of all of us when Campeggio plucked up courage to tell our master that the decretal authority which the Pope had vested in him had been withdrawn. The poor old man had come with reluctance and left with conscientious formality. Had I been in his shoes, I should have mounted my mule and made off quietly one dark night for the coast.

Henry, with the dice box still in his hand, was rendered scarlet and speechless. But his impetuous brother-in-law, the Duke of Suffolk, sprang up and banged the table with both fists. "It has never been merry in England since we have had Cardinals amongst us!" he shouted rudely.

Yet even then our own magnificent Cardinal had the last word. "You, of all men, have little cause to say so, Charles Brandon," he pointed out, with truth and dignity. "For when you married the King's sister in Paris without leave, certain it is that but for my intervention you would have had no head upon your shoulders."

But that was over and done with, and radiant Mary Tudor, who had been so briefly Queen of France, had already borne Suffolk two daughters.

"Where is that decretal of the Pope's?" bellowed Henry, cutting through their quarrel.

"Since his Holiness declared it invalid, I have burned it," said Campeggio, courteous to the last.

But Henry did not believe him. "We still have one Papal legate in our realm, and if we can but lay hands on that precious piece of parchment I may be able to persuade Wolsey to use it," he said, as soon as they were gone.

"And probably find all the bullion which he is sure to be sending out of the country by his fellow bungler, now he has incurred your displeasure," snarled Suffolk, still sore from that just rebuke.

From my lair behind the arras, before Hal Norris had well finished ushering them on their way, I heard the King give orders that half-a-dozen trusty pikemen of his guard should ride after the "crafty Italian" and search every saddlebag in his baggage. I was indeed seeing the workings of diplomacy from behind the scenes, and their incredible baseness shocked me. Yet I swear that a few months back, while the influence of the Queen was still with him and he had not yet come beneath the spell of that Boleyn witch, Henry would have been incapable of offering such a brutal indignity to Papal authority and hospitality. It was contrary to all his early training and to his true love of the Church. But his gouty foot was probably paining him like fire, and his need for Anne was certainly like fire in his veins. Never had a king been kept waiting so long for so tantalising a girl, and his patience was wearing thin.

An evening or two later, the King waved his gentlemen of the bedchamber away and called for me to sing to him while he slumped dejectedly before the fire. The news had just been brought to him that Cardinal Campeggio's baggage contained nothing but a pitiful assortment of shabby soutanes and worn and comfortable shoes. But I do not think it was only the loss of the decretal he was thinking of. I think he was remorseful for having caused a fellow-sufferer from the gout such shamed embarrassment, and hating himself very thoroughly.

And Thomas Wolsey, the magnificent, was left to bear the brunt of it all.

The King sent for him one gruelling day in July. They were closeted together for over an hour, as they had so often been during the past years, with Wolsey holding forth and a younger, easier master content to do as he advised. What was said between them this time no man knows. But I happened to be loitering on the landing stairs when Wolsey came glowering down to his waiting barge. He brushed past me unseeingly, his sagging jowls atremble, and did not so much as acknowledge the raised oars of his watermen. "A hot day, your Eminence," remarked the amiable Bishop of Carlisle, who was waiting to be rowed back with him to York House steps.

And I saw the bleak look on Wolsey's face as he snapped back, "You might call it hot indeed, milord, had you been so chafed as I have!"

I went on whittling at the small wooden puppet I was fashioning as though I had not heard, but as the splendid barge pulled out into midstream I wondered how long it would be before York House was handed over as a sop to royal displeasure, as Hampton Manor had been because a Kentish girl coveted it. Although I had many a time mocked him, at that moment I remembered with gratitude how much Wolsey had done to put learning within the reach of ordinary young men like myself and how hard he had worked in the cause of equal justice for all. If he must indeed fall from kingly favour, as Suffolk had foreseen, the descent of one so high would be painfully steep, and he, in his self-confident importance, so ill-prepared.

He took himself off, rather belatedly, to attend to his bishopric of York. The King, having cooled down, sent Norris after him with a ring in token of continued friendship, and invited him to live, withdrawn from Court, at Esher in Surrey. And during those uncomfortable, uncertain weeks, Katherine, unbecomingly swelled with dropsy, still appeared in public as Queen.

Her daughter, now sixteen, was old enough to wonder why no princely bridegroom was forthcoming, and to wish, no doubt, that she might marry the Countess of Salisbury's lovable son, Reginald Pole. For all I know, now that there was to be neither French nor Spanish marriage, the Queen may have wished it too, for, although he had never sought political power, Pole was a Plantagenet. But Henry unwittingly stamped out that romance when he asked his learned, self-effacing cousin to support him in the matter of divorce, and Reginald Pole, driven by his honesty and his affections, spoke out for the Queen. Perhaps he was the one man from whom Henry Tudor ever took such plain speaking. But after that there was nothing for it, as far as the scion of the Plantagenets was concerned, but to live abroad, where he entered the priesthood, and so silenced any suspicion that he might have been courting the King's daughter with an eye to the throne.

When not too occupied by his own concerns, Henry tried to show the young Princess even extra affection, and I am sure he took it for granted that, when the break came, she would prefer to stay with him. She adored him, and he had always been the fount of fun and lively Court life, whereas her mother, who seldom spoiled or petted her, had always been devotedly concerned with the training of her mind and character. But during those last weeks when Katherine was still the Queen I used to watch them together. The Princess, looking younger than her years because she was so short, would stand closer than ever to her mother's chair, and often her small fingers would be gripping tensely at the carved arm of it, while her short-sighted brown eyes scanned the company present, as if watching for any movement which might threaten to part them. Often I have seen a doe stand like that—a small creature knowing nothing but the softness of the bracken and the warmth of protecting fur, rising, piteously vulnerable, on some hillock to take its first alarmed look at approaching danger from the hunt.

And so we of the royal household lived in uneasy service, covering our own sympathies or ambitions as best we could. And in the end the glittering crown came to rest upon the Boleyn girl's sleek, raven head, not by means of solemn convocations of Pope and Cardinals, but by the chance remarks of an unimportant tutor, teaching privately in Essex. A modest man with modern Lutheran views and a remarkably fine feeling for the beauty of words. Save as a fellow of Jesus College he had no renown, but during a royal progress Gardiner and Fox, the King's secretary and almoner, happened to be lodged in the house of Master Cressy, whose young sons this man taught. Finding a kindred spirit, they must have sat and talked, as scholars will. And as with everyone else in England at that time, their conversation soon turned to the all-engrossing subject of the royal divorce, of which naturally a royal secretary and almoner were well equipped to give an unworldly tutor all the latest news.

He came fresh to the problem with unconventional and uncluttered mind. "If the Church can give his Grace no definite decision, why not turn to the Universities? To all the best and most disinterested theologians of Oxford, Cambridge, Padua, Bologna, Paris?" he suggested, probably more for the sake of enjoying a good evening's argument than because he cared much what happened to Henry Tudor's wife.

I can just imagine their shocked faces. "But it would mean offending Holy Church!"

"Not the Church. Only the ineffectual head of it," he may well have said, in the relaxed company of congenial friends.

And although it must have sounded to them like blasphemy, his suggestion opened up a whole vista of new ideas. When the Court was back at Greenwich, and all the scare of the sweating sickness over, Gardiner and Fox told the King about it. And Henry, in his eagerness for any fresh means of escape, threw aside the weighty theological books he had been studying and the excellent treatise on the subject which he himself was composing. "That man has got the right sow by the ear!" he declared inelegantly. "What is his name?"

"Thomas Cranmer," they said, in unison.

No one at Court had ever heard of the man, but from that moment events began to move towards more than a second marriage—towards far more than most of us Englishmen had ever imagined. To something which was going to shake all Europe.

Already the King began to feel free. He took Anne Boleyn to visit the King of France, in the hope, I imagine, of winning his fellow sovereign's approval. And this time there was no polite subterfuge about her going as one of the Queen's ladies-in-waiting, because the ailing Queen was left at home.

I well remember the wild excitement among the younger women, with Anne herself trying on new gowns and singing happily about the palace, preening herself to please King Francis, who had spoiled her with flattery when Mary Tudor had been Queen of France. But Mary, now Duchess of Suffolk, refused to accompany her. And the King of France's sister, also sympathising with Katherine, saw to it that this Mistress Boleyn, whom everyone was talking about, should not get beyond English territory. She was too sick to receive guests, she said, and very cleverly offered as deputy hostess a lady whose reputation would have done Anne's no good. So when Henry and all his fine gentlemen, dressed almost as sumptuously as they must have been for the Field of the Cloth of Gold, rode out to be the guests of Francis in Boulogne, Anne Boleyn was forced to remain fuming in her lover's town of Calais.

I was left with her, to "lighten her spirits," the King said. But, having no desire to get my ears boxed by a woman in a fury, I spent most of my time more pleasantly down at the wool staple and the harbour. Richard Fermor's Calais agent welcomed me, but he was an extraordinarily busy man, so I spent many enthralled hours watching ships come in from a score of different countries, many of them—to my vast interest and delight—belonging to my former master or bringing merchandise to stock his warehouses.

And there by chance I met Thomas Cromwell, either keeping an eye on some private business of Wolsey's or both eyes on the chances of more fortunate employment with the King. To which end, perhaps, he thought it politic to be civil to me. He had a precise, lawyer's way of talking, and as he had been in Calais several times he was able to point out to me several interesting features. He, too, appeared to be interested in the ships, though less as craft than for the volume of trade they represented. "Look at that merchantman coming alongside now, flying the lion of St. Mark. She will be bringing spices from the East to enrich our merchants," he said. "One wonders how much such a cargo is worth."

I was able to tell him approximately, and he looked sharply round at me, surprised no doubt that a jester should have solid knowledge of such things.

"I served Master Fermor of Northamptonshire, one of the biggest staplers of London and Calais," I explained proudly. "See, Master Cromwell, that is one of his ships being laden down by the sheds now. The *Joanna*. He exports more wool than any other merchant in the midlands."

"Fermor of Northamptonshire," he repeated, as if catching up some train of thought. "He married one of his sons into the Vaux family, I think?"

"And his father-in-law was Lord Mayor of London," I added, quite unnecessarily.

We leaned elbow to elbow on the harbour wall in the late October sunshine, and it so happened that that morning half the bales of wool and sacks of wheat in Calais seemed to be marked with the name of Fermor. "He must be a very rich man," observed Thomas Cromwell, before moving on to some more profitable occupation. And, chattering fool that I was, I felt vicariously flattered. For how was I to know that before long Thomas Cromwell would be Chancellor of England, and that his memory was as long as his bulging black eyes were sharp?

Such pleasant idling ended when Henry brought the King of France for a return visit to his own town of Calais. Our Governor greeted them at the landgate. Merchants, sailors and bi-lingual English colonists cheered wildly as they rode through the streets. And Francis and his modish courtiers soon flattered Anne Boleyn back into good temper. They treated her as if she were already Queen of England. And, carried away by the semblance of that royal state, she must have been sure enough of the coming reality to throw aside discretion at last and give herself utterly to her lover. Any of us who were responsible for the entertainment of that gay, sparkling company were far too busy to find time for gossip, but it was clear to see that these carefree weeks away from the conventional restraint and the outspoken condemnation of England were for Henry Tudor and his "sweetheart Nan" their *lune de miel.*

And the proof of it came one evening a few weeks after Christmas when we were back at York House, which the King had renamed Whitehall. I was teasing the Countess of Salisbury's ladies while we waited for his Grace to come to supper. Hal Norris, George Boleyn, young Weston, from Sutton Place, and William Brereton were grouped about the window-seat discussing a new type of siege gun. And Thomas Wyatt, standing by a side table, in the throes of some poetic composition no doubt, had just helped himself absent-mindedly from a dish of those delectable apples with which his estates at Allington always supplied the royal table. When suddenly, on a gust of laughter and followed by her crowding women, Anne appeared.

"This new man, Thomas Cranmer, is going to prove a very useful Archbishop of Canterbury, now that old Warham is dead. About Thomas More as Chancellor I am not so sure—he is less biddable," she announced, addressing all her friends collectively in that wild, careless way of hers. For, callous as she was towards people who did not please her, nothing, I think, ever changed her affection for that group of friends. She trusted them, and no royal elevation ever made her in the least haughty or condescending towards them.

Wyatt looked at her across the half-eaten apple in his hand. Possibly, like me, he wondered what she had been drinking. "Is *everyone* called Thomas these days?" he asked fastidiously.

"At least there is one fewer of you since Wolsey went," she said. For Wolsey, summoned back by an angry master, had died on his journey to London, declaring to the kindly monks of

Leicester Abbey that had he but served his God as faithfully as he had served his King, Heaven would not have left him so naked to his enemies.

"That man must have worked prodigiously," remarked young Weston, from the window steps. "Apparently it takes *two* men now to perform his clerical and lay functions."

"Or perhaps," suggested George Boleyn, "the King has learned the wisdom of not vesting so much power in one person."

"It leaves more for himself, and of course he could always play off one against the other," corroborated Anne boldly. And, picking up her skirts, she danced across the room from her brother to Wyatt— Wyatt, who had enough diplomatic sense to scowl at their indiscretion and who had long since written to her that lovely sonnet of renunciation *Forget not yet*. And she begged sweetly, "Give me an apple, Tom."

I saw him stretch out a hand to choose one from the dish, but she snuggled wickedly against him and reached for the one he already held. "No, no, a bite of yours will do, Tom. Why should we two not share an apple? After all, is it not true that I might have been an ordinary country wife and mistress of Allington?"

White-faced and furious, he pushed her from him, but she only went into fresh gales of inexplicable laughter. And when George Boleyn, seeing his friend tormented, asked curtly what there was to laugh about, she answered, "Only that several times this week I have found myself yearning for a good Kentish apple."

Embarrassed by her strange, uncontrolled behaviour we all stopped whatever we were doing to stare at her; and the Countess of Salisbury, who had been sitting by the fire, gathered up her embroidery as if to go.

"Do you know what the King says that means, Tom? My foolish hunger for apples?" Anne persisted, without attempting to lower her voice.

Wyatt stood there by the table, rigid and wretched. Only his hurt gaze followed her as she went laughing hysterically about the room. I think he did not realise how much she cared for them all and how near she was to regret. "He says it is because I am with child," she boasted triumphantly, brutally, to the man who had always wanted her for his wife.

There was the sound of men's cheerful voices and the smart thud of halberdiers coming to attention outside the door. One of her ladies whispered to Anne warningly, and she instantly restrained herself. And then the King came in and led her in to supper. He may not have heard what she said, but everybody else, from milord of Norfolk to the greasiest scullion, must have known of it before morning.

Chapter Fifteen

ALL THE WAY FROM Dover the people, watching the King's procession pass through their towns and villages, had stood in sullen silence. Now, in the streets of London—not having seen their beloved Queen for months—they were shouting, "We do not want the Bullen whore!" When the Pope at last listened to Queen Katherine's pleading and pronounced her marriage to be valid, the Commons, led by some brave man called Terns, sent a petition to King Henry begging him to take her back. And the Pope, who had no wish to quarrel with him, wrote privately warning him of ex-communication if he did not "put that woman Anne Boleyn away."

But they were all too late, for he had married his mistress secretly. So secretly that even we of the royal household were never sure of when and where the short ceremony took place. Whether immediately on our coming ashore at Dover, during their brief visit to the Boleyn manor of Blickling, or in some unfrequented attic after the Court came back to Whitehall. All we knew was that Anne had been created Marchioness of Pembroke—the Welsh stronghold where the first Tudor had landed—and that her father was now Earl of Wiltshire and her brother Viscount Rochford. I believe now that the royal marriage had just been celebrated soon after daybreak one bleak January morning when I passed an unknown monk hurrying furtively down the west turret stairs. But at the time, had I passed a whole procession of monks in that improbable place, they would have made no impression on my mind, for Joanna Fermor was to be married that very week. To Oakham Skevington, from John Brown's house in Aldermanbury.

It had to come. A man must get his daughters wed. And God knows I had tried to steel myself to accept it. Ever since I had entered the King's service I had tried to find compensation in the hundred and one interests which crowded my days. But since the Fermor family had sent me their "glad news" life had become a blank, with only the cruel picture of Joanna's fragrant loveliness in that solemn money-maker's arms for my ever-present torment. I had been bidden to the wedding, but would sooner have faced the gallows tree at Tyburn than go. Even though Father Thayne, who was coming down to London to marry them, had written me with rare understanding, reminding me that only by endurance and renunciation can we acquire the power to help the sorrows of others. Which power, he added in his inimitable way, must be attended by rare opportunity for one who met so many different kinds of people as I.

But I could not reach up to the level of his goodness. Whether they needed help or not, I banged the door of my own small room to shut them all out, and jerked my hated motley from its hook. There were to be many guests and great festivities at dinner that forenoon—a sort of unacknowledged wedding feast, presumably. I should be expected to scintillate with wit, and I had not thought up a single line of appropriate patter. John Thurgood, my good friend and Master of Revels, had warned me that I was becoming too quiet of late, and that some of my jokes had fallen flat, so that expectant company had been heard to murmur, "Poor Will Somers is losing punch."

Well, Will Somers's jesting would be sharp enough today, striking out like a sharp sword of criticism in all directions, thrusting without pity at men's vulnerable hidden weaknesses, in an effort to pass on some of his own hurt to others—which was the reverse of what good Father Thayne would have me do. I would have a stab at priests like Wolsey, who kept wives in private and got rid of them when the bright light of success began to shine, and at secular scholars like Cranmer, who let themselves be ordained hurriedly into vacant Archbishoprics so as to do their royal master's dirty work. I would slip in a sly thrust at milord of Suffolk for casting a matrimonial eye on his wealthy ward, Lady Willoughby's daughter, while his sweet wife Mary Tudor lay mortally sick, but still alive, in their country manor at Westhrope. And I would flick all present with an uncomfortable reminder, in the midst of their gluttonous revelry, of that other sick woman who had been a fêted queen, and who had now been ousted from this her home to live in loneliness in some borrowed country house at Buckden.

And for a finale I could, with John Thurgood's connivance, arrange a topical little allegorical scene in which half-a-dozen prosperous-looking middle-aged men, each with a wife beside him, anxiously searched the intertwining boughs of half-a-dozen trees.

"Landowners with a promising crop of mulberries," some wit in the audience might guess, raising a spate of giggling.

"Nothing so juicy," I would correct him. "These are their family trees. All pleasantly entwined and growing ever upwards. Grazier to merchant, merchant to titled gentry. Upward and rich." And I would snap my fingers for the actors in fustian to come in, each with his axe.

"Then why do they now call their servants to cut out a bough here and a bough there?" someone would surely ask.

"Because they grow too close!" I would interpret. "Ask your-selves, my friends. Is it not going on all over England? In your own homes, perhaps. People suddenly worrying whether their marriages be right and lawful, where once there was security. Middle-aged people, grown comfortable to each other as old shoes, beginning to worry about their marriages, where once we had a pattern in high places. And fathers bringing in lawyers—see, here they come, with deeds and inkhorns—stuffing their purses by proving, with all this intermarrying among the top crust of families in this island of ours, that your children's betrothals will not be in any degree incestuous."

Indeed, I would lay bare the whole rotten expediency of modern marriage, which should be a spontaneous thing, for love alone, and women not mere pawns. I, who knew too much, would for once say too much. And probably the King would rise up in wrath and expel me from his service. And there would be nothing left but to go back to Shropshire and milk cows at a groat or two a day for my comic-looking, valiant-hearted uncle.

But I did none of these daring things because Mistress Emotte Fermor came seeking me, and banged peremptorily on my inhospitable door. Gaunt, ageing, invaluable Mistress Emotte in a soaked hooded cloak, who had walked all the way in the rain from Aldermanbury. And probably put half-a-dozen pert pages in their place until, worn down by her determination, they directed her aright. I embraced her as if she were a messenger from Heaven, dried her cloak and muddy shoes before my meagre fire, and put her in my only chair. "It is about Joanna," she said.

"I know. She is being married tomorrow."

She laid a compassionate hand on mine, knowing what it meant to me. "I am not so sure. Father Thayne, who should have performed the ceremony, cannot come."

"Is he sick?" I asked.

"No. But I am sure he soon will be, kept without proper warmth and food this bitter winter. Cromwell's men came while my brother was over in Calais on business. And because Father Thayne would not be talked down by them, they took him away to Buckingham gaol."

I knew immediately what she meant, and my own heartache was momentarily forgotten. "Cromwell's commission, enforcing the Statute of Praemunire," I said. "And of course he refused to sign."

It was the old law of Richard the Second's reign, revived. By it, with the help of Thomas Cranmer, Henry had been declared head of both Church and State—denying all ecclesiastic authority of the Pope in England. And the entire priesthood must deny their former loyalties and subscribe to it.

With clever diplomacy things were made easy for the rest of us by a kind of general pardon—for what, God knows!—issued to the laity after Wolsey's fall. We were not obliged to say what we thought or felt, so that time might gradually accustom without accusing us. Half England cared passionately for tradition and the teaching of their fathers, some were indifferent, and many of the intellectuals were all for the New Learning—the Bible to be printed so that all men could read for themselves, the call of Erasmus to see Christ more vividly portrayed in the pages of the Gospels than in gilded images, freedom to manage our own affairs without interference from Rome. Most of us, of whichever persuasion, had the sense—or the cowardice—to keep our mouths shut on the topic, save before trusted friends, and for myself it was an easy kind of comfort to find the Mass said just as ever in the King's own chapels, with all the candles and colour and music which he loved. We all knew about this commission and the inspection of the smaller monasteries, the dissolving of the Holy Trinity Priory in Aldgate, and the cross-questioning of important Church dignitaries, but I had not realised that the hunt was going on among worthy parish priests and private chaplains in little villages as far away as Northamptonshire.

"Father Thayne is so frail—and Buckingham gaol so grim," was all I could find to say.

A tear splashed down on to the thin, capable hands in Emotte Fermor's lap. In the old days, when I was a lad making a crazy nuisance of myself at Neston, I do not think she had ever been seen to cry. I like to think that it was partly her coming to care for me which had softened her. "It is like one of the family gone—the best and most secure part of us." She turned to catch at my sleeve as I came to perch comfortingly on the table edge beside her. "Is there nothing you can do, Will? Everyone says you are so popular at Court. Could you not speak for him to the King?"

I shook my head sadly. "Not about anything arising from this break with Rome. It touches his immediate need for a divorce too closely."

"It is all that wicked Kentish harlot's fault!" she cried angrily, as most women did. It would have taken too long to explain to her that it was not—quite. And all about the movement in Europe and at our own Universities which might eventually have made this heart-rending schism happen anyway.

So I said, to cheer her, "Well, the Skevingtons and the Fermors and the Browns between them should be able to find another priest easily enough. What about the Vaux's chaplain, who married milord's sister to your nephew, Master John?"

Mistress Emotte looked at me in surprise. "Had you not heard? They have taken him, too. Just when Thomas Vaux was off to Jersey for his new Governorship. It is enough to blight a girl's wedding day. But it is not only the getting of a priest which puts us all in a pother. It is the Skevingtons themselves who are being—difficult."

"Difficult?" I repeated roughly. "What in Heaven's name about? They have more money than Master Fermor himself, a manor in Rutland, a fine town house—and the sweetest bride in all Christendom! And Skevington *fils* is not impotent, is he?"

"Not so far as I know. My brother says he has more than one brat in Flanders. But he *is* a kind of cousin. A nephew of Sir William Brown, who was Joanna's grandfather. And now, with all this fuss and litigation about the Queen's marriage—"

"But that is because she was first married to Prince Arthur."

"Well, besides being a kind of cousin, it seems that Oakham Skevington was once betrothed to a daughter of a Fermor cousin of ours who, as far as I can recall, imported Toledo blades—"

"And he wriggled out of it when her father's business failed through our quarrel with Spain," I retorted, suddenly seeing with the eye of memory the page of an account book in which I had recorded the generous financial help which Richard Fermor had given him at the time.

"Oh, I do not pretend to know the rights of it all except that they say the relationship is too close and there was a pre-contract," sighed Mistress Emotte. "But they are all there arguing about it in the Browns' house now—Master John himself, the bridegroom and his father, and Joanna's sister-in-law, Maud Vaux. And some creepy little lawyer whom the Skevingtons have called in."

It was my topical allegory of the family trees come to life. I sprang up in a fury, knocking my jester's cap with a harsh jangle of bells to the floor. "And the bridegroom is *letting* them argue?

Letting them put Joanna to such embarrassing humiliation? Where is Master Fermor?"

"Not yet back from some urgent business in Calais. There was a bad storm in the Channel, they say. But we have heard that his ship is safely in and expect him before nightfall."

"When he will soon send their lawyer packing! And tell his future son-in-law what he thinks of him. And in the meantime, what does poor Joanna herself say?"

"Joanna says nothing. She loves her father, and has ever been a dutiful daughter, as you well know. But I have seen her catch at her sister-in-law's arm and ask, 'Do you think, Maud, that there *may* be something in all this arguing?'" Mistress Emotte shrugged, but there was the hint of a smile at the corners of her straight-set mouth. "The wish may be father to the thought, if you ask me," she added.

I had not asked her, but such gratuitous encouragement was enough for me. Joanna did not *want* to marry him. And, come to think of it, how could any girl with a sense of fun and beauty want to marry Oakham Skevington? "Did she know you were coming here?" I asked.

"She may have guessed," prevaricated Mistress Emotte, rising to depart in order to avoid the issue.

I grabbed her by the elbows to detain her. "Did she—God forgive my hopeful vanity!—did she ask you to come here, Mottie?"

"She said we had all been so busy with the wedding preparations—and that I needed a little fresh air...."

"In this torrential rain?" I enquired, grinning at her discomfiture.

She was almost of a height with me and could not avoid my eyes, which must have been brightening from gloom to ecstatic triumph. She had to smile and surrender. "She has been like a dead thing with no laughter save in her father's presence, to reassure him. A man must make sensible marriages for his daughters," Mistress Emotte added, staunchly defensive. "And this, mind you, would seem to my brother a very good one. Mixing friendship with business, and a fine fortune to come."

"I know," I agreed caustically. "And let her not for worlds miss the fine fortune!"

"Only how was Richard, being a mere man, to know—"

"To know what?" I demanded, still holding her.

"That my poor niece could not love even the most suitable of husbands—now."

In that moment there was no more subterfuge between us. "While you were with us at Neston she grew to depend on you, and she is not one to forget," said Emotte Fermor, picking her words carefully. And hope, bittersweet, sprang up in my heart. Bitter because if, with childhood left behind, Joanna had come to love me, what could it bring to her but a sharing of my pain and frustration? For, although I had her father's trust and liking, even should this Skevington union come to naught, what match could I ever hope to be for her? She, a rich man's daughter, connected by marriage with a lord. And I, once a rustic clerk in her father's employ, and now a landless, jingling Fool, a figure of fun, dependent on the Tudor's whim.

But, as her aunt had said, Joanna had come to depend on me, and if she needed me in this crisis of her life, go to her I must. All the more so because her father, whom in my heart I still served, was inadvertently away.

A shaft of thin sunshine was breaking through the clouds. I took my unexpected visitor down into the courtyard and asked a groom of the royal stables to take her, riding pillion behind him, back to the City. Helping her to mount from the stone block, and kissing her hand as if she were royalty, I promised to do my utmost to follow her to Aldermanbury as soon as dinner at Whitehall should be over.

As soon as she was gone I put on my motley. I seized a pen and scribbled down some doggerel at my little table. And when the company assembled for dinner, with Anne Boleyn, resplendent in some of Queen Katherine's jewels, on the King's right hand, with the younger courtiers flattering her and even the older ones being politely subservient, Will Somers's jokes were not sharp at all, but slyly broad and mellow, as befitted a wedding party. Once as I passed him the King gave me a friendly cuff, as if appreciating my understanding of what had not as yet been announced. But there were hundreds of others to whom the thing which he had done must be announced, and he was worried and preoccupied. He must have guessed the people's mood. And it was their reaction, I think, which he feared most. He could behead a recalcitrant noble or two, but not a whole mob of citizens. His father had encouraged the enterprise of tradesmen in order to curb the power of the titled class who had made a shambles of England during the interminable Wars of the Roses. And now it was the competent sheriffs and aldermen who ruled the City of London, and the Members of Parliament who yapped at his heels. And peasants and 'prentices who dared to voice their feelings.

If it had not been for uncertainty about their reactions I think he would have announced his marriage there and then. And in this uncertainty I saw my chance to get away. So when Anne Boleyn and some of her ladies began clamouring to see my new puppet show at supper time, and the King approved, I said as casually as possible, "But I am going to London after dinner, so must beg to take leave of you, Harry."

"Going to London—now—today? With all our guests to be entertained?" said the King, glowering. "What for?"

"To bring you all the latest Court news," I said.

"But why go *from* the Court for that?" he asked.

I glanced meaningly from him to the new Marchioness of Pembroke, as I picked up young Harry Fitzroy's beribboned lute.

> *"London citizens can always show*
> *What's done at Court e'er thou and I do know,"*

I warbled, plucking at the strings.

"I almost believe that to be true," admitted Henry, regarding me with undivided interest for the first time that day.

So to the amusement of the company, and with an occasional sharp twang at the strings, I wandered about the dais, pattering my hastily composed script.

"If an ambassador be coming over
Before he do arrive and land in Dover
They know his master's message and intent
Ere thou can'st tell the cause why he is sent.

"If of a Parliament they do but hear
They know what laws shall be enacted there.
And therefore for awhile, adieu Whitehall.
Harry, I'll bring thee news home, lies and all."

I had twanged the last line or two leaning over the King's chair, close to his ear, and he laughed with the rest, knowing it to be all too true. He wanted that news of the man in the street very badly, and there was no one he could trust better than me to gather some. "I perceive you are in a hurry, Will," he said, "and we will await your return with uncommon interest."

And so he let me go to London.

Chapter Sixteen

THE LAST COURSE HAD cleared before I had changed my motley for the well-tailored cloak and doublet I had bought with gifts of money given me at Christmas. As I hurried through Charing village and along the muddy Strand, some of the masthead lamps were already glimmering from the Thames, and by the time I had passed under Ludgate and come by St. Paul's to Aldermanbury the early dusk of a dank January evening was beginning to close in. From my former visit I was not unfamiliar with the ground floor of Master John Brown's fine house, so I asked the servant who admitted me to tell Mistress Emotte privately of my arrival and waited cautiously in the outer hall, a place of heavy oak panelling, impressive Flemish tapestries, and a great wall torch as yet unlighted.

As I waited I could hear voices coming from the great hall, and by glancing through one of the doors of the serving screen had a momentary view of the interior. John Fermor's high-born wife, who had been Maud Vaux, was sitting with her back to me by a leaping fire. "But the wedding-gown is already finished," she was protesting, half bored and half resentful on her sister-in-law's account. But John himself, his uncle John Brown, and the Skevingtons, *père et fils*, were too deep in discussion with a legal-looking little man to heed her. They were all seated about the long table at which I had once so joyously drunk wine in reunion with my former Northamptonshire master.

"They have been going on like that ever since the servants cleared the board," a rich, amused voice said quite close to me. Realising that I had not been alone in the semi-darkness, I turned with a start to find a stocky, cheerful-looking priest standing behind me. "You, too, are waiting?" I observed foolishly. "Have the Browns asked you to officiate in place of poor Father Thayne?"

"They have not, young man. They attend the church of St. Mary the Virgin, whereas I have the cure of souls at St. Magdalen's, near-by in Milk Street. But their Rector is sick abed, and the Browns are very well loved hereabouts—as well they should be, with all they have done for our sick poor. So, hearing of the sad imprisonment of their niece's family priest—as one hears the least tittle of news from servants and street vendors in this lively city—I came to see if I, Thaddeus Morton, could be of any help."

"Yet you are not wholly of Father Thayne's persuasion?" I suggested, observing the plain white collar about his neck, such as the new Archbishop Cranmer and his followers were beginning to wear, and thinking irrelevantly that no two parish priests could have looked less alike.

My companion's mundane cheeriness changed to a very real earnestness as he tried to give me an exact answer. "It is true that I see much which to my mind needs reform. I should, for instance, like to see some of the rich Abbey lands given to small farmers from whom common pastures have been enclosed. I would give the printed Gospels to the poorest dock porter in my parish, together with opportunity to learn to read them. Yes, I suppose I have modern views. But I doubt if I have that good man Thayne's courage."

I liked Thaddeus Morton from that instant, and would have enjoyed staying to talk with him. But the servant returned with Emotte's message that Mistress Fermor was in the solar on the first floor and would see me, so I made eagerly for the stairs.

As I shot past the rubicund little priest I caught him grinning at my eager haste. "They say it is unlucky—" he was saying, incomprehensibly. And it was not until I was half-way up the wide, polished flight that I realised with amusement that, what with my new suit and my questioning about a priest to officiate and my knowledge of the household's affairs, the good man must have mistaken me for the intended bridegroom.

In the pleasant solar there was no gloom at all. It was the family living-room of a wealthy Master of the Mercers' Guild, whose father and whose great-uncle had each in turn died Lord Mayor of London. Thick curtains of Dutch velvet had been drawn, and candles lit in silver sconces of rare Florentine workmanship. By their light two young maids, down on their knees with silk thread and scissors scattered beside them on an eastern rug, were putting some finishing touch to a shimmering wedding-gown spread like a swooning bride across a long chest carved with the City arms. Emotte stood by to superintend their every stitch, and beyond them, by the fire, stood Joanna—pale in spite of the glow, and lovelier even than I had remembered her. And so utterly lovable that my heart choked the words of greeting in my throat.

She bade me welcome and sat down, indicating for me a stool on the opposite side of the hearth, but all her actions seemed stilted and embarrassed. As if that exquisite, detestable dress stretched between us made her already Oakham Skevington's wife. As soon as the last stitch had been made and the last thread severed, Emotte bundled the excited, giggling girls away with vague promises that they should see the bride dressed on her wedding day. And with that shimmering creation delicately shrouded from the dust, our tensions relaxed and we sat for a while about the fire and talked, Joanna, her aunt and I. Like a family reunited we spoke of the storm, of their recent fears for Master Fermor's safety, of our deep concern for Nicholas Thayne, of the poor Queen. Knowing my professional interest, they described for me a masque which they had seen performed at Northampton castle, and then questioned me about the rumours they had heard of Anne Boleyn's marriage.

"I would not choose to be married in the same week as that woman!" exclaimed Joanna. And the words reminded Emotte of some wedding feast detail which she had forgotten—or at least she said they did—and, making a note on the tablets hanging from her girdle, she went hurrying from the room.

"In truth," added Joanna, as the door closed sharply behind her, "I would not choose to be married at all." As our eager conversation ceased she came back piteously to the present, and all the brightness suddenly went out of her. "I would not have believed I could be so wretched here in my mother's home where I used to be so happy as a child—with my father delayed abroad just when I need him most—and my betrothed discussing the advisability of our union much as Jordan discusses the mating of our herds in the stockyard."

The things I muttered about Oakham Skevington were quite unfit for her to hear, but the strained look on her face broke into a smile. "Oh, Will, I am so thankful you have come!" she cried. "I have so hungered for you!"

She must have risen, and taken a quick, involuntary step towards me, and, quicker still, I had crossed the hearth and had her in my arms. "Every day—every night—every hour—since I left Neston I have hungered for you, my little love," I vowed thickly, against the gold of her hair.

To my joyful amazement she clung to me every whit as eagerly as I pressed her sweet body against my own. And presently she lifted her tear-stained face from my breast. Her eyes searched mine. "Do you think that either law or Church will really find some objection to the marriage on the grounds of consanguinity?" she asked.

"No," I said bluntly, not knowing how far I brought comfort or humiliation. "All this digging up of connections by marriage and objections to marriages is far-fetched nonsense forced into the public mind by the King's divorce."

"Yet I pray they can persuade my father that there is," she sighed.

I held her sweet face between my hands and gazed down at her lips as if to draw the last vestige of truth from them. "You would rather go back to Neston—unwed?"

"A thousand times."

"You have thought of the gossip there would be?"

"I know. But I cannot—cannot marry that man."

Reason fled from me. "Nor *any* man?" I persisted.

She would not answer, so I lifted her chin between my fingers so that her eyes must give the denial which her lips would not speak. And a surge of happiness consumed me, for what I read in their warm responsiveness wiped out all past loneliness and longings. I would have kissed them in passionate gratitude, but Joanna was mature now, not only with a woman's understanding response to passion, but with a woman's common sense and a background which gave her knowledge of the ways of the world. "If only my father could be persuaded to *this*," she murmured, as if dismissing the impossible. Tenderly, compassionately, she placed forbidding fingers against my demanding mouth, reluctantly she tried to free herself from my embrace. And suddenly, rather wildly, I began to laugh.

"What, in the name of sorrow, can you find for mirth?" she demanded, indignantly.

"That priest—down in the hall," I spluttered.

"What priest?"

"From St. Magdalen's, Milk Street. He is waiting to marry you to someone, but no one seems to know that he is here. He said just now—that it was unlucky—"

"What is unlucky?"

"That I should rush upstairs to see the bride. But rather let us say it is lucky that I put on my best suit to do so. You see, my love, he thinks I am the intended bridegroom."

"Will! Are you crazed?" she cried, her mind quick as ever to follow mine.

"No. Just a clever opportunist, as the King is always saying. Do you not see, Joanna? We could call him up here. He has his breviary. He is only too anxious to marry some happy pair. Emotte and one of those romantic girls could be our witnesses. And by the time your father comes there would be nothing left to argue about."

Her eyes lit up. She no longer struggled against the temptation of my demanding arms. "You mean—this willing priest instead of Father Thayne—and *you* instead of Oakham?" She scarcely breathed the magic words. By springing the suggestion on her, by not giving her time to think about her father, I think I could have persuaded her. Of course I was crazy, as a man light-headed with hunger is crazy. I had no house to take a bride to, no assured income, no honoured name to give her. But, in the end, it was not those indisputable material facts which stopped me.

It was the reminder of Father Thayne, and the memory of words which he had spoken several years ago. I seemed to stand again in Jordan's room at Neston with the six golden sovereigns belonging to her father in my outstretched palm, struggling with temptation. Through the long waves of memory I heard my confessor's warning words, "There is one dragon which you have slain, Will. But there are more subtle ways in which you could cheat a good master than by stealing money." And this was one of them, with the fiercest dragon of all waiting to devour my trustworthiness or be slain.

God knows how hard I fought to damp down the consuming fires of my blood—fires all the hotter because more than most men I had kept myself for her. I took my hungry hands from her and forced myself to let her go. White-faced and mirthless we looked at each other, and at the gulf of worldly circumstances which separated us.

There was nothing more to say—or rather, nothing more which either of us dared say—and mercifully our silence was shattered and our decision made sure by a clatter of horses on the cobbles outside, by a barking of dogs and a banging of doors, and by Emotte coming in to tell us that her brother had arrived. Or perhaps, dear understanding woman, to warn us.

In the general excitement she had left the solar door wide. We heard Master Brown come out from the great hall to welcome him, and the returned traveller's happy, hearty greeting to his brother-in-law. "I do not know which were rougher—the Channel waves or the Kentish roads!" he was saying laughingly as his brother-in-law's servants clustered round to take his cloak and baggage. "And to leave you and your people to make all the preparations for tomorrow—Why, John, my son, it is good to see you." Presently we heard Master Skevington greeting him half apologetically, as they passed into the great hall, and then a low murmuring of his voice and of

Oakham's. But there was no reciprocal argument, no explosion of wrath as we had expected. Only Richard Fermor's voice, cold and carrying, and without any trace of his former heartiness. "I hear what you say, Sirs, and will answer you. But I will see my daughter first." And then his firm, quick step on the stairs.

When he came into the upstairs room we had none of us moved—prompted, perhaps, by a feeling that it might have been in some way deceitful to have done so. He had endured a stormy Channel crossing, and all the way from Dover he must have ridden hard. There were tired lines about his eyes, and for the first time I noticed a sprinkling of grey at his temples. He threw a brief word of greeting to his sister, but his shrewd, searching gaze went straight to Joanna.

For once she did not run into his arms. All demonstration of affection must have been curbed by the half guilty thought that she had too recently been held in mine. And no one but a zany could have failed to see that she had been weeping. "Your Uncle John seems to have been having trouble with these Skevingtons—" he began.

But there was something, in my defence, which she wanted to make clear first. "I wanted Will Somers to come here," she said, direct in her complete honesty.

"So I went to Whitehall this morning to tell him," added Emotte, completing the circle of love's defences.

He cast one quick, appraising glance at me. He might well have questioned what the devil I was doing there. But he was that type of man who, having once put aside even a half-justified suspicion, would have to be hard driven to niggle with it again. "A good thing you both have a well-proven friend about you this time," he said briefly. And in that illuminated moment I knew how abysmally low I should have felt had I stolen his daughter.

"I suppose you have been weeping because Oakham Skevington was a party to these trumpery objections. Do you still want to marry him?" he asked brusquely. Either he was hurt because she had not embraced him or he was an extraordinarily angry man.

Joanna shook her head, unable to speak.

"But all the preparations are made—the meats cooked, the guests invited," faltered Emotte, trying to warn her, as I had done, of the foolishness a woman must inevitably feel returning home unwed. "Even that lovely bridal gown with the satin specially fetched from France—"

"It will keep," said the man who had paid for it, shortly. "You have always been a dutiful daughter, Joanna, trusting me to do what I think best for you. You would have been entirely happy, I believe, in that first union I arranged for you with the Browns' young cousin—God rest his soul! You had the same background. As adventurous young men his father and I had fought together in the wars. But now with this Skevington match I am not sure...." He crossed the room and lifted Joanna's unhappy face towards his own. "For your dead mother's sake as well as yours I must know. Are you hurt only in your pride, or in your heart? If I stop this marriage, as I have a mind to do, do I strike a blow at you, or only for my own stubborn Fermor pride? Do you want to marry the man?"

She looked straight back into his searching eyes, and was able to do so, thank God, without shame. "No, Sir. And now less than ever," she said, yet withholding from him the whole reason.

"Then you do not have to," he said. "Stay here, both of you, while I deal with them."

Without so much as stopping to kiss her he strode downstairs again and, not having been included in his command, I followed him at a discreet distance. I suppose the Reverend Thaddeus Morton, tired of waiting, must have left shortly before he came. But by the great carved newel post at the bottom his brother-in-law, John Brown, awaited him. "That all this unpleasant tarradiddle should have happened in my home, which is ever yours and hers, Richard!" he was saying, in a low voice.

Their hands and arms met in a warm clasp of understanding friendship. "I only regret that you should have been so harassed, John. But if you will allow me still further to abuse your hospitality by letting me use your street door as if it were indeed my own, I promise you we shall soon be well rid of them."

They went together into the great hall and, unnoticed, I flattened myself just inside against the serving screen. What went on there mattered more to me than to any other man. Brief as it was, I would not, for all my hopes of Heaven, have missed the scene that followed. For sheer surprise drama John Thurgood and I could never have touched it. But to me, with half my heart upstairs with Joanna, it was more than impersonal showmanship. It was the future of the woman I loved.

Richard Fermor went and stood with his back to the roaring fire, hands thrust beneath his short, swinging cloak. Firelight flickered on the plain richness of his travel-stained clothes and on the jewelled dagger at his Florentine leather belt. I recognised the familiar stance which he adopted when other merchants tried to get the better of him with some nefarious deal. The little lawyer chose that moment to clear his throat and start shuffling his papers, but Fermor waved him aside. "I thought, Skevington, that we had gone carefully into this matter of our children's betrothal months ago when it was first mooted?" he said.

"Quite, quite, my dear Fermor," agreed his new shipping partner propitiatingly. "But in the warning light thrown upon these matters by the royal divorce I thought perhaps we should be well advised to—to—"

"To discuss the close connection there would be between Joanna and myself through my sister's marriage into the Brown family—" concluded Oakham, a shade too eagerly.

While the younger Fermor hovered indecisively on the edge of the group, his uncle ranged himself quietly beside the older Fermor. And I thought, "This is where the real wordy battle begins." But there was really no argument at all. In fact, no one really spoke except the bride's father. No one had much chance to.

"Being neither a philanderer nor a weather-vane myself, I have no desire for further discussion," he said. "Northamptonshire is full of promising young men who want to marry my daughter, and whose fathers' manors are more conveniently near my home. And it seems," he added, rounding on the reluctant bridegroom, "you never were much to Joanna's taste."

"But our shared contracts—our ships—and that new Venetian deal—" spluttered the older Skevington, realising too late perhaps how much was bound up in this marriage and how the goodwill of his foreign markets had improved since his new business partnership.

Richard Fermor's anger was a heart-warming thing to see. "By St. Blaise!" he cried, using the oath of the wool-combers' saint, "you can keep your ships and I will keep my daughter," and his voice must have carried to the listening women upstairs. "Not for all the gold in the Indies would I let your dithering son have her now. When she marries it will be with a man who wants her beyond all doubt, and who is prepared to outface royal fashion to keep her. And now, with my brother-in-law's leave, I will wish you good-night, Sirs. And you, you quibbling quill scratcher, get out, too," he added to the unfortunate lawyer. "I am tired from my journey, but my own legal man will see you in the morning about all matters resulting from my broken partnership."

Young John Fermor went with them courteously to the outer door, but I would willingly have taken upon myself that office and shown them out more brusquely into the murky night.

"I am sorry so to have disturbed your home for nothing, and you must let me recompense all your people who have helped," apologised Richard Fermor, throwing himself wearily into a chair as soon as they were gone.

"Let us drink and forget it," said John Brown, calling for the servants. Had they noticed me in the sudden bustle of men laden with fresh logs and flagons I am sure they would have called me to join them, and hospitable Master Brown might have offered me a bed. But the day had already brought too much clamour to my heart. I must be alone to think, or not sober enough to remember. I waited only to see them comfortably established around the fire and my former master resting in a homely haze of fire and candlelight.

"I fear this will do your trade no good, Sir," said his son, coming back in time to hand him a beaker of the best Bordeaux.

"But it has done my spleen against that pair a great deal of good," retorted his father, stretching his feet to the blaze while a willing servant pulled off his mud-caked boots. "Have I frightened your lady wife away?"

"She has gone upstairs to be with Joanna, I think. But now that you are all in London we both hope you will stay with us awhile when Uncle John can spare you. Stay at least for the Coronation."

"Coronation?" repeated his father and his uncle in unison. "What Coronation?"

"Queen Anne's, of course," said that up-to-the-minute purveyor of Court news. "If a King's mistress becomes a wife and mother all in one amazingly short matter of months surely she must be crowned. At Westminster, some time early this summer, is my guess."

He was certainly one move ahead of me, who but a few hours ago had been with them both. And that reminded me of the excuse upon which I had come. I slipped out from the shadowed end of the hall to the accompaniment of Richard Fermor's indignant protest that he knew of only one Queen, and her name was Katherine.

I walked unseeingly past the dreamlike grandeur of the Guildhall and down through Milk Street, where I encountered Father Morton, lantern in hand, locking the door of his church. "Has the bride's father come safely home?" he enquired, as I stepped into the wavering circle of light.

"Yes, but neither he nor Master Brown will be troubling you. There is to be no wedding," I told him.

"Now God help you, my son," he exclaimed. "I am truly sorry." He gripped my arm with a fervour which changed to shocked amazement when I burst out laughing.

"I thank you, reverend Sir, but I am not the bridegroom," I explained in contrition. "I am but Will Somers, the King's jester."

"Then God help you, just the same, for the people of London say you have persuaded his Grace to many a kindness." He wrung my hand as if truly pleased to meet me, and added with a twinkle, "And perhaps, if you have not already a wife, I may have the pleasure of officiating at *your* wedding some other time?"

"I am not married, nor ever like to be," I said bitterly. But in spite of my churlishness he raised a hand in blessing. And I carried away in my mind a comforting picture of him standing against the arched darkness of St. Magdalen's door, illuminated like a rosy beacon of warm humanity.

From the quiet of Milk Street I came into the chaffer of Cheapside. Traders' torches flared in the wind, and there seemed to be lights in every window of the tall, gabled houses. It was just that time when market folk were taking down their stalls, and 'prentices were shouting the last of their wares at reduced prices before the closing of their masters' shops.

"What d'ye lack? The last lady's pomander left, and going cheap!" one impudent lad yelled at sight of me. "Or an embroidered wedding shift, fit for the Kentish whore."

Men's minds seemed to harp on weddings that day. Marriages made, marriages broken and marriages never to be.

I pushed the persistent young devil aside and, thrusting open the door of the Mitre tavern, called for the drink I so badly needed. All was warmth and cosy commonness inside, flavoured with the smell of hot spiced wine and dregs and dogs and sweaty humans. I wedged my thin body among a crowd of hilarious citizens upon a fireside settle, and with a buxom doxy warm on my knee and a frothing tankard in my hand, I heard the latest Court news hot from London city.

"No, this man Cranmer wouldn't do it hisself…. Some monk or other, they say. A friend of mine in the halberdiers seen 'im slipping away in a boat at Whitehall stairs…." Ribald laughter and scraps of shrill conversation came from the direction of a redheaded troll sitting on a table to entertain a group of travelling players with the latest London news. "After all, they'd had their sport in France them two, and the King was in such a hurry he wed her afore it was light…."

"An' not an hour too soon," cackled her friend from my knee. "I had it from that pock-marked wench who cleans house for the tailor at the corner of Mercers' Lane. One of them proud pieces from the palace came in last week with a pattern to be matched. Wanted another width o' peacock green damask so the Bullen could let out her skirt!"

Both women rocked with coarse laughter, and the whole parlour of the Mitre rocked with laughter, too. There were no discreet undertones or polite evasions in Cheapside.

I do not remember much of that night, but by the time I returned to Whitehall next day I had a head that would scarcely pass in at the gates, and enough Court news scraped from decent houses and the stews and streets of London to persuade King Henry that his heralds might as well blazon all his future intentions from the steeple of St. Paul's.

Chapter Seventeen

J OHN FERMOR'S GUESS ABOUT a Coronation proved right, and
although his father absolutely refused to stay for it, he and Joanna
remained long enough for me to see them sometimes. I tried to
let nothing spoil our mutual pleasure in being together, for although
Joanna must soon go back to Neston where some other marriage
would inevitably be arranged for her, at least I no longer had the
present torment of picturing her in Oakham Skevington's arms.

During that spring I was often at the Browns' house in Aldermanbury, and so heard of the City's preparations for Anne Boleyn's
triumph. While Thurgood and I were busy planning masques and
merriment for the palace, Master Peacock, the Lord Mayor, had
been ordered by the King to provide a splendid water pageant on
the Thames. He and the sheriffs and aldermen were to fetch Anne
from Greenwich to the Tower for her crowning at Westminster
on Whit Sunday. They were to turn out the artillery, to arrange
a barge for a bunch of serenading bachelors, to provide a wherry
mounted with cannon lent by the Lieutenant of the Tower, and
I know not what. "And I hope those obsolete old demi-falcons
explode and they all sink to the bottom of the Thames!" I heard
him mutter among his trusty merchant friends. And although both
banks and London bridge were black with spectators, and anyone
who could afford a place in a boat helped to crowd the shining
surface of the river to see the lavish spectacle, most Londoners
seemed to be of much the same opinion.

"Stuffed in our scarlet robes and civic chains on a sweltering May day!" grumbled his worshipful the Lord Mayor, reviving himself with a stoup of Master Brown's best French wine.

"And look at the motto she has chosen—'Me and Mine,'" exclaimed his host, to whose lot it had fallen, as Master of the Mercers' Company, to decorate the bachelors' barge.

"Different indeed from the motto 'I serve' which our real Queen used, and lived up to, when she was Princess of Wales!" said Richard Fermor.

"And now her daughter will be called upon to serve, but in a very different capacity," I prophesied, having recently heard the boastful conversation of the new Queen's ladies.

The three prosperous merchants turned from watching the final work of one of their journeymen carpenters on a huge model of the Boleyn falcon to survey me dubiously. "You mean her Grace will have to wait on this new brat? Well, you should know, Will, coming from Court," admitted my former master sadly. "But has not our Princess suffered enough? God forbid that this jumped-up woman should try to humiliate her still further!"

"Jumped-up is the word," agreed his brother-in-law, John Brown, turning his attention again to his carpenter's unwelcome task. "Save that her mother was a Howard this new Queen of ours comes from no better stock than my own. Like my own father and uncle, her grandfather, Geoffrey Boleyn, was but a plain merchant before he became Mayor of London."

"The people do not like her, with her presumptuous 'Me and Mine,'" growled the greying carpenter, purposely letting his chisel slip a little so that the falcon developed a foolish smirk.

And even Anne herself, being rowed in state up their river or riding through their streets, must have seen very plainly that they did not. "Why did they stand and stare in silence, as if they cared only for the getting of a free show? Why did they not suddenly cheer enough to wake the dead as they used to from the moment your first wife appeared? Why were no caps thrown in air?" she demanded afterwards, beating furiously on her royal husband's massive breast. And, seeing that the King knew not how to answer, and that this was something which for all his commands and his spending he could not remedy, I took the opportunity of creeping up to her, cap in hand, as if to whisper the reason, all very serious and secret in her ear—yet taking good care that all about us should be a party to it. "Have you not heard, my gracious lady, that since your return from France the men of London are suffering from the scurvy? It hurts to uncover their heads and is, I fear, a complaint which will take a long time to heal."

There was a hastily suppressed titter from some of the grooms and pages, and if looks could kill I should have fallen dead at the lady's slender, ermine-clad feet. Nor would I have greatly cared, my love Joanna having gone back to Neston. But Anne disliked me anyway, almost as much as Wolsey had done. And now that the King had broken with Rome, and Cranmer, our new Archbishop, had called together some sort of an assembly and passed sentence that the King was free to marry her, she must have felt that she had climbed as high as any Cardinal. She was born under a lucky star, the astrologers and soothsayers said. Yet when her child was born, in September, it was a girl.

And we were all spitefully glad, or sorry for her, according to our loyalties or our natures. And while the Princess Mary, as heir presumptive, and many of the important noblemen and bishops were crowded into the lying-in chamber as witnesses, most of the rest of us hung about passages and ante-rooms waiting to hear how the King had taken his disappointment.

"His Grace was remarkably forbearing—at least in his wife's hearing," Hal Norris told us hurriedly, coming out on some errand. "He went within the bed-curtains. 'Sweetheart, we are yet both young,' I heard him say, which must have made her pluck up heart."

"And the child?" asked Thurgood, who was standing near me.

"'Frail-looking, yet the spit of her father,' the midwife says. He is naming her Elizabeth."

"After his adored mother, Elizabeth of York," I said softly.

And almost immediately the busy gentleman of the King's bedchamber had passed through our midst.

"Well, let us hope the poor creature will be worth all the fuss and pother of getting her legitimately born!" snorted a clerk of John Fisher of Rochester, who was like to lose his bishopric over it.

Remembering those entertaining hours when Anne Boleyn had shone so gaily among her friends, I was glad that Henry had been kind to her. Yet almost the first favour she asked of him was that Queen Katherine's daughter might be made to wait on her new half-sister—or so Lord Hussey, the Princess's chamberlain, told me a few days afterwards.

Although I myself had foretold this, I was shocked and distressed. "You are sure that this is true, Milord?" I asked, forgetting my own troubles for a time.

"His Grace is still so bewitched by her that he will give her her way. You may be sure, my good Will, that as soon as this nursery Court is set up at Hunsdon or wherever it may be my own lady will be sent for from her present home at Beaulieu, and I shall lose my position."

"Will she be disinherited, do you think?"

"Not immediately. This new man Cromwell is far too wily to take chances. If they cannot rear the child his Grace would be left without any legitimate heir at all. For although he has been careful to marry young Fitzroy to Norfolk's blue-blooded daughter, he must know that this country would never accept a bastard king. And since Bosworth every living Plantagenet looms like a threatening shadow over the Tudor mind."

I looked over my shoulder to make sure that no one overheard such dangerous words. The poor man must have been sorely tried, having had to bring the Princess hurriedly and unwillingly to such an unwelcome duty. But it always amazed me in those tortuous days at Court how people of various opinions and factions trusted me. I suppose he must have known that while, like many others, I conformed ignominiously for my keep, my sympathies were wholly with his young mistress. And perhaps I was less ignominious in this than some, because, for his personal kindness and much that we enjoyed in common, I loved the King. When we are young we love our idealization of people, I suppose, and only as we grow older do .we love them as they really are.

In the general excitement and confusion of the whole palace it was easy enough to slip away from my duties and wait upon the Princess Mary before she left again for Beaulieu. There was no press of people about her doors these days, and the apartments allotted to her were in an old wing once used by Cardinal Wolsey's pupils. Margaret Plantagenet, Countess of Salisbury, was resting. When Mary Tudor gave immediate orders for me to be admitted only two ladies were with her, and at a sign from her they moved away with their needlework to a window seat at the far end of the room.

"Will! Will! It is good to see you again!" she cried, her sad face lighting up with pleasure. She was dressed as always in quiet good taste, but I thought too sombrely for her age. She was only seventeen, but most of the spontaneous fun and open-hearted warmth seemed to have been already drained out of her. The ordeal of waiting in that stuffy bedchamber for her rival to be born had told on her. And it was weeks since she had seen her ill-used mother.

"They say the Queen is really ill," she said, refusing to acknowledge any other. Yet she turned her head aside as she spoke; shamed, perhaps, by having to ask such news of me, the King's fool. But though I might be no better informed than she, at least she knew that I would not lie to her.

"I enquired of a messenger who came from Buckden—"

"To bring some of my mother's jewels. I saw them in the Boleyn woman's room," she interrupted sharply.

"It may well have been. He said her Grace had taken to her bed. But is it any wonder?" I said. "Have not you yourself been ill of late?"

"My father was good enough to send Doctor Bartelot, and now I am better. But I wish it could have been Doctor Butts who always treated me when I was small."

"This new physician is said to be very clever."

"Alas, it takes more than medical cleverness to cure some deep-seated sicknesses. I have just been translating something from Plato in which he says that the ills of the body sometimes stem from the sorrows of the soul."

She was so well equipped intellectually, yet so completely vulnerable, having never until now had need of sharp worldly wisdom. "At least you still have Lady Salisbury," I said to comfort her.

"You say 'still.'" She turned to me with a small echo of her old laughter. "Do not, I entreat you, dear Will, begin suggesting that *she*, too, may be taken from me! I do not know how I should face life without her. Though it is true that she grows old," she added more soberly, "and God may mean me to prepare for even that possibility."

"By then you will have a husband," I said, squatting companionably on a stool beside her.

"My cousin, James the Fifth of Scotland, has asked for me. But my father has refused. Lest I, too, become a Queen, perhaps," she added bitterly. "Though one would expect that they would be only too glad to be rid of me."

"He may not want you to leave England until he has a son. There is no doubt, your Grace, that your father loves you," I said, recognising the crux of her hurt and seeking for some means of explaining it to her. "This union of his with a younger woman is in no way the same as marriage with your mother. He is as some men are in middle age—bewitched beyond normal reason. Beyond consideration of others, or more enduring loves.... But God knows it is treason for me to talk to you like this—Will, the buffoon—a man of no family...."

She laid a hand on my shoulder. "But you *have* a family. You have us, the Tudors," she said, and there were tears of sincerity in her beautiful, short-sighted brown eyes. And I knew that what she said was in a sense true, for did they not all three talk to me frankly, and had not the King had me painted with him in his room while we made music—he and I alone together?

"Then you will understand how I must go on serving the King and caring for him even when he sends your mother away, or makes you wretched?"

She nodded and, withdrawing her little hand, sat for a while in thought. "Although I should hate to leave England, unless it were to go to Spain, perhaps it would be a good thing if I were to marry," she said slowly.

"And have children," I added, watching for the tender smile that curved the too straight line of her lips.

"Ah, that would be worth everything! But it is hard and bewildering to have this and that prince suggested as my husband—ever since I was small—not really caring for any of them, and always, always having them snatched away."

"Oh, my poor child!" I whispered compassionately, because of all the Tudors I loved her best. "But it is harder—infinitely harder—as I believe you may already know—to care desperately for one whom you cannot have."

She did not pretend to miss my allusion to Lady Salisbury's son, Reginald Pole. "Perhaps I was too young to care *desperately*," she said, with her usual frankness. "But my mother told me there was such a one in *your* life. And yet you play the fool and keep us all merry. Is she some fine lady about the Court?"

"No. My love and constancy go back farther than that. But I have recently seen her in London."

"And does she return your love?"

"I believe so, now, to my humble amazement."

"If ever it should be in my power to help you—" she began, with an unconscious assumption of her mother's graciously regal manner, which sat quaintly upon her. "Promise you will tell me, Will."

"I promise. But the matter lies in our own consciences."

"Then at least give me her name, that I may remember her in my prayers."

I gave her the name, and knew it to be in safe keeping. Then, realising that the two ladies were still chatting in soft undertones at the far end of the room, I got up from my stool. And, as if suddenly aware of them too, the Princess said in a more ordinary voice, "I have had a most lovely letter from my mother, but there is something in it which I do not understand."

She rose and crossed the room to a writing desk carved with the pomegranates of Aragon. Lifting a key which hung on a chatelaine chain from her waist, she set it in the lock and drew out a letter sealed with the same device. Skimming through the well-worn pages, she paraphrased for me some of its contents. "Her Grace urges me to obey my father in all things, save only if it should offend God. Should I be recalled to Court, she warns me not to meddle. For my studies she recommends various books, which she will be sending me; and, lest I should mope, for my recreation would have me make music with my virginals or lute. After all, there would be little hope of our happy evenings with masques and dancing now, would there, Will?" Mary Tudor broke off with one of those tender smiles which were becoming all too rare, and turned to the last page. "My mother asks me to recommend her to Lady Salisbury and pray her to keep a good heart in these trials because, she says, we seldom come wholly to the kingdom of God but by suffering. Those are very beautiful words, do you not think, Will?"

"Very beautiful—and true," I answered, out of my own experience.

"Save that she signs herself—and always will—'Katherine the Queen,' that is all. And there is nothing, nothing in that lovely letter—a letter which might be written by any wise and loving mother to her daughter—from which even the most suspicious man could impute evil—or treachery—is there?"

"Why, nothing, of course," I agreed, looking at her with surprise.

"Yet my lady mother writes here—and underlines it, look you—'I think it best you *keep your keys yourself.*' As you see, I have obeyed her. But what does she mean?"

I saw the words myself in the fine Spanish script of a woman proud enough to ignore intrigue, and took a thoughtful pace or two about the room. After a childhood so enriched by security and love, such words must indeed have been bewildering to Mary Tudor, who already seemed to age too quickly and to become more withdrawn. "No one could gain anything by taking any of my letters out," she murmured, glancing back at her unlocked desk.

"No. But someone could put an incriminating letter *in*," I explained, hating to add to the sum of her unhappiness. "Her Grace, in her wisdom, may have thought of that."

For a few moments there was silence in that dull, sunless room. Then the King's elder daughter said in a voice which had already broken from childish lightness to a rather attractive deep duskiness, "Are we indeed so beset by enemies, my mother and I?" And with those simple words she set the stage for future family drama, showing quite clearly upon which side she stood.

Presently she roused herself from that dark reverie and locked away her precious letter. "Well, now we know why she warned me to obey the King my father in all things," she said, with a new, uncurbed bitterness, careless of who might hear. "Tradition demanded that as heir presumptive I must come here to be present when my father's second daughter was born, and now, so Lady Salisbury tells me, I may have to carry the chrisom at her christening. Walking meekly behind the woman who was once my mother's least and most flighty attendant."

She was spared that. She went back to Beaulieu next day, and it was the Duke of Norfolk's daughter Mary, she who was married to Henry Fitzroy, who carried the anointed cloth for the babe. But the respite was only short. After all the fuss of establishing the Princess Elizabeth's nursery home at Hunsdon, with healthy country air, a conduit of fresh water specially laid for the infant's use, more baths and jakes than in any of the King's own palaces, and Lady Margaret Bryan installed as Governess, I met Lord Hussey hurrying to the water steps at Greenwich, looking more harassed than ever.

"The thing which I feared has come to pass," he told me, thankful, I think, to speak to someone whom he could trust.

"You mean, milord, that your position as Comptroller to the Princess Mary is lost?"

He nodded wretchedly, although, to give the man his due, I believe his concern was as much for her as for himself. "I have the King's orders to disband her house and dismiss all her people and to bring her again from Beaulieu, but this time to Hunsdon, where she will be treated, I fear, as little more than another attendant to her stepsister."

"And live under the supervision of the new Queen, who will show her every spite!" I exclaimed in horror. "But how can this be expected of a Princess of Wales?"

Lord Hussey paused on the landing-stage, staring down unseeingly at his waiting barge. "Between ourselves, Will, she will no longer *be* Princess of anything. By a new Act of Succession she is to be declared a bastard and disinherited. The King is making the offspring of Anne Boleyn his heirs."

We stood silent in the wintry sunshine, the thoughts of both of us going out to a girl who must suffer greatly—and to a sick, wronged woman in lonely seclusion at Buckden. "I am sure that Lady Bryan, who has much past affection for the Lady Mary, will do all she can to soften the position in such an anomalous household," he said, as if trying to drag comfort from a threatening thunder cloud. "But nothing can console her for parting from the Countess of Salisbury."

I had that morning received by John Fermor's servant a posy of late rosebuds lovingly pressed in a letter from Joanna. I drew the precious packet from my breast and, dividing them, thrust half into my companion's hand. "I beg you, good milord, give these to milady when you get back to Beaulieu," I entreated.

He looked surprised, but obligingly folded them into his pouch, enquiring gruffly if there were some message to go with them.

"Only that they are from the King's fool, who will ever love her," I said.

Chapter Eighteen

LIFE WAS VERY DIFFERENT at Court. A kind of hectic gaiety had to be maintained, with revels and masques, but little of the old spontaneous homeliness. For some months the enamoured King had little need of me, which suited me very well because half my heart was at Neston and most of my pity at Hunsdon. Much of the modern trend in wit and music was supplied by the new Queen herself and by her brilliant group of personal friends, and although they continued pleasant towards me Anne's black eyes frequently snapped unconcealed dislike. She was ever bringing to her husband's notice an ill-mannered young musician called Mark Smeaton who languished for her far too openly. He could certainly sing, and maybe I disliked him because I was jealous of his voice and feared that he might supplant me.

About this time Lady Butts, the wife of the royal physician, told me that the Lady Mary was really ill and that Katherine of Aragon had written imploring Henry to send her daughter to her that she might nurse her in her own bed at Buckden. But urged by Anne and fretted to brutality by Katherine's unbreakable persistence in signing herself as his wife, Henry had disregarded her plea and sent Charles Brandon, Duke of Suffolk, instead.

"With five hundred men-at-arms," Lord Vaux, home on a visit from his governorship, told us afterwards.

"To intimidate one obstinate old woman," grinned George Boleyn, who was now milord Rochford.

"And my good brother-in-law did not mince his words, I hope?" said Anne the Queen, listening bright-eyed. Thomas Vaux had been sent to Buckden more or less as the King's spy, and like many others Anne made the mistake of supposing that his sympathy as well as his instinct for survival drove him to obey.

"He told her that she must cease appealing to Rome and accept Archbishop Cranmer's decision, and that she and all her household must take this new oath of supremacy over which so many of our priests are in trouble. That she must acknowledge his Grace to be head of the Church in his own realm."

"And myself as his lawful wife," added Anne, coming with dancing steps down from the window seat of her sunny room.

"I fear she will never accept either," reported Thomas Vaux sadly. "Although the alternative put to her was removal to Fotheringay."

"Fotheringay!" I remember how the ominous word escaped the lips of several of us, because even for a woman in robust health that notoriously unhealthy fortress amidst ill-drained river marshes might well spell death. Even Anne's closest friends averted their eyes from her shamed face, guessing that it was she who had first suggested the place.

"One would think that for her women's sake she would have given in," snapped milady Rochford reproachfully.

"Oh, no. She let them go, and had the laugh of us," said Vaux. "For as quickly as Suffolk turned them out into the snow, there were the local gentry waiting with warm cloaks and horses to take them hospitably into their own houses. And, worse still for poor Suffolk, Buckden courtyard was full of local men hastily armed with a travesty of out-of-date swords and bill-hooks whom he himself had called in to augment his regular troops outside. And when the Aragon woman walked painfully to the open door of her manor with the assistance of a handful of women and a priest and an apothecary whom, out of pity for her sickness, he had left her, all these ragged locals shouted and doffed their caps in passionate loyalty. 'Take me to Fotheringay if you must, milord,' she said, making sure that every man-jack of them heard her. 'But I warn you before all these honest folk you will have to carry me over the threshold by force.'"

"And there is where we get this new word 'arrogance' that Will Somers here has so expressively coined," sighed Hal Norris, half admiringly. "What did milord of Suffolk do, Thomas?"

"Do? What *could* he do? Charles Brandon is no fool. He knew as well as I did that the moment he laid hands on her even the rawest cowherd in that rabble would have killed him." Thomas Vaux, whose own family priest had been imprisoned like Father Thayne, probably did not admire himself over-much for the non-committal attitude which he took, although, with the Tudor becoming daily more despotic, he was no more despicable than many of the rest of us. "And so we left the poor lady and rode home together," he concluded drearily.

"With an escort of five hundred which had failed to get the better of her," I could not forbear from remarking.

"But we were sometimes rather glad of them when the people shook their fists at us in Huntingdonshire and the outskirts of London," he admitted, with likeable honesty.

An uncomfortable silence fell on the assembly, so that the new Queen called to the ever-hovering Mark Smeaton to make some cheerful music. As usual I prepared to take myself off from a voice which I could not emulate and a personality which I disliked. But Thomas Wyatt, scarcely conscious of the conceited fellow, stopped me by the door. "It is not natural cruelty which makes the Queen so inhuman towards her predecessor and our poor Lady Mary," he said in a low voice—though why he should have troubled to defend her so loyally to me, the King's jester, I do not know, save that he was ever sensitive to the unspoken thoughts of others. "No girl, as I knew her before this blaze of glory burned her, was ever more open-hearted. It is so often *fear*, do you not think, Will, which makes people relentless?"

"Fear?" I answered in astonishment, my mind harking back with a kind of retrospective pity to poor, powerful Wolsey whom I had so often baited and she had so successfully expunged. "With *all* her enemies laid low?"

"Yes, growing fear," insisted the man who understood her best. "Fear first implanted months ago when at the apex of her triumph she was carried to her Coronation and felt the people's hatred—and sensed their awful justice. And unconsciously increasing fear *now* lest she should repeat the pattern and fail to produce a son."

I shrugged, half flattered that he should care what I thought. "It may well be so," I agreed from the doorway. But Wyatt, like Vaux and Surrey, was a poet. He exaggerated, and imagined things, I told myself. Until the day when we heard that Katherine of Aragon was dead. And that should have been Anne Boleyn's most triumphantly secure day of all.

The poor sick woman had been moved after all, but to Kimbolton not Fotheringay, although there was little to choose between the two places, people said. As soon as Henry heard the news, he had left Greenwich for Westminster. He would have to hold a special Council meeting, compose as tactful a letter as he could to her nephew the Emperor, and make arrangements for her funeral.

Before leaving, with his second wife still abed, he had given orders that all our half-rehearsed masques and mummeries for Twelfth Night were to be abandoned, and told Master Heneage, who had charge of the household, to see that Court mourning was provided for all. So, having no work to do and sensing that my master would have need of men who cared for him, I flung a cloak over my motley and crowded into the royal barge to be rowed up the half-frozen Thames. The oarsmen's breath hung like smoke in the still January air and the rushes stood like stiff, silvered rods along the ice-bound banks. And save for the barge-master's curt orders no one spoke a word save the King and Thomas Cromwell, deep in private discussion in the shelter of the richly painted cabin in the stern.

As soon as he arrived in the palace of Westminster, Henry sent for Fritton, the master of the royal wardrobe, telling him to bring some of the mourning garments which had recently been worn for his late sister Mary, and for his tailor, who was soon loosening the seams of his Grace's black velvet doublet until such time as a new suit could be ready, while his assistants were rigging out the royal attendants in an anteroom. Before going in to a hastily summoned Council meeting Henry stood patiently enough for Dragonot's ministrations, but most of the time he was talking over the man's bent head to Archbishop Cranmer who had come along from Lambeth, or to Thomas Cromwell, who had been appointed Vicar-General so that he might the better enforce the Act of Supremacy.

"The widowed Lady Willoughby—mother of Suffolk's new wife—begged permission to go to Kimbolton," said Henry, expanding his chest to the tailor's tape and throwing out orders at random. "If the spirited woman was prepared to ride there through this weather, I would not have had her refused admittance. After all, as Mary de Salines, she was with my brother's betrothed when they first came from Aragon. Over all the years there has been great love between them and such a visit should give a dying woman comfort...."

"The Spanish Ambassador was also with her," remarked Cromwell, in that flat voice which expressed nothing of his thoughts.

"That we cannot help," said Henry, pursing his small mouth. "A little more fullness to the shoulder pads, Dragonot, 'tis more slimming. And be sure to send enough cloth to Kimbolton for Lady Bedingford, the custodian's wife, and at least half a dozen other ladies to attend as mourners. And black jerkins for eight yeomen who will bear the coffin. Peterborough Abbey, you suggest for the interment, milord Archbishop?"

"It is near Kimbolton and," added Cranmer, with a gentle, deprecating cough, "not too near London."

It was characteristic of Henry Tudor that he was quick to appreciate these two convenient factors and then covered them with another which satisfied the nice fastidiousness of his conscience. "And beautiful enough for the last resting place of so virtuous a lady. Have the comptroller of our household send the very finest linen we have for her—for the head."

Tears were suffusing his light-blue eyes as he gave this last intimate instruction. At that moment I swear he had forgotten how abominably he had treated her, and saw himself only as the bereaved husband. The fitting was finished, and as he turned towards the door of the Council Chamber with a black-feathered cap on his head the sight of my garish motley in the midst of so much sobriety must have offended his sense of fitness. "Here, Will, my friend, you always loved her and we shall be out of tune with jesting," he said with a gusty sigh, pressing my shoulder as he passed me. "I will have one of Dragonot's men fit you out with that black doublet and hose that young Richmond wore."

So after everything had been arranged even to the colour of the pall, and the news of Katherine's passing was generally known, we were rowed back to Greenwich on the evening tide looking like a boatload of decorous ravens.

"All your labours and John Thurgood's spent for nothing, Will!" muttered some of the younger men, lamenting only that Court etiquette would deprive them of their Twelfth Night fun. But as we trooped wearily up the water stairs at Greenwich it seemed that they were going to see something of it after all. There were lights streaming from the Queen's Gallery, and as we went under the gateway into the inner courtyard we were greeted by strains of gay dance music and a surge of excited, laughing voices.

Henry stood as if rooted to the spot at the foot of a wide flight of stone steps, listening with incredulous anger. His head was raised towards the lighted windows, and presently he snapped his fingers impatiently in my direction. "You and Thurgood obeyed my orders and stopped all your preparations for that Twelfth Night mummery?" he demanded.

I was at his side in a moment. "Sir, you must know that even without your Grace's orders we should have had no heart for it," I said quietly. And I know that he believed me.

"Then who has dared to disobey me?"

Servants and torch-bearers flattened themselves against the stairway wall and dared not answer. Nor dared they move to warn those who so heedlessly romped above. And so the King went up with his sad-faced jester and the rest of his sombrely clad attendants close at his heels, and stood in shocked amazement within the great carved screens, staring incredulously at a scene of joyous revelry. Every torch was lighted, musicians scraped their fiddles in the gallery above us, costumes and discarded draperies cluttered the disordered dais, young men and girls capered in some strange dance, and by the blazing central hearth Anne, the Queen, dressed in flaunting yellow with some exotic fur flung about her bare shoulders, played Circe to a group of young men prowling in imitation of enchanted beasts. Mark Smeaton, mounted on an upturned barrel, was raising his baton to start the musicians off in a fresh tune when he caught sight of the King.

His face went white, his mouth sagged open, his baton hung suspended. "What is the meaning of this orgy?" roared the Tudor.

Warned by the sudden silence, Anne turned and saw him. Even then her gasp was more of surprise than fear. Probably she had seldom seen him dressed in black before. It made him look like a stranger, with all the semblance of a widower's grief about him, even to his puffed and reddened eyes. To her less complicated nature it must have seemed that he only indulged in some tiresome, necessary display of mourning which was a mere farce compared with his recent genuine grief for the loss of his sister Mary.

"Did Heneage neglect to give my orders for Court mourning?" he asked, with cold and terrible politeness.

"N-no, your Grace," admitted Anne, glancing down at the flaming skirts spread so dramatically between her outstretched hands, and halting uncertainly on her eager way towards him.

"Then why are you and these other women mumming away the night in unseemly, atrocious yellow? Answer me, some of you!" he burst out, seeing a Boleyn for once tongue-tied before him. "Why do I return from arranging about my wife's funeral to find you indulging in ill-timed festivities like a troupe of cold-blooded mountebanks when even my jester knows better?"

It was Anne's turn to be furious. Her sleek, dark head, crowned with a bacchanalian vine wreath, jerked higher. "Your *wife*!" she challenged indignantly.

"My late brother's wife," he had the grace to correct himself.

She came a step or two nearer and would have laid pleading hands against his unresponsive breast. "But, Henry, I thought... have you not said a hundred times... have we not prayed for this moment?" she whispered in a genuine perplexity, which but enhanced her strange beauty.

But for the first time Henry did not seem to care whether she was beautiful or not. "Take off that unseemly dress," he ordered sharply, "and go pray for some sense of decency."

"The hypocrite! The self-righteous hypocrite!" I heard her mutter, as I turned to follow him out. "Let him go to his dead wife's bed and warm him."

But, even allowing for his facile self-pity and powers of self-deception, perhaps Henry was not wholly a hypocrite. In spite of all his cruelty, his thraldom by her Circe spells and subjection to her spite, some part of him must have felt bereaved that night. He had lived with Katherine in amity for nearly twenty years—the best years of a gifted, athletic man's life. And this married life, as I had so recently been trying to explain to his broken, bewildered daughter, was something altogether different from the fierce desire which had burned out the better part of him in early middle age. Something far less potent, but more indestructible.

With the inwardly excited but outwardly subdued gentlemen of the bedchamber I followed him to his room. "Have they told the Lady Mary, Harry?" I asked in a low voice when his anger had died down and Hal Norris was warming the royal bedgown before a roaring fire.

"I sent a courier to Hunsdon immediately. I ought to have sent you, Will. You would have known how to comfort her. I wish that she were...."

I believe he had been going to say he wished that she were here with him now, but he let them prepare him for bed and then sat down again in a fit of depressed abstraction. Only once did he rouse himself, and that was to call back a page who was carrying away his clothes and to take back from him the hastily selected black velvet wallet which had been hanging from his belt. And from it he presently extracted and unfolded a letter, and then waved his gentlemen away. Supposing that he wished to be alone I would have joined them as they bowed themselves out had he not laid a detaining hand on my shoulder. "Her last letter, sent from Kimbolton," he murmured, more to himself than to me. And, spreading his legs towards the fire, began to re-read it.

But even for the mighty Tudor it had been a tiring day. A day which dug up past memories and emotions, and had ended in a burst of justifiable fury. Sitting there in his warm, fur-lined bedgown, he began to nod and doze. His strong hands, backed with hairs that shone stiff and ruddy in the fire glow, gradually relaxed. And the letter with the dangling seal of England and Aragon slipped to the black-and-white tiled floor. I bent to retrieve it, lest a cinder should fall. Knowing that she was beyond human help or danger, what would Katherine have said to him, I wondered? Had she died haughtily, as a daughter of Imperial Spain? Or upbraiding him, as she had every right to do? I folded the letter reverently between my forefingers and thumbs, and as I did so the last sentence in her fine clear handwriting sprang, warmly illuminated, to my gaze. "More than anything in this transitory life mine eyes desire the sight of you."

So she really loved him in spite of all. With the kind of love which was beyond the comprehension of women like Anne Boleyn. And with those most beautiful and elemental words she had silenced unfaithfulness and ridicule and cruelty.

I laid the letter reverently on Henry Tudor's knee. I knew then that I was right. That whatever others said, he had not been wholly hypocritical that day.

And as I waited for him to rouse himself and climb into his high, lonely bed the thought came to me in the stillness of that luxurious room that, just as Thomas Wyatt could see past the crude selfishnesses into the once carefree, friendly heart of Anne, so perhaps it was given to me, the King's fool, to see with deeper understanding than most men into my master's mind. Perhaps he himself was half aware of this, and that was why he sometimes laughingly called me his *ultra ego*, and steadfastly refused to put Mark Smeaton or any other bright young performer in my place. And why he showed me so much indulgence and liked to have me sit with him and dropped defensive pretence when we were alone.

I liked to think it was so. It seemed to make my leaving Easton Neston more worth while.

Chapter Nineteen

O F COURSE, THE KING's remorse was short-lived, all the more so because Anne was soon with child again. But this time Henry was taking no chances. He and Cromwell had their heads together drawing up some sort of statute by which the succession should pass to her male issue or, failing that, the King should be free to nominate his heir. True, there was little red-headed Elizabeth who seemed lively enough; but whoever heard of a woman ruling? And the fact that men were beginning to look again, reluctantly, at Henry Fitzroy had made bad blood between the pregnant Queen and her uncle, Thomas of Norfolk, who had given his daughter to the pasty-faced bastard in marriage. "In the end a dutiful daughter may prove of more use to me than an ambitious niece," he had been heard to say, in that surly way of his.

As Anne's time drew near people even began to lay bets on the two hopes so that the strain of uncertainty affected her health, and her outbursts of temper gave her women an uncomfortable time.

"Even her looks begin to suffer," remarked my friend John Thurgood, while we were preparing a guessing game with which to entertain the company after supper. "See how washed out she looks beside her vivacious Rochford sister-in-law."

"Which is probably why she has been keeping that pale, sedate Mistress Seymour so much in attendance of late," I answered, with my usual reluctant appreciation of her showmanship.

"She must be sick indeed to take such an unwary chance; she who is usually so observant," sniggered one of her women who had overheard us, and who had recently had her ears boxed for some clumsiness.

And we, wooden-pated males that we were, wondered what the disgruntled waiting woman had meant, until it was all over the palace that the Queen had caught the King fondling Jane Seymour on his knee.

"What happened?" we asked after supper, of the excited page who had witnessed the exciting encounter.

"The Queen had been resting all afternoon the way his Grace said she was to."

"No wonder the amorous old sly-boots made such a point of it," chuckled Thurgood incautiously.

"But the sun was shining and suddenly her Grace took a notion to go out in the garden. You know how she decides to do a thing," went on the lad, thrilled to find himself momentarily of so much importance. "Sir Thomas Wyatt's sister tried to dissuade her. Maybe she knew where Mistress Jane had gone. But the Queen wouldn't listen. Said she must go out and find the first snowdrops as she used to do at Blickling and Hever. She didn't even stay to let us change her soft fur shoes. And that was how, when I opened the door for her and ran after her with a wrap, she came upon them in a kind of ante-room leading to the garden passage—suddenly—just like that," explained the lad, clapping his two palms together.

We could all picture the scene, but Thurgood, as an efficient Master of Revels, was ever one for dramatic detail. "What were they doing?" he asked, rather unnecessarily, I thought.

The lad, having but recently left his father's wholesome country manor for the laxity of the Court, went red to the ears. "Well, Sir, he was kissing her mouth—and the lady didn't seem to be making any pother about trying to hold him off, if you know what I mean. Her skirts were spread across his legs and her arms about his neck. And—what with the Queen's soft shoes and they not hearing us—well, he just went on kissing her."

"A pleasant sight for a woman carrying his child," I murmured caustically. "What did she say to them, Diggory?"

"I don't rightly know, Master Somers. It was as if all these new cannon we heard being tried aboard ship at Woolwich were suddenly fired at their unsuspecting heads. The King sprang up, tumbling Mistress Seymour from his lap. He even moved in front of her as if to protect her when the Queen called her a mealy-faced mopsy and a Bankside bawd. You could have heard her angry screaming voice all down the gallery, and Mistress Wyatt came running and tried to stop her. She and the other ladies looked terrified, but you know how the Queen doesn't fear anybody, not even the King, when she gets beside herself like that. And instead of roaring at her to be quiet he kept trying to soothe her. 'Everything shall be as you wish, sweetheart,' he kept saying, meek as a monk. I can't think why."

"Because of the unborn babe," Thurgood explained to him.

"He'd care more about that than about any woman," I corroborated.

"I see. But the funny thing was," went on Diggory, beginning to giggle, "Mistress Jane, whom we boys always call 'the tame mouse' among ourselves, just stood there looking far more composed than either of them. 'By our Lady's body, Madam,' she said, when still more grossly taxed, 'I promise you I am as much a maid as when I came to Court.'"

And probably that was just what Queen Anne feared, I thought, remembering how successfully she herself had played for high stakes with prolonged chastity.

In the end, it seems, Margaret Wyatt and some of the others who loved the Queen had borne her, half swooning, back to her room, and Jane Seymour had been sent away for a short while, to her home at Wolf Hall.

For days Henry trod warily as if his highly strung wife were made of brittle Venetian glass. But it was the wine which the glass held that was precious to him. And certainly no one could say that what spilled it a few weeks later was the fault of either of them.

Henry had taken up tilting again. To look and feel young before a newly returned Jane, perhaps. He was over forty and had to have a larger suit of armour made, but in order to prove his old prowess he challenged her brother, Sir Edward Seymour. We were all out there in the early spring sunshine, to watch him, and it was like old times to see King Henry in the lists again—perhaps all the more so, I thought, because Queen Anne was not present, but resting in her lying-in chamber. Everyone seemed more free and easy. Bannerets were fluttering in a stiff breeze from the ladies' gallery, heralds blew stirring fanfares, squires were standing about holding their masters' lances and heaumes, horses whinnied and reared. The King's first course along the barrier was indecisive, and his great dappled charger shied at a fluttering banneret before ever he had spurred him to a second. It may have been the weight of the new armour or because he was out of practice, but for all his fine horsemanship Henry could not curb the great, restive brute. It threw him with a crash of metal down into the dust—threw him and rolled on him, breaking open the fistula on his leg so that a vein burst open and he was like to bleed to death. And after that resounding crash and the women's screams and the urgent thud of men's running feet, it was as if a terrible tangible silence had suddenly fallen on the world.

He was quite unconscious as we loosened his greaves and carried him indoors. While the surgeons did what they could I looked round at the strained, grey faces about me and realised that for all of us, whether high born or low, life had suddenly become an incredible, bewildering blank. Whether they liked him or not, it was certain that England needed him. Without the Tudor there was no one. No one of sufficient stature to keep the country free from invasion or the old interminable civil wars. No mastiff to snarl all the contentious, ambitious curs to silence. During those few minutes before he opened his eyes and let out an oath of pain as Butts tightened a bandage, I saw full justification for his obsessional desire for a son.

And it must have been during those anxious moments that Norfolk slipped away and hurried to his niece's apartments to tell her that the King was at the point of death. There were many who made a point of remarking afterwards that unless she bore a living son his own daughter might well become Queen. Little as I liked him, I found it difficult to attribute such cruel malice to any man. But if Henry's death meant that the world, as we knew it, would stop, what must the news have meant to her? He had made her what she was and, although she had probably loved no one but young Percy of Northumberland, during the three years that she had been married to the King only his protection had stood between her and the people's hatred.

She brought forth her child prematurely, and although his own life still hung in the balance Henry spared her his best physicians. But Anne's child was born dead. And, of course, it was a boy.

Although she pleaded that fear for his life had killed their hopes, Henry insisted that her wild hysterical jealousy of Jane had been the cause. "You will have no more sons by me!" he stormed in the hearing of her huddled women, as soon as he was able to limp to her bedside. And since he always had to have a scapegoat, in his heart he must have been blaming her for the whole up-turning of a Church and kingdom—for an upheaval which had once seemed so urgently necessary, and now, from his point of view, seemed all to no purpose.

She seldom saw him again, but spent her time wandering sadly in the garden, wishing herself back at Hever, no doubt. And I am sure her women tried to keep it from her when Thomas Cromwell was asked to give up his rooms next to the King's so that Sir Edward Seymour and his sister might occupy them. Sober Edward and his ambitious younger brother, Thomas, now provided the same specious sop to decorum which had once been furnished, more light-heartedly, by the presence of George Boleyn. Poor George Boleyn who, because he had once lounged late at night across the foot of his sister's bed trying to cheer her through her terror of not being able to produce a boy, now found himself appallingly accused of having helped her to produce the still-born one.

Nothing, however vile, could be kept from her at the trial. Jane Rochford, his wife, who had always been jealous of his affection for his favourite sister, helped to convict him of incest. Besides this, trumped-up charges of adultery with other courtiers were brought against Anne, smearing foulness against the bright page of her friendship with a group of gifted and gallant young men. Thomas Wyatt's former renunciation of his youthful matrimonial hopes saved him, and the King would have spared Hal Norris if he would have stooped to incriminate her by so much as a word. Only Mark Smeaton, tortured by the rack, admitted some imagined guilt. Not being of noble birth, he went out by the hangman's rope, and his sweet voice went with him. But it was a sad day for all of us when, in spite of all Anne's pitiful entreaties, Rochford and Hal Norris and two of the Queen's other friends, Weston and Brereton, were executed on Tower Hill.

Even when we had heard her sentence, few of us believed up to the last moment that Anne herself would be beheaded. Even the women of London, who had not been able to say anything bad enough about her, were shocked to pity. "No King has ever had a woman put to death before," they kept saying, standing about at street corners or gaping outside the tall Tower walls. "Not unless she was a witch."

"No *Plantagenet* king," some of their husbands added ominously.

"But then," I thought, trying to find some figment of excuse for such brutal behaviour in my master, "she really did bewitch him."

The King of France, who had protested in vain, sent his own expert swordsman from Paris lest her slender white neck should be roughly butchered by an axe. And almost before the Tower guns had told London of her passing Henry Tudor had married Jane—quietly, in the same little room at Whitehall where he had married Anne. And just as she had seemed unabashed when caught cuddling on Henry's knee, so now she showed no qualms about being so summarily made way for. She had served and revered Katherine of Aragon, and so to her way of thinking it was Anne Boleyn who had never been anything else but a usurping strumpet.

I think Henry was happy with her. To a man who slept well and had an easily appeasable conscience it must have been like coming into some peaceful harbour after all the buffeting storms of her predecessor's turbulence. And this marriage must have been a comfort to him when his natural son died. He had given Fitzroy the family title of Richmond, and Norfolk's blue-blooded daughter to wife, but even he could not stay in his bastard the wasting sickness which had taken his brother Arthur Tudor at Ludlow. Along with such hardened types as Suffolk and Cromwell, the young man had gone to gape at Anne's beheading, which might well have pushed him nearer to the throne, and had disgraced his manhood by vomiting squeamishly before half the sheriffs and aldermen of London. After which he had gone home quietly and sunk into a quick decline.

So when Jane became pregnant Henry would have given her the moon. But, being a kindly gentlewoman of considerably less ambition than her two brothers, Jane did not ask for the moon nor even for Katherine's long-purloined jewellery, but only that her first beloved mistress's unfortunate daughter Mary might be forgiven and brought to visit her at Hampton. For which I shall ever hold her memory in gratitude.

With such a dutiful consort Court life became considerably more peaceful. The horror of that May morning on Tower Green gradually faded. But for many of us there was a sad emptiness. Often, as I led the evening's fun, I would find myself listening for the sound of George Boleyn's lively lute or the absurd rhyming contests of Francis Weston and Will Brereton, or the kindliness of young Hal Norris's spontaneous laughter. Without the gay, golden promise of their youth the world was a poorer place.

And gradually, almost imperceptibly, the thickening shadow of Thomas Cromwell began to hang over us. More powerful and sure and deadly than any sudden, swift spite of Anne Boleyn's. As Vicar-General—yet without ever having taken holy orders—he served his royal master well. The King never made a boon companion of him as he had of suave, entertaining Wolsey, but beneath Henry's deceiving air of bluff naïvety he always had known most astutely how to pick his servants in every walk of life. He would even force men into office who had no ambition for it, like Archbishop Cranmer or—in much humbler estate—myself. But, with a kind of rough justice, it was usually those who eagerly wormed their way up to the dizzy peak of being essential whom he threw down when their usefulness was done.

Thomas Cromwell was all-powerful when Jane was Queen, and one had to admit that the man deserved it, for his capacity for hard work was incredible and carried out with a toad-cold objectiveness devoid of personal enmities. The gradual dissolution of the monasteries was already beginning to change the face of England, and by switching much of the economic power to the Crown was building up an almost despotic monarchy. Parliament was consulted, as a constitutional save-face, but dared less and less to oppose the wishes of the King. Successful courtiers, who in their hearts hated Cromwell for the martyrdom of good, brave men like Bishop Fisher of Rochester and Sir Thomas More, were glad enough to profit by a gift of Church lands. Holy Trinity Priory in Aldgate was gone. The church of the Crutched Friars was now part tennis court, part carpenter's workshop. The new Queen's younger brother had a greedy eye on rich pickings from Romsey Abbey, and the stones of many a noble nave and refectory were being ear-marked for the building of fortresses for the defence of our Channel coast. Often, in hours of leisure, I wondered how long my beloved Much Wenlock would stand. Homeless monks and nuns, besides the destitute whom they had fed, roamed the roads and begged.

But all this was the more obvious side of Cromwell's work. Somehow he had to repair the inroads which Henry's extravagance had made on his able father's carefully hoarded wealth, and make up for what must have seemed to him the political lunacy of two royal marriages with mere subjects who had brought no rich dowry or foreign alliance. And this he did in devious ways, marking down the wealthy and biding his time to bring some serious charge against them so that all their possessions should be confiscated to the Crown. His spies were everywhere, his cat-and-mouse kind of patience inexhaustible. And the Pilgrimage of Grace, as the jargon of the day called that foredoomed crusade when men of the older faith rose bravely in the north in protest against destructive reforming zeal, only provided him eventually with more opportunities to fleece them.

Though the Queen herself begged that both men and monasteries should be spared, Henry told her not to meddle. Reluctantly he called in Norfolk, because he was his best soldier, and when he and Suffolk between them had finally put down the last fighting flare for Papal supremacy, and Robert Aske and other honest leaders had paid for it with their lives, so many were known to have sympathised that it was easy for Cromwell to bring suspicion on many a family up and down the country who, although living outwardly in orderly subjection to the King, yet in their hearts could not acknowledge him as supreme head of the Church. Again and again law-abiding citizens were arrested on a charge of Praemunire, although even the lawyers seem to have become confused as to its exact implications, and those of us whose worldly assets were negligible went on with our lives uncaring, or—if we cared—at least learned to keep silent tongues. For me this was rendered all the easier because in all save acknowledgement of Papal authority the services in the royal chapels went on unchanged. Henry loved the music and the ritual and the richly coloured vestments, and was a regular worshipper. "In spite," some unsettling voice would chirp up in my mind as I caught sight of his reverently bowed head, "of Anne Boleyn."

As the weeks wore on even I, who was never able to make friendly contact with the reserved, humourless new Queen, found myself praying for her safe and easy delivery. Mary Tudor, who had been so shorn of love, must often have prayed for her, and even that she might bear a son, although this would put aside all chances of the crown for herself. And devout Mary Tudor's prayers would surely carry more weight with the Almighty than those of ribald Will Somers. And at last the day came when all those prayers were answered.

Ever since dawn Hampton Court had been in a state of pandemonium, with physicians and bishops and ambassadors arriving, ladies looking important and pre-occupied, and servants scurrying with steaming cups and chafing dishes up the back stairs. The September day dragged on, and with it the Queen's long, painful labour, but at the actual momentous hour of birth the palace was extraordinarily silent. All the dignitaries of Church and state were crowded into the lying-in room, and lesser officials and pages hanging about for news outside. Tension had gone on too long. Somehow I did not want to join them, or share in the nervous, excited whispering. Slowly, thoughtfully, I walked back to the King's deserted bedroom. I was *persona grata* there, and with a friendly word the servants on duty opened the door for me. I wandered about restlessly, picking up the King's harp, which was so much finer than my own, and plucking a note or two of sweetness from its strings, then wandering to the fireplace to kick a falling log into place. How should I feel, I wondered, were I waiting for my child to be born, sharing vicariously in the long agony with which my wife's tender body was being torn in payment for my joy with her? But Henry did not love as I loved. Such thoughts would not be in his mind. His anxiety was all for the child, based on the prideful reproduction of himself which lesser men shared, and yet rendered desperate by mightier, more impersonal issues. I found myself slipping into his mind, though it was so utterly different from my own. Almost tenderly, I picked up the bedgown which had fallen to the floor and draped it welcomingly across his chair before the fire. Memories and disgusts of the last few turbulent years receded, and for some reason or other I found myself smiling at the recollection of my Uncle Tobias's comic visit to Court, and of Henry's jovial kindness to him.

And then the bedchamber door was suddenly thrown open on a gust of excited sound, and as long as I live I shall not forget the warmth and joyful strength of Henry's entry. His great frame seemed to fill the arched stone doorway, torchlight illuminated the ruddy gold of his close-cropped head and short, square-trimmed beard.

"God has given me a living son!" he cried out. And his voice filled the room, sweeping all Plantagenet claims and insecurity before him in a burst of Tudor pride.

With all those important lords and prelates at his back he caught sight of me, the only occupant of the room. He must have recognised the welcoming gesture of the warming bedgown, realised that the news was no repetition to me, and read the affectionate joy in my eyes. In that high moment he saw me as some part or appendage of his family.

He strode forward and seized both my hands in a grip that hurt. "Will! Will! I have a son!" he repeated.

Chapter Twenty

THE CHRISTENING IN THE chapel at Hampton Palace will ever remain to me a blur of colours and incongruities. Mary, an ardent daughter of Rome, carrying the new-born babe who had supplanted her and handing him to Cranmer, the reforming Archbishop. Little red-headed Elizabeth, borne in Thomas Seymour's spring arms, smiling in unwitting innocence at those who had been instrumental in bringing her own unremembered mother to the block. And her Boleyn grandfather, so tragically bereaved of brilliant son and exalted daughter, brought pitifully to holding a taper and a towel for the baptising of a Seymour heir.

I had squeezed myself into a corner of the King's private gallery so that I could look down upon them all. Upon tall, dark Norfolk and thick-set, bearded Suffolk and all the other nobles resplendent with gold chains and followed by pages bearing christening gifts which would have paid the upkeep of their manors for a year. And upon the ladies in pearled caps and kirtles and billowing damask skirts. Plainly dressed by contrast and firmly standing her ground close to the infant prince was his nurse, Mother Jack—the only woman, I swear, of whom Henry Tudor ever stood in awe. And in the midst of all that throng, the exhausted Queen, brought on a pallet from her child-birth bed, with her husband sitting beaming beside her.

For once there was a becoming flush on Jane's pale cheeks, and more and more frequently as the long ceremony dragged on I saw her pass a trembling hand across her forehead. Sometimes, when her husband's attention was engaged elsewhere, she would close her eyes and lean back against her cushions as if all the lighted candles were swimming in a dizzy haze and the triumphant blaring of the heralds' trumpets jangled in her fevered head.

From my vantage point I was amused to note the cunning with which the child Elizabeth tried to conceal her yawns, and touched to see how protectingly milady Mary took her hand as soon as the King rose to leave and the procession formed to follow him. There was no need for further rivalry, since both of them were relatively unimportant now.

Midnight had sounded from the courtyard clock before Queen Jane's attendants bore her back along the draughty passages to her bed. And a week later she was dead. Jane, who only a few months ago had made a stir in London by riding her horse beside Henry's across the frozen Thames, and who had sat patiently for Hans Holbein to paint her portrait.

More shocked, perhaps, than sad, Henry shut himself up alone to face this new development in his life, not suffering any of us to come near him. But next morning he was off to Windsor, leaving Mary to mourn the dead. Off to make arrangements for the late Queen's interment there, he said. Sickness and the trappings of death he never could abide. But in all the years that followed he invariably referred to Jane as "my wife." While Katherine's body lay beneath a black and silver pall in the cold grandeur of Peterborough, and Anne's headless corpse had been bundled hurriedly into an arrow chest and pushed beneath the paving stones of sad St. Peter-ad-Vincula in the Tower, Jane was laid to rest in the family vault at Windsor, to await her lord the King and lie beside him through the years. It was Henry's acknowledgement that she was the mother of his son.

In a more devious way I owed a debt to her, too, for it was during the two years of his widowerhood that Henry needed me more, and I became far more to him than a mere jester. For a long time after Queen Katherine's death I had gone on wearing the black suit which he had given me, or some other sober garments, and although nothing was said it seemed to me to be tacitly agreed between us that I should not resume my motley. Had Henry wished me to he would have said so when John Mallard, his chaplain, was having us painted together for a page of the exquisite psalter he was preparing in the Italian style for the King's own use. It was Henry himself who insisted upon my being included. "Because Will is part of my daily personal life," he said. And there we are pictured together in his bedroom, all done in rich colour beneath the lovely words of the psalm *Speravi in misericordia dei in eternum.* Painted for all posterity to see, he sitting in his Glastonbury chair playing the harp and I standing near him in sober black humming over the tune as we so often used to do, and the trees beyond the garden archway and the very tiles on the floor all just as real as life. Though I cannot say that the artist has flattered either of us.

If it had not been for my separation from the woman I loved, these would have been my happiest times at Court. Not only did the King like me to make music with him, but sometimes we fell to discussing this and that, and these were the long evenings when a close bond was forged between us.

Having begotten a son, Henry no longer seemed to want women. Only his ships. And books. And—as he says in that song of his which is so popular—music and good company. He was in his mid-forties and rapidly putting on weight, so that men who wished to be in the fashion had to wear great purled sleeves and swinging coats similar to those which the tailors so cunningly designed to hide the royal bulk, and wide-slashed shoes like those which a resourceful craftsman in Cordwainer Street thought up for the easing of the King's incipient twinges of gout. The running sore on Henry's leg was often very painful and, in Doctor Butts's opinion, he had never been the same since his charger had rolled on him at that ill-fated tournament. He no longer jousted, and was less inclined for mummery and jesting. He would walk with a gaggle of courtiers in the gardens at Windsor, Greenwich or Hampton, but was content to watch younger men score bull's-eyes at the butts. Fine theologian as he had been, he seldom troubled to read through a book now, but would pass it to some of the more learned courtiers and then set two men of opposing views to discuss it, which provided us all with many a worthwhile hour. Or he would take barge and go down-river to Gravesend or Woolwich to watch his galleons being built. "A good ship is more satisfying than a woman," he would say, straddling the poop and imagining himself to be a ship's master. And although Thomas Cromwell kept suggesting advantageous foreign marriages Henry Tudor discussed them half-heartedly and sporadically, behaving in the interim like an irritating boy bent on enjoying to the full a school holiday of freedom.

When the King of France's daughter and one or two other ladies were mentioned as prospective brides, Henry seemed to expect them to be lined up for preliminary inspection, until Francis, in a fury, sent word that the ladies of his family were not brood mares to be looked over by buyers at a horse fair. And by the time the lovely little Duchess of Milan had gently intimated that she would be honoured to consider proposals from the King of England if only she had two necks, I think he began to realise that he was not the handsome matrimonial catch of Europe which he had once been. Henry hated being made fun of, particularly through the polite mouths of foreign ambassadors. Blinking his sandy lashes as he always did when momentarily abashed, he would puff and pshaw, and then call for our horses and ride off to Hunsdon to see his son. There, at least, he would be the dominant male giving his own orders. Or so he thought. But there was always Mother Jack to contend with.

"If every mouthful the poor mite takes is to be first tasted in case of poison, and every garment he wears tested against the plague," she protested, after Henry had spent a laborious morning drawing up a new and more stringent set of nursery rules, "his Grace will be smothered by inspecting busybodies and scarce able to breathe God's fresh air."

It was the clash of wills behind which they hid years of grudging respect and affection for each other. After one ferocious glare, Henry tried to ignore her, and turned his attention to the small prodigy who had been brought to him. "He is sturdy. He comes on apace," he declared triumphantly, which was probably music in the old lady's ears. "See, milords, my son can almost walk alone!" And an endearing sight it was to see that great strong Tudor hold out his hands and cluck to the babe who, to be sure, did not seem quite so optimistic about it. "Come to your father, my brave lad!" encouraged Henry. The infant, who was the living spit of his mother, gave him a sweet, obliging smile and tottered forward, then tripped over his elaborate clothing, lost balance and sat down hard on his tender rump. His round, pale face creased into the preliminary misery of tears. He let out a long enraged howl.

And before his unfortunate father could set him on his tiny feet for a second venture, Mother Jack had swept him up into the accustomed comfort of her arms. "Your Grace cannot expect him to walk alone at scarce a year!" she defended her charge indignantly.

"He must make a beginning," blustered Henry, almost as red in the face as his yelling offspring.

"And grow up bandy!" snapped that dauntless woman, to the huge delight of her admiring audience. "Which he probably will anyway with all this dandling on your great knee until he pukes, poor poppet!"

She swept the disgruntled Prince off without further ceremony and tucked him into his cradle, and with crooned endearments rocked him to sleep.

How wonderfully one helpless child can kill all pretentiousness in a group of grown persons! "Could it be that the good body was once *your* nurse, Harry?" I teased.

"She was, though only assistant to Mistress Anne Luke," he admitted ruefully. "And smacked me betimes where it most hurt."

"Which would seem to give any woman an unfair lifelong advantage!" grinned Norfolk's son, Surrey.

"And my mother, God rest her sweet soul, ever upheld her," explained the King. "Which is why the old crone is so cantankerous today."

"Probably her Grace the late Queen Elizabeth knew that Mother Jack would give her life for you," I suggested.

"As she certainly would for her nursling Ned today," agreed Henry, considerably mollified. "That being the reason why I gave her the appointment and why I allow myself to be so—so hectored."

"Or because the Welsh dragon has met his match?" I murmured among the general laughter. But he preferred not to hear my impertinence, and spent the rest of the morning talking kindly to his elder daughter, whose docile submission must have soothed him as much as it saddened me.

I stood at a respectful distance watching her. Mary was a woman now, far more grave and reserved than nature had ever intended her to be. Gone were all the sparkle and spontaneity of her happy childhood, leaving her face plain as her mother's, and pitifully wary. Only her brown eyes were still beautiful, and they were sad and shamed. Shamed because at long last she had been driven to deny the Pope's supremacy and her own legitimacy, to the end that she might sometimes come home and receive a breath of family kindness for which she, of all lonely people, yearned. Yet she must have known that Cromwell's spies were nosing about her household, whether here at Hunsdon or elsewhere, making sure that she did not go back on the document which she had been made to sign. Even her attractive husky voice had grown gruff with the strain of argument, and only when she bent over her small half-brother's cradle did the beauty come back into her sallow face.

"We must be getting back to Whitehall, dear daughter, lest I find friend Cromwell waiting at the gates with some fresh foreign bride," Henry excused himself with heavy humour, as soon as we had dined.

"At least the man works while most of us go hunting or sit rhyming," Surrey had the grace to say.

"And brings in the money," added the King succinctly.

Although most people hated Thomas Cromwell, he was always pleasant enough to me. On the rare occasions when he had time to notice me, that is. Perhaps he thought it as well to keep in with someone who, however unimportant, had the King's affection. But I sometimes wondered whether he remembered how I used to bait his former master whose interests he had served faithfully until the end.

"Do you ever hear from Easton Neston these days, Somers?" he asked, a few days after the Hunsdon visit, when I happened to be standing beside him in a small ante-room waiting for the King to come from Mass.

It sounded like one of those casual questions which any important personage might put to a subordinate to avoid an awkward silence during some moment of propinquity. Yet, as his bull-like eyes swivelled round upon me, I felt an illogical conviction that he knew of the letter from Joanna lying warm and cherished against my breast. Could one of his ubiquitous spies have been down at the wharf waiting hopefully for Bart Festing, Master Fermor's London agent, who had just come down from Neston? But, of course, that was absurd. Of what possible interest could my leisure hours be to a busy man like Cromwell? "Quite recently," I replied.

"And where is that modish son of his these days? The one who married so well into the Vaux family and used to come to Court with milord sometimes."

"He has been living in Calais for some time now so that he can attend to that end of the business," I told him.

"I am sure he must be much needed there," said Cromwell pleasantly. "Only last time I saw him he was telling me how enormously their trade with Europe was expanding, and how much spice his father was importing for this country from the East. A pleasantly frank young man. Years ago a colleague of mine, John Clark, met him in Florence, Somers, when on milord Cardinal's business, and young Fermor was able to help him out of a temporary embarrassment by a loan of two hundred pounds, in return for which we ordered some expensive silks from him."

I recalled perfectly how Wolsey had failed to pay for the silk, and how I had ridiculed him into doing so. Probably Cromwell himself had seen the entries in the York House ledgers. If he hoped that I would enlarge upon the Fermors' growing profits from spices as glowingly as Master John had done, I did not rise to the bait. "The Fermors' main export is wool—to Flanders," I said non-committally. And then realised that as the Vicar-General of England had begun life in the wool trade he was probably able to assess the value of the Fermor exports quite as well as I. My mind went back to a day when he had leaned with me on the harbour wall at Calais watching the loading of Fermor bales into Fermor ships, and telling me that as a young man he had owned a fuller's mill on Putney Heath.

The man knew too much about everything. For the first time I looked at him with real dislike. At his pudgy, expressionless face, his capable hands and the black jowl that always looked as if it needed shaving. I did not know how soon and how thoroughly I, too, was to hate him. Nor do I know to this day what half-understood warning made me take my afternoon stroll in the direction of the wharves that day. To watch this clever painter Holbein painting one of his Hanseatic merchant friends at the steelyard, I probably told myself. But I meant to see Bart Festing, too. To repeat to him that oddly disturbing conversation perhaps. To assure myself that all was well.

I had barely turned into Thames Street when I saw him, riding head down against the wind towards me. Clattering like a madman along the narrow cart-obstructed street. Had I not shouted out his name he would have passed me, blindly. As it was, to my astonishment he slid from his saddle and grasped me by the arm, almost pinning me against the steelyard wall. "God be praised, Will, what sent you? Just *now* when I had to see you," he gasped almost incoherently.

"What is it?" I asked, seeing the pallor of his face and trying to steady him.

"Old Jordan has just ridden down from Northamptonshire," he gasped. "They've arrested Master Fermor."

"*Arrested* him?" I repeated stupidly.

"This Praemunire thing—"

"Praemunire! But he is one of the King's most loyal subjects. You know how careful he has always been to conform, and how he never discusses religious matters except among his closest friends."

"I know," agreed Bart Festing. "But last week he rode into Buckingham to visit poor Father Thayne in gaol. He'd heard the old man was sick with the damp and cold, and took him a couple of his own warm shirts and some money for better food. He has done it before, often. As you probably know, he used to be a sheriff of Buckingham himself, and the present sheriff, like a good friend, has always turned a blind eye. So who can have made trouble? Who could have seen, right away there in Buckinghamshire?"

"One of Thomas Cromwell's spies," I said, and my voice rasped with harshness. I walked back with him in silence to his familiar work-room on the busy, sun-lit wharf near Dowgate. I was piecing things together. These same bales and ships all those years ago in Calais harbour, John Fermor's bragging tongue, all those apparently casual enquiries.

Faithful, irascible old Jordan was awaiting us, head in hands, worn out by his anxious, unaccustomed journey. "They are bringing him to London for his trial," he told me, as we came in.

"And Mistress Joanna?" The question shot from my lips like ball from cannon.

"She wanted to follow him."

"Alone?"

"Mistress Emotte is too sick with a bout of fever to accompany her. So the Master bade her stay and await the result of the trial at home. What do you suppose the verdict will be?"

Bailiff Jordan had many a time set me in my place in the old days, but we were all in this together and he was looking to me for help. I laid a comforting hand on his bowed shoulder. "There is only one kind of verdict when Cromwell's agents prosecute," I said.

He clutched at my hand and slewed round towards me. "Could you not speak to the King, Will?" he entreated. And I saw that the more sophisticated Festing's eyes were entreating me, too, albeit more doubtfully.

I shook my head sadly. "There are two things no one dares importune the Tudor about these days—his treasury and his supremacy of the Church."

"But what has riding a dozen miles or so to do an act of Christian kindness got to do with denying the supremacy of the King?" burst out Festing, slumping down before a desk piled with bills of lading.

"Nothing, my good Bart," I agreed bitterly. "Except that it acknowledges the supremacy of Christ. But it is the sort of pretext being used daily to scoop a successful man's money into the Treasury."

"And what will happen to all this?" he asked. His gaze wandered wretchedly over his samples and ledgers and beyond them to the busy porters, all unaware of disaster, still bringing merchandise ashore from hold to warehouse. It was his commercial life, and I should have been full of compassion for him. But my heart was torn for Richard Fermor, my mind already making wild plans for the protection of his unmarried daughter.

Chapter Twenty-One

IF I COULD NOT go to the King about Richard Fermor's unjust fate, I went to Cromwell—which I hated doing far more. But one might as well have looked for mercy in a stone wall. Particularly at a time when he dared not relax his efforts to fill the royal coffers. Edward Seymour, recently created Earl of Hertford, was proving himself a sober and exceptionally able young man. Not just another modish, jumped-up poet courtier, but someone with a mind almost as astute as Cromwell's own though linked with a finer conscience towards humanity. A man, who, with the King's favour, might one day prove a serious rival.

"Set your mind at rest, my dear Somers, if you formed some attachment while you were at Neston," he told me, probably without any intention to insult. "Everything will be done decently and in order. When a landowner is arrested my men always have strict orders not to molest the womenfolk or disturb the household in any way until after the trial."

"And you are always quite certain which way the verdict will go?"

"And as for the servants," he went on, ignoring the sarcasm of my question, "those of good character will no doubt be taken on by whoever the property passes to."

"How pleasant for them!" I said, wishing for once that I had my fool's bladder to blow a rude noise on.

But there was no perturbing Master Cromwell, and at least I learned from him the time and place fixed for Richard Fermor's trial.

Plagued by rheumatics as he was, old Jordan had hurried back to Neston to try to calm the frightened farmhands and household, but Festing and I sat through the brief travesty of a trial in London. We heard our master—obviously still unable to believe that his whole life's work and all he owned could be jeopardised by so small a charge—speaking out bravely in his own defence. He scorned to deny his errand of mercy to a sick and beloved priest who had offended against the King's Act of Supremacy, but maintained his own loyalty, giving the names of influential friends who would testify to his orderly private life and offering the court opportunity to inspect his books in proof that he had always made his money honestly and paid all taxes except those personally remitted to him by the King himself. I was on my feet, hoping to be allowed to bear witness to this. But when Cromwell prosecuted for the Crown, no defence was of any avail. The prosecution called witnesses to prove that the accused had taken money and clothing to a proscribed priest, and that was enough. The judge pronounced a verdict of imprisonment and confiscation to the Crown of all possessions and estates under the Act of Praemunire. And that honest and good-living man, Richard Fermor, was hustled out of court like a criminal. And taken under guard to the Marshalsea prison. We had not even been allowed to speak to him.

"I would not give a thieving scullion such short shrift! It was scarce worth the pain of coming!" muttered Festing furiously, as the court began to clear.

"At least he saw us and knew how much we cared," I said, still staring at the empty place where the condemned man had stood.

Festing kicked at a stool on which one of Cromwell's lawyers had sat. "You were fortunate to change to the King's service before this black day came," he said.

"Perhaps," I answered, realising that at least I would not suddenly find myself out of good employment as he would. "Why do you not sail to Calais, Bart? As things are here Master John would be a fool to come back, and you could help him to salvage and consolidate what remains of the business over there."

"Calais is but another part of England," he demurred.

"True. But although the Fermors' is a family business, I doubt if Cromwell will pursue the matter beyond these shores."

"I think you are right, Will," he agreed, after a moment's consideration. "I will warn my wife and try to sell or rent my house. At least," he added, with a bitter laugh, "I shall have no difficulty in getting passage aboard any of a dozen good ships whose masters are well known to me."

"But will not your house be confiscated along with the other Fermor property in Thames Street?" I asked, knowing that it stood alongside.

"That they cannot do. Master Fermor gave it to me for a wedding gift, and the deeds are in my money chest."

It was for his ability to make quick decisions that Master Fermor had particularly valued him, but before leaving the almost deserted court-room I laid an urgent hand on his arm. "But first, as you are my good friend, will you do something for me?" I entreated.

"You know I will. With all my heart," he promised, surprised. "It is so seldom that *you* ask anything. What is it, Will?"

"Ride to Neston—now—to-night. I have to entertain at this banquet for the envoy returning from Cleves and cannot get away. Break the evil news to them and bring Mistress Joanna back with you."

"Here—to London—though she surely will not be allowed to see her father once he is in prison? Will she come?"

"She will come if you tell her that I ask it."

He gave me a long look. Perhaps on his business visits to Neston he had gleaned from Emotte how it was with us. Like a good friend he nodded assent, and asked no further questions.

"Take her to Master John Brown's house in Aldermanbury. Tell her I will come to her there."

We came out into the street, where people were still standing about discussing the trial in shocked voices. "I must fetch my horse from Thames Street and will at the same time tell Gerda to begin packing up our possessions," he said.

"Give her my humble duty," I said, remembering her as a kindly, comely Dutch woman whom he had married when on some business journey to Bruges. "And, Bart, if Mistress Emotte is still unfit to travel, I pray you make sure before leaving Neston that she is safely housed with some of their good friends." I felt as if I were playing the role of one of Richard Fermor's absent sons. But I had to hurry back to Whitehall. To be funny at dinner. To help Thurgood prepare a masque mounted in the Flemish style, since everyone was talking of the possibility of a royal union with Cleves. To think up some fresh means of entertaining Dr. Nicholas Wotton, the returning envoy, after supper, together with all the distinguished guests who were agog to hear his news. The King's revelry must go on. And, oddly enough, judging by the bursts of laughter, I must have been at the top of my form. Or perhaps it is easy to be funny about brides. Or, again, it may just have been that Henry was delighted with the miniature which Hans Holbein had been sent to paint of the Duke of Cleves's sister, and was in merry mood at the prospect of marrying again.

It was past midnight before I got away to the small room which was all the privacy I could call my own when at Whitehall. Wearily I flung myself on my bed, with mind at liberty again to go over the morning's devastating events. I wondered how much Richard Fermor would sleep in the Marshalsea. And how I could manage to get entry there. I had heard that it was strictly controlled by the King's Marshal, and that, because most of the prisoners were political, visiting was seldom permitted. And there seemed to be something else which I had heard about this grim prison over on the south bank, but it eluded me. For the first time I tried to realise what the full repercussions of this blow would be to Richard Fermor himself and to so many people whom I knew and had affection for.

A ship's bell clanged dismally as she nosed her way by lantern light down-river into the Pool. Presently the tramp of martial feet crossed the outer courtyard. The guard had changed and all was quiet again when I found myself sitting up, gripping the sides of my wool-stuffed mattress with excitement and staring wide awake into the darkness. Some train of thought about the Marshalsea began to stir. Back over all the scenes and people, the pageants and the executions, to the time when I was new at Court. When Henry was younger and less autocratic. Something to do with a woman—a ragged woman carrying—incongruously enough—a richly embroidered cushion. I had been resting on a stile by the river…. Gradually it all came back to me. That woman whose pirate son was condemned to death, and who had been so insistent that I should do something to save him. And afterwards the man himself, a great muscular fellow standing among the daily crowd of hungry beggars, come to the gates of Greenwich to thank me. Had he not told me that a merciful or short-staffed head gaoler had given him work at the Marshalsea, of all places? And had he not muttered that usual formula of gratitude, "If ever there should be anything that I can do for you—"? Well, there was certainly something which he could do for me now. If he were still there. And if only I remembered his name. But so many years had passed, and a King's jester meets so many strangers. Strain my memory as I would I could not recall the name.

At the palace all the talk was of preparations for this marriage with Anne of Cleves. Neither Cromwell nor anyone else had time to discuss an extra prisoner in the Marshalsea. Cromwell was Chancellor of the Exchequer now and all manner of other titles had been heaped on him, such as Earl of Essex, Great Chamberlain of England and Governor of the Isle of Wight. And had he confined himself to refilling the Exchequer from Church lands and private estates here at home he would have remained the invaluable King's whipping boy which he was. Men hated *him* for acts from which a pleasant, smiling King benefited, and the King could never have found anyone so well trained to replace him. But foreign policy was, I submit, beyond his money-making mind. Lest France and Spain should combine against England, he persuaded his master into a Lutheran alliance with insignificant Cleves. Religious parties were all one to Cromwell, but he stood as the man behind the marriage and, as I should have thought he might have learned from Wolsey's fall, it is dangerous work meddling with Henry Tudor's private life where women are concerned.

But what could I care for these things when any hour now I should be seeing the woman I loved? And she must have set out from Neston as soon as she had my message, because Festing, hurrying back to Thames Street to see to his own affairs, sent word that he had left Joanna at the Browns' house in Aldermanbury. Master Brown and her aunt were away, but the servants were taking good care of her and she was awaiting my coming.

What could eager lover want for more?

I rewarded Festing's messenger extravagantly, called for my horse and clattered through the palace gate and along the frozen mud of the Strand towards the City. A keen north wind nearly caught my cloak from me at street corners, and I thought, "Heaven help that poor Cleves woman if she has to cross the Channel in this gale!" In Cheapside shopkeepers and 'prentices were already decorating their wares with holly, but I scarcely noticed them. Nor anything in the world till I stood in the pleasant room where I had last parted from Joanna, and saw her again. She looked pale and weary, but rose eagerly from her aunt's chair to welcome me.

"That we should meet again only when your world is smashed!" I stammered almost incoherently.

"Yet our meeting is the one thing that can bring me comfort," she said. "Oh, Will, Will! How could they do such a terrible thing to my father, who was respected and loved by everyone and who cared for all the people he employed?"

"All of them will suffer as well as you and Emotte and I."

"If only I could see him!"

"I will try to find a way, sweetheart."

"Everyone comes to you when they are in trouble, expecting you to perform miracles, do they not, Will?" she asked, with a small, brave attempt at laughter.

But I, the professional fool, was far from laughter. The decision for our future was firm in my mind. I came close to her and lifted her face to mine. "This time I want you to do something for me," I said.

She had regained some of her usual poise. She even smiled, with heart-warming sweetness. "You know that I will do anything, Will. But what can I do for anyone—now?"

"Marry me."

The two words hung momentarily in the quiet room. Her whole mind had been wrapped in bewilderment and grief. She looked up at me with surprise and a kind of searching uncertainty. Save in moments of levity, she was a mature and thoughtful woman now. "You were always kind. You are asking me because I am homeless and penniless. Because, without a dowry, any other marriage arranged for me will almost certainly have—melted away." She tried to free herself from me. "No, no. You are a coming man whose name is in the mouths of all. Everyone says so. And a man whose future depends upon the King is not helped in his career by this sort of entanglement with a family that has given offence. Do not be anxious for me, my dear. There will always be a home for me with the Browns—or with one of my married sisters," she added, with a shade less certainty.

I took her by the shoulders and shook her gently. "And live like Emotte—the invaluable prop of some other woman's home? No, my sweet, you will marry me and live in your own home, though it be a very poor one for a successful stapler's daughter. In most of the palaces I have but small bachelor lodgings appointed me, and to those, with Cromwell's spying, over-shadowing presence, I cannot take you. So you see what sacrifice I am asking of you. But if you love me...."

She looked lovelier than ever with the pink colour creeping into her face again. "Have I not always loved you, Will, ever since I was sick and you used to make shadows of fantastic creatures by candle-light on my wall?"

I kissed both the little hands I held. "I know, dear heart, but, sweet as it has been, that kind of love will not satisfy me now. I have always loved you, Joanna, since the day I first saw you standing in the chapel doorway with flowers in your arms. Loved you and hungered for you so that neither success nor royal favour nor all the other things which I truly value can ever count against my hunger to possess you."

She pulled my face down to hers, and kissed me long and tenderly. "Never think for one moment that I say this because I am now shorn of so much else," she vowed, with tears in her eyes, "but that, I swear, is the completeness with which I, too, have loved you for a long time now."

It was the moment of ecstatic happiness for which I had lived so patiently—even monkishly, as Henry often said. For the first time I held her in a lover's embrace, untrammelled by pricks of conscience. Selfishly, I thanked God that she was homeless and penniless. There could be no betrayal to my first, best master if I took her and cared for her now. I pressed the softness of her body against the hungry hardness of my own, kissing her eyes and mouth and the whiteness of her throat, releasing her only when she was warmly responsive and half breathless. Then, because there was so much that we must talk of and so little time, I drew her down beside me on the window seat. "This proposed marriage with some Northamptonshire neighbour—does it mean anything to you that it is not to be?" I asked.

"Only unspeakable relief. He is a good man. My life would have been pleasant and easy. My father chose him carefully from the others, and then seemed to delay, making excuse that he needed me. I think he knew—"

"About us?"

She nodded. "And that any marriage such as he would be likely to arrange could be nothing but a duty to me. I should have married into some wealthy or titled family eventually, I suppose. But most fathers would not have—cared about my feelings."

"You must know that I admire him more than any man I have ever known." Joanna gave me a warm, grateful smile and, springing up from my side, said almost merrily, "And so, Will Somers, I am willing to marry you next week if you say so."

I took her hand and swung it between us, grinning up at her as she stood before me. "Not next week, Joanna Fermor—but now, today," I corrected firmly.

"Today!" she cried out. "By all the Saints, how masterful you grow! It must be associating with royalty!" The unashamed joy in her face suddenly changed to dismay. "But what priest of the Reformed Church would marry us, today or any day? You, the King's jester—and me, the daughter of a man so recently imprisoned for offending against the King's statute of Praemunire?"

"I know of one. And not far from here."

"You are sure?"

"Not sure. But he was only too anxious to marry me to you once. When you so narrowly escaped that unspeakable Skevington, and he mistook me for the bridegroom."

"You mean that round, jolly Parson Morton of St. Magdalen's in Milk Street, with whose mistaken offer you tempted me here in this very room?"

"That same man. What a memory you have for names! I spoke to him in the Lane afterwards and found him to be a liberal-minded man. Let us go to him now, Joanna." But though she sent for her cloak with a willingness which delighted me, when I had taken it from the servant and put it about her I detained her as I fastened it about her pretty throat. "It will mean secrecy—separation perhaps. All the things we hate. It will be necessary to trust each other utterly," I had the honesty to remind her.

She did not answer in words, bless her, but pulled me gently towards the door and down the stairs, and hand-in-hand we walked the short distance to Milk Street.

"What a way to go to one's wedding!" she giggled once, having slipped at the edge of a filth-filled gutter and splashed her already travel-stained stockings. And thinking, perhaps, of all the fuss and preparation there had once been for her first frustrated nuptials in the house we had just left.

"So be that we are going to it anyhow—at last!" I said fervently, drawing her more safely beneath the over-hanging eaves. "Though I am sorry you have had to choose between that shimmering bridal gown and me."

I tugged at the raucous bell of the priest house, and Parson Morton himself appeared. "You once offered to marry me," I reminded him, without waste of time.

He stared with surprised, bright eyes, but recognised me at once. "You are Will Somers, the King's fool," he said.

"And this lady is a niece of Mistress Brown of Aldermanbury—the same bride who was to have been married then."

He pulled us inside and we told him our story, hiding nothing from him. "I heard of the trial. So many cruel things are done in Christ's name..." he said ruminatively. "You wanted this fair lass when she was to have married young Skevington, though you kept it always in mind that she was your master's daughter. But only now, when her family's prosperity is lost, do you propose to marry her, which seems to me to spell real love." He tramped about his small, dark room, fitting the thing together in his mind. Then fetched up before Joanna. "And you really wish this, my daughter?"

"More than anything, Reverend Sir," she assured him.

"I should wait until Master Brown returns, I suppose, and consult him," he muttered. But instead he took us into his church and left us while he went to light the candles and put on his vestments, and to call his old housekeeper and the sexton as witnesses. Joanna and I stood, handfast and quiet, in the gloom of that old building with its empty niches where statues of Our Lady and the Saints must so recently have stood. What had been growing in our hearts over the years was strong enough by now to wash out all need for words. But I remember whispering, "It must be a terrible thing for you to lose your lovely home—like being turned out of the Garden of Eden." And Joanna squeezing my hand and whispering back, "You—always—will be my home."

And then the solemn words of marriage were being said, and we were man and wife.

Afterwards, in the little vestry, when Thaddeus Morton brought out pen and ink to register our names according to the King's new decree, he asked us where we lived.

"Greenwich, Hampton Court, Whitehall..." I answered airily. But he waved aside the vague grandeur of such names.

"Those are indeed the King's palaces, but what place shall I enter as your married home?"

Joanna and I turned to each other with raised brows and laughed. We were forced to admit to him—and to ourselves—the absurd truth that we had none.

"My husband will find us one," said Joanna, with large optimism—which was the beginning of her complete trusting.

"Say that first piece again," I ordered. "I liked it."

"My husband," she repeated dutifully, with shining eyes.

"You are both crazed," chuckled the good vicar of St. Magdalen's. "But wherever you find a home I make no doubt the good God will bless it with abundant happiness. And when you have settled into it come back here so that I may baptise your children."

Chapter Twenty-Two

M<small>Y HUSBAND WILL FIND</small> us a home," she had said, calm as the unruffled leaves on a lily pond. She, the gently reared daughter of a capable business man, putting her faith unquestioningly in a professional fool! Unutterably proud yet desperate, I prayed as earnestly as I had ever prayed for anything that I might never betray her touching trust in me.

And either because the Almighty listens to fools or because I had lived on my wits for years, before we had turned into the bustle of Cheapside an idea had come to me. "The Festings are going to Calais!" I said, pulling up short with her hand through my arm.

"Oh, Will, and they are wanting to sell their house," she cried, quick to pick up my thought. "As we were riding to London he was telling me how wisely you had advised him about joining John, and how they must try to find a purchaser or tenant. And his careful Dutch wife hates the thought of leaving it to strangers."

The Festings' home was a narrow, gabled house with upper stories jutting out over Thames Street which Master Fermor had had built beside his wharf. Its frontage would seem dismal and noisy indeed to anyone accustomed to the wide, airy fields surrounding Neston Manor, but from the back windows there was a sunny ever-changing outlook across the busy Thames and southwards to the Surrey shore. And those windows, being Gerda's, gleamed like crystal.

Their door stood wide and we found them packing house linen and clothing into three great cedar chests, assisted by Bart's elderly clerk and a young maid who kept dissolving into tears at the thought of their departure.

"Why, Mistress Fermor!" exclaimed Gerda, curtsying as best she could with a bolster in her rosy arms.

"Mistress Somers," I corrected, proud as Lucifer.

"Of all swift workers!" exclaimed Bart Festing admiringly, and dropping the rope with which he was lashing up a bundle of particularly precious household possessions in a sail, he sent Craddock, the clerk, for wine with which to celebrate.

They were genuinely glad. Gerda put my bride into the only available chair and fussed over her, and they both listened delightedly to my suggestion. "The master's daughter living *here* in our humble home!" they kept saying.

"*Tempora mutantur*," I quoted sadly.

"And neither my father nor I have *any* home now," Joanna reminded them.

"My poor pretty one." Mistress Festing, who had no children of her own, put a motherly arm about her. "If this is what you both really wish, nothing could suit us better, could it, Bart?"

"There is no time to sell, and Gerda has worried the night through lest hurriedly accepted tenants ill-use our carefully chosen furniture."

One had only to look round to see that, like many a merchant's agent, he had bought good stuff in advantageous markets, and that everything had been kept polished with Dutch thoroughness. "Not woven tapestry as you both are probably used to in palaces and manors," said Gerda, following my appraising gaze. "But all our walls are hung with good wholesome painted linen from Antwerp. And, oh, how thankful I shall be not to have to leave my best feather-bed and pillows to flea-infested strangers!"

On my insistence Bart and Craddock and I went across to his office on the wharf to agree a rental and to draw up a properly signed and witnessed agreement. "Your home will be here for you when you come back," I said, trying to cheer him. "And it could be a *pied-a-terre* to shelter the master if we can get him out of prison."

"You have hopes?" they both asked eagerly.

The all-powerful shadow of Thomas Cromwell seemed to blacken them all out. "I shall never give up trying," I said cautiously.

As we came down the outside steps to the wharf trying to steady ourselves against the blustering wind, seamen and porters crowded about us. "Any fresh news, Master Festing?" they asked morosely. Some of them recognised me and called to me to tell the King, who so loved ships, that six good merchantmen were moored idle. It was always the same. Because one or two stories of my having been able to help the under-dog had got about the city and become household words like some of my absurdities, people seemed to think that I could approach the Tudor about anything. They never could realise that I had to choose my opportunity—and above all the King's mood. But I could and did tell them that no matter who acquired the Fermor estates, a man with as much business sense as Cromwell certainly would not allow the wharf and all that valuable shipping space to stand idle for long. And because I happened to be a familiar figure in all the King's palaces they believed my words as unquestionably as the gospels in Master Tyndale's newly-printed Bibles, and took comfort.

And back to Whitehall Palace I must go, bridegroom or no bridegroom, leaving my treasure unenjoyed. The clock of All Hallows was striking noon, and the royal procession would be forming to go into hall for dinner. And the King would soon miss me. "I am sure our good friends will spare Craddock here to escort you back to Aldermanbury," I said to my new wife, feeling about as inadequate as a pricked bladder.

But Joanna did not want to be escorted anywhere. She preferred to stay here in what was going to be her new home—if the Festings would have her. After all, they were her father's people, and would not advise or interfere as the Browns might do. "If I shall not be an added burden to you at this busy time," she said.

"My sweet lady, we are honoured," Gerda assured her. "But you do realise, Master Somers, that we shall be sailing in three days' time?"

"You cannot stay here alone when I am on duty, Joanna," I

said. Much as I liked to think of her here, in our own place, I felt that I should take her back to her aunt's house where I knew she would be safe.

"There is Tatty, our willing little maid, crying her eyes out because we are going. And she has already taken a vast liking to you, Madam, and would, I am sure, ask nothing better than to stay and work for you."

"And Craddock sleeps at the docks and will keep an eye on them," Festing promised me.

And so it was arranged.

"Listen, my sweet," I said, taking Joanna's hands in mine. "The Cleves princess, Heaven help her, is due to arrive at Dover tomorrow, or—if the storm does not abate—by next day. From there she and milord Southampton, who is fetching her, and all the usual welcoming retinue will ride to London, breaking their journey for a night at the Bishop's palace at Rochester and then setting out for the great official welcome on Blackheath. But the King has taken a notion to ride to Rochester with milord of Suffolk and one or two more of his cronies disguised as merchants, and so pay her a surprise visit there."

"I thought it was all planned that he should meet her at Blackheath with all this elaborate reception we have heard so much about," said Festing.

"I know. That is to be the official welcome," I said. "But last night at supper his Grace was planning to pay her this surprise visit first."

"But surely the poor creature will have been seasick and want to rest," remonstrated kindly Gerda.

"And looking her worst, all ill-prepared," put in my wife. "It doesn't seem kind. Why must his Grace do this?"

Because she was showing more anxiety for some foreign princess than she had shown for herself, I kissed her worried brow. "'In order to foster love,' he told milord of Suffolk. 'Or because you still love dressing up, you romantic old roisterer,' jibed Suffolk, they both being full of sack and high good humour at the prospect of so unusual an outing. So as soon as they have word that the

Flemish Princess has landed you may be sure they will set off for Rochester. And you may be equally sure that the moment they are over London Bridge I shall be on my way here."

"To foster love?" enquired Joanna, with a provocative grin.

"Love like ours needs no fostering. For my own part, it is already full grown to the point of starving," I said, reddening her cheeks with an ardent kiss before them all. "And so I warn you, that you may be prepared to solace me when I come."

And so, striving to weigh my unlooked-for possession of her against that long delay, I took my leave, promising Bart Festing to send a quarter's rent before he left for Calais. My tastes had always been simple, my expenses few. In the King's service so much in victuals, travel and amusement was free. Save for a gift to my aunt in Shropshire, whenever I could find opportunity to send to her, there was no one dependent on me. Though I made it a rule to take no bribes, rich men who had enjoyed an evening's fun and visiting foreign envoys frequently made me presents. My savings were considerable and lay snugly in the royal cofferer's care. And when I got back to the palace my good friend John Thurgood, in whom alone I confided, offered to deliver the money for me. I think he was as desirous of meeting my bride as of doing me a service at this all-important juncture in my life.

"She is sweet as a field of spring flowers, and gay as sunshine," he said, stretching himself out in my room on his return. "You are a lucky man, Will, but your constancy deserves it."

"I would to God I could have won her fairly in any way but by her family's misfortune," I said. "And that I could keep her openly as my wife in some place where there are gardens and the things to which she is accustomed."

"It may not be for long," said Thurgood, trying to cheer me. "And 'tis a quiet nest for love."

"Too quiet, perhaps, if Joanna frets too much about her father. And what to do for him I know not, John."

"Nothing, I fear, with Bull Cromwell in power," he sighed, getting up reluctantly to go about his own affairs. "Listen, Will. There will be little to do here until all this Blackheath pageantry is over, and higher level men than us, such as milord Marshal, will have all the managing of that. So I can well cover up your tracks here. You can easily be free to get away the moment the King and Suffolk and Sir Anthony Browne set off on this escapade of theirs for Rochester."

I needed no second bidding. "Success or no success, Court life would have been a desert indeed without you, John!" I said, grateful for his years of ungrudging friendship and professional co-operation. And when he had gone, with a thwack on the shoulders and a ribald wish for my new married state, I had the temerity to visit the King's own barber and then put out my fine mulberry velvet which had been ordered for the coming of the new Queen, and dressed myself with as much nervous fumbling as any bridegroom. "You are no Adonis. You can't be fashionably fair like the Tudors and all those gallants who dye their hair with saffron to imitate them," I told myself, peering anxiously into the silver-framed mirror which milady Mary had given me. "Your cheekbones are too high and your face too lean, but at least you've kept your figure and your eyes and teeth are good. Dressed like a gentleman of the more sober sort, you look the kind of man a woman might willingly acknowledge as her husband. But"—and here I came to the question which always nagged at the back of my mind—"could any woman in her heart want to have a husband who was the King's fool?"

As one prospective bridegroom to another, and because I really wanted to, I went down into the courtyard to wish the King godspeed. He and the Duke of Suffolk and Sir Anthony Browne were already in their saddles, dressed in plain brown worsted with unfeathered caps and as conspiratorially excited as a trio of plump schoolboys.

"Do we look like a party of honest merchants?" Suffolk was asking, looking down at his unaccustomed garb self-consciously.

"Here's Will. He should know, having lived with some of them," cried Henry, at sight of me. "Do we look like honest merchants, Will?"

I viewed them with mock solemnity, walking critically around each, so that all the attendants and grooms began to titter. "You look like *merchants*, Harry," I assured him. "But as to *honest*—well, let your consciences be the judge of that."

"He must be alluding to you, Charles, for managing to keep your ward's dowry by marrying her," laughed Henry. "But, since we talk of disguises, if *we* look like merchants *you* look like the lord of a manor, this morning, Will. Whither are you going?"

"To my honeymoon," I said, without hesitation.

"Then there are two of us."

I went close beside him and laid a hand on his stirrup. "So I wish you happiness with all my heart, and pray you find the lady to your liking," I said, in a sudden glow of affection for him. For all our sakes, I wanted this fourth marriage of his to be a happy one. And he knew as well as I how, even in the midst of our fooling, we sometimes said things in deep sincerity which strengthened the strange bond between us. "Where will you be spending *your* honeymoon, Harry?" I asked lightly, to cover our moment of emotion.

"Where else but at Greenwich, since it is conveniently on the Kentish side for my bride's arrival," he answered, all jovial with anticipation. "And where will Master Somers of Mummery Manor, in all his wedding finery, spend his?"

"In the City of London," I told him promptly.

"An odd, public sort of place to choose for dalliance, surely?"

"But I chose it because only milord Mayor has jurisdiction there, and so your Grace cannot recall me before the moon be waned and the honey all tasted."

Everyone was smiling good-humouredly around us. "An excellent idea," he agreed, making a last effort to restrain his plunging mount. "And when do you propose to go?"

"Now, this same moment as yourself," I told him. "For were we not both born in the month of June under the self-same sign?"

He laughed again and waved his plainly-gloved hand. "We must compare our experiences later. *Amuse-toi bien, mon brave!*" he called back over his shoulder.

The three of them, followed by a groom or two, clattered through the gateway, and it was as if the exciting centre of things were gone. Courtiers and servants went back in twos and threes to their various occupations. The courtyard began to empty. "A lanky, nonsensical fellow, that fool! But for some reason the King allows him far too much liberty," I overheard a long-nosed, ambitious bishop say disapprovingly, as I passed him and the parson-poet Skelton on my way to the stables.

And then I heard from behind me John Skelton's mocking voice answering him in ribald rhyme,

> *"How good for kings*
> *To hear of things*
> *From fools who find*
> *No axe to grind."*

Probably he shocked his ecclesiastical superior, but he delighted me immensely.

And the funny part was that because I had told the exact truth in open courtyard no one had dreamed of believing me, and if anyone missed me during the following week probably the last place in which they would think of seeking me would be the City of London.

One of the grooms had my grey gelding ready saddled for me. And I rode like the wind to Thames Street—or it might well have been to Heaven—where the Festings were already gone and my bride awaited me. And whatever romantic surprises or gorgeous spectacles of nuptial welcome royalty may have been enacting to an amazed world outside our ken or caring, Joanna and I had no need of them. No matter what other homes we might live in, that narrow, typical London house among the docks would always remain in our memories as the enchanted casket of our first married ecstasy.

During those few precious uninterrupted days we scarcely ever left it save for an evening saunter across Tower Green beneath the stars. We had waited so long and so hopelessly to be together. There were so many things to talk of, so many years of lovers' longings to assuage. And we found that we satisfied each other in mind, body and emotions. Poor as my parents had been, the education my father had given me was much the same as that enjoyed by merchants' sons. Contact with her father had dispelled much of my youthful gaucherie, and Court life had given me a worldly wisdom which, save in social graces and experience in managing a gracious manor, Joanna lacked. We valued intensely every facet of a happiness which we had never hoped to possess. If we had waited long enough to lose the shy romance of very early youth, we had found an undreamed depth of magic in our marriage.

But when the bells of St. Paul's and all the other London churches began to ring out, and we saw the wealthy Flemish merchants setting out from the steelyard in all their best finery to welcome their Princess, and a wild scurry of small boats filled with sightseers rowing down-river we knew that the bride must have arrived at Blackheath, and that soon the King would be escorting her with all the bejewelled company into Greenwich Palace. And that I, the Court jester, should be expected to be there.

"I shall often be back," I promised, making my hurried preparations. "Late at night sometimes, or when the King is out hunting or having a long session with Cromwell or one of the foreign ambassadors. This is our *home*, Joanna."

But she was standing disconsolately by the window of our bedroom staring out across the Thames, perhaps to hide her tears. "I believe I can see the Marshalsea prison from here—tall and grim on the Surrey side," she said, and I knew that her tears were mostly for her father. "Oh, Will, have we been wickedly selfish, being so happy here in this warm room while he is imprisoned over there across the water? With family and freedom gone, his full life all in ruins. Even hungry, perhaps—"

I turned her from the window and held her tight, so that she wept for a while against my shoulder. Any evening we might have walked across London Bridge and stood beneath those prison walls, but what good would it have done? "If only we could see him—speak with him," she murmured, making a brave effort to dry her eyes.

"Cromwell's orders about visiting are extraordinarily strict. You may be sure I made every enquiry," I said. "I even woke in the night with a wild idea—"

"Yes?" she asked eagerly.

"It was useless, through my own carelessness. You see, my sweet, I was once able to save a man from hanging. And I believe he became a gaoler at the Marshalsea."

"You mean the sailor accused of piracy whose mother pleaded for him?"

"Yes. Did I tell you about it?"

"When I was in London. She caught you in a softened mood, you said, that day your Uncle Tobias came about Frith Common. Miles Mucklow, you mean?"

I held her at arm's length and stared at her in amazed admiration. "Joanna! Joanna! I always said you had a marvellous memory for names. But how, in Heaven's name, when I myself had long since forgotten?"

"Oh, my dear foolish one," she cried, "do you not see how your life has been such a full one—so busy with becoming a celebrity—while mine has been so quiet that I have lived on your letters and all the interesting stories you ever told me? I wrote them down, some of them, lest I should forget any part of you—after I grew older and must be married to another."

I held her to my heart in silence. What could a man say in return for so sweet a confession? An ordinary, low-tongued, time-serving buffoon like me? Life would not be long enough to show her how gratefully I loved her.

She brought my riding cloak and smoothed down my fine maroon doublet. "Fit for a new Queen," she teased, quick again to laughter. "But I am glad you wore it for me first."

"What will you do while I must leave you?"

"Tatty and I will furbish this dear house from attic to cellar while you are gone lest dear, kind Gerda should find fleas!"

"Au revoir, my love," I whispered. "Even though I should be set upon by footpads between the bushes in St. Martin's Lane for my new velvet purse I shall die the most fortunate of men, dumb with gratitude for all you have given me."

"I cannot imagine my Will dumb. Call loudly 'Oh, mihi beati Martin!' so that honest men run to your aid and the saint of travellers will let you live for me," she adjured me gaily, following me to the stairs. But at the open door she caught at my cloak and entreated with sudden seriousness, "And you will try to speak to the King about my father?"

I wished that she would not ask me. I knew how unlikely the Tudor was to interfere with any clever move of his Chancellor's. "Perhaps—if this new marriage mellows him—or if God makes something unexpected happen to smooth the way…" I promised hurriedly, with small conviction.

Chapter Twenty-Three

I F I HAD ENTERTAINED any hopes of speaking to a King who was a mellowed bridegroom, they were rudely shattered from the moment I re-entered Greenwich Palace. The courtyard was crowded with hangers-on from the gorgeous spectacle on Blackheath, but many of them seemed to be already preparing in a subdued manner to return home. Instead of the wild bridal merriment I had expected to have to lead that evening, an awed hush had fallen over the interior of the palace. Ushers stood about looking frightened and uncertain, even the incorrigible pages moved decorously, and the servants laying the tables for supper might have been preparing a funeral meal for a batch of mourning relatives. Thomas Cromwell, who had brought off the whole diplomatic *coup*, and whom one would have expected to find very much in evidence, was nowhere to be seen. And the only sight I caught of the King was a brief glimpse of his back-view, as he strode along a gallery, with his short coat flapping out on either side of him like the wings of an enraged swan, and then disappeared through his bedchamber door which a couple of scared-looking ushers pulled firmly shut behind him.

Thoroughly nonplussed, I went in search of John Thurgood, whom I found in one of the smaller galleries putting his new troupe of tiny monkeys through their tricks, while Hans Holbein sat in one of the wide window seats moodily sketching them. "What line do you want me to take this evening, John? Has anything cropped up that I can use for a topical joke?" I asked, rather conscience-stricken that I had left him to make all the preparations for so important an occasion.

"Not unless the whole Flemish marriage is a joke. And even so, in the King's present mood, it would be dangerous to be funny about anything. That is why I am playing safe with these," he explained, flicking his fingers towards the monkeys.

Since the German painter must just have returned from Cleves, I looked to him for enlightenment, but he went on sketching glumly.

He had been about the palace for years and spoke English fluently, and most of us liked him personally besides admiring his work. "But surely there was never such a state welcome," I said. "What went wrong at Blackheath?"

"Everything went wrong *before* Blackheath," vouchsafed Holbein at last, with a brush between his teeth.

I remembered Joanna's indignation on behalf of a bride who would not be looking her best. "You mean—it is always a mistake to take a tired woman unawares?"

Holbein looked up then, his expressive brown eyes smouldering with anger. "She had been horribly seasick. We all had. She had even taken off her stays, so her women tell me."

I gave a low whistle of comprehension. "And the King did not like her."

"He called her a Flemish mare."

How brutal the Tudor could be! And how hurt in his liking for the lady was Holbein! "But I myself heard him extolling that exquisite miniature you sent," I said.

"Which is said now to have been over-flattering—to please Cromwell. As if I, whose whole life is painting, would prostitute my art to please any man!" He got up, scattering a genius's unfinished sketches of monkeys in all directions. "She looked as I painted her, Master Somers. She *is* like that, for all who have eyes to see. A tall woman—angular if you will—with calmly hooded eyes looking out straightly on to the world." He had screwed up his eyes as if visualising his recent model, the stick of black crayon in his hand seemed to be measuring her, and his deep voice shook with enthusiasm. "The nose too long for beauty, but the mouth kind, with a suggestion of quiet humour. There is a placidity—a beauty of the soul—a—a—how do you say?—sensible healthiness."

His enthusiasm almost discomforted us. "A pity the poor lady had to travel in such a storm," was all Thurgood could think of to say.

"Yet, ill as she felt, she persuaded Sir Thomas Seymour to teach her English words and card games, to fit herself for her future lord. And your seamen, who had hated the thought of crossing with a boatload of foreign women, finished up by swarming up the ratlines to cheer her when she disembarked at Dover."

"Where will you go, Hans Holbein?" I asked, watching him gathering up his plain cloak and cap, and realising that his brilliant career must be momentarily blighted.

"As far as possible from palaces," grunted that unostentatious son of Augsburg.

"To paint some more rich Flemish merchants down at the steelyard?" I said, having seen some of the fine portraits they had commissioned him to do, and suddenly wishing that he had made a picture of Richard Fermor to hand down to posterity.

"Till this blows over," he said with a shrug.

I stooped to pick up two of his half-finished sketches, folded them carefully and put them in my pouch. Even the most casual lines of the artist who had so splendidly depicted Henry, the late Queen Jane, her infant son and half the notables at Court, must be valuable. "I suppose that Cromwell's stock has fallen, too?" I asked my friend, as soon as Holbein was beyond earshot.

Thurgood's clever little monkeys had finished the rehearsal of their act and he sat back on his heels, while they jumped about him clamouring for the tit-bits with which he always rewarded them. "All I know is that the moment the great guns boomed out salutes for the royal arrival, the King conducted his bride-to-be to her apartments. Then he snapped his fingers sharply to Cromwell—as I might do to Mitzi here—to follow him into his own room. They were closeted there alone for nearly an hour, so Culpepper, that new young gentleman of the bedchamber, says. Then Cromwell comes glowering out and calls a Council meeting. This afternoon, of all times! So there were no more festivities and most of the guests took themselves off. And no instructions from milord Chamberlain for this evening. Heaven alone knows what it all bodes!"

"Perhaps the meeting was called to make final arrangements for the wedding," I suggested, trying to keep my thoughts from straying back to the quiet happiness of my own.

"If so, surely the King himself would have been present. But those two Dutch gentlemen who came with the bride were called in—Waldeck and Hostoden, or some such names—together with the Duke Philip of Bavaria, who seems to have come as a suitor for the Lady Mary. And Holbein, who speaks their language, was telling me just before you came that the poor men were bewildered at being cross-questioned about some pre-contract between the Cleves Princess and the young Marquis of Lorraine. Some idea that was mooted years ago by the late Duke of Cleves, her father, but never implemented."

"Then the King has changed his mind and must be trying desperately to find means to avoid marrying her," I said, bitterly disappointed, because it seemed to wash out any faint hope of begging a mellowed bridegroom for Richard Fermor's release.

"A pity he ever sent for her!" said Thurgood, not relishing another uncomfortable period like the end of the Boleyn reign.

"Or that he noticed that young Howard girl first!" I said. I had not meant to speak of it, but this was our common misfortune, and I understood my master all too well.

"You mean the auburn-haired orphan sired by that fine soldier Lord Edmund Howard, who was younger brother to the Duke of Norfolk?"

"Yes. The Duke's detestable old stepmother brought her up, it seems. And now, after neglecting her since childhood, I suppose they suddenly realised that she had big appealing eyes and the right colour hair, and that the King is at the age to make a fool of himself over a cuddlesome girl of seventeen."

"But surely he would never look with more than a passing lascivious eye at a penniless chit like that?"

"He might. Like all the Howards, she has royal blood. I saw him watching her from one of the windows in the long gallery while she was playing shuttlecock on the terrace with some of the Lady Mary's maids. Young and fresh as a rose, she looked, although her cousin George Boleyn once told me she was no better than she ought to be. 'Who is that sweet child, Tom?' Henry asked. And poor Tom Culpepper, who clearly wants to keep her charms for himself, had to tell him, 'Katherine Howard, my cousin, Sir!'"

"And you really think that Norfolk has pushed her upon his Grace's notice purposely, Will? In the hope of getting another royal marriage in their family at the expense of this carefully planned Protestant one?"

I got up from the stool on which I had been sitting. "Bear me witness that I always refused to credit it when people said that Thomas Howard rushed to his other niece, Anne Boleyn, to tell her that her husband was at the point of death so that her son might be born dead, and leave the pathway for his own daughter open. But now—now I am willing to believe anything." As I passed behind him I pressed my hands affectionately upon his shoulders. "Oh, John, John!" I exclaimed sadly. "How Court life stinks!"

"There are certainly some men about who make me prefer my monkeys," he said, finally shutting them into their cage and beckoning to one of his property men to take them away. Then he uncoiled his lithe body from the floor and came and threw an arm about my shoulders, his round, cheerful face quite serious. "It is because you are freshly come back to it—from an unblemished happiness which is the nearest we humans get to Heaven. Come and tell me about your new home, Will. It must be hard indeed to leave the sweetness of a new wife, but never forget the odd sparks of goodness which you and I have often found in the most unexpected people even here."

Most certainly it had been hard, and most truly I stood in need of such invaluable friendship. "The goodness of people whose devotion to truth as they see it ignores worldly gain or safety," I said, enlarging on the comfort of his theme. "People like Queen Katherine and Sir Thomas More and frail, brave old Bishop Fisher.

Though they died, their names burn like a row of steady candles lightening the darkness of our world."

"And the gay young goodness of men like Hal Norris," supplemented Thurgood.

"And the thrice-blessed goodness of all those kind kitchen folk who bring us surreptitious plates of food when we have had no time for a decent bite all supper time," we both spluttered laughingly, almost in unison, coming down to everyday things.

At supper we saw our prospective Queen, dressed in a strangely round-cut gown of cloth of gold strung with jewels, and surrounded by the plainest bunch of *jantlewomen* imaginable. Some unkind rumour was going round that the fair hair showing beneath her elaborate headdress was a wig. She certainly was not the type for Henry who, like most big men, liked his women small, feminine and dainty. To those of us who knew him well it was evident that he was making an immense effort to play his part as chivalrous host. But from the hurt glare in his eyes, coupled with the fact that few of his guests had sufficient English to understand the subtlety of a joke, any attempt at humour seemed out of place. Thurgood had solved the difficulty nicely, I felt, by entertaining the foreign ladies with the charming antics of his monkeys, who danced and pranced and curtsied to them to the lively strains of a jog played on the virginals. For myself, I attempted nothing, save when some time-serving wit tried to be funny about our defenceless foreign guest and I took it upon myself to teach him better manners.

"And speaking of monkeys," he said in a high, mincing voice, "how amusing is this new fashion of ladies wearing wigs to ape the Tudor hue!"

I had no means of knowing how much that is English Anne of Cleves understood, either of our language or of the reason for the strained atmosphere which prevailed. "Had you travelled much in Europe, Sir, you would know that for a great lady to wear her own hair would be as mean as for her to wear a coat of her own spinning," I told him sharply. I thought she looked towards me, but it was difficult to tell. As Holbein had said, and shown—her eyes looked straightly out on the world. And they were very tired and anxious eyes just then. She and her ladies asked leave to retire early, which was just as well, because at the crack of dawn on the next day, which was Sunday, Henry sent word to the Princess's apartments that he would be ready to marry her at eight o'clock—perhaps on the principle that things which cannot be avoided are best done quickly. We watched him, all resplendent in cloth of gold and crimson, striding up and down impatiently because the poor woman kept him waiting. "If it were not to satisfy my realm, or to avoid making a ruffle in the world where you have arranged it, I would not do what I must do this day for any earthly thing," I overheard him complain to Cromwell.

And one of the captains who had fetched her from Cleves and who happened to be standing within earshot, too, said to me regretfully, "Well, it pleased his Grace to dislike her, but to me she always appeared a brave lady."

The King went to her bedchamber that night in ceremonial nuptial procession and, according to her women, for many nights afterwards, but during each day he was as irritable as an ill-mated bull. More often than not he looked through me or waved me out of his way. Which was a blessing in disguise, because it left me free to go more often to Thames Street for stolen hours of happiness, and at the first opportunity I crossed London Bridge to try my fortune at the Marshalsea.

The very strength and age of the building dismayed me, and I was kept waiting for a long time at the porter's lodge. I had put on my shabbiest clothes so that I might pass for a turnkey's friend, and asked if I might speak to one Miles Mucklow. To my great relief the man was known, and at last came to me. "I have brought a message from your mother, Miles," I said, in the rough voice of the people, frowning him into silence before he could speak. "The man she now lives with has been killed in a tavern brawl and she begs you to pay her rent." It seemed to be a story in keeping with my surroundings. Staring open-mouthed, he yet had the sense to listen to my cock-and-bull story and to promise gruffly that if I came with him he would spare me a few groats for her. And once outside the lodge I was able to explain to him my real errand.

"A pleasant gentleman, Master Fermor," he said. "And I remembered you the moment I set eyes on you, Sir."

"And you once said that if ever there was anything you could do for me—"

"An' I'll not go back on my word," he vowed.

After a careful look round he led me up a narrow, ill-smelling stone stair and along a maze of foul-smelling passages, and, taking a great key from the jangling mass of iron hanging from his belt, unlocked a low-pitched door. "Only half an hour until I go off duty," he warned me in a whisper. And then I was in a small, cell-like room, alone with Richard Fermor. It had been as easy as that.

"Will!" he cried, in amazed joy, rising from a kind of truckle bed and throwing aside the book he had been reading.

I grasped both his hands, too moved for speech. My eyes searched his face, and I rejoiced to find it not too ravaged by the terrible shock of his experience.

"Did you wheedle a pass from the King—or that unspeakable Cromwell?" he asked, almost laughing in his eagerness.

"No. From that huge, hirsute gaoler, Mucklow—I once did him a service."

"Good indeed! He is more humane than most of them. He has been to sea, so we sometimes talk about ships and foreign ports when he has time. To talk to anyone helps to keep one sane. But to talk to you, Will, will be like a visit to Heaven."

"A brief visit, I fear."

We laughed awkwardly to cover our emotion. He cleared away a litter of possessions so that we could sit side by side on the roughly blanketed bed. "You will notice that I am not too badly treated," he said. "As a political prisoner I was allowed to bring books, ink, paper, warm clothing—even a lute to pass the time, though I am not the wizard with it that you are."

"And warmth?"

"As you see, they bring me a brazier—at a price! Sick as Emotte was when I left—home—she sewed money into my belt. And I still have a few assets in London which escaped even Cromwell's cruel nose. You know, Will, when I feel murderous, or despairing, I have only to compare my lot with poor Nicholas Thayne's."

"I have bad news for you from Buckingham. Bart Festing tells me that Nicholas Thayne died soon after you visited him."

"Small wonder, in that cold cell!"

We crossed ourselves and sat in silence thinking of his kindly goodness. "How few of us stand up to the world for what in our hearts we believe to be the truth!" said Fermor.

"And how he loved the family and the gardens at Neston!" I said, remembering how it was he who had first manoeuvred for a homesick lad the comfort of a meeting with Joanna. "But Father Thayne could take so much of his spiritual life into prison with him, whereas you—who have built up all those smoothly running strands of commerce, all those vast interests in various countries—"

He let his hand drop upon my knee. "I try not to think what is happening to them lest I go mad."

"Festing has gone to Calais to join Master John," I told him.

"I am glad. But, above all, what news have you of my daughter? What will become of her now, Will? I know that the Browns or other friends will take her in. But since having so much time in here to think, I have realised how selfish I have been in keeping her with me. She should have been comfortably married by now."

"She *is* married, Sir," I said quietly.

"Joanna married! You mean that good Northamptonshire fellow came forward after all and took her—dowerless?"

The moment of confession had come. I stood up and faced him. "No," I said sharply. "Joanna is married to me."

He let out a sound which might have indicated surprise or anger. He, too, sprang up, head held high. It could have been the instinctive pride which, years ago, would have repudiated such a thought with furious resentment. Then, slowly, his stance slackened into reasonable acceptance. His gaze passed round his prison room, assessing his misfortunate state. Then came to rest on my unyielding face, assessing me.

I was glad that he still thought of his daughter as being far above me as the sun and stars. No one could have been more utterly in agreement with him than I. But even so, through completely unforeseen circumstances, God had given her to me. "I do not always go about in darned hose and faded doublets," I said, grinning down at my unprepossessing attire. "It was to persuade people that I am Mucklow's bosom friend."

Slowly the smile on my face was reflected warmly on his. "In the filthiest rags you could be nothing less than our friend and equal, Will Somers. And I am glad and—grateful," he said, gripping my hand in his. "Where have you taken her?"

I told him about the arrangement we had made with the Festings, and how Joanna herself preferred this to going to her relatives in Aldermanbury.

"I realise that you cannot at the moment take any daughter of mine to Court, even had you adequate lodgings," Fermor said with a sigh. "And Heaven knows that I, on my side, would not have her breathe the same air as Cromwell!" He was not one to dwell on his bitterness, so went on quickly to speak of Emotte. "How I wish I had made over Wapenham to her! I always meant to do so in my will. I am afraid it is not in very good repair, but at least she would be near all her friends."

I remembered the disused priest house at Wapenham, the living of which had been in his advowson, and which was only a few miles from Easton Neston, and well understood his regret, as it would have made one small piece of his former world salvaged. He was much concerned for all who had worked for him, but his last thoughts and messages were all for his beloved daughter.

"I will go straight back to the wharf and tell her everything you have said. She will be overjoyed that I have seen you," I promised.

"Tell her I am well and warm, that her watch which she made me bring still ticks away the hours till I see her again, and that I am glad she has gotten herself so good a husband," he said, standing firm and dauntless in spite of all his cruel misfortune.

And then—in what seemed to be the flash of minutes—Miles Mucklow came to see me out.

Chapter Twenty-Four

IT WAS A STRANGE Court to which I returned, and all agog with whispered rumours. The King did not like his new wife and she had neither coquetry nor the art of flattery with which to win him. He complained to Cromwell that she waxed stubborn, at which we could scarcely wonder. He complained to Cromwell that he could not bring himself to beget sons on her, and most of us guessed that he was impotent. Since it was bullet-headed Cromwell who had urged him into this unfortunate marriage, he complained to him about everything. He had given him the earldom of Essex in gratitude for his negotiations, and now that there was nothing to be grateful for he grudged it to him.

The Tudor's eyes and appetite were ever turned towards the dainty Howard morsel which Norfolk and his scheming wife dangled so painstakingly before him. And in his chafing anger he agreed with Chancellor Cromwell that Lord Montague, the Countess of Salisbury's elder son, was conspiring with his brother Reginald Pole against him and that Lord Lisle, the Governor of Calais, was secretly acting as their go-between. Had not the Poles tried to stir up trouble because he divorced his first wife? And now they would meddle and rouse up his people—and his people's ineradicable sense of fair play—because he was trying to divorce his fourth. These arrogant Plantagenets were best swept out of the way. So Cromwell—who could probably have concocted some plausible charge against the Archangel Gabriel himself—had tried to regain the royal approval by convicting Montague and his kinsman, Courtney of Devon, of treason, and having them executed. For which the people hated *Cow Crommuck*, as they called him, more than ever.

"It seems only a few months ago that Montague was with us at Queen Jane's funeral," lamented milady Mary, as some of us were walking back with her from the bowling alley where the news had been brought to her. "Oh, God be thanked that Reginald Pole is safely in Rome!"

"And now a Cardinal, I hear," I said, knowing how much she had always cared for him and trying to cheer her.

"But have you heard, Will, that they have taken my beloved Lady Salisbury to the Tower—at her age, when she feels the cold so much. Though what offence they can bring against her blameless life I cannot imagine, unless it be that she was ever kind to me," said Mary Tudor bitterly.

"Or because, like any good mother, she refused to bear witness against her own sons," said her waiting woman, Bess Cressy, who was carrying her woods.

"Or simply because she is the daughter of the murdered Duke of Clarence, and niece to Edward the Fourth and Richard the Third," added Susan Toenge, her favourite lady.

"Or because Cardinal Reginald keeps crying milady Mary's wrongs in Rome," muttered Jane, the Princess's pampered female fool, who was in some ways no fool at all.

To take her mind from her own troubles I told milady of the imprisonment of my former master and—because I had long wanted to tell her of my happiness—I told her of my marriage to Joanna. With her usual goodness of heart her Grace wished us well.

But for her there was worse to come. In a final effort to regain the King's approbation, Cromwell excelled himself in rounding up victims. Mary's former tutor, Dr. Featherstone, and her late mother's chaplain, Father Abel, were dragged on hurdles to the flames at Smithfield together with a Protestant martyr, Dr. Barnes, because he denied the doctrine of transubstantiation. Which naturally provoked the witty French ambassador, Marillac, to many a caustic comment on the crazy inconsistency of our country. And then, as if poor Mary Tudor had not suffered enough, Cromwell's spies brought the aged Margaret Plantagenet, Countess of Salisbury, to the scaffold.

"All they could find against her was a bedgown embroidered with the arms of England—the Plantagenet leopards before the Tudor dragon joined them—which she had a perfect right to," Susan Toenge told me, when I hurried immediately to the Princess's apartments.

I found her Grace pale and exhausted with weeping. "Next to my mother I loved the Lady Margaret above anyone on earth," she said. "I was so happy to see her again when Queen Jane had me back at Court. And now I have no one of my own left." All her submissive protestations of filial loyalty had forsaken her, and it would have been vain at that moment to have reminded her that she had a father. "Oh, Will, Will, it was kind of you to come!" she cried. "You see how just as an ordinary act of human kindness was used as incriminating evidence against your Master Fermor, so a piece of family embroidery and a refusal to betray her sons has brought my friend and mentor to this terrible death. In public—at Smithfield—where we all used to be so gay, do you remember, watching tournaments and May Day dances." As if only physical movement could help her to bear the horror she visualised, Mary crossed to a window to stare out unseeingly. "The Lady Margaret was proud like my mother. She refused to bow her head before a common executioner. And while the men yelled their execrations at him and the women pleaded with tears, he chased his ageing victim round and round the block. Hacking—hacking—"

"My sweet lady, stop!" I cried, catching her blindly groping hands in mine while Randal Dod, her devoted manservant, and the women who loved her pressed around to carry her to bed. But she had sunk down upon the window seat and I signed to them to let her be a while first. To one so long shut up with grief, to sit and cry unrestrainedly must mean relief. We all remembered her as a happy, trusting child, and recognised the effort she must have made to hold such strong emotions so rigidly in check. At last she pulled herself upright, hands to throbbing temples and eyes blind with tears. "She is with my mother now in Paradise," she said huskily. "But if ever I had the power to revoke such things…"

"Oh, my lady!" exclaimed Bess, shocked by the set expression on her face.

Even in that hard moment Mary Tudor laid a reassuring hand on hers. "Well, well, my young brother will be King. Perhaps it is just as well that these matters will never rest with me." She rose with a sigh, and went, leaning on Dod's strong arm, and followed by her women, towards her bedchamber. Although she was a fine horsewoman, ever active of gait and still young, she walked that short distance like an old woman. Which brought home to me in a rush of compassion how much she must have suffered, in humiliation, fear and hurt love.

And as I stood looking after her with a hand still on the high, carved back of her chair, I was recalling an odd conversation I had had a few days earlier with Hans Holbein. He was already back in favour, and had been working on a portrait of the Prince which Henry wanted him to finish, and a quiet companionship had grown up between us two so that I often watched him at work, trying to learn something of his art and a good deal about my own country through the eyes of a foreigner. "His little Grace should be strong as his father when he grows to manhood," I had remarked cheerfully, as he put the finishing touches to a pink and dimpled arm.

"*If* he grows to manhood," the great artist had said.

He was bending over his palette and I wondered if I could have heard him aright. "But with that colour, those rounded cheeks—and Dr. Butts so pleased with him—" I expostulated, too low for the women amusing the Prince to hear me.

Casually, as if to select a different brush, Holbein turned to make sure that no one stood behind us. "I painted young Richmond. He had them, too," he said, adding a firmer line to the rattle which the pictured child held. "And there is that painting of your unfortunate Prince Arthur."

"You mean—" I had gasped, staring at him.

But he had become absorbed in his work again. "Only that

sometimes a painter sees more than a physician," he had answered cryptically, as Mother Jack came bustling forward to make sure her charge was not over-tired.

And now, as I watched the door close behind King Henry's elder daughter, this strange, almost casual conversation seemed to take on a still greater significance. I had seen all the happy ties with her mother's Court broken, everything their religion stood for swept away. And I wondered if it were a dangerous thing to make one small woman suffer so much. A woman who might, just conceivably, one day come to power—power to retaliate. A woman with a long-leashed desire to do the impossible—to build up again the world as she had first, and so happily, known it. And I wondered if the cruelties of Cromwell and the acquiescence of her father could ever bend back again, pliant as a whip, to scourge England.

I spoke some part of my thoughts to Edward Seymour, although by now my anxiety had veered to the immediate effects of such brutalities upon my royal master. "Surely the people will never forgive him," I said involuntarily, as we chanced to ride heel by heel behind his Grace through a sad and silent City.

"Oh, yes, they will forgive the King anything," said Seymour, Earl of Hertford, "as long as he appears to consult Parliament and makes our defences strong against the French."

"But—killing women? Even when it was the Boleyn, whom they did not love, they were sullen like this for days."

Seymour bent to adjust a rein more exactly. He was an exact and careful man. "Like all effective monarchs, ours has always been careful to keep a whipping boy. In the past the people blamed Wolsey. Now they will blame Cromwell."

"But they must know that none of these cruelties could be done without the King's consent."

"True. But seeing something is so much more persuasive than knowing it, particularly with people who do not think overmuch. They do not see him daily as we do, nor realise the way in which he has gradually changed. He has always been the right kind of figure-head, bluff and hearty and popular. Listen, Will Somers. If you had never lived at Court, and saw this same hearty figure of a man at ceremonial occasions or riding through the streets, how could you know that he had become altogether different inside?"

I could see that this was true enough. To us it had been a slow, sad realisation which we had had to live with. "It is his leg—" I began. But even the doctors were now forbidden to discuss the diseased state of his health.

I looked at Edward Seymour with new interest. I felt that my ill-advised groping for reassurance would be safe with him. He was neither handsome nor lovable like his younger brother, the swashbuckling Sir Thomas. But he was strong and humane and more deep-seeing than I had supposed. The Prince, for all that he was said to lisp precociously in Latin, was still but an infant. And although many an arrogant lord walked before Seymour in processions, nothing could alter the fact that he was the Prince's elder uncle and might one day become Lord Protector of England.

But I had been playing at being prescient of late. I must shake myself out of such weighty thoughts and play the fool, which was what my wages were paid me for. I fell behind milord Hertford and some of the other riders so that I might think up some means of cheering the whole household when we got back.

Although Mary Tudor had her own household she was now often at Court, and one bright spot in a calamitous spring was the very real liking which seemed to have sprung up spontaneously between the new Queen and herself. At first sight one might have judged them to be an oddly contrasted pair, but they were much of an age and both knew the humiliation of not being wanted. Mary helped her stepmother with the vagaries of English speech and customs and toned down her flamboyant taste in dress, while Flemish Anne, by dint of kindness and complete naturalness, broke down milady's tense reserve and even made her remember how to laugh.

"And now, just as we are getting used to hearing laughter at Court again," I told Joanna later, in the precious intimacy of our little home, "the King takes a blow at both of them."

"Oh, Will, is it something serious?" exclaimed my wife with her ever-ready sympathy.

"Not perhaps as serious as some people seem to think. Or rather,

I should say, the loss may prove to be more ours than theirs." I went to fetch a couple of tankards of well-spiced sack from the buttery, and pulled Joanna more comfortably against my shoulder on the settle before a cheerful fire. "I do not know how much you have heard, my love, but the King has now actually divorced his Flemish wife and, having thus offended Cleves, he was obliged to tell his daughter to return the handsome diamond cross which young Philip of Bavaria had given her."

"Is *every* marriage negotiation for our Princess to be broken off?" exclaimed Joanna.

I turned to kiss the tip of her small, indignant nose. "Did that prove such a calamity for us, with love waiting at the end?" I teased. "And Jane the Fool blurts out that her mistress could not send the lovely bauble back quickly enough. 'Duke Philip is a very kind gentleman,' says Jane, in that squeaky voice of hers, 'but my lady will be spared the pain of marrying a Lutheran!'"

Joanna had to laugh at my imitation of poor nit-wit, shaven-headed Jane. "But on what grounds can the King divorce *this* Anne?" she wanted to know.

"Oh, the usual convocation of clergy declaring the marriage null and void. On three points. That it was unwillingly entered into by the bridegroom, never consummated and marred by the bride's pre-contract to Lorraine. I suppose that one of the advantages of being Supreme Head of the Church is that one can make and unmake one's wives. If one is in the unenviable position of wanting to! It was all very quickly done. After all, Cranmer and the rest should be quite experienced by now. No good purpose would be served by the defendant being present, they said, because she was not familiar with our language. There had been one or two cases of plague in London as there always are in hot weather, so an excuse was made to send the Queen to Richmond while all this was going on. Though, as the French ambassador so pungently says, had they been very grave the King himself would have been the first away. And immediately the divorce was granted Henry sent Suffolk and Southampton and that toad, Secretary Wriothesley, there to tell her."

"Whatever in Heaven's name did she say?"

"Nothing, at first. She swooned from shock."

"Or fear? After all, whether she understands much English or not, the poor lady must have heard about what happened to—the other Queen Anne."

Others had said the same, but I had always maintained that the Flemish head was safe enough. "She probably had, but the King would no more have dared to do that to her than to Queen Katherine, whom he was trying to get rid of for so long. You see, neither of them was his subject, like Jane Seymour and Anne Boleyn. He would soon have had half Europe about his ears. No, my dear, this Anne is to be styled 'his dear sister' and to rank after the Lady Mary, to keep her household at his expense. And he is giving her Richmond Palace. And I think she probably fainted with shock at hearing how much money he was giving her with it—particularly after hearing about the meagreness of his own daughters' households."

"Oh, Will, you are making fun of it all. But after she recovered from the shock of—fear or relief or whatever it was—how did the poor Queen take it?"

"With remarkable serenity, they say."

"You mean she did not insist that she was his legal wife, as Queen Katherine did? After all, you have told me that he often slept with her."

Since I had come expressly to sleep with *my* wife, I took the opportunity of kissing her closely. "Perhaps she did not enjoy it very much, sweetheart," I suggested.

"Neither should I enjoy having a great fat man like that in my bed," giggled Joanna, snuggling more warmly up against me. "But what of her brother, the Duke? Surely he will make some sort of diplomatic protest?"

"He certainly will," I agreed, not caring much at the moment whether he did or not. "But now that France and Spain are making an alliance, little Cleves will not count for as much as Cromwell had hoped."

"And now Cromwell himself is in the Tower under sentence of death?"

"Well, nobody can be sorry for that," I said, thinking of the poor Countess of Salisbury and milady Mary's distress, and how things might now be made easier for the Fermors. "And up to the last, while he was in the Tower, the King still made use of him, forcing him to bear witness in a letter that the marriage was made unwillingly. And they say that the divorced Queen has written to her brother, Duke William, entreating him not to make trouble and assuring him that she is well used in England."

"But how will she be called, being now the King's sister?"

"My Lady of Cleves."

"And you mean to tell me, Will, that after being brought to England and so insulted she has just meekly done everything the King wanted?"

I had to laugh at recollection of the King's face when he was told. "A shade too meekly, perhaps," I said. "He is so accustomed to having women fight for the right to call him husband that I fancy the easiness with which she let him go must have shaken him considerably." As I went to the door to call to young Tatty to prepare our bed half my mind was still on my master's marital affairs. "After all, Joanna, she may not have wanted to go back to all that strict maternal supervision we heard about in Cleves, and she may *prefer* having her own life to having Henry. And, as I say, in his grateful relief he has heaped manors upon her and given her far more money than she would ever have had the free spending of as his wife. *And* Richmond."

"Why do you say Richmond like that, with a kind of ecstatic sigh, as if it were part of Heaven?" asked Joanna laughingly, as I pulled her to her feet.

"Do I?" I said, as we went upstairs together. "It must be because I have seen the gardens and those bulbous fairy turrets from the river. And because the King himself always speaks of it that way. It was his family home and his mother lived there, and I suppose he thinks of it as a place full of love and sunshine and laughter, where the cares and cruelties of an ambitious world fall away."

Chapter Twenty-Five

I WAS GLAD WHEN Lord Vaux came back from the Channel Islands after his Governorship was ended. I knew he would do what he could in the Fermor cause, and now that Cromwell had been executed our efforts might meet with more success. Wriothesley would have his day, but Seymour was the coming man.

"How different the Court seems, Will!" Vaux said with a sigh, when at last he had time to walk with me alone along the *vrou* walk, as the servants had come to call that pleasant path at Hampton which the Flemish Queen and her ladies had liked to use.

"A place for older, more materially-minded men," I said, and knew that we were both thinking of those cultured young gallants who, but for the Boleyn witch, might yet have graced the scene. "But Surrey is still with us to make verse. And now we hope to have yours, milord."

He shrugged my praise aside with a new and becoming modesty. He had matured during his travels.

"What is all this I hear from my sister Maud in Calais about her father-in-law? Is it really possible that he has been imprisoned and stripped of everything? And all for visiting their priest, a crime of which I have often been guilty. You know that ours was imprisoned for refusing to take the Oath of Supremacy, too?"

I gave him all the family news and told him how I had seen Richard Fermor in the Marshalsea. And how I had had the amazing happiness of marrying his daughter.

"Maud wrote to tell me about that also—and how relieved they were for Joanna. Then, since my sister is married to your wife's brother, you are in some sort my kinsman, Will Somers," he said, holding out a ready hand. "So perhaps you had best stop addressing me as milord and call me Thomas. Have you told the King you are married?"

"I told him I was going on my honeymoon the day he himself set out to meet his bride. But, as I intended, he took it all as a part of my fooling. But I hope to tell him in all seriousness when I find an opportunity to plead for my father-in-law."

"I, too, will speak for him if I can," he promised. It would, of course, be to his sister's advantage if he could.

"Say rather *when* you can. More and more it becomes a matter of choosing one's moment. You will find the King much changed," I warned.

"Physically, you mean?"

"Ever since he has had that running fistula his temper has been more uncertain."

"You think it is the syphilis?"

"The doctors are not allowed to discuss it. Whatever it is, it seems to change his nature. Though he grows more despotic, I believe that inside himself he is more fearful and suspicious."

"Which might account for such barbarous cruelty to the few remaining Plantagenets."

I nodded. "Yet in some ways his powers wane. He is amorous of Katherine Howard, but with nothing of the devastating passion he had for her cousin Anne. He is always pawing this one in public as old men will."

"According to Norfolk he really means to marry her."

"Some say Archbishop Cranmer has already made her the King's wife."

"His *fifth*!"

I shrugged. "I have lost count," I said. "And interest," I thought. From then on anyone whom the Tudor might marry would be but one of his women to me.

"After all, in this age of grace, plenty of men—like Suffolk, for instance—run through at least four," Vaux was saying broad-mindedly.

"They marry them the moment they are come to puberty and wear them out in continuous childbirth."

"And then, when the first heat of their desires dies down, they marry again and again into rich families to increase their estates."

"Listen to a couple of old cynics in their late thirties!" grinned Thomas Vaux, giving me a friendly dig in the ribs. "Or is it that few men love and cherish their wives as we do?"

We had reached the old moat wall, and sat there awhile in the warm afternoon sunshine in companionable silence. I think he felt strange at Court with so many new faces and was sadly aware of deterioration and loss of brilliance, and each of us found comfort in having someone connected by family ties and interests to whom we could unburden our minds without cautious forethought. "That hussy Katherine," he began presently. "It is not her fault, poor wench. After her gallant father died she was dragged up with the Dowager-Duchess's maids. But even before I went away there were stories going the rounds about her which, if the King should come to hear of them, would stop all thought of matrimony. And if he finds out *afterwards* there will be no more joyous poems from Surrey, I am afraid. Nor any more ambitious family plans from his father Norfolk."

"Whatever may have happened in the past she is ardently in love with Tom Culpepper now. It is plain for all to see," I said.

"A pity about this Flemish Princess," said Vaux ruminatively. "At least she has dignity, judging by her portrait. Tell me, Will—and I swear it shall go no further—can you really believe that marriage was never consummated?"

I shook my head doubtfully. "The one thing the King wants—and has always wanted—more than he has desired any woman—is strong, legitimate sons. If you ask me, he would scarcely miss the chance to come by one."

"Then presumably he is impotent."

We were talking dangerously, but suddenly Thomas Vaux began to laugh. He leaned back and laughed aloud, his neat, pointed beard quivering with mirth.

"What is it?" I asked, hating to miss a jest in a world which was becoming all too solemn for me.

He clutched my arm. "Suppose Henry underrated his virility," he spluttered. "Suppose, Will, just suppose—that after all that solemn tarradiddle at the divorce proceedings—my lady of Cleves found herself pregnant—at Richmond—*now!*"

"Now she is called the King's sister? And he married to the Howard. What a situation!" I elaborated, joining in his laughter. "In truth, kinsman Thomas, it would be the biggest joke in all his Grace's reign."

We were still laughing helplessly when a swish of skirts on the grass and a woman's voice recalled us to decorum. His lady wife had come through the gardens to look for him. "My good Thomas, I thought you must have thrown yourself in the Thames for very boredom with this changed and wearisome Court. But since you and our good friend Will here have found something amusing I pray you let me share your mirth," she entreated charmingly.

We slid from the wall and brushed the dust from our hose. I bowed and milord offered her his arm. "No, no, my love. 'Twas but one of Will's more disreputable jokes. The kind with which he amuses the King in his cups," he excused himself—mightily unfairly, I thought. "Though I doubt," he added, looking back at me to bat an eyelid, "whether this particular one would amuse his Grace over much."

But kings and jokes all went out of my mind when I arrived at Thames Street that evening and Joanna whispered against my shoulder that she was with child. I exclaimed over her and kissed her, feeling that I held my whole world in my arms. "We will call him Richard," I announced, knowing that she would wish this, too, and certain that we should have a boy. And that evening we walked across Tower Hill and out through Aldgate to the pleasant hamlet and fields of Shoreditch, in moonlight and the peak of married happiness, eagerly deciding what school he should attend and what profession he should pursue.

"There will be no inheritance from my father and he may not have the ready wit to become a jester," Joanna reminded me.

"One of your father's friends would right willingly apprentice him to the wool trade. Or he could be a vintner like the Chaucers, or a mercer like the Browns. Most of the money these days is made by merchants," I mused.

"He could be a printer like Caxton or a learned translator like Tyndale. There are sure to be more and more books, Will."

"Or an explorer like Magellan, sailing right out into uncharted seas to prove the world is round," I suggested, still hot for my boyhood's hero.

"Oh, no!" she protested. "For then, as we grew old, we should never see him."

During the months which followed I tried to be with her as often as I could, to cherish her and keep her thoughts from grieving for her father. I exhorted a delighted Tatty to take the utmost care of her mistress. Lady Vaux came to visit us, bringing Joanna peaches and grapes from their country garden. John Thurgood, who had long since fallen victim to my wife's charms, could scarcely be kept away. He took her books of amusing plays and, somewhat prematurely, a small set of puppets which he had carved for our small son to play with. And one unexpected visitor we had that winter was Colin, my eldest cousin from Shropshire, come to settle about some taxes in London and to tell me that my dear old Uncle Tobias was dead. My aunt sent her grateful love to me for such small things as I had sent her, farm and family were prospering and Colin himself was now the father of two sturdy boys by the Tarleton girl whom he had been courting in the neighbouring village of Condover.

"And the Priory?" I asked, well knowing what sort of answer to expect, having seen the sad desolation of Merton Abbey when staying with the King at Oatlands.

"Being gradually demolished. The fine nave be all pulled down and the choir where you used to sing—an' the stones, some of 'em, gone to build Master Tyrrell's pig-sties. Only the Prior's house be saved to house some stranger. Even the great kitchens, where the lay brothers used to dole out food to the destitute, is become an inn."

"And the good monks themselves?" I asked, remembering their finely trained voices.

My honest, shock-headed cousin shrugged. "Homeless an' roaming the roads, I reckon. Beggars themselves by now, most like."

Tatty made up a bed for him in the attic and showed him some of the sights of London. And Joanna fed him and showed him every kindness. But when it was time for him to mount his strong farm horse I had no desire to go with him. Now that Uncle Tobias and the Priory were both gone I felt that I could never bear to see Much Wenlock again.

And when Joanna's time was drawing near there came that most welcome visitor of all. That indomitable woman, Emotte, who made the journey with the only maidservant left to her and stayed with us until Joanna was up and about again.

"There is nothing you could have done for which a man could be more grateful," I told her with a fervent embrace when my son was safely born.

"*You* went to see my brother in prison," she said, in that short, unemotional way of hers.

"And, God helping me, I will one day get him out," I promised. Her loving look and my wife's eyes shining at me from the bed made me feel a poor, inadequate sort of knight errant. "But with the King one has to await the right moment," I explained apologetically, as I had so often been forced to tell myself.

But through a series of unexpected happenings and the kindness of two great ladies my moment was to come sooner than I had dared to hope.

For fear of making trouble for Miles Mucklow I had not gone again to the Marshalsea, but, being swollen with paternal pride, I felt that I must give Richard Fermor news of his new grandson. I took him the loving letter and the dainties which Joanna had prepared, but Mucklow dared not let me stay for long. "The Governor is all on edge about people coming in and out just now because of all these fresh cases of plague," he explained. But in the excitement of seeing Richard Fermor the words washed over me at the time. There was so much news to tell, and so short a time in which to tell it. He had heard about the Cleves marriage and Cromwell's execution, and most of the Court gossip. But he was avid for family news and delighted about his small namesake. To my great relief, my father-in-law looked reasonably well. He kept up his spirits by reading and writing a useful account of foreign towns which he had visited. He was allowed to take exercise in some inner courtyard and refused the money which I had brought.

"How do the other prisoners manage to live?" I asked, as he showed me the modest supply of money still left in the cunning lining which Emotte had made to the leather of his Florentine belt.

"The baser kind spend much of their time making counterfeit coins which some of the gaolers have found a brisk market for at a stiff commission—particularly among unsuspecting foreign visitors," said Fermor, sampling one of Joanna's honey cakes with relish. "But many a poor devil would starve, I fear, were it not for milady Mary's donations for them."

"The Lady Mary!" I exclaimed, marvelling that I, who had known her from her childhood, should yet have had no inkling of this bounty. "But she herself has had so little—in the past, I mean, when she was sharing her household with the young Lady Elizabeth, and when but for her kindness the child would have had scarce enough clothes to stand up in. Do you mean that she has always done this?"

"And to the Fleet Prison as well, I believe," Richard Fermor told me. "Her mother always helped the prisoners, and whatever the Lady Mary's personal privations, her Grace has never let the payments cease. There is not a man here, however debased, who does not bless her name."

I returned home because I knew that Joanna would be longing for news of him, but had to hurry back to Whitehall before sunrise. Yet in the grey light of dawn I saw a cross chalked on a door quite close to our house in Thames Street, and almost stumbled over the half-naked corpse of a woman callously thrown out on a stinking laystall at the corner of Paul's Wharf. Instantly the words of Miles Mucklow came back to me. "More cases of plague," he had said. One heard it so often, and small wonder, with the filth thrown from bedroom windows to overflowing gutters, and cattle still being slaughtered within the city walls. But here in our own street, so near my loved ones! I almost turned back to drag them from our comfortable home, but had nowhere to take them. Let them sleep while I thought what best to do. Perhaps someone at the palace could help me.

The King, they said, had been asking for me. But I pushed past the pestering pages and made my way to the comptroller of the household's rooms. Perhaps in this overcrowded hive at Whitehall he could find me some accommodation. If not I was prepared to tell him my private concerns and beg leave to bring my unsanctioned wife and child into my own lodgings, risking the royal displeasure. But Sir John Gage's clerk did not know where his master was.

"Then go and find him," I snapped.

"But, Master Somers, he may well be with his barber at this early hour."

He was a meek little man, already over-burdened with work, and to my shame I hit him, in one of those sudden brief outbursts known at Court as Somers's rages. "I care not if he be with the Devil himself," I bellowed. "Go find him."

There was a light step behind me. "Will!" exclaimed a shocked contralto voice. I swung round, still aggressive, and there was milady Mary immediately behind me, coming along the gallery on her way from early Mass.

"What is wrong with you, Will? What has the poor man done?" she asked, waving her ladies to a standstill behind her, while the little rabbit of a clerk bolted back into his burrow rubbing his reddened jaw.

"Everything is wrong," I said roughly.

"But surely not so wrong but what, with God's help, we can put it right?" she said quietly. By her use of the plural pronoun she was deliberately associating herself with my stress. And suddenly I had a mental picture of her, denying herself a much-needed new gown and writing instructions in her own careful hand that the money should go to feed a horde of miserable ne'er-do-wells in prison. If she helped them, surely she would help me, whom she cared for?

"It is the plague, milady—in Thames Street," I burst out, finding myself unutterably glad to tell her.

"And you want to move your wife and new babe to safety—and have nowhere to go?"

"I *must* get them away." I saw again the dead, disfigured body of that young woman lying in the filth at Paul's Wharf, and remembered that the King's daughter had once said to me, just as Miles Mucklow had, "If ever there should be anything that I can do for you—" I looked round at the quiet, contented faces of her ladies, with the reflection of their prayers still like a soft radiance upon them. It was the first favour I had ever asked for myself since I came to Court. "I suppose that your Grace could not—"

She followed the direction of my eyes, guessed my hope, but shook her head regretfully. Then she walked away from me to the window and back, her head bent in thought. Small as she was, she somehow looked remarkably like her mother then, less carefree than others because her thoughts must ever go out to her responsibilities in the world. It was the *trait* for which the people had always loved them both. When she came back to me her hands were folded severely beneath her wide sleeves, but her brown eyes were smiling. "You know, Will, that I cannot take the daughter of a political prisoner into my household even if I would. I am too—"

In Cromwell's time she might well have said "beset with spies"—but she changed the sentence with a deprecating smile. "My household is still carefully *surveyed*, shall we say? But do not look so downcast, dear Will. I have an idea. This very afternoon I go to visit my Lady of Cleves at Richmond and I will ask her if she has room in her household for your wife. She loves children, is not suspected of Papist tendencies, and since she has so uncomplainingly made her home there no one seems to concern themselves with what she does. Indeed, she has far more liberty than I."

I seized her hand and kissed it. "You would do this for me—" I mumbled, wildly incoherent with gratitude.

"It is not much. She is easily approached and very kind. And have you not always come to me when I have been in trouble? Have I not told you, you are as a part of our family? So be at the water steps when my barge returns and I will tell you what milady

Anne says." She would have left me then, but seeing that I did not answer, she added anxiously, "What is it, Will? Does my plan not please you?"

"Oh, your Grace, I cannot think of any refuge I would choose for my family rather than Richmond. But—but could I not bring them *now*—in your Grace's barge? Lest the plague should spread—"

She looked at me with raised brows and the suspicion of a smile on her lips. Perhaps she was laughing at my cowardice for them—she who had faced so much—but I could not care. "How you love her! I have never before seen the King's irrepressible fool all of a tremble." She nodded assent and beckoned to Randal Dod to tell him we should be of the party. "It must be wonderful to be loved like that!" I heard her murmur with a sigh, as she passed on to her apartments.

And so my wife and child went to the safety and sunshine of Richmond. To that place of sunshine where cares and cruelties fall away. My Lady of Cleves, on her Grace's recommendation, received my wife with every kindness. She even seemed to remember me from out of all the welter of English people whom she must have seen at Court.

"I think *you* were once kind to *me*," she said, when I tried to thank her. "Ze leetle matter of ze wig." Seeing that I did not remember, she explained in her rapidly improving English. "The Norfolk Duchess tell me it is ze custom in your country to wear one. She even brought me one, yellow and crimped. So that my Dutch cap will not cover it and I look ugly. Some ill-bred man laugh and I hear you—how you say?—downdress him."

"I did not know how much you understood, milady," I said, recalling the incident.

"Kindness, in any language, is always easy to understand. And that first night at supper I was so much afraid."

"You did not show it, Madam."

"No," she agreed thoughtfully. "It is always better not to show when one is afraid. But coming into a strange country—I was so much afraid of all those gentlemen and ladies. Most of all the ladies, who could laugh at my so different clothes and ways…"

"And of the King, I suppose," I said, listening to her with great sympathy.

But to my surprise she laughed, surprisingly and wholeheartedly. "Nein! Nein!" she said. "I vas never afraid of your King. Not after that first terrible day at Rochester. A man—one manages him—like...." She did not say "like a spoiled boy," but her smiling glance slid to my half-naked, red-haired son sprawled on the daisy-strewn grass a few yards away.

The Lady Mary, who had never managed a man in her life, looked slightly shocked. While my wife and I, trying to control our laughter, hoped above all things that life would one day give us an opportunity of seeing our hostess managing Henry Tudor.

Richmond Palace was far too vast for the Flemish lady's household, and with a sweep of her wide generosity its mistress assigned to us a pleasant lodging in the wardrobe court, large enough to accommodate me whenever I could leave my duties to come, and with a little room for Tatty. I had only to take boat across the river whenever the Court was at Hampton, as it was more and more often these days. And we soon found that there were often other small children about the gardens because the King's divorced wife, denied a family of her own, seemed to have adopted half the destitute infants of the neighbourhood. And it did not take long to discover that these orphaned infants were cared for with practical common sense, rather than with the spasmodic sentimentality with which other wealthy ladies sometimes indulged this whim.

"Everything is so well run," Joanna told me later, full of admiration for Flemish efficiency. And because she herself had so painstakingly learned to control a thriving manor house beneath Emotte's expert tuition, she was able to repay some of milady of Cleves's kindness by taking charge of the herb garden and supervising servants in the stillroom.

"Do these servants never quarrel?" I asked on one of my happy visits, being freshly come from the frequent backstairs wranglings and jealousies of the King's household.

"I often hear them *laughing*," said Joanna, sinking down amid spread skirts upon the greensward beside me, and helping our sturdy, auburn-haired son to crawl towards a coveted dandelion. "But, being rather more adept at baking and brewing and butter-making than they are themselves, milady manages to keep them too pleasantly occupied to have much time for *quarrelling*."

Spurred to efficient management herself, she sat up and began to give me my orders. "Have you remembered to send the Festings the rent for all these weeks we have not been using their house of happy memories? And will you sometime take me back there to make sure Gerda's beds are aired?"

"I sent the money by the Captain of the *Hopewell* last week. And I will take you back," I promised, like a model husband. "But not until the last danger from the plague is over, because I find you extraordinarily precious." Having a long evening ahead of me when I must help to entertain the new Howard Queen's more youthful company, I stretched myself out gratefully on the grass to enjoy the pleasant view of cattle grazing in lush meadow grass across the river. "God has been very good to us, Joanna," I said, stealing one of the hands from her lap. "Here in this secluded place we seem to be free from politics and all social strivings and ambitious bickerings."

"And from God-Almighty kings!" laughed Joanna, who sometimes resented the unpredictable exigencies of my unique profession.

Chapter Twenty-Six

B UT, LIFE BEING WHAT it is, we were not to be free from kings for long. Henry was nothing if not impulsive. And now that he was married to a pleasure-loving girl-wife, he rose at dawn to keep down his weight with a game of tennis, took to archery again and was more than ever inclined to plan some expedition on the spur of the moment.

"Let us take barge and go to Richmond this warm August morning," he suggested to a half-dozen or so gentlemen who were breaking their fast with him at Hampton.

I stopped dead in the middle of an absurd story I had resurrected for the benefit of a visiting Frenchman, wondering just what I had better do about Joanna. Sir Thomas Wriothesley's mouth opened and stayed open like a carp's. Archbishop Cranmer coughed deprecatingly. And Lord Vaux and the others glanced towards where the new Queen Katherine was sitting with her ladies to see how she had taken her husband's tactless suggestion.

But Norfolk's little niece was as unaware of dangerous shifts of royal favour as her uncle was ever on the lookout for them. And she was utterly devoid of malice. "I pray you commend me to my Lady of Cleves and ask her for the recipe for that excellent herbal drink for headache which she gave me when she was here," she said, smiling sweetly at her husband but holding a hand to her head.

"Then you will not be coming with us?" In a swirl of wide, silk-lined sleeves and swinging short coat Henry was at her side.

"Your head aches again, my poor poppet?" he said, instantly all concern.

"A little. So I pray you excuse me. But could we not invite your Flemish sister to visit us at Hampton one day soon? It would be pleasant to see her again."

Henry was delighted. Never had two women been so amenable. "I will do so, my love. And do you rest quietly until our return," he urged. He had not been watching the quick satisfaction on Tom Culpepper's face as I had. Tom, who was on palace duty that day. Clearly the Howard girl had wits, but kept them for more immediate and personal issues than whether the King's interest might ever stray back to Cleves again.

So a dozen or so of us prepared to crowd into the royal barge to watch this peculiar encounter. "Will the lady have enough victuals for us, being taken unawares?" Cranmer had the kindly thought to ask.

"She must be used to being taken unawares by now," Thomas Vaux reminded him as we waited on the water stairs.

"And even if she was once caught without stays, she is unlikely to be shamed by any shortage of victuals," I assured them.

"I would not miss this for a fortune!" Vaux whispered to me behind the Archbishop's back. "But what will you do, Will, if the King learns about Joanna?"

"God knows!" I said, flopping down into the swaying barge and mopping my brow.

The oarsmen seemed to have rowed only a few strokes before we were drawing alongside the palace at Richmond. It seemed only a moment of time before the King was being received by a very surprised looking Flemish steward. But there was no panic. "My lady is in the rose garden," he said, bowing low, and soon we were trooping after them through orderly and spotless courtyards and out into the privy garden by another archway. And there was the lady who had so briefly and so recently been Queen of England diligently repairing some of the priceless but neglected old tapestries with her ladies grouped about her, and my wife among them with a wooden cradle by her side. They rose like a row of dutiful children when their teacher appears.

To say that they all looked surprised, and my wife positively horrified, would be less than the truth.

"Who is it, Guligh?" asked the Lady Anne, whose back was towards us.

And when her massive steward announced that it was his Grace the King, she rose considerably more slowly than her ladies, letting her piece of the long tapestry fall unheeded to the grass, and made the lowest imaginable obeisance. She was not the most graceful of women, but probably did it to give herself time. When a well-born woman is suddenly confronted by a man whom she has not seen since he called her a Flemish mare and divorced her she probably needs time. But when the King greeted her—a trifle too exuberantly in his last-minute nervousness—as his dear and esteemed sister, she rose to the role and to the occasion marvellously.

"I do not need to zay how we are honoured," she greeted him pleasantly. And then, with a swift, calculating glance at the rest of us, she said to Guligh, "Tell the servants to lay eight extra places for dinner." And to herself, no doubt, "Can the wretch *never* let me know when he is going to appear?"

She began to present to him Madam Lowe and the rest of her ladies, but Henry was scarcely interested. Roused by so much sudden movement my small son had begun to whimper and Henry's eyes were riveted on the cradle, which was so close to our hostess's chair and so incongruously the centre of this spinster household. I saw my wife step forward, apologetically, ready to remove him to obscurity. But the Lady Anne was quicker. With a covert glance at her erstwhile husband she scooped up the yelling infant, gathered him into the most maternal of embraces and began to soothe him as if he were more important to her than even her exalted guests. If there was the suspicion of a grin on her wide mouth, it was effectively hidden against his cheek.

All conversation ceased. And so almost immediately, did the whimperings. And the King of England, standing staring in astonishment, said, "He has Tudor hair."

I felt Thomas Vaux grip my arm in an ecstasy of enjoyment. But for my own immediate problem I could have matched it with my

own. It was his mad, unlikely jest—or rather a mischievous counterfeit of it—being enacted before our enraptured eyes.

"It *is* a boy?" asked Henry, moving a step forward to peer into
the rosy little bonneted face.

"Oh, yes, your Grace. And well grown, do you not think, for
three months?"

We could almost see the King making mathematical calcula-
tion. Three months, and nine months. And just a year since he
had divorced her. He put out a podgy hand and touched the babe,
as if to make sure that he was real, and my offspring obligingly
belched and smiled blandly back at him—red hair, blue eyes and
all. Clearly Henry coveted him. And clearly he was the most bewildered man in Christendom.

"I trust her Grace the Queen is well," Anne was saying politely
in her careful English, as if all unaware of his dilemma. "Or if she
should be indisposed that it may be for the coming of a fine boy
child like this one."

As we all knew, apart from migraines feigned in order to spend
more time alone with Tom Culpepper, the Queen's health gave no
cause either for anxiety or rejoicing.

"The Flemish woman plays him like a fish!" muttered Vaux at
my ear. "Whoever started this rumour that she was stupid?"

And Henry, unable to bear the uncertainty any longer, blurted
right out with what was in his mind, "Is he yours, Madam?"

Never have I seen a look of such shocked virginity on any
woman's face as milady of Cleves achieved. "Sir! What do you
accuse me of? A defenceless woman in a strange land. And before
all these gentlemen.…"

And Henry, knowing only too well that she had already been
insulted past what most women would bear, and fearing that his
words might put an end to her patience, or to her brother the
Duke's, fell into her trap and discredited the bluff of their divorce.
"Anne, my dear Anne, I did not mean that," he hurried to explain,
lowering his voice. "Only—is he—ours?"

Cranmer and Wriothesley, who had helped to frame the decree
partly on the King's assertion that the marriage had never been

consummated, drew in their breath, cringing almost visibly with discomfort. The rest of us were merely her delighted audience. And naturally she needed an audience. For this was her way of vindicating herself, as Katherine of Aragon had tried to do—only Anne's version was so much more painlessly performed. "But how can your Grace suggest such a possibility, since I am your sister?" she asked, the shocked expression on her face giving place to something approaching blank imbecility. She beckoned to Joanna. "I was going to present to you this lady of my household, Joanna Somers, who is the baby's mother."

"And my wife," I told him, pushing my way proudly past all my betters and so exhilarated by Anne's masterly performance that I had forgotten to fear his displeasure.

Henry turned and looked at me with limp relief. I think for the moment he believed that I was merely helping him out of an awkward predicament in which a witless foreign woman had somehow involved him. "You mean that that attractive red-haired atom is yours?" he said, passing a hand over his perspiring forehead. "How do you call him?"

"Richard," I told him, knowing well enough that in all subservience the name should have been Henry. "After my wife's father, Richard Fermor."

"Richard Fermor, a Calais stapler," recalled Henry. "I well remember his bringing you to Court, and walking with me from the bowling green, and our interesting talk about our trade in foreign countries. A practical, well-informed man."

"Whom Cromwell recently imprisoned for infringing your Grace's Statute of Praemunire," Wriothesley had to remind him. "He was caught visiting and giving money to a proscribed priest."

"A well-loved family priest, too old to take to new ideas, who was dying," put in Lord Vaux, coming to our rescue.

"All Master Fermor's estates were stripped from him, else I should not have presumed to marry his daughter, whom I have loved ever since I served him most humbly as a clerk," I said.

Henry raised Joanna from her curtsy and patted her hand approvingly. "As pretty a love story as ever I heard. You ever had good taste, Will. And Thomas Cromwell was ever a good minister to the Crown," he said non-committally, evidently having no intention of interfering with anything which had enriched the depleted royal coffers. "But why did you not tell me, all this time, that you were married?"

"Harry, I did," I insisted. "That day when you were leaving Greenwich to meet your—the bride you then had. Do you not remember my saying that I, too, was going on my honeymoon?"

"And you talked some nonsense about spending it in the city of London. Go to, man! No man believed you, specially not I, who have always called you a confirmed monk."

"'Yet in his folly a fool sometimes speaks the truth,'" I quoted, and would have liked to add "and it is obvious that the monk spent his time more profitably than the masterful king," but did not dare. Impotence and money were two subjects upon which one did not twit the Tudor.

Having a stag party of guests, Anne of Cleves, like a wise woman, lost no time in feeding them. And when the anxious Archbishop saw the laden tables he nodded to me as one who gives a minor prophet best. I saw to it, for our hostess's sake, that it was a merry meal. And for me it was a happy one because for the first time in the King's presence my own wife took part. There was a good thick pottage followed by roasted venison, boar's head served with mint jelly, and a delicious eel pie, a dish on which the King doted. And every course was served piping hot.

"I shall have to borrow your cook," said Henry, guzzling up the last of his gravy. Whereat some of the Flemish ladies began to giggle delightedly. "Then you will have to take back milady Anne," her life-long friend, Madam Lowe, told him triumphantly. "For she made that tasty eel pie with her own hands."

For the first time our hostess looked embarrassed. She may have gathered that in this strange land it was considered derogatory for high-born ladies to use their hands for anything less elegant than embroidery. And her own were so eagerly capable. "It is true that some of my ladies and I were having a trial of cookery just before your Grace arrived," she admitted, looking down at them apologetically.

But Henry, for his part, was looking at her with a new, if puzzled, respect. He had had five wives and most of them had been talented. They could discourse in Latin and design altar cloths, make music on a variety of instruments and shine socially. Even the foolish child he now had could dance adorably with younger men so that he did not want to take his eyes off her. But not one of them, so far as he knew, had ever been able to cook. And not even his own master cook at Hampton could concoct an eel pie like the one he had just eaten. So he rested his hands contentedly across his enormous stomach and awaited the next appetising course of mulberry tart and cream.

When at last the Archbishop had asked a blessing our hostess left the King to doze awhile. Like the rest of us, she probably suspected that when a man is fifty, living up to a skittish young wife must be quite a strain. But when he roused himself and the servants began to clear she asked him if he would like to look round his palace and see the slight alterations she had made. It was tactful, of course, not to say "my" palace; but it was not until we had trailed round after them for an hour or more that most of us realised what a temptation it must have been to say "vast improvements" instead of "slight alterations."

"I was glad to see you repairing that neglected tapestry which my father brought from Antwerp," he had said graciously, but she was set on showing him the kitchens.

"I see you have converted one of the big bread ovens into a serving hatch," he noticed at once, not quite so graciously.

"Which is why your dinner was hot," she countered. "During my—my stay—at Hampton it always worried me that the servants had to bring the dishes all that way from the kitchens and up the length of the great hall, so that by the time they reached our table they were cold. I should have liked to build a small kitchen in that courtyard behind the watching chamber and have had a serving door made leading straight through to the dais."

It was a feasible idea and Henry, who hated half-cold food and was interested in domestic matters, listened attentively.

She showed him the well-stocked benchings in her cellars, the plump pigeons in her dovecots, the well-tended fruit in her walled orchard and the ripening grapes in her vinery. For the first time she was meeting her former husband on her own ground, talking to him about things which she understood and in which he was interested. Seeing what she had done for Richmond perhaps he was beginning to think, as we were, that the three-thousand-pound annuity he had made her was not so lavish after all.

And finally she went before him up the carved staircase to the best bedchambers and opened the door of the one which had been his mother's. The one which most women in her position would have used for themselves. And as she did so a sweet scent of rosemary and thyme drifted out to us. "Why, you have kept it just as it used to be," I overheard him say in the kind of voice men use in church. "Even to her hour-glass…"

"And the embroidered stool beside her bed where I expect you stood to bid her 'good morning' when you were a small boy," said Anne, very gently.

"And there are fresh rushes—"

"I have them changed every week and myself cut up the bay leaves to sweeten them," she told him. "I hoped it would please you, Henry."

He went into the quiet room and she had the good sense and delicacy to close the door behind him. We all went downstairs and streamed out into the sunlit garden again, where milady of Cleves talked politely with her strangely assorted guests—or, to be exact, listened to them while they talked. She was that kind of woman, and however well she had carried off such an embarrassing and unexpected visit, it must have been a strain even to so healthy a woman as she.

The gnomon shadow on the sundial by which I was standing had slid round quite a way before the King came out to rejoin us. He came almost unobserved and quite unattended, and for the time being he was a kinder man. He was neither strutting nor straddling, and had more the look of the good sportsman he used to be. But Anne pretended not to have seen him and suddenly decided that her other guests must inspect the beautiful Flemish horses her brother had sent her, and rounded them up for a visit to the stables. All except myself and Thomas Vaux, who was talking to Joanna a few yards away on the other side of the sundial. And as she passed me I felt a sharp nip on my arm. "*This ees your moment,*" the Lady Anne hissed in my ear, and went straight on, keeping the rest of the party on the move like a flock of chattering fowls, so that by the time the King had crossed to the centre of the garden where four box-edged paths joined we three were there by the sundial alone.

I knew that she was right. This was my moment, and she—the discarded foreigner in our midst—had made it.

I went a pace or two to meet my master. "It is good to be home, Harry," I said.

He nodded, but did not answer, and I saw that his eyes were abrim with tears.

"It must be terrible to be shut away from God's sunshine, and all this loveliness of the changing seasons," I said, waving a hand towards green sward, trees and flowing river.

He had come to the sundial and, standing with his fingers resting on the edge of it, looked round at me questioningly. He knew me well enough to suspect that my remark was leading up to something. So without further preamble and with tears in my own eyes I entreated him to pardon that good man, Richard Fermor.

The look of grateful love that Joanna gave me repaid the constancy and every effort after decent living of my life. She and Vaux had broken off their conversation abruptly at the King's approach, and now she went down on her knees with suppliant hands before him, and Thomas Vaux spoke with manly forthright-ness of the value which good honest merchants were to England, reminding Henry how his father, Nicholas Vaux, first baron of Harroden, had thought fit to give one of his daughters in marriage to Richard Fermor's son.

"Fermor is well served by his friends but he had his trial and now his wealth is put to other uses," said Henry, with bull-like obstinacy. "Yet I would not keep so upright a man in prison," he added, mellowed by his surroundings and recently stirred memo-ries. "That is, if he has anywhere to live," he added hastily, afraid perhaps that I might want to find place for him, too, at Court.

"There is Wapenham. Oh, your Grace, let him have Wapenham, that he may see the fair Northamptonshire countryside again!" cried Joanna.

Henry looked down at her consideringly, and she was fair enough to move a monster. "Wapenham?" he repeated. "What an ungainly name! What is Wapenham?"

"An empty priest house which he owned. A few miles from Easton Neston," she explained. "The new owner does not use it and it grows sadly neglected, with all the fields untilled. My father intended it for his unmarried sister." I was watching my wife's face, and to my surprise I saw her lips curve into a smile, and her eyes, bright with merry inspiration, seeking mine. "*His* sister is a capable, forthright woman too, who can cook," she told the King conversationally. "Rather like milady of Cleves, who has been so kind to us all."

Holding our breath, we watched the King frown as he often did when feeling himself unfairly defeated. Still in painful suspense, we watched his forefinger trace the time on the dial. "Then we will let him have it, and send word to the Governor of the Marshalsea," he said, after what seemed the longest seconds in my life. "Get up, you pretty, wheedling hussy, or you'll have the very blood out of my heart. You and that ingratiating husband of yours make a fine pair. And I make no doubt you will bring up that unfortunate young red-head to the same kind of tricks!" He turned to milord Vaux rather in the manner of one who finds relief in being able to address someone reasonably sane. "It is high time we left or we shall find the tide against my oarsmen and our hostess wearied with us." He slipped an arm through Vaux's because at times the ulcer on his leg made walking difficult. But he yawned contentedly. "It is a long time," he said, as they took the path to the river, "since I spent such an interesting morning."

Behind his broad back Joanna and I fell into each other's arms in relief. We treated ourselves to a brief, ecstatic, triumphant embrace. We had to part. There was no time for words. Yet, woman-like she managed one pithy sentence which proved her a true merchant's daughter. "*Make him put it in writing*," she adjured me, cautious even in her gratitude.

I kissed milady of Cleves's hand with alarming fervour, and just managed to slip into the tail-end of the barge party and secure a place near the King. "Do you remember, Harry, once saying that only a good woman should be the mistress of Richmond?" I asked, as we both gazed back from the water at its fair towers and gardens.

"Well, she does," he answered, and made no further remark until we were back at Hampton.

Not until after supper that evening did he address another remark to me. I had persuaded John Thurgood to amuse the company with a game of "forfeits," which was always popular with the ladies because they usually paid theirs in kisses. But the King's forfeit, which he owed for failing to answer a purposely impossible question about the vegetation on the moon, was that he must write his signature with a kitchen skewer in ox blood on a roll of legal parchment. And the parchment which the page brought him was an order for the return of Wapenham to its original owner. To my great relief Henry, one arm uxoriously about his young Queen, signed it and handed it to me, since I was hovering so anxiously behind his chair.

"You are like a persistent gadfly, Will," he said, with an affectionate grin. "And I perceive you would scarce trust me the length of this hall with my own Crown Jewels."

Chapter Twenty-Seven

AVING BEEN PERSUADED, HOWEVER reluctantly, to do a kindness, King Henry enjoyed a sense of beneficence, and so rather characteristically proceeded to do more. He sent for me next day and bade me borrow horses from the royal stables and fetch Richard Fermor from the Marshalsea and then accompany him to Northamptonshire. He himself was planning an important progress, with Queen and Court, through those northern counties which had been so disaffected during the Pilgrimage of Grace, and intended making his headquarters for some weeks at Pontefract Castle in Yorkshire. So he gave me leave of absence for a month so that I could help to put the neglected parsonage at Wapenham in order. "You have not had a real holiday since you have been with me, Will," he said. "So take that endearing wife of yours with you and make up for all the times you have been parted from her, so that she comes back with the beginnings of another boy. Make it a happy family reunion for Fermor, who did me the service of bringing you to me. Joined, no doubt," he added with a sly chuckle, "by that sister who is supposed to be so touchingly like my own sister of Cleves."

I collected Joanna and our babe from Richmond so that she might share in the joy of welcoming her father. We took him first to the house in Thames Street to which the Festings had hurriedly returned on receipt of a letter I had sent by the King's post to Dover, so that they could bring him news of his son and of such business as was still being carried on from Calais. And I was glad to see that Master John had sent more tangible greeting in the form of cash, in case his father should need it.

But the elder Fermor would have none of it. "The profits, such as they are, are his and Maud's," he insisted, "for I shall now have nothing to leave them. If I can pay my way with the glebe lands at Wapenham I must be thankful." And before leaving London he insisted upon waiting upon milady of Cleves to thank her for her kindness to his daughter and, finding congenial interest in his practical, travelled mind, she insisted upon his staying to enjoy one of her excellent dinners.

We sent the joyful news of his release to Emotte who, leaving the good friends she had been staying with, joined us there. She and Joanna, with Tatty and the one young maid who had remained with Emotte, worked with a will to put the old place to rights. Jordan came back and one or two of the older men from Easton Neston. More would willingly have come, even at lower wages, but Richard Fermor insisted that he could not hope to do more than make the land self-supporting.

The month we spent there was a complete change from Court life and the exacting publicity of being the King's Fool. I went about in an old leather jerkin, doing bits of carpentry and helping in the fields—all willingly undertaken tasks at which Jordan still told me, quite truly, that I was inept. Having Joanna at home seemed to make up for much of her father's loneliness in prison. Small Richard throve on the good country air, and played havoc with all the pent-up maternal instincts in Emotte's nature.

"We shall never have the heart to take him from her," said Joanna, watching the tall, gaunt woman, who could not sing a note in tune, pacing the room with our son in her arms while crooning him to sleep.

"If we left him for a while and you came again at Christmas to fetch him, it would mean something for them to look forward to and might keep your father from riding so often towards Towcester and staring hungrily at the house and fields and sheep that were once his," I suggested.

My precious month was up and I had to be back again at Court. But since the King seemed to live more and more at Hampton I should often be able to cross to Richmond to see my wife, and we should both be happier now that our marriage was no secret. I feel sure that had I pressed him, Henry would have allowed me larger lodgings so that I might have my family with me there, but Joanna and I had discussed this and decided that our love was something which we wished to keep apart from the public aspect of my work.

And I was glad that we were perfectly agreed about this, particularly with the present Queen. I make no doubt she would have been kind to Joanna. The trouble was rather that she was too kind, and often to the wrong sort of people. An atmosphere of ugly gossip was growing up around her. If you went into a room or gallery too quickly there were sure to be women with their heads together, whispering about her, or a group of young gallants sniggering about the latest tit-bit of scandal, such as the oft-repeated story of the evening when the King had been kept waiting in his bedgown outside her bolted door while the tittering pages heard sounds of hurried scurryings within. Everybody watched her cousin, Tom Culpepper, with a kind of salacious curiosity. It was difficult not to if one had any sensitivity at all. He was a very personable young man and the King's favourite gentleman of the bedchamber, and to prepare an obese middle-aged husband to go to bed night after night with the girl you love must be a tearing experience. Almost as difficult as having to dance with her beneath the indulgent husband's adoring gaze, and try to hold her so that no one can guess how passionately you held her during those rare dangerous moments of contrived privacy, nor how the very touch of hands sets you both trembling.

And now there seemed to be people about poor Katherine out of her dubious past—people who had come pushing their way in like bees round a honey flower and whom she, foolish child, was afraid to send away lest they would not keep their dirty mouths shut about what favours they had received or knew that others had received. There was a handsome looking braggart of a poor relation called Dereham, and a friend called Mary Lascelles, who probably knew all the goings-on there had been in the women's dormitory in the Dowager-Duchess of Norfolk's ill-managed household. And a low fellow who had taught Katherine music and probably much else besides.

"Why don't you throw yourself on the King's mercy and tell him?" I found myself wanting to say to her. "For all you are called his wife, I know him far better than you do. He *can* be merciful. If you choose your moment and tell him yourself, and don't leave it until some fiend of a busybody forestalls you. He is human enough to see that it wasn't your fault. That it was the old Duchess's fault for not looking after you when you came to her, an orphan of good parents whose father had fought for England. And your uncle of Norfolk's fault for poking you forward into a position for which you have no ability, save that of being cuddlesome. For suddenly remembering you, the neglected family burden, because it occurred to him after Cromwell's fall that another niece on the throne might serve to bring the power of King's chief adviser back to himself again."

Kind and accessible though she was, a jester cannot say such things outright to a Queen. But I have blamed myself since that I did not try, more subtly, to warn her—to persuade her to tell the King something of her past. Close in his arms, she might have found pity. I am sure the worst he would have done to her would have been to send her to some convent. Though perhaps to pretty, wanton Katherine Howard this would have been a worse punishment than death? But during her brief year and a half as Queen I had been preoccupied with my own affairs and, truth to tell, the unschooled little beauty with the wide eyes and tip-tilted nose had never interested me much. And now it was too late to warn or give avuncular advice, for her mother's nephew Culpepper was on the scene. Thomas Culpepper who was all too obviously of the present, not the past. And who—if half the tales told about secret bedchamber visits while the King was busy at Pontefract were true—would evoke no pity at all.

"What do you suppose will be the outcome?" John Thurgood asked me on my return from Northamptonshire, under cover of the minstrels' merry dance tones to which she and Culpepper danced. "Think of her cousin, Anne Boleyn, and what happened to her—even though, judging by the meagre evidence, she may well have been innocent."

"I do often think of her," I said. "And of the bitter blow it will be to the King's pride should he ever find out about this one. Why, only last evening, he was petting her and calling her his 'rose without a thorn.'"

Thurgood was not the type to wish unhappiness to anyone. "Sooner or later someone is sure to tell him," he said regretfully, looking round at the sour, disapproving faces of most of the elder men who, like the King himself, no longer danced.

And the telling came soon indeed. After Mass the following morning, when Henry, because it was All Souls' Day, had asked his confessor to give special thanks for the good way of life he now had with his thornless rose, Katherine.

As he came out from his private pew I saw Cranmer hand him a letter. I do not think any man living would have dared to *say* whatever he had written in that letter about the Queen. Henry read the words with a brow like thunder, turned his back on him, and so thoroughly disbelieved the whole sordid story that he read it aloud, contemptuously, to the three members of the Privy Council who happened to be with him. Probably he took it to be another Protestant attempt to discredit Norfolk which the gentle primate had been gullible enough to be hoodwinked by. Henry went on his way to the tennis court and left him standing there. But the seed of suspicion had been sown. Naturally, when he had simmered down, Henry asked how the Archbishop had come by such venomous scandal. And it came out that a woman called Mary Lascelles, who had been in the old Duchess of Norfolk's household at Horsham, had told her brother what went on there. And he, fanatical puritan that he was, had sought an interview at Lambeth and repeated it to the Archbishop—neither for spite nor gain, but for his conscience's sake, with a devastating honesty which carried conviction. "Go see this man and look into these palpable lies," Henry must have said to Wriothesley or someone, when the source of Cranmer's concern had been explained to him. "But let no alarm or slander reach the Queen."

But the sleuths were at work and truth will out. To the shocked amazement of all of us the next thing we heard was that Madox and Dereham had actually confessed. Madox said that he had amused himself with her when she was yet too young to be seduced, and Dereham that he had lain with her many a night and, being a poor relation of the Howards, considered himself contracted to her in marriage until the King himself fancied her.

It must have been a blow indeed to Henry. And yet, as 1 could have foretold, he had pity. "She was too young to know better! That hell-hag of a stepmother of Norfolk's should have cared for her as a gentlewoman and not put her with the upper servants." I heard him say it, groaning and holding hands to head, when he came into his bedchamber after hearing Wriothesley's report. He was grieved past caring who heard. If she had run to him then and implored forgiveness he would have protected her. But only Culpepper was there, white-faced and guilty, and his hands shook like aspen leaves as he held the royal nightgown to the fire to warm. And because of his shakiness and pitiful guilty fear it fell to me to try to comfort our master.

"She complained of the jolting of the roads," Henry said, pacing back and forth before the fire, "and during all our journey I cared for her tenderly, even abstaining from her bed when she complained of being tired, because I hoped—and she pretended to hope—that she was with child by me. And now the doctors say it was nothing. And I, poor duped fool, know that had she been capable of child-birth she would have been disgraced by bearing one long ago to this Dereham fellow, or who knows what menial."

I coaxed him to sit on the edge of the great four-poster bed. Gently, I pulled off his doublet and embroidered shirt and, stretching a hand behind me for the warmed shirt which Culpepper silently handed, slipped it over the tousled auburn head. Looking down at it so closely, I noted how that vibrant, brilliant thatch was thinning and greying. Compassion stirred in me. "And you are all the more distressed because they greeted you on your return with alarming news of the Prince's health," I sympathised. "By and large, it has been a sad homecoming for you, Harry."

"You always read my heart, Will," he said, with an appreciative pat on my shoulder. And, to my dismay, leant forward with bowed head and began to sob. "If he—my Ned—should die—" he said brokenly.

"You have daughters," I dared to remind him within the shelter of the half-drawn bed curtains.

"How could I leave England to be ruled by a woman? Mary married to some meddling foreign prince?" he demanded. But for once he seemed to review them thoughtfully with that contingency in view. "Mary is a good woman, like her mother. But obstinate as an abbot's mule—she would drag my country back to the Pope."

Trying to soften him, I told him how I had found out about her caring for the prisoners. "She was a charming child, but she has soured," was all he said.

"Is it any wonder?" I should have liked to ask, but even in this moment of close sympathy did not dare. "And what of the younger one?" I asked instead, trying to lead his mind away from present troubles.

"Young Bess?" he said, and for the first time smiled. "I suppose men would say she is the spit of me, with her hair, and her man's acuteness and the way she stands and orders people about—"

"And her cunning, Harry?" I ventured.

He kicked at me playfully with his unshod foot. "A pity she was not born a boy," he said with a sigh, and sat staring for a long time at the tiled floor. But I knew it was her dark-eyed mother and not young Bess of whom he was thinking. And presently he proved me right. "Will," he asked, "do you suppose the wench knows about—my second wife?"

"Almost certainly. After all, she is ten and too quick in the up-take not to," I said.

"Then how does she—" He stopped, unable to put into words a question he must have been too proud to ask for many years.

I was quick to remove the necessity. "Lady Bryan, who, having always had charge of her household, should know, once told me that her Grace has never been heard to mention her mother," I told him. A sigh of relief escaped him, though I myself mistrusted the result of such repression of youthful thoughts. But his feelings towards his younger daughter must have been kindly because, although she was still considered to be illegitimate, he did not reprove me for using the title "her Grace."

He was sleepy by then, and the present peak of grief for an erring wife and anxiety for an only son were past. Memories of his second wife seemed to be merging with the immediate memory of his fifth, and almost submerging it. Culpepper and I helped him to lift his heavy bulk on to the high bed and pulled the rose-embroidered covers about him. But as I nodded to Culpepper and slipped from the room, I noticed that he did not lie down beside his master as usual, but remained, fully clothed, sitting very still by the dying fire. I could not help feeling sorrow for him. If ever a man must have been fearing the next bit of scandalous revelation it must have been he.

It was his rival, Francis Dereham, who supplied it—though to give the man his due, not willingly. Like Katherine herself, he was never vindictive. Henry had sent his defiled little wife across the river to the Convent of Sion which, since its dissolution, he was converting into a hunting lodge for himself. But Sion House was only just across the river and this inconclusive move was not enough for Norfolk's enemies. Any fine morning the King, riding to hounds, might see her again and relent. For had she not managed to elude her guards that last day at Hampton and run screaming along the gallery and almost succeeded in throwing herself at his feet as he came out from chapel? So Cranmer and Wriothesley rode to the Tower and had Madox and Dereham tortured in the hope of getting something more damning out of them. The music master had nothing more to tell. And Dereham stuck to his assertion that, although he had persuaded the Queen to take him into her household as secretary, he had never sinned with her since her marriage. He had never had the chance, he said bitterly, as the rack on which he lay began to pull and stretch his fine young limbs.

"She wouldn't even look at me," he cried, at the next excruciating turn of the wheel. "It was always the other one—"

Cranmer and Wriothesley came close and leant over him, one of the rack men told me afterwards. "What other?" they asked, in merciless unison.

And in his agony at the next turn of the cruel contraption he moaned Tom Culpepper's name.

The Queen's two lovers stood some kind of trial at the Guildhall with the Duke of Norfolk, of all people, as chief examiner for the Crown. The result was a foregone conclusion, and the death sentence was carried out conveniently before Christmas at Tyburn. Dereham was hanged and quartered, and Tom Culpepper, because of his gentle birth—or because the King had once loved him—was beheaded.

Henry never spoke about any of them all that Christmas. He was hurt in his vanity as much as his heart. He had been made to look a fool waiting outside his own wife's door before a couple of sniggering pages while Jane Rochford helped to hustle her mistress's lover safely out. He, once the marriage catch of all Europe whose proud divorced Spanish wife had died still loving him, had been cuckolded before Court and country. That he never would forgive. He moved his Court from Hampton of happy memories to Greenwich. He showed friendly gratitude towards Archbishop Cranmer, and gave orders that everyone should enjoy themselves as usual during the festive season.

> *"At Christmas play and make good cheer*
> *For Christmas comes but once a year,"*

I quoted from the popular poet Tusser, trying to start off the season on the right note and to make a bright spot in the lonely life of the young Princess Elizabeth. But it was difficult to be merry with a queen in disgrace and the uncertainty of her fate hanging over us, and for once I was thankful that my wife and babe were far away on their visit enjoying the simpler pleasures of Wapenham.

And still more thankful was I that they were well out of it all when the Constable of the Tower received a warrant signed by Henry for the execution of yet another wife.

Early one sad, misty February morning Thomas Vaux and I stood on the opposite bank and watched the great black barge covered with an awning pull out from the mooring creek where the lawns of Sion slope down to the Thames. There were halberdiers aboard and Suffolk, we knew, had been given the unpleasant duty of taking Katherine to the Tower.

"One pays for being the King's friend," remarked Vaux, his voice floating flatly on the grey stillness of the riverside mist. And some of the stark verities which touched our lives at that time were too obvious to need answering.

Even without the extra big awning the two women in the barge would have been but shadowy figures to us, and both Katherine and Lady Rochford, condemned for her part in helping Culpepper to the Queen's bed, were probably wrapped in black, warm garments, sad as the morning.

"A brittle beauty, made by Nature frail," I heard Thomas Vaux murmur, as he watched the oarsmen pull out skillfully towards mid-stream. I suppose he was speaking of poor Katherine Howard, but the words may well have been taken from one of his own vivid poems.

"An unusually strong current," I said, as they shot forward. "It will be difficult for so big a craft to shoot between an arch of the bridge on this high tide. But thank God for the mist!"

Stamping his cold feet and drawing his cloak more closely about his neck, Vaux looked at me in questioning surprise.

"In the city these new coal fires will have turned this white mist to fog," I pointed out. "So she will not see her lovers' mouldering heads stuck on poles above the bridge."

We turned away to warm ourselves, while small, sensuous, nineteen-year-old Katherine was rushed by the too swift tide of river and Life to the same block which had not so long since been scrubbed clean of the blood of her cousin Anne.

"She stooped to comfort milady Rochford before mounting the scaffold, and died meekly confessing her sins against the

King," an unctuous parson told us in the depressed quiet of the palace afterwards.

But the Captain of the halberdiers, who had been reviving himself after an unpleasant duty with some of the cellarer's strongest wine, lurched to his feet and reported daringly, "These things she may have done. But I was standing within a few feet of the executioner, and know that last thing before she died she cried boldly, with all the blood of the Bigods and Mowbrays, the Plantagenets and Howards which was in her, 'I die Queen of England, but God knows I would sooner be the wife of Tom Culpepper.'"

Chapter Twenty-Eight

I T WAS LIKE THE time when Henry had been a widower before, with Court life settled down into a predictable, unexciting routine. Except that now it lasted for only a few months. He did not hunt any more, but would attend Council meetings or see foreign envoys in the forenoon, fall asleep after dinner, and often in the evenings he would send for me to amuse him. As he usually retired early I was often free to row down to Richmond and spend the night with my wife. I seemed to spend a small fortune on hiring watermen.

One midday Henry came bustling back from dinner to his private apartments looking particularly pleased with himself. "You have heard of the new law they are passing to safeguard me from further pain?" he asked, in that disassociated way he had of throwing all the onus of his own wishes on to his advisers, and quite forgetful of the fact that it had been the Howard girl who had suffered most of the pain. "In future any woman who comes to the royal marriage bed with former unchastity unconfessed will be guilty of treason."

I laid down the lute I had been tuning. "In future?" I gasped.

He did not seem to hear me, being busied with searching through a pile of music scores for something which he wished me to play. He handed me a French love song, which I took to indicate the direction of his thoughts. He settled himself to listen in appreciative silence while I sang the thing through, and when the last sweet cadence had died away I could contain my curiosity no longer. "Is your Grace seriously thinking of marrying again?" I asked, carefully keeping all emphasis from the last word, which would so soon be on all men's lips.

"For feminine companionship, not for any hope of a family," he admitted smugly.

"Yet she must come to you a virgin?" It seemed to me grossly unfair. And surely it would be asking for trouble to tie a girl, still avid for the half-guessed sweets of love, to a diseased mountain of a man like him? What he needed was some motherly woman to nurse and cosset him. "After your last experience why not try a widow, Harry?" I suggested.

He looked up sharply, pulling at his spade-like golden beard. The idea was new, but worth considering. "Some lesser man would have had the love bird's first sweetness," he objected.

"And therefore she might be the less likely to flutter outside the gilded cage."

I had made the suggestion in part because it seemed unlikely that any girl, however innocent, would now risk the charges which might be trumped up against her should the King's affection wane or veer. But Henry took the thought and mulled it over like a good untried wine.

As a result there were Privy Council meetings and secret consultations; and one day, emerging from one such meeting, Thomas Vaux beckoned me to join him in a quiet corner. There was a look of astonishment on his pleasant, contemplative face. "You are always plaguing *us* with guessing games, Will. Now guess whom the King is going to marry," he said, in the half deprecating manner of someone who has scored unexpectedly high at the butts.

"Not a *sixth*!" I murmured. "It will make him the laughing stock of Europe."

"Katherine Parr, who married Lord Borough of Gainsborough when she was thirteen, and then milord Latimer, who has just died," he went on, too dazed to heed my remarks.

I burst out laughing. "Three Katherines. And this one twice widowed! Then he has taken my advice most thoroughly."

"Each of the husbands was a widower when she married him, the last even richer than the first," elaborated Vaux, as if reciting some carefully recollected family history.

"What better reason could our Tudor need?" I asked cynically. "Although he did mention companionship."

"Katherine Latimer is a very learned and pleasant lady whose conversation his Grace has often enjoyed," said Vaux defensively. "But that is not my point. Do you not realise, Will—and you from Northamptonshire—that she is sole heiress of my grandparents, the Greens of Green's Norton, and sister to my late mother who was my father's second wife? So that she is my aunt!"

I let out a low whistle. "And she will be Queen," I said, duly impressed at last.

Mercifully, Thomas Vaux was not devoured by ambition like so many of the men about the King.

"This will bring you close within the Tudor family circle," I added, with the thought stirring in my mind that he might one day be able to help Richard Fermor still more. "That is, of course, if the lady herself be willing. Everybody must know that handsome Thomas Seymour is courting her."

"And she certainly cares for him. Although one would scarcely have expected the flamboyant younger Seymour to be attracted by so staid a woman as Aunt Katherine when every pretty chit at Court is making eyes at him."

"Perhaps he cares more for big money bags than big eyes," I said.

A chattering posse of courtiers was coming our way. It was as well for milord Vaux of Harroden not to be seen gossiping in odd corners immediately after a royal conference on so delicate a matter. "And however much my kinswoman may want to wed him, you may be sure Tom Seymour is too astute to push his charms in the King's way just now, and will take himself off to sea or some-where," he added hurriedly, before he left me.

And so, after a quietly dignified wedding, the reluctant bride of fair estates and impeccable character became King Henry's sixth wife. She was able to talk to him knowledgeably as had his first Katherine. She often read to him in Latin. And she was there, calm and efficient, through all the worries of war we had at that time.

There always had been the difficulty of keeping a balance of power between Spain, France and England, which must have given Henry many a sleepless night. And now the ever-ready alliance between France and Scotland had sprung into the very real fear of a simultaneous invasion from over the northern border and from across the Channel. Jane Seymour's elder brother, Edward, Earl of Hertford, held off the Scots, and Thomas Seymour certainly found plenty of occupation at sea. When King James the Fifth died after the battle of Solway Moss, Henry would have negotiated a betrothal between our Prince Edward and the baby daughter Mary whom James left, if only to prevent a later alliance between her and the Dauphin. He was astute enough to see that union within our isles could give us greater solidarity than any spectacular European marriage. But the Scots, instigated by the French, would have none of it.

The French were digging deep trenches along their coast and mounting falconet cannon on their walls. The Spaniards were with us this time and at last our ships and men were ready for a joint invasion. Henry, heavy as he had become, rode down to embark at Dover. And I, his fool, rode gladly in this company—not because I had orders to, but because it took away the stigma of buffoonery which I had felt when I first saw my long-discarded motley. And, hard as it was to part from my loved ones, I would not for the world have missed that campaign.

Men saw a King of England, splendidly mounted on an enormous charger, riding to war again. And they forgot the cruel taxes they had been grumbling at, the debased coinage, desecrated shrines and abbeys, the executions, and the homeless monks and unfed beggars on their roads. In every town, as we rode through, they turned out to cheer or to join. We English are so illogical, quarrelling like curs among ourselves, but standing as one man the moment some foolhardy foreigner butts in. Grasping greedy we can be in times of peace, but giving our all without question when it comes to war.

Soon after we had landed the Spaniards made a separate peace with King Francis. But the angry Tudor hung on. He besieged Boulogne, and by the tail end of that summer we had taken that important seaport with all the French equipment abandoned in it, and he returned home a hero. Knowing how often his people had groaned beneath his despotic dictates, their spontaneous cheering must have been sweet to him. There was a happy reunion between him and his Queen, who had acted so successfully as Regent and had his two younger children in her care. But I doubt if any reunion could have been as happy as mine with Joanna, whom I found awaiting me at Richmond.

All that winter we knew the seething French were preparing to retaliate, but when they landed on the Isle of Wight the resourceful islanders were ready for them. It was not the first time they had had to contend with French invaders. They fought them on the slopes of Bembridge Down, destroyed the bridge over a small river there, and then cut them to pieces when they came to fill their water casks in some place called Shanklin Chine. For months they had been driving stakes into their beaches, and strengthening their forts at Sandown, Cowes and Yarmouth with stones shipped across from demolished Beaulieu Abbey on the mainland. And whether deterred by a score or two of well-aimed island guns or by the tricky waters of the Solent, the French Admiral d'Annebaut never reached Portsmouth but scuttled for the safety of his own shores again.

The King had insisted upon riding once more to Dover. "If I can no longer go to sea with my ships at least I shall be there to meet the enemy," he said. And dined aboard the *Great Harry*, which was the pride of all his Navy and of his heart.

But after the scare was over those of us who saw him daily knew what the effort had cost him. In spite of his indomitable determination, he was failing. During that last autumn of his life, although he had to be lifted to the saddle, he somehow managed to make his usual progress. Hampton, Oatlands, Woking, Guildford, Windsor—he visited them all. And each as usual was cleansed and made sanitary again during the absence of the Court. But, try as we would, Thurgood and I could not make Christmas at Windsor the merry season it had been. Suffolk, the King's friend and brother-in-law, was dead. Gifted Holbein, to my grief, had fallen a victim to the plague.

After Christmas Henry came back to Whitehall. And there Queen Katherine showed him infinite patience, carrying out his physician's orders, giving him his potions and sometimes sitting for cramped hours with his bad leg resting across her lap. She slept in the same room with him when the gentlemen of the bedchamber feigned illness rather than endure the stench from the putrefaction of his ulcer. And, above all, she was kind to both his daughters, having them with her at the palace as much as possible. In gratitude for this, and out of old rooted affection for my master, I tried as often as I could to relieve the tedious strain of her devoted nursing.

Henry had become so heavy and unwieldy that the head carpenter had devised a great chair in which he could be lifted from room to room, sometimes by means of pulleys. He hated the necessity for this so much that he would often hit out at the strong young halberdiers who came to move him. And how could they, or anyone who had not known him in his prime, realise how their ministrations must infuriate and humiliate a king who had been the champion wrestler of his day and who had challenged all comers in the lists? They had not in their minds, perhaps, the picture of a strong, laughing, generous Henry Tudor which I tried to keep fresh and vivid as an antidote to all hatred and misunderstanding and repulsion. And although Henry was often violently irritable with all who tended him, he was seldom so with me.

"You are comfortable to me, old crony," he said, opening a wary eye to make sure who it was as I took my place quietly beside his bed.

"Like an old slipper," I answered. Not too tactfully, perhaps, because he had just thrown one after his departing wife. I hoped that she was out in the thin wintry sunshine getting the stench of the sickroom out of her lungs or playing with young Elizabeth to sweeten her thoughts. Poor lady, she had been three times stepmother to old men's children, and unless Thomas Seymour waited for her, and did not have to wait too long, her chances of ever bearing a child of her own seemed slender.

Henry heaved himself up in his bed and I put his harp into his hands, hoping to coax him to play. But his gaze was still resentfully on the array of medical phials from which the poor Queen must have been trying to physic him. "Why are good women always so dull?" he asked, plucking crossly at a string or two.

"Perhaps because, men being what they are, it is difficult for them to be both good and gay," I suggested, playing over the sweet air of his own "Greensleeves" on muted strings.

"We look for perfection every time we fall in love," he grumbled, half singing to his harp.

"Women are but human, poor creatures. And it would be uncomfortable to live with an angel, would it not, Harry?"

Unconsciously, we were turning our conversation into a kind of part-song, twanging a string of lute or harp at the end of each sophistry.

"At least this one puts up with my vile sores."

"And does not have lovers in odd corners."

"Only Seymour in her heart," I thought.

"A woman above par," punned Henry, with regained good humour and something of his verve.

"And kind to clever, motherless Elizabeth."

He stopped drawing odd sounds from his harp, and became all serious. "That was the worst thing I ever did, Will. To render a young child motherless. It is the one relationship in which we *do* find something of the security of Heaven."

"All women are not real mothers because they are capable of giving birth," I said, remembering how Anne Boleyn had seemed to care above all for wit and gaiety.

"Then I must have been fortunate in mine. You scarcely remember yours, Will?"

"And was still unconsciously aching for her when, as a grown man, I came to Court. But now I have found some part of her in my wife."

"Who, miraculously, contrives to be both good and gay."

I beamed upon him fatuously for the compliment. "She is going to give me another child," I told him. And I like to think now that he was the first person I told. And that the glance he shot me held pure, friendly pleasure unmixed with envy. Then he sat quite still against his pillows, blinking his sandy lashes. "What are you going to call *this* one?" he said.

More than anything I had wanted to call him John for my faithful friend Thurgood, and because this was Joanna's brother's name it would have served well. But I knew what Henry wanted and was touched beyond measure that he should care for that souvenir of himself in my son. There was so little I had to give him, so short a time in which to give it. "We hope to call him Henry," I said, after the most infinitesimal pause. And if ever an actor tried to put conviction into his lines, I tried then.

"Your second son, after your second best master," he said, without rancour and with a most satisfied and ungrudging smile.

We sat in silence for a while, he in the great bed and I on my stool, until a gleam of wintry sunset began to glint on the diamond panes. It slid round the richly embroidered wall tapestries, illuminating an English lion and Henry's Welsh dragon standing on their hind legs to maintain a crown. The bed curtains hung open about the posts at the foot of the tester. A log fire burned cheerfully on the hearth. It was the hour before the candles were brought—the hour for confidences between friends.

And Henry, the old reprobate, gave me gift for gift. He laid the little harp across his raised knees and rested his arms across it, allowing me a look into his mind, not as King but as a human being—a more intimate résumé of his life, perhaps, than he had ever allowed even to Charles Brandon of Suffolk, whose father had been his own father's standard bearer at Bosworth. "It is strange to look back," he said slowly. "Not at the Field of the Cloth of Gold and the political hagglings and the glittering feasts and tournaments which all the world knows of. But at my own private life—now that it is nearly over. One comes to realise that one's parents are so much wiser than one knows. You see, my first wife was the only one brought up as I was, with all the skills and learning and sense of responsibility to fit her to be a Queen. Looking back, it was a golden time—the years with her—full of contentment and success. And Katherine loved me. Probably she was the only one of them all who ever did. But *I* was never in love, hungrily with all my senses, save with that witch Anne Boleyn. God knows how I denied my body, waiting for her! I wrote her some of the most beautiful love letters a woman ever had. I turned my world upside down to get her.

"Oh, my heart, and oh my heart
My heart it is so sore!
Since I must needs from my love depart
And know no cause wherefore,"

he sang softly, in that exquisite tenor of his. For a while he seemed to be caught back in time, right away from age and sickness. Then he sighed deeply, as if letting go of something which had been all the core and colour of life.

"Then there was Jane—pale, gentle Jane," he said, with the relieved smile of a man who comes to something infinitely easier to deal with. "Perhaps I chose her by contrast. Jane, who gave me my son. Jane, whom I shall probably be joining soon—at Windsor."

"And that other Anne?" I prompted, striving to keep his melancholy thoughts from death, which he had always so much feared. "Surely no two women called by the same name could have been less alike?"

He laughed, with the same kind of affectionate raillery I kept for Emotte. "I cannot think now why I ever found her ridiculous," he admitted. "But, truth to tell, I often have a strong suspicion that she and those Flemish *vrous* of hers are laughing at *me*. And do you know, Will, when—when I was widowed this last time the Duke of Cleves quite thought I would take her back. Poor Cranmer had the oddest letter from them urging me to do so. He asked me how he should answer it. And when I remembered her kindness to your Joanna and that happy day at Richmond and—"

Henry began to chuckle richly, "and that eel pie, I found myself sorely tempted."

In his shoes I should have been more than tempted, but I scarcely dared to contemplate the utter consternation which such magnanimity would have caused tall, sensible, inestimable Flemish Anne. "The people would have been pleased," I was forced to admit.

"Because she has the common touch, as my first Katherine had," he agreed. "Some people are born with it, and it cannot be acquired. Not to have it is a cruel handicap to many a good ruler, and often the only salvation of a bad one. Consider my father. The most tolerant, hard-working, progressive king this country has ever had. He made men respect him, but no one could have called him popular. And when they shouted for me so eagerly at my accession it was partly because I was eighteen and tall and open-handed and had my mother's Plantagenet hair. But mostly because I could compete with my own archers or wrestle with a blacksmith on his own village green and laugh at their jokes and use their own oaths."

"And because you had what all the distinguished visitors from Europe called 'immense promise,'" I added softly.

"Promise," he repeated sleepily. "God knows I meant to confirm it—then."

"And now these other two Katherines," I prompted.

"The one so deceitful and the other so much kinder to me than I deserve. You knew them all, didn't you, Will?"

"All six of 'em," I answered.

"And in your stubborn old heart loved only the first," he accused, with a yawn.

The harp would have slid to the floor had I not saved it. Henry turned his head wearily on the pillow and fell into a light doze, which was good for him. And a few minutes afterwards a page opened the door quietly and his wife came in. There was a lightness to her step and a smiling happiness in her eyes, so that I wondered if she had seen or received a letter from Thomas Seymour. But she looked instantly, in duty bound, at the bed. I rose, with a finger to my lips.

"Ah, he sleeps," she whispered, with relief. She had no special liking for me, but I think she spoke to me more freely because I was now distantly connected with her nephew, Lord Vaux. "I have been listening to the Lady Elizabeth playing on the virginals. She is a talented child. I must try to persuade the Council to let her live with me."

And I knew by the new happiness in her eyes that she was not picturing Elizabeth in any palace, but in Thomas Seymour's home. It was rumoured that he would be made Lord High Admiral, and some fine house should go with the appointment. He had a way with women and the precocious child always sparkled for him, so such an arrangement in the future should make up to her for much neglect in the past. Never a dull moment, they say, with a sailor in the house....

Chapter Twenty-Nine

JOANNA BROUGHT A LIVELY young Richard back from Wapenham in time to spend Twelfth Night with her aunt and uncle in Aldermanbury, and several times I visited her there. With the King lying so ill there were no festivities for which my services were needed at Whitehall. John Brown and his wife were grateful for what I had been able to do for her father, and in these changed times showed only relief at my having married her, and took great pleasure in our boy.

Towards the end of January, on the last afternoon of her visit, they left us to talk alone in the great hall. Richard was with his great-aunt and we sat side by side upon the fireside settle.

"The King has promised me his harp—that lovely Welsh-made instrument," I told her. But Joanna was scarcely listening to my enthusiasm. She laid aside the small garment she had been making and began to fiddle thoughtfully with the lacing of my doublet. "I have not told you before, Will, because I did not want to worry you during our Twelfth Night happiness here. But when we were bidding this short farewell to our kind friends at Richmond before Christmas, Mistress Wingfield, one of milady of Cleves's women, drew me aside and told me in confidence that if the King should die milady may be asked to vacate the palace. There can be nothing certain yet, of course, but it is thought the Council may want it for the Prince, or for one of the King's daughters."

"It is only reasonable, I suppose," I said most regretfully. "But would this not be a great upset for the Lady Anne?"

"It may be. But she is not one given to useless worrying, as you know. And the King has so richly endowed her that she has several other houses to choose from. Dartford and Bletchingly, for instance."

"Sir Thomas Carden is her tenant at Bletchingly."

"Yes. But she prefers Dartford. She has grown used to our river, she says, and although Dartford is in Kent it will still be a home near the Thames."

I put my arms about her. "I cannot have you so far away as Dartford," I said decidedly.

"How did you know about Sir Thomas Carden?" she asked.

"Because for some time he has been considered officially Master of the Revels."

"Oh, poor John Thurgood!"

"John works hard and is the most conscientious man alive. But—though I hate to say it—he does not move with the times. Were I not to prod him he would still be producing the same kind of masques as we had when I first came to Court."

"I suppose there will be a great many changes?" said Joanna anxiously.

"There are bound to be—under a new King."

"Oh, Will, how strange it sounds. Almost as long as we can remember it has been great strong Henry the Eighth—and soon we shall have a child of ten! Will *you* have to go, too?"

I hugged her reassuringly. "No, no, my love. Not unless I wish. Edward Seymour will be Protector of England, and he is well disposed towards me. But I am tired of living in one palace while my wife lives in another."

"I hope it will not be because of me—if you give up your appointment as royal jester?"

"It will be mostly because I am tired of fooling in public, my sweet."

A pleasant-looking maid came in to put fresh logs on the fire, through the open door drifted the sound of Mistress Brown playing "London Bridge has fallen down" on her virginals, and our sturdy son sitting down on his behind with a bump and a shout of delighted laughter every time the bridge fell down. "I begin to wish we could build a house of our own and live in a real, comfortable, middle-class home like this with a reasonable amount of family privacy."

"We could borrow some money from my uncle and buy some land and rear sheep perhaps," suggested Joanna doubtfully.

"You know how good old Jordan always says I am at *that*!"

"Then what *will* you do?" said Joanna the practical.

I stretched luxuriously before Master Brown's roaring fire. I was an odd, unpractical fellow, I suppose. "Do you remember when we walked through Shoreditch fields before young Richard was born, planning what he should grow up to be? And how you mentioned men like Caxton and Tyndale, and said that as time went on and there were more grammar schools people would want more and more books?"

"Why, yes, I think I do," she said doubtfully.

"Then I have a mind to give up being the King's fool and write a book," I announced, seizing an imaginary pen and thrusting a hand through my wiry hair in a burst of unlikely inspiration.

Joanna leaned back against the settle and laughed at me as she used to laugh years ago when I made shadows of little animals for her on the wall at Neston. "Wonderful! Wonderful! A harp and a book," she jeered lovingly. "But, Will, my precious idiot, we shall have to eat!"

"Too true," I agreed, coming down to earth. "Specially with another mouth to feed soon."

"I am glad you told the poor King we planned to call him Henry," she said. "After all, we hope that John Thurgood will be with us often, and—who knows?—if you go on loving me so extravagantly we may have other sons. No, no, Will!" she protested laughingly, fending off my immediate embrace. "I cannot have you making love to me in the great hall with the servants coming in and out. Look, it grows dark, I can hear old Bardolf bringing round your horse and you should have been back at Whitehall by now."

It was too true, and I was growing tired of all this coming and going. I cantered back, splashing up the mud along the Strand, with my mind still on that comfortable, cheerful house. Among these pleasant fields out Shoreditch way perhaps? And wondering if, with no appointment at Court and my wife having no dowry, I could scrape enough from my savings to buy one good enough for her.

As soon as I set foot in the palace, although the torches and candles were lit, I felt the frightened gloom of approaching crisis. It was in the unusual hush and the secret consternation on people's faces. "The physicians say he cannot last long," an officious usher hurried to tell me.

"Does his Grace know?" I asked sharply.

The man shrugged in an affected gesture which he must have copied from the French ambassador. "No one dares to tell him."

There were several who might have, I thought. Archbishop Cranmer, whose place it really was. The Queen. Or Edward Seymour.

A very young page came running up to me, life's first introduction to the reality of death written starkly on his white, pimply face. "The King has been asking for you, Master Somers," he blurted out, all terrified importance.

"Now, by God's soul, they are not going to ask *me* to do it!" I thought, in panic. But Sir Anthony Denny, one of the gentlemen of the bedchamber, had loyally done what the physicians dared not. They were all in a huddle outside his door when I had hurried there along endless passages, not even stopping to shake the wet of the blustery January evening from my cloak. They seemed to be holding some pretence of consultation, but the flatness of their voices showed that there was little more to consult about. Evidently, I was expected. Hurriedly, I tossed my dripping cloak to the servant who admitted me.

Although there were several people present I did not stop to glance at them. They seemed to be grouped just inside the door. The great state chamber was very still. My eyes went straight to the monstrous mound beneath the bed covers, and that was very still, too. But when I reached the foot of the bed I saw that Henry's eyes were open, looking at me. I hated myself for every moment I had kept him waiting.

"I am going on a long journey, Will," he said.

Sickness was already toning down the redness of his face to grey. In spite of the royal composure with which he spoke, I detected fear in those small, light eyes.

Instinctively, to cheer him, I went to the window, pushed open a casement and stuck out my head. "No, Harry, you must have been misinformed," I said, after making a great to-do of looking this way and that. "There are no horses, nor grooms, nor any baggage carts down there."

"The kind of journey on which one does not take—baggage," he said.

"It is sometimes best to travel light," I said, coming back to the side of the great bed. I felt he had just been through enough. I did not want to let this develop into one of those awful moments of sepulchral solemnity, and because there were others in the room I tried to cling to something of my bantering fool's way of talk.

"There are some burdens—burdens of conscience—I wish I could go without. Like proud old Margaret of Salisbury. And that poor, misused, Howard child's screaming...." His voice was so thin that I had to bend down to catch what he said.

"One takes along the good deeds, too," I reminded him. "The courage, the long friendships, the many kindnesses."

"There are not so many of those as I would now wish. Not enough to outweigh those—those other deeds. Though God's love can forgive me all my sins—even worse than those I have committed."

It was not until that moment that the thought came to me. "I can take at least one ugly bundle from your burden, Harry," I said, talking in that half-fooling way. "Give Richard Fermor back his estates and make one of your most loyal subjects happy. Every day he rides to look over the gates of them like a man shut out from Paradise. And you know, Harry, where you are going you will not any longer need his money."

It was some moments before he answered, and then, for a moment I thought he was evading me. "Take care of my harp,

Will, my old friend. I could not bear anyone else to play my songs on it. And take Richard Fermor the deeds of his estates. Better send one of those gaggling clerks to me while I can still sign my name to it." He roused himself up a little and spoke more strongly. "My name, Henry Tudor, which has made the whole world shake." He pulled himself up and looked challengingly about him in a most impenitent pride, while I bent to kiss the swollen hand that would just have time to make Fermor master of Easton Neston again.

"And Will—" he added, feeling the passionately grateful touch of my lips.

"Yes, Harry?"

He turned and glared at me in a way which would have intimidated anyone who did not know him through and through. "Tell me, you incorrigible beggar," he said, with his old gruff affection. "In all the years you have been with us, have you ever asked anything for *yourself?*"

"Only your unchanging affection," I said brokenly.

And that was the last time I ever spoke to him or stood near him alone. Of course, I was in the room sometimes, but it was always crowded with lords and prelates and important people. I knew that he talked earnestly with Edward Seymour about the future of his ten-year-old heir, who was at Hatfield, and to my great joy he sent for his daughter Mary, telling her with affection how much he regretted not having arranged a happy marriage for her, and begging her to show loving care to her young brother. And I was there, on my knees at the back of the room, when Archbishop Cranmer came hurriedly just before midnight to ask if he died in the faith and to pray for his departing soul. The doctors said their patient had been unconscious for hours, but Cranmer always swore that the King understood and pressed his hand.

And why not? "The love of God can forgive me all my sins," he had said.

Chapter Thirty

Now that King Henry the Eighth is dead I can stop playing the buffoon and go over it all in serious thought. Now that his great, disease-ridden body has ceased to struggle for breath I can go back to the splendid beginning. After twenty years of faithful service which far exceeded the normal role of Court Jester I may, without disloyalty, even write of it.

With that varied service in mind I have just sought audience of the comptroller of the royal household, Sir John Gage, and asked leave to tender my resignation.

"*Le roi est mort. Vive le roi!*" he reminded me.

Certainly we now had young Edward on the throne and he would need a jester. His sister's fool Jane, perhaps, or that gentle rhymster of Cranmer's could amuse him. But I was too old, I said.

"Too old at forty? Or run out of quips at last, Will?" Sir John asked kindly but absently, being harassed by all the new arrangements he must make in the royal household.

"The right *kind* of quips," I said. For how could one shock a delicate, whey-faced lad of ten with the lusty kind of merriment that had called forth his father's mighty laughter? And a lad hedged about by Protector Seymour's stern avuncular prudery, at that.

The comptroller must have appreciated my point for he made things easy for me. "You can still be King's Jester officially, and come back to us on special occasions, which will give you a livelihood, but would mean that you must live in or near London. And, of course, there will always be bed and board for Will Somers in any of the palaces. And a host of friends of your own making." He turned back to his document-laden table to ring a small hand-bell. "Well, I will instruct one of the clerks to make up the wages owing to you," he said, assuming a more business-like tone. "Besides which his Grace the late King has left you something."

"I know. His own harp," I said, grinning warmly at the very thought. "Several times he promised it to me, those evenings when he was sad and we used to make music together. 'Will, you monkish old celibate, I am sure to go before you,' he would say, with that fat chuckle of his. 'For 'tis wives that wear a man out.' And I do assure you, Sir John, there is nothing I could value more than that finely strung instrument. I shall play it evenings in some ordinary little home."

I bowed formally and turned away. But Sir John went on speaking, and that hint of kindly laughter was back in his voice. "It need not be such a particularly *little* home, Will," he was saying. "King Harry set aside a sum sufficient for you to build a comfortable house to raise your family and play your favourite tunes in for the rest of your life. You have a boy, I think, who is his Grace's godson."

Suddenly I realised what an unworldly zany I had been never to have expected such benefit, even in a Court full of grasping time-servers. Henry must have realised it, too, for had not his last words to me been, "Have you ever asked anything for yourself?" Standing there, with a warmth of gratitude at my heart, I felt the crowded years roll back. It was as if the recent sight of the Tudor's gross, tortured body heaving itself impatiently beneath the hands of scared physicians had been completely expunged. Instead I recalled the tall, athletic Tudor as I had first seen him, half Welshman and half Plantagenet, standing in the pride of his manhood with the morning sunlight about him. Standing on the bowling green at Greenwich Palace, strongly muscled legs apart, ruddy head thrown back, roaring with laughter at some foolish jest which I, a new-come country bumpkin gaping at the sport, had had the temerity to make. Outstanding he was then, as always, among his gaily-dressed group of courtiers. Not merely because he happened to be King of England but because he could surpass them at any sport, yet compose a learned Latin treatise as expertly as a sonnet, and because when he led their laughter their world seemed a good place for a man to live in. And now—after all the exciting, cruel, incredible years—I could still hear his mellow voice demanding my name and vowing, "By the Holy Rood, Will Somers, I like you for a witty, impudent knave! By your master's leave, who brought you here, we will keep you as our Jester." And keep me he did, for twenty years or more, and used me kindly. Which, as any aspiring young man knows, could be my making and leave my name a household word. Although at the time it tore me to pieces to be parted from Richard Fermor, the best master that ever man had. And from all that was Richard Fermor's.

Groping blindly, before tears unmanned me, I pulled open the comptroller's door at Whitehall, and closed it behind me, shutting out the past.

Could it be, I wondered, that a man goes back to his Maker as he was first moulded, all comely and generous, and not as Life, or some black-eyed witch of a woman, makes him? I, who for years had been teasing others with riddles, would leave my glittering, demanding world of wit and motley, and try by weighing and remembering to solve this biggest riddle of all. I would live with my wife and family in some pleasant place out Shoreditch way and write it all down. Strange things that could happen to humbly born men like myself. Royal confidences and kindnesses and passions which it is given to few humbly born men to remember.

Reading Group
Guide

1. Who is the central character in *King's Fool*?

2. In chapter two, Will says of himself, "I am one of those miserable sinners who hunger to be noticed. I need to bolster up my inadequacy with applause, as stronger men need breath." What other characters does Will meet who also represent this type of "sinner"?

3. In chapter five, as Joanna is extended to the first of the possible suitors her father finds for her, Will learns his "first valuable lesson about the power of ambition and the price which women are often called upon to pay for it." What other women does Will encounter who teach him more of the same lesson? In what ways do women today pay the price for men's ambitions?

4. Throughout the book, Margaret Campbell Barnes uses the hindsight of history to draw out the irony in Henry's obsession with producing a male heir. In chapter nine, King Henry says to Will, "And what would happen to this country in the hands of a woman?" What do we know did happen? What is the irony behind his fears?

5. What moment in the story do you think marks the turning point in Will's relationship with the king from one of service to one of intimate friendship?

6. In chapter thirteen, Will describes watching Queen Katherine of Aragon's trial as "like storing in one's mind a momentous hour of history." Throughout the book, he is indeed an accidental witness to history. How does Will's unique perspective and the author's use of the first person narrative give the reader a fresh view of a familiar story?

7. The book splits quite evenly into two halves: The first is Henry's reign and marriage with Queen Katherine of Aragon. The second half is the years following, with all his other wives. We almost see two different kings, as well. Was there a specific turning point for the "two Henrys," or was the change gradual?

8. Henry's actions are driven by many different influences, though it can at times be hard to discern the root of his motivations. What are the political factors driving his actions? What are the religious factors? What do you think are the real, personal fears?

9. Thomas Wyatt says of Anne Boleyn in chapter eighteen, "It is so often *fear*, do you not think, Will, which makes people relentless?" What is it that Anne fears? Is fear at the root of her dislike for Will?

10. After Anne Boleyn loses their second child, Henry blames her "for the whole up-turning of a Church and kingdom." Can this blame really be laid entirely on Anne? Who else should be held responsible?

11. Throughout the book, how does Will's attitude toward and relationship with the king change? What are the factors that cause this change?

12. Of all Henry's wives, it is his two foreign wives—Katherine of Aragon and Anne of Cleves—who seem to manage him best. Why do you think that is? What qualities do each of these women exhibit that give them the ability to stand up to him as they do?

13. History has painted King Henry VIII as a tyrant, and he is most notably remembered for his remarkable number of marriages. Discuss Barnes's portrayal of Henry. What about this Henry can you identify with, relate to, or even sympathize with?

14. What is the irony in the title *King's Fool*?

Brief Gaudy Hour

by Margaret Campbell Barnes

"It is all over," moaned Mary, lifting a face reddened and blotched with tears.

"You mean between you and the King?"

Anne regarded her younger sister with curiosity and awe. It was two years or more since she had last seen her, and it was difficult to imagine that this girl with whom she had eaten, played, and slept could be the King's mistress. But then Mary was so sleekly beautiful. Anne put out a hand and lifted a tress of the soft fair hair which she had always envied. It seemed to her like living gold, and the tendrils of it curled instantly, confidingly, round her slender fingers. Soft, confiding as Mary's nature.

"Do you care so much?" asked Anne.

"I w-wish I were d-dead!"

But then Mary had always cried easily. George had been wont to twit her for it. Whereas with herself such abandonment of grief would have betokened a broken heart. If she were ever fool enough to break her heart over a man!

"But you didn't love him?" she expostulated.

Mary's blue eyes, awash with tears, regarded her reproachfully.

"You couldn't have!" persisted Anne.

"No. Not love perhaps."

"I know that you must feel angry, and a fool, and hate to meet people," said Anne, groping for what her own reactions would have been. "But you can go home for awhile. Until people have something else to talk about." Her gaze, accustoming itself to the dim and fading light, wandered round the disordered tent until it came to rest upon a richly enamelled necklace which would have looked well against her own white throat. "And, of course, you will miss all the dresses and the jewels," she sighed.

"That is the least of it," lamented Mary, who could look just as delectable in a dairymaid's smock. "It was the cruel way he did it. Urging me to come to France in his train, flattering me, and then, when I had given him everything, just dropping me like a wornout glove."

It was the old story. How could Mary be so simple? What had she expected, wondered Anne, feeling infinitely more worldly-wise.

"Did he tell you himself?" she asked, curiously.

In spite of her grief, Mary gave vent to a little splutter of laughter at the bare suggestion. "Kings don't have to deal with unpleasant details of life like that," she explained bitterly.

"How then—"

Mary sat up dabbing at her eyes and pulling her expensive miniver wrap about her. "He just didn't come any more," she said drearily. "I used to lie awake waiting. And when he was well on his way to Calais, our father told me he had orders to conclude my marriage with Sir William Carey immediately."

"Are you with child?" asked Anne.

"How should I know yet?"

How strange to bear a child who, but for a bar sinister, might have ruled England! Another Fitzroy, like Bess Blount's handsome boy. But evidently Henry did not mean to acknowledge this one. It would be inconvenient, perhaps, at a time when the Pope was being approached about a divorce. Anne wondered irrelevantly if her first niece or nephew would look like the King. She tried to think of something comforting to say. But it was a long time since she had lived with her sister, and they never had been as close companions as herself and George. "You were to have married Will Carey anyway," she reminded Mary.

"Perhaps you will grow fond of him. He is quite a pleasant sort of person."

"But only a knight. Considering that I gave his Grace the flower of my womanhood, he might have done something better for me!"

Coming from someone heartbroken it seemed so small a grievance.

"It is really only her self-love that is hurt," decided Anne. "It could not be her heart."

She sat for awhile in the gathering gloom imagining how she herself would have behaved in her sister's place. Never, surely, could she have been so meek and tearful about it all!

"Mary," she essayed presently.

"Yes?"

"What is it like to be the King's mistress?"

Mary answered almost dreamily, "It is exciting. The way people watch when he speaks to you in public, and knowing how some of the women envy you. The covert glance, the thrill of a passing touch, and everybody really knowing. It is much more exciting than marriage."

Mary was smiling now and turning the King's opal on her finger. Her face was flushed, and there was a warm reminiscent quality in her voice which made Anne feel uncomfortable. But the gloom lent itself to confidences.

"I meant what is he like as a lover?"

"Oh, of course he is not young, if that is what you mean. But he has wit and poise. He is always master of the situation. Being wanted by him makes one feel surrounded by luxury and importance."

Mary drew up her knees beneath the coverlet and sat hugging them. "And you know, Nan, I think even if Henry Tudor were not royal at all, there is something about him that would make other men's love-making seem tame."

"It could be," admitted Anne doubtfully. But it was all beyond her comprehension. Her mind had strayed to poor Will Carey, who would be forced to take the King's leavings. Probably Mary had not sufficient imagination to be sorry for him.

But why should she bother? She had her own way to make—her own life to live. She was confident that she could do well enough for herself.

AN EXCERPT FROM

My Lady of Cleves

BY MARGARET CAMPBELL BARNES

THE SIMPLEST ENGLISH WORDS had been scattered from her mind. And when she raised her eyes she saw another man standing in the wide span of the doorway. The fat man who had laughed on the bridge, laughed because he was so confident of making a good bargain. But he wasn't laughing now. And when he doffed a plumeless cap from his closely-cropped, red-gold head, Anne knew him to be Henry Tudor and herself to be the bargain.

Their eyes met across the disordered room—met and held. She knew that she must look like a startled rabbit. She saw the same disappointment repeated in his eyes—but far more poignantly. She watched his cheerful, rubicund face work painfully like that of a child deprived at the last minute of some promised treat. He looked half ludicrous, half pitiful, so that even in her humiliation some mothering instinct in her wanted to comfort him. But she was far more sorry for herself.

Henry recovered himself almost immediately. He strode into the room, brushing Sir Anthony and the staring women aside, and bade her welcome with a fine gesture. Although his presence seemed to fill the room, he no longer looked fat or ludicrous. One was aware of him rather as a mighty personality. One knew that whether he were clothed in cloth of gold or worsted, he would always—inevitably—take the center of the stage. Mentally, he was master of the situation and his ruddy vitality was such that other men, crowding respectfully into the room on his heels, looked nondescript as the figures on some faded tapestry. In her distressed state of mind, Anne felt him towering over her. His voice was warm and cultured and kind; but she had read her doom in both men's eyes and all she could think of was Hans Holbein in her bedroom and Nan Boleyn on the scaffold. And because—after all the strain she had been through—her legs felt as if they would collapse under her at any moment, she very sensibly went down on her knees before her future husband.

Henry was magnificent. Nothing he had rehearsed in his reju-venated lover act could possibly have been more gallant than the way in which he lifted her up and embraced her and forbade a daughter of Cleves ever to kneel to him again. He made her sit down while he presented his friends. Probably he saw how ill she felt and Anne only hated herself the more for behaving like a weakling.

"Even if I'm plain as a pikestaff, at least I'm healthy enough to rear him a dozen children!" she thought savagely, remembering all her mother's reassurances to Wotton on this important point.

Because he hated gaucherie, Henry made an effort to set her at ease. Much as he might have gentled a horse, he sat and talked with her. When he inquired after her comfort and whether everything possible had been done for her, poor Anne could have screamed, remembering how very much the Duchess of Norfolk and Lady Rochfort had managed to do for her in one short hour in this very room. And all the time she could feel the man controlling some inner fury and trying to avert his eyes from her unbound hair and the feminine disorder of the room, as if by not looking at them he could make them cease to exist. She could almost hear the punctilious Duke of Suffolk inquiring afterwards if it were customary in Cleves for well-bred women to strew their living rooms with clothes chests, and could have died with shame on observing that her discarded stays were protruding from beneath the cushion which the careless Hagalas girl had so hurriedly thrust over them.

Anne was amazed to hear him ask by name after most of the people she had met on her journey, and touched to find that he himself had planned even the smallest details of her reception at Calais and Dover. But that was before he saw me! she thought, longing—yet dreading—to be alone with the knowledge of his disappointment, to absorb it and to adjust herself to the new outlook on life it would necessitate.

She guessed that the cooks were preparing an elaborate meal; but she was spared the tedium of this, for when at last the Bishop's steward came in to announce dinner, the King said something to Cranmer in Latin about what we have already received and got up to go. Being on his best behavior, he turned to chat for a few minutes with her ladies on his way out; but, after raking the lot of them with a selective eye, he seemed to think better of it. Anne could scarcely blame him. Now that he was really going, several quite amusing remarks occurred to her, most of which she found herself capable of saying in impeccable English. But he turned abruptly on his heel.

Just outside the room, Katherine stood flirting with one of the younger men who had been sent to Calais. Although it was still broad daylight, the servants had set torches to light the dim, monastic gallery, and the light from one of them shone down on her exquisite little head, warming the mischievous curve of her cheek and her moist, red mouth. Evidently the young man adored her, but Anne saw her make a little secret gesture to check his ardent talk. She lowered her eyes respectfully, and flattened her childish body against the wall to let the King pass. But he stopped squarely in front of her. He cupped her little chin in his great hand and gazed at her disconcertingly, although half his mind was still elsewhere.

"You look like a rose with the dew still on it," he said, and sighed prodigiously. Presently he let her go and turned to the young man beside her. "What did you tell us her name was, Tom, that morning she annoyed milord Cromwell by playing shuttlecock at Greenwich?"

"Katherine Howard, your Grace," said Tom Culpepper, blood hotter than any torchlight flashing his own ingenuous face.

"Ah, yes. I remember thinking what a charming name it was." Henry turned to the delighted Duchess. "And when you bring the new Queen to court, Madam, be sure you bring this child as well," he ordered affably.

An Excerpt from

The Tudor Rose

by Margaret Campbell Barnes

"Come and sit beside me, Bess. Margaret Beaufort, Countess of Richmond, has sent us a message, and as it is confidential we will send the others away." With a wave of one bejeweled hand Elizabeth Woodville cleared the parlor.

"The Countess sends me word how gifted and personable a young man her son has grown," she said.

"Naturally, since he is her only son." Elizabeth smiled.

"But all reports confirm the trend of her devotion…and his mother says that it is high time he took a wife," added the dowager queen.

"Probably he will marry the Duke of Brittany's daughter," remarked Elizabeth, with polite indifference.

But her mother leaned forward and placed a hand upon her knee. "The message was particularly for you." She said impressively.

Elizabeth came out of her own private thoughts with a start. During her short life she had become accustomed to being offered as matrimonial bait for some political reason or another, but the implication of her mother's words appeared to have no rhyme or reason. "A message for me about Henry Tudor of Lancaster?" she exclaimed. The scornful abhorrence in her voice was as unmistakable as it was purely hereditary.

"Better a well-disposed Lancastrian than a treacherous Yorkist!" snapped the dowager queen.

"But my father would never have heard of such a thing," stammered Elizabeth, realizing that the suggestion was being made in earnest.

"Were your father alive to hear, there would be no need of such a thing," pointed out his widow. "But times have changed and we must change with them."

"Have you forgotten, madam, that Henry Tudor is attainted of treason and still in exile?"

"He might be persuaded to come home."

When an ambitious woman's world crumbles about her, she can still meddle in the advancement of her children, thought Elizabeth. "Nothing would induce me to marry him," she said, and having always rendered sweet obedience to both her parents, was amazed at her own words.

The Dowager Queen flushed red with anger. "I think you forget, Elizabeth, that in your father's will he left me charge of my daughter's marriages. Even our enemies who dispute your legitimacy cannot dispute that," she said.

"So you must plot with a Lancastrian? White rose or red, I suppose it can be all the same to you Woodvilles!" accused Elizabeth Plantagenet, for the first time insulting her mother's birth.

Before such rare defiance, the Queen dowager's vivacity wilted to self pity. "You do not consider me at all," her mother was wailing as Elizabeth dutifully dabbed rose water to her brow.

"It is the boys who need considering," said Elizabeth. "In what way would your proposal benefit them? Judging by what my father told me of Henry of Lancaster, it would not get Edward back the throne."

"No, but it might save their lives. We could make it a condition... you could offer him your precious blood, in return for a promise that he would keep your brother honorably in his household."

"As for promises, has not Uncle Gloucester sworn exactly the same thing? Why should I sell myself in the hope that a Lancastrian's word may prove more reliable than a Yorkist's?"

"Because your uncle has already broken his word. He has not kept them in his household but in prison," pointed out their mother.

Elizabeth stood aside as the solicitous waiting women came to escort the dowager queen to her room.

"I begin not to believe much in any promises," she said sadly.

About the Author

Margaret Campbell Barnes lived from 1891 to 1962. She was the youngest of ten children born into a happy, loving family in Victorian England. She grew up in the Sussex countryside and was educated at small private schools in London and Paris.

Margaret was already a published writer when she married Peter, a furniture salesman, in 1917. Over the next twenty years, a steady stream of short stories and verse appeared under her name (and several noms de plume) in leading English periodicals of the time, including *Windsor, London, Quiver,* and others. Later, Margaret's agents, Curtis Brown Ltd., encouraged her to try her hand at historical novels. Between 1944 and 1962, Margaret wrote ten historical novels. Many of these were bestsellers, book club selections, and translated into foreign editions.

Between World Wars I and II, Margaret and Peter brought up two sons, Michael and John. In August 1944, Michael, a lieutenant in the Royal Armoured Corps, was killed in his tank in the Allied advance from Caen to Falaise in Normandy. Margaret and Peter grieved terribly the rest of their lives. Glimpses of Michael shine through in each of Margaret's later novels.

In 1945 Margaret bought a small thatched cottage on the Isle of Wight, off England's south coast. It had at one time been a smuggler's cottage, but to Margaret it was a special place in which to recover the spirit and carry on writing. And write she did. All together, over two million copies of Margaret Campbell Barnes's historical novels have been sold worldwide.